THE PARTISAN

In the spy game, every move matters...

★ **PATRICK WORRALL** ★

UNION
SQUARE
& CO.

NEW YORK

UNION
SQUARE
& CO.

NEW YORK

UNION SQUARE & CO. and the distinctive Union Square & Co. logo
are registered trademarks of Sterling Publishing Co., Inc.

Union Square & Co., LLC, is a subsidiary of Sterling Publishing Co., Inc.

First published in the UK in 2022 by Bantam Press, an imprint of Transworld
Publishers.
This 2023 paperback edition published by Union Square & Co.

ISBN 978-1-4549- 5076-9
ISBN 978-1-4549- 5077-6 (e-book)
ISBN 978-1-60582-316-4 (galley)

For information about custom editions, special sales, and premium purchases,
please contact specialsales@unionsquareandco.com.

Printed in Canada

2 4 6 8 10 9 7 5 3 1

unionsquareandco.com

Cover illustration by James Weston Lewis
Cover design by Marianne Issa El Khoury/TW
Interior design by Kevin Ullrich

In Loving Memory

Vytautas Giniotis
(1960–2020)

Jadvyga Keiniene
(1936–2021)

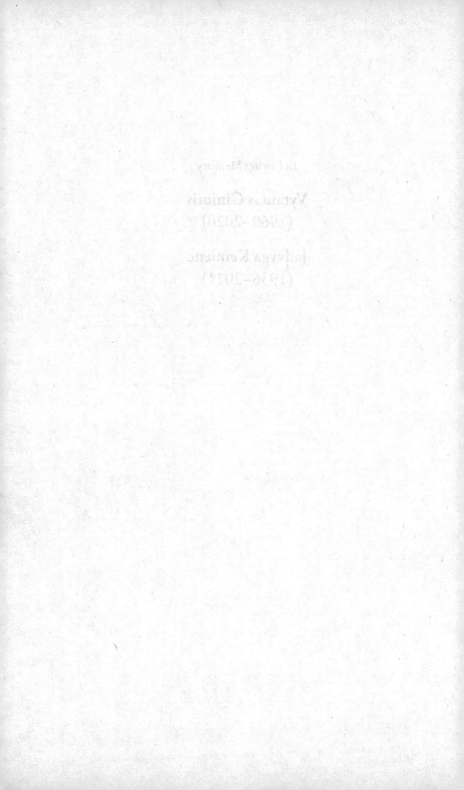

"My life I never held but as a pawn
To wage against thy enemies; nor fear to lose it
Thy safety being the motive."

—William Shakespeare, *King Lear* (Act 1, scene 1)

PROLOGUE

The quality of the light was the first thing that struck her when she went to Madrid in the spring of 1960. The afternoon shadows were the deepest and darkest she had ever seen.

Like all old men, the doctor was a creature of habit. He always shopped for groceries on Saturday afternoons. She tailed him to a place near Atocha station that sold international food. He bought black bread, beer and slices of cured sausage that resembled Westphalian salami. He stopped to ask the shopkeeper's six-year-old about his schoolwork, bending down with some effort and talking to the boy with unfeigned interest. He had always been good with children. The young ones in the camp had trusted him and called him "Uncle Erik."

When he turned for home, she headed back the way they had both come. He walked with difficulty these days and she had some minutes to get into position. The apartment next to his was unoccupied, and she had burgled it the day before with the tip of a long, thin stiletto, leaving the front door unlocked so that, when the time came, she could walk through the empty rooms and out on to the terrace at the back. The removal men had left deep scratches in the wooden parquet floor and cigarette ends scattered across the brown concrete of the balcony.

The narrow street. She knew the idea that everyone in Spain took to their beds for an afternoon siesta was a myth—at least in this part of the country. But a pleasing stillness hung over the street and there were few signs of life. She scanned up and down, then slipped over the low wall that separated the balconies. The doctor always left his back door unlocked. She walked through the galley kitchen on stockinged feet. When she sensed, rather than heard, movement in the next room, her hand flew to the inside pocket of her thin cotton jacket. A tortoiseshell cat padded across the living room and butted its head against her shin as she stood in the kitchen doorway.

The doctor's bedroom was on the opposite side of the living room. She waited just inside the door, watching through a crack as the old man entered the apartment. She saw immediately that reports of his chronic ill health were true. He held on to the wall to steady himself as he shuffled through to the kitchen, and it seemed to take him an age to unpack the groceries and stow them away. She could hear him clucking at the cat. When the doctor came back into the living room he was breathing heavily. He was facing the bedroom door that hid her. She pushed it open, and the cat trotted across and nuzzled her ankles again.

Erik Urban studied the intruder's face and said: "I'll met by moonlight, proud Titania." Except that it is broad daylight. I see you have already met Kaiser—the shameless traitor."

"I think he likes my stockings. He's making static electricity."

"It has been a long time since he had a woman to rub up against. I could say the same about myself. With your permission, I am going to walk very slowly to my favorite armchair over here. And sit down. So. I always knew this day would come. I did not know they would send you, O Queen of Cats! You are getting quite the reputation, you know?" He winked at her.

"I trust that you have only heard good things, Herr Doktor."

He smiled at this, then followed the cat's progress across the living room rug. The smile weakened, and he said, in very soft German, "What will become of you, my boy?"

The woman moved to within a few paces of the doctor's chair. Her feet were planted wide apart as she reached inside her jacket.

"Is there a form of words?" the old man asked. "I had heard there was a form of words. Otherwise, you could be . . . a common housebreaker."

She took a breath. "I have been authorized to carry out an executive order issued by the president of the state of Israel. Do you understand why I have come to you?"

"That's very good," the doctor said, as if speaking to himself. Then he realized he had failed to answer her question and said quickly: "Yes.

Yes, of course. I understand everything. It will sound strange to you, but I have been looking forward to this for a long time."

"Is there anything you want to say?"

"I have tablets."

"What?"

"I obtained tablets. I did not have the courage to use them, God forgive me. They are in the top drawer over there. I will not move a muscle. Will you permit me to take them? It will be easier for both of us."

The woman found a white paper bag in the drawer containing a cardboard box with a bottle inside. She tossed it to him and watched him fiddle with box and bottle. His movements were so clumsy that she thought he was playing for time, but then she remembered he was supposed to be recovering from a stroke.

At last, he tapped the tablets on to the palm of his hand. There was a bottle of clear spirits on the side table next to his chair, with the glass he had drunk from the night before. He poured three fingers into the tumbler and took a small sip, followed by a proper mouthful. Then he froze. The hand that held the tablets was trembling. He looked at the woman pleadingly.

She nodded emphatically and said: "It's time. Do it now." It helped. He swallowed the first pill. Nothing happened and he took another, gasping from the fire of the alcohol in his throat. He took the rest hungrily. The third, the fourth, the fifth, the sixth. She feared some kind of trick, but when he spoke there was nothing left in his mouth. "Do you see them when you close your eyes at night?" he asked, sinking into the chair and letting his head flop back. "The others. The ones before me?"

"Sometimes."

"Mine come to me every night. When I lie down and shut my eyes, there they all are—waiting. Just like in life. They always waited so patiently. There were so many. But I remember all the faces."

His speech was beginning to slur. His breath was a rasp that filled the room. The glass thudded on to the rug.

"What do they say to you?" She reached forward and took his wrist in her hand, feeling the slowing pulse. She had to know.

His eyes closed for the last time and it took him a while to process her words and form a reply.

"Nothing!" he said, with an effort. "They just look at me. I didn't mind them at first. I used to shout at them—tell them to get lost. But in recent times . . ."

"Yes?" He was trying to say something, but could not get it out. She put her ear next to his lips. The voice seemed to come from far away. "They crowd around me," he whispered in German. "The small children. *Die kleine Kinder.*"

I

LITHUANIA, 2004

In the spring of 2004, an elderly woman traveled from her home on the island of Elba to the Republic of Lithuania, using three different passports to complete the journey.

Flying from Elba to Rome, she used a well-worn Norwegian document that gave her forename as Greta—the name she had answered to since childhood. From Rome to Berlin, she was, as far as any prying eyes would have been concerned, a citizen of the state of Israel with an entirely different first and last name. On the final leg of the journey, from Berlin to Vilnius, she used a stiff new Lithuanian passport that identified her as Zofija Jenseniene.

It was done from habit rather than any real need to cover her movements. The woman was seventy-seven years old and had long retired from the kind of dangerous work that required such precautions. She had reached the age at which few of her fellow passengers paid her any attention. If someone had studied her, they might have noticed that her eyes were a dramatic shade of green, with a hint of the Central Asian steppes in them. She had high, angular cheekbones that gave her face a cat-like quality. Her hair was white and thinning and she had cut it as short as a Roman soldier's. She wore expensive technical clothing of the kind favored by skiers and mountaineers.

At the airport in Berlin, Greta drank tea—English-style, with milk—and ate chocolate and salted almonds. She bought a postcard showing the Brandenburg Gate and wrote a message on the back to her eldest son that began: "Greetings, from the lair of the Fascist beast!"

When she hailed a cab at the airport in Vilnius, the driver popped the boot for her but did not help her with her case. She sat in the back and they drove south toward the Rūdninkai Forest. The country all around was flat and pleasant. There were lots of storks. When they were passing Žagarinė she noticed that the meter was already showing double the price they had negotiated.

"What's going on with that thing?" she asked. "Tourist tax."

"I am not a tourist. I am from Samogitia."

The driver thought this unlikely. The woman's clothes and the way she spoke—with frequent pauses for forgotten words—made him guess that she was a wealthy Lithuanian-American. She had probably spent her life in Chicago and was seeing the fabled mother country for the first time. She was, he felt sure, destined for disappointment. "I pay what we agreed," the old woman said. "No more." They pulled up at a set of temporary traffic lights on the last good road before the deep forest began.

The driver shrugged and said these new guys (he meant the government) were stiffing everyone, Mother, and he had no choice but to obey the law, when he saw that the woman had put a hand on the back of his seat and was leaning forward. He reluctantly turned to meet her gaze while the engine idled.

She put her face very close to his and let him feel all the force behind her eyes. "*Draugeli*," she said. "My little friend. Do you think I am going to be cheated by the likes of you?" He turned off the meter.

A friend of Greta's son had told her about the memorial and given her directions. She recognized no landmarks now and would never have found the spot without his help. There were no roads in this part of the forest the last time she was here.

The young man had warned her of what to expect, so when at last she made it to the top of the steep slope and saw the marble slab, there should have been no surprise. There was no logical explanation for the stabbing sensation she felt in her stomach.

The inscription on the slab read: "This marks the spot where two young girls, members of the renowned partisan band Three Sisters, were buried in the summer of 1944. Lithuanian patriots, the girls were killed after a long gun battle with the German SS."

Greta walked around, stamping her feet against a fresh breeze that raked the wooded hilltop. Then she sat awkwardly on a tree stump. Every so often she looked again at the words on the marble as though she had misread them the first time. In the car park at the beginning of the newly cleared woodland trail, the taxi driver would be sitting and smoking sullenly. Or perhaps he had driven off in disgust and abandoned her.

She held on to herself very tightly but, at length, the tears came. What does it matter anyway? she asked herself. Who else will cry for them? After a while, she wiped her eyes, and indignation began to build inside her. Everything about the monument was wrong.

On a computer in the business suite at her hotel, she searched for the government ministry responsible for it. She remembered the departmental logo that had been etched into a corner of the marble slab, next to the twelve stars of the European Union. She navigated her way slowly across the department's web pages, struggling with the written Lithuanian language. She found a good likely contact, a Mrs. Indrė Žukauskienė, and tapped out a message.

No one replied. Two days later, Greta wrote another message, then called the ministry. People asked her to hold on, then cut the line while she was waiting. They told her she had the wrong department. They said no one with the name Indrė Žukauskienė had ever worked there. They told Greta that she was supposed to fill in a form, not send an email. They told her Mrs. Žukauskienė was on maternity leave and could not take messages.

Right at the end of her week in Lithuania, Greta received a call from Indrė Žukauskienė. The young woman really had been on maternity leave, the messages had only just been passed on, and could Mrs. Jenseniene see her in Vilnius?

They met in a café near the castle. Indrė Žukauskienė ordered cakes and coffee for herself and tea with milk for the peculiar forceful old lady.

The waiter brought everything over. He paid the young woman a great deal of attention and Greta could not help but smile.

"You seem too young to be a mother. I forget that people still get married and have children early in this country. It's a good idea. I left it late and found it hard to keep up with my boys."

"You said that you grew up in Lithuania but emigrated to Scandinavia?"

"There is a little more to the story than that." Greta sipped her tea and could not help grimacing. The water was lukewarm, and the waiter had heated the milk with the nozzle of the coffee machine. "Thank you for meeting me, and I don't want you to think that I'm ungrateful for the memorial. It's good that people want to remember what happened back then. But we have to get the details right."

"Absolutely," said Indrė. "Will you tell me what you think is wrong? I will make a full report."

"The first thing is that the girls were indeed Lithuanian patriots, as is written, but they were also Jewish, and that is too important to be left out. Also, there was no long gunfight. It was over in seconds, I'm afraid. And the men were not SS. They were Wehrmacht—regular German Army. That is an important detail too."

The young woman was too professional to show any surprise. Her brow creased as she wrote on her spiral pad. "How can you be sure that the girls were Jews? There was a Jewish partisan group active in the forest around that time, but we think that the Three Sisters were Lithuanians."

"It was possible to be both of those things at the same time, my dear. That is something that some of you appear to have forgotten. I know they were Jewish because I grew up with them. Their names were Vita and Riva. And whoever found their graves must have known they were Jews, because I carved the Star of David into the rifles I left to mark the place. On the wooden bit, you know . . . I can't remember the word."

"The butt? The butt of the rifles? You . . . carved?"

"I didn't have much time, but I scratched six-pointed stars into both rifle *butts* with a knife. I had taken it from a German soldier and stabbed him to death with it. The blade was notched where it had struck his collarbone, but the point was still sharp."

The younger woman pushed her plate of apple cake to one side. An hour earlier, she had been singing a song to her infant son about a squirrel in a red hat.

Greta delved into her handbag and took out a folding map of Lithuania and a leatherbound organizer with half a dozen loose documents inside. Some were handwritten letters. She spread a paper napkin on the table and laid a black-and-white photograph on top of it.

Three smiling girls. The one in the middle was unmistakably a young Greta. Her arms rested on the shoulders of the others. They all wore rough clothes, like farm workers. The girl on the left, the slightest, had her hair up in a headscarf and a cigarette hanging from her lips. Her arms were crossed over her chest. She held a stubby Mauser semi-automatic pistol in one hand and a Luger in the other. The girl on the right was the tallest, and she had taken the most care with her hair and make-up in preparation for the photograph. She had a Schmeisser submachine gun slung across her body. None of the girls looked older than sixteen.

"I was beautiful then," said Greta. "Of course I thought I was ugly at the time. That's the way with women, isn't it? I hope you know how beautiful you are now, Indrė, and that you enjoy it. So, you see how I knew the girls. We were not related by blood, but I am the last of the Three Sisters. I killed the men who killed them."

Indrė continued to write carefully for some moments. Then she said: "I'm going to order more coffee. Would you like another tea?"

"Yes, please, but first I need to tell him how to make it properly."

2
TENERIFE, 1960

After Madrid, Greta spent two quiet months in southwest France, staying in a small hotel close to the Spanish border. Every Sunday she rang the same three numbers, one in Paris and two in London, using a different public telephone each time. On the first Sunday in July 1960 the calls took longer than usual. The next morning, she bought clothes for a beach holiday. Just before Bastille Day, two plane tickets and a counterfeit passport arrived at her hotel in a stiff envelope.

That evening, she drove to a small vineyard in the Corbières region and was welcomed like a long-lost daughter by the elderly couple who owned it. Madame was preparing Greta's favorite meal: stewed boar with cognac and wild mushrooms. After dinner, Monsieur went to the bedroom where Greta always slept, took her ancient suitcase from the top of the wardrobe and left her alone with it.

Greta fingered the items inside: a necklace with a Star of David pendant, a scrap of handmade linen, an envelope stuffed with photographs and letters. It was all that remained of her mother, her grandmother and her childhood friends Vita and Riva. She felt emotion rising in her throat. She knew that it would overwhelm her if she let it. She put the things back and shut the lid of the case firmly, closing the locks with both thumbs. "Not yet," she murmured. "Not yet."

Southern Tenerife was unbearable in high summer. It was cooler in the north. In La Laguna people had heard of Florian, but no one knew where he was. Greta caught the look of pity in their faces. It was not the first time a woman had come through, looking for him. She hired an asthmatic Seat 600 and took the slaloming road up to Taganana. She knew to take the downhill sections in low gear. The brakes would not last if you rode them.

The seasons changed minute by minute as the little car wheezed up into the Anaga mountains. Bands of cold mist gave way to blistering sunshine. She stopped at Casas de la Cumbre and ran her hands over the bark of the strange trees that clung to the hillside. These woods were very different from the forests of her youth but being among trees always calmed her.

A sudden squall of rain swept in and she ran into a doorless stone hut to shelter. She bit into a large bar of La Candelaria chocolate. An ancient shepherd put his head through the doorway and there was a little comedy of embarrassment as she rose quickly and tried to leave, and he insisted that she stay. He shared bread and olives with her and offered her wine from a tartan Thermos flask. If a traveler from Mars landed in these woods, thought Greta, the local people would offer them wine and bread. This was still Spain, even if they were closer to the Sahara than the Pyrenees.

At Taganana there was talk of Florian, and she drove around the coast to Benijo, following a hunch. She picked her way down the steep steps cut into the cliff face. She saw him over on the right, where the gray-black sand of the beach met rocks the size of houses. He was the only man she had ever seen who wore his hair so long that he had to tie it in a ponytail.

He was on all fours, performing callisthenic exercises, surrounded by ten or twelve young men and women aping his movements. Almost twenty years ago, at the height of the war, a British newspaper had called him The Most Dangerous Man in the World.

Florian was still handsome, though age had given his face a sour, patrician look. His mouth drooped slightly at the corners. After they finished exercising, his group ran into the sea and their whoops of delight carried to Greta on the breeze.

Afterward, Florian sat bare-chested and cross-legged, and the others gathered close around him. She could not tell if they were performing a breathing exercise together, or whether they were listening to him dispensing some wisdom.

Before the war, he had been one of the first Europeans to travel to Tibet. He had enjoyed great success with a book that laid out the traditional exercises done by Buddhist monks there to keep themselves limber between long bouts of sitting meditation. He had changed his name and altered his appearance after the war. She wondered if his contacts in Germany collected book royalties on his behalf and forwarded the money to him.

He stood up and she saw that he was tanned and very lean, with the stomach muscles of a much younger man. When they broke for lunch, he draped a flowing linen shirt over his shoulders but did not fasten the buttons.

At the café in the village in the afternoon, Greta spotted two women who had been exercising on the beach with Florian. She walked past and complimented them gushingly on their dresses and their matching straw hats, which were made by local villagers in the traditional Canarian style.

One of the women asked Greta to join them. She was a Milanese journalist of about thirty. The other woman was from Holland: tall and handsome and very grave. She could not have been older than nineteen. The Italian told Greta that they were learning about Buddhism from a German academic who knew the secret of raising his body temperature at will by meditating and controlling the flow of his breath. The woman pointed out Florian to her as he passed them on the other side of the street, and Greta said: "Oh, my, he's handsome." The Dutch girl looked at her and her eyes flashed.

That night Greta slept badly, curled up on the back seat of the tiny car. She rose at sunrise to bathe in the sea. She put on a flowing cotton dress that flattered her figure. It had deep pockets into which she dropped a handful of Spanish currency, a tiny glass bottle labelled as Murine eye drops and a knife that opened automatically. She looked at herself in the driver's mirror. Her hair was below her shoulders now and the seawater made it wavy. Her skin always took a deep tan and held on to it. Her shoulders were slightly sunburned. The overall effect was tousled but attractive.

In the early afternoon she saw Florian and the Dutch girl arguing in the palm trees by the seafront walkway. She wasn't close enough to hear what they were saying, but the girl raised her voice several times. Florian's stayed calm and low. He drew the girl to him and kissed her on both cheeks but she pulled away in disgust and marched off. Greta saw her ball her hand into a fist and rub away a tear.

When the sun set over the ocean that evening, Greta took a walk along the beach, following the line where the tide made the black sand wet. She wandered close to the spot where Florian and his group were ending their second exercise session of the day. It was all very casual and natural. They were shaking themselves off after their workout and the Italian woman shouted a greeting and beckoned to Greta as she passed. The Dutch girl was nowhere to be seen. Greta walked up to the group. She smiled shyly and shook hands with a few people. Florian stood apart, shaking a towel. She glanced at him, making eye contact briefly, broke it off, then looked at him again, holding his gaze for longer.

There was a group dinner that night, and Florian told a story about Tibet while they waited for the food. When the lamas were in charge, before the Chinese invaded, the Tibetans were only ever allowed to wear two outfits, one for summer, and one for winter. The whole population had to swap from one costume to the other on the same day, which the monks decided by casting a horoscope. The spring might come late one year, but if a particular date was considered auspicious, everyone would have to stow away their yak-fur coats and go about shivering in summer tunics, even if the ground was still thick with Himalayan snow.

The waiters brought platters of grilled fish and small, wrinkled potatoes cooked in seawater. It was simple but good. An earnest, intense Brazilian man sat next to Florian and monopolized him for the rest of the meal. When the Brazilian left his seat for a few minutes, Florian leaned over to Greta and said: "I'm going to seize my chance to escape. Would you like to come back to my place?"

The apartment was sparsely decorated. In the corridor there was a teeming, garish painting of the life of the Buddha in the traditional Tibetan style. The Enlightened One was a huge presence in the middle of the canvas. Smaller versions of Him acted out scenes from His miraculous life in a circle around the outside.

Florian went through them one by one, telling the stories with great fluency: The Dream of the White Elephant; The Years of Austerity; The Bowl of Rice under the Banyan Tree. He stood close to Greta and leaned against the wall with one arm. He had been a great seducer of women in his time, but he was nearly sixty now. This guarded young woman had arrived out of nowhere and he could not quite read her.

Greta realized that this was the moment Florian was going to try to kiss her. She ducked under his arm and went past him, touching his back as she did so to soften the blow. She went into the kitchen and called: "Is there anything to drink?"

"There's whiskey in one of the cupboards."

Greta found an unopened bottle of Black Bush and two good crystal glasses. She shouted: "I've never tried this kind."

"I don't like the Scotch," Florian called back. "Bad memories. I prefer the Irish. More neutral." She heard him chuckle at his private joke.

When she came into the lounge with the drinks, he was sitting at one end of the sofa, his body turned in to the center. He was wearing loose white cotton drawstring trousers and a cornflower blue linen shirt, open almost to the navel. His chest was nearly hairless and his stomach looked very taut. His long iron-gray hair was tied with an elastic band. He looked at her warily. His face was lined from age and exposure to the sun but he had fine cheekbones and a strong jaw. She sat at the other end of the sofa, leaving a space between them.

She raised her glass and took a big swallow. He did the same. Then he put the glass down firmly on the coffee table. She sensed again that he was going to try for a kiss.

Greta crossed the space between them on the sofa quickly, slipped her hand down his trousers and took hold of his cock. He was still a vigorous man, and she felt it swelling in her hand. He leaned back and closed his eyes, exhaling slowly. She said: "I'm in control. Understood?"

"Yes."

"Men used to treat me badly. Not anymore. We do this my way."

"Oh, yes."

She picked up the glass and held it out. "Have some more to drink first. Take it! Or do you want me to stop? All right, then. Good boy." She watched him drink and swallow, then put the glass back on the table for him.

Greta stroked him rhythmically. His breath was deep and slow. Men are farmyard animals, she thought. Hold them in the right place and you can lead them all the way to the slaughterhouse. After a while she felt his erection begin to subside. His head rested on the back of the sofa. He was breathing very deeply.

She let go of him and pulled her hand out of his trousers. "How are you feeling?" He did not respond. The clear solution she had dropped into his whiskey had taken effect. Greta waited for two minutes and spoke again, loudly and clearly: "How are you feeling now, my Obersturmbannführer?" There was no flicker of response on his face. She allowed herself to give in to disgust and let her body shiver uncontrollably. She glared at the hand that had held him as if she wanted to cut it off.

There was nothing of interest in his bedroom. Nothing at the back of the drawers and no false bottoms. Nothing hidden behind the paintings. She threw clothes carelessly out of drawers and cupboards.

She found a small safe at the bottom of the wardrobe, hidden by shoeboxes. It had four dials, like a bicycle lock, all set to zero. She thought about shooting it open but the noise would wake the neighbors.

Greta knelt in front of the safe and stared at it. No obvious course of action suggested itself. She nodded. It's time, she told herself. I am just going to have to kill him, without proof or confession. Sometimes it has to be this way.

A sudden thought occurred to her. She set the dials to two, zero, zero, four, then turned the handle. The door of the safe popped open.

Photographs of women. A French passport in a German name that was not quite his real one. American dollar bills. Stacks of coins packed into sealed paper tubes. Each held about ten coins and was very heavy. Greta tore the paper with her thumbnail and squeezed out a coin.

She stood up, stepping back into the light to look at it properly. It was pre-war—a twenty-mark piece with the German eagle on one side and the coat of arms of the city of Hamburg on the other. The coin was highly polished and she caught the reflection of movement behind her. Her hand flashed toward her pocket.

Some instinct of danger had troubled Florian's drugged sleep, sounding a discordant note that wound through his dreams and took on the insistent tone of an alarm. He opened his eyes and the crushing heaviness in his body told him something was wrong. He tried to stand and found that he could not. Panic sent a surge of adrenaline through his system. It fought the sodium pentothal and propelled him to his feet. She had given him a respectable dose, but it could not overpower a lifetime of instinct and training. He shook his head to clear it and moved silently toward the bedroom.

He had wrapped his left arm all the way around Greta's neck before she could stop him, so that his elbow was pointing forward, and the blade of his wrist was pressing hard against the side of her throat. She dropped the coin as he wrenched her backwards, lifting both her feet from the floor. He put his right forearm against the back of her neck and squeezed the biceps with his left hand. There was intense pressure on her carotid artery. She would be unconscious in seconds—but the knife was already in her hand.

The blade slid out and she sliced him across the knuckles, cutting deep. He let her go and stared at his hand, seeing white bone below gashed red flesh.

Greta flashed the knife in Florian's face, cutting him from the corner of the mouth right out to the ear. His hands flew up instinctively and she stuck the switchblade straight into his belly, low down, just above the groin on his left side.

She butted her head into his chest, jumped back and drove forward until he was pinned against the bedroom wall. The hand holding the partisan knife switched to a reverse grip, so the blade was closest to her little finger, the knuckles pointing up and the elbow flared out to the side. She wrapped her other hand over the end of the handle and shifted her feet so she could get all her weight behind the movement as she dragged the embedded knife from right to left across his lower abdomen, ripping him open entirely.

Florian held his arms across his lower body like a mother cradling an infant, trying to prevent his intestines from spilling out. He slid down the wall and sat there, looking down. His eyes flickered up at Greta, but she saw the consciousness drain from them as he toppled sideways. She saw the bright glossy colors of his exposed organs. A cloud of damp steam rose from the open wound. His bowel emptied itself and the sour smell began to fill the room.

LONDON, 1961

"Not every job will be as hard as that, okay?" said Yakuv.

"Remember Madrid?"

"That was a strange one," said Greta. "Like a dream."

"So you said. Do you want another of those? Ice cream and chocolate sauce?"

"Cold vanilla ice cream, hot espresso. I've had enough, though."

"You're practically inhaling it. I don't want to get too close in case I lose a hand."

She snorted with laughter, through a full mouth. He gave her a disapproving look, with his El Greco face—long and lean and Iberian, with the fussy little pointed beard. It was patched with gray now, and he was bald on top. When Greta had first met Yakuv, fighting Hitler's armies in the forests of Lithuania, he had had a mass of black curls piled on top of his head. The story was that his Russian handlers had nicknamed him "Trotsky" and he had cut his hair short ever since out of wounded vanity. He could not bear to lose the beard, though.

She wolfed down another spoonful and he winced. "How is your weight now?"

"I've lost a few pounds. It always happens when I get ready for a show."

"What about the teeth? Let me see. Not bad."

"Thank you for the recommendation." She ran a fingernail across the surface of the enamel of her new white incisors. "They felt too big for my mouth at first. And sensitive. I couldn't even eat ice cream." She pouted.

"A woman must suffer to be beautiful. It is her fate."

"How *profound*. I always forget you're a poet."

Yakuv raised two fingers. "Poet and soldier, okay? Two jobs, like everyone at home. Like my brother-in-law is a dentist as well as a tank commander."

Zampa's on the Gray's Inn Road, in the mid-morning lull. They had a corner table and sat sideways in their chairs so they could see all the entrances and exits. Yakuv looked sulkily through the big plate-glass window at the gray sky. The London winter drained the color from everything and turned it into wartime newsreel. A woman stalked along the street past the front door of the café, dragging a child by the hand. She had the collar of her long black coat turned up against a swirling wind that made the rubbish dance along the pavements. Most of her face was hidden.

Greta lifted the glass to drink the melted ice cream at the bottom. A few drops escaped and ran down her chin. She saw Yakuv grimace with exaggerated disgust and she laughed. It had been a long time since she had let herself laugh like that.

Before she had finished, he leaned in and whispered: "Don't get too comfortable. Someone is on your trail, little vixen. I hear things. You know what I hear? That the name *Greta* is never far from the lips of certain personnel in the Soviet Embassy in London. They do not have a photograph of you. They make discreet enquiries among acquaintances who might possess such a thing. I could make a lot of money."

"I can see those MGB oafs coming from a mile away."

"Perhaps. But listen to this. A man who belongs to the Fourth Directorate of Soviet intelligence has also been seen in various locations around this miserable island. A capable man, I might add. This is unusual. Where does he pop up? In London and in Cambridge. What a coincidence. Who do I know who spends her life running between those cities, flirting shamelessly with the toothless old professors, for reasons I cannot begin to guess at?"

"Distant neighbors," said Greta, suddenly serious. "That is news. But I can't see the Fourth flying over here to give the MGB a helping hand, can you? They hate each other more than they hate Russia's enemies."

"The wolf hunting alongside the bear. You are right. They would claw each other to death first, would they not? And yet my source is impeccable. I don't purport to have an answer to this riddle. I pass on what I hear, okay? This is how I pay down my debt to you, one coin at a time."

He tailed off, peering past her out of the window. Greta turned to see what he was looking at: a young woman in a white raincoat standing on the opposite pavement, facing the café.

"It's not her."

"What?"

"The woman waiting for the trolleybus. You're wondering if it's the same one who walked past a minute ago with the child, in a different coat. It's not. The height is wrong, the shoes. This woman has bare legs too. The mother had stockings on. You can't just whip them off like that when you're out on a job."

Yakuv looked at her for a few seconds, then said: "Fly back with me tonight." She nearly coughed a mouthful of tea into her lap. "There's a house near the beach in Eilat I'm thinking about for you. I want you to see it. You have a bank account full of dollars that you never touch. I'm working on a passport now."

"I thought I was still on probation."

"Nonsense. It's been three years. A couple more jobs? We're talking full citizenship." He raised his mug in a salute. "The foreign minister of Israel sends her personal greetings."

"As if that lady would take an interest in some poor little Lithuanian *shiksa*."

Yakuv grinned. "I walked past the Queen of England's palace this morning. I wasn't impressed. My queen? Lives in a very simple apartment in Rehavia. She invites me into the kitchen and prepares Turkish coffee while I tell her all about your exploits. With most of the details cut out, naturally, to preserve deniability."

"Naturally. How flattering."

"All I'm saying is that you have friends. Why don't you let me help you? Whatever you've got yourself into here, I can help. You can always reach me through the *shnayder*."

"You mean you want to know if my personal business will create problems for your queen in Jerusalem. It won't. It's a small historical matter. And I have friends here who help me."

"Mindaugas." He snorted. "Is that the name? I remember him from the war. A farmer's boy from Samogitia, catching flies with his mouth open."

"And you were a skinny kid with a bad chest from the Vilna ghetto. But you became strong. Mindaugas is solid." She rapped her knuckles on the cracked Formica tabletop. "Like a Lithuanian oak."

Yakuv sat back in his chair and nodded reluctantly. His mother had been told he would not see his first birthday. He had gone on to stand in the wings of history, playing a hand in the collapse of empires and acting as midwife at the birth of a new country.

He looked out at the street again. A 543 trolleybus had arrived and the woman in the white coat was getting on.

"You can't stay in this miserable country forever."

Greta reached out and touched his hand. "I know you can't stand it here. I appreciate you coming over. It's difficult for me to get away just now."

"Cold, gray place," Yakuv said bitterly.

"You just hate the British because they threw you in prison once."

"I don't hate anyone. My philosophy? Forgive and forget."

This time Greta did not manage to keep all the tea in her mouth and she had to snatch up a napkin. Yakuv could not help smiling at her reaction.

"I am only half joking. Listen, okay? There is a serious point. You think I am in the business of revenge. No. Settling debts is my business. When they are paid off, I move on. Israel moves on. Vengeance is not a sufficiently developed moral principle. One cannot build a new kind of country based on it." He gave her a searching look. "A human being cannot construct a full life based on this principle either."

She was dabbing at herself with the napkin and did not want to look him in the eye.

He said: "I mean it. I can do something else. What's your second career? What are you going to do when this is all over?"

"Some people have only one talent."

He pointed to a spot on her chin. "You have a little . . . There. That's it." Then he said: "Well done in Tenerife, okay? I know it was hard going. And handing in the gold? Much appreciated."

"I thought it might have belonged to someone. Maybe they can trace the owner."

He smiled grimly. "You mean the owner's distant relatives. They'll certainly try. But the money? Not worth handing it in. It just creates extra paperwork for me. A bit of currency like that? Just put it in your pocket next time."

After he had settled the bill and she was putting on her tweed coat, Yakuv said: "You never told me how you got the safe open in Tenerife. That was a clever piece of burglary."

"Just a lucky guess. Twenty oh-four." He looked at her blankly.

"The Führer's birthday."

That afternoon, Greta ventured out into unknown territory: the stretch of the Central Line west of Marble Arch. It was busy at first, and she had to stand. She felt it once, twice, three times: a hand skimming her waist and hip. A man was tracing the outline of her midsection lightly with his fingers. He wasn't bold enough to squeeze her.

As they pulled into Notting Hill Gate she turned and gave him a dazzling smile. A Teddy Boy, though no longer a boy. Thinning quiff, gray sideburns, teeth like the rotting supports of a fallen pier. When he smiled back, she said: "If that hand comes near me again, I'll chop it off." The man left the train.

Further west, she recognized some of the names. Northolt called to mind images of dogfights and vapor trails in the blue English sky. Someone else's war is always a sideshow, she thought. The only real war is the one you fight.

At Ruislip Gardens she walked southwest, following a brook that ran along the edge of the airfield, until she reached the woods and the allotments. She saw Viktoras from a quarter of a mile away, over the top of a hedge. He was digging. He had the same bushy mustache, and his upper body was as bulky as ever. Greta came up behind him as he was bending down to peer into a long, low greenhouse full of cucumbers. "How are they looking?"

He did not turn immediately. He gripped the spade tight. When he looked at her, it was with a smile that did not reach the eyes.

She was wearing her long tweed coat and a beret. Both her hands were in her pockets. She let him see that something else was in the right pocket.

"As big as torpedoes!" he said. "I can show you a way to pickle these in fifteen minutes that tastes like you did it for months."

"That sounds good. Let's talk. Put the spade down first."

She could not get used to seeing Viktoras on his own like this. In her head, the big man and her wicked little uncle were an inseparable duo—a classic, mismatched music hall double-act. A photograph of them taken in 1942 remained stamped on her memory, so that when she thought of one man, she always pictured the other next to him. They were standing hip-to-hip and propping each other up in the photo. If you looked at it from arm's length, the men merged to form one gray mass, a single animal with four legs and two heads. Viktoras provided the muscle, while Greta's uncle, she knew, was the malign brain of the beast.

It looked like whoever had taken the picture had made some crack just before the shutter closed because the men's mouths were stretched wide with hilarity. There was a knock-kneed silliness about them:

they were laughing so hard they could barely stand. Both were wearing the *Feldgrau* uniform and runic badges of the fifth division of the Waffen SS.

The shed at the top of Viktoras's sloping allotment was the size of a double garage. They sat on camping chairs, two sword-lengths apart. There was a card table, the green baize stained and worn away in patches. He wiped his filthy hands with a yellow cloth, then poured himself a measure of clear liquid from a bottle with a handwritten label. Greta waved away the offer.

"Your information was excellent," she said. "He was in Tenerife exactly when you said he would be. And he wasn't hard to find, with that long hair."

"I hear he is some kind of guru now. Like Gandhi?"

"Something like that. Viktoras?"

"Yes?"

"It's 'was,' I'm afraid. Florian is in hell now, with all the others." He seemed to pride himself on not reacting to things like that, so she added, cruelly: "It was a difficult death. I had to perform a Caesarean section."

Viktoras sipped at the grubby mug and wiped the mustache with the back of his hand. "I hope these Jew filth pay you well."

"You know they do because you take your cut. But it's not all about money for me. You know that too."

She produced a small red and black notebook from her pocket, like a rent ledger, and placed it on the table. She remembered what Yakuv had told her: they were in the business of settling debts. Well, here was an account book.

"You told me about the Einsatzgruppen," she went on. "But I know you were in Viking Division too. I know you were at Bad Tölz."

That got through. He gave a start, like he had been slapped in the face.

"I know that you helped other SS volunteers get out after the war," she went on. "Lithuanians, Latvians, some others. At the very least, I need the names of all the Germans you know who made it to Spain.

The Israelis won't be interested in all of them, but they need a full list, so they can check it against their persons of interest. There's a process. They don't go after anyone without good evidence. I try to keep the Lithuanians out of it if I can."

Viktoras put the mug down, and his hands gripped his knees. Something about his body language made her slip a finger into the trigger guard of the Baby Browning in her pocket.

But when he finally spoke, it was with a pleading tone.

"All we wanted was to save Lithuania for you—our daughters and our sons. It was always the same, my whole life. We were the bone the dogs fought over. Pulled in every direction. Sure, I wanted the Jews out. All the rest of them too: Germans, Russians, Polacks. I wish could have thrown them all on a bonfire. Burn the weeds and make the land green again. We took German guns to fight the Bolsheviks, sure. We needed training too. They offered it and I took it."

"I've seen photographs. A synagogue on fire. You and my uncle—close enough to warm your hands . . ."

"The Jews of Lithuania were always working for the Russians!" Viktoras shouted. "If you scratched a Jew, they were Russian underneath."

"But you did more than scratch them, didn't you? You and your boys."

She stood up and pushed the notebook closer to him. It was wrapped in rubber bands and it bulged in the middle. "There's money in there. The same as last time. You'll recognize my uncle's handwriting. His memory failed him when it came to Lithuanians who joined the SS, but he was good on other nationalities. I want you to confirm all the names he wrote down and add as many others as you can."

He picked up the book reluctantly, hefting it for weight. "You're like a Jew landlord." He was his old hard self again. He had been in more interrogation rooms than she had fingers.

"Every name you add helps keep yours off the list." She stood up and backed toward the door, both hands still in her pockets.

"Not for me either," he said vaguely. "What?"

"It's not all about money for me."

He studied his hands, spreading the thick fingers wide. They were caked with black dirt and there were rings of dried blood around the nails. "Sometimes when I'm finished here for the day, I look at these and I don't know how I'll ever get them white again. My daughter won't let me in the house like this. She makes me wash in the yard, like an animal."

"Keep scrubbing, old dog. You need to scrub a little more before you get clean, and before you and I are done."

4
MOSCOW, 1948-61

When Yulia Sergeiovna Forsheva was seven, she went to her father and announced that she had learned the game of chess and had already beaten the boy who was supposed to be the best player in her class.

Sergei ignored her. He was lying on a sofa under a blanket drawn up to his neck, reading the chess column on the back page of the *Komsomolskaya Pravda*. He wrote notes in the margin with a pencil. He never read anything else in the newspaper. Most of the books he owned were stored in boxes then: the novels and volumes of poetry and short stories. He did not read for pleasure in those days, before the death of Stalin.

They were in the old flat, the one he had designed himself. Yulia knew that her father was an important man and worked on something called modular housing, among many other projects of great significance. The family did not have a dacha then. Sergei had the tired eyes of a much older man. He suffered attacks of what her mother called "weakness of the nerves" in winter. He said that bad men had once taken him away to live in a place even colder than Moscow, and when that kind of cold sinks into your bones, it stays there forever.

"I will show you, Papa."

A couple of minutes later, Sergei peered over the top of the newspaper and saw that the little girl had set up his chess set on a small table close to his elbow. She knelt on the floor at the other side of the table and looked up at him expectantly. She pushed a white pawn forward two squares. Yulia was an appealing child with plump cheeks and very large brown eyes.

Her father frowned and waved a hand. "This is not the way to learn."

"But I know all the rules."

"Congratulations. Now you can fritter away some idle time playing with your friends. Sometimes you will win, sometimes them. You may as well flip a coin."

Yulia put her elbows on the table, rested her chin on her fists and stared at her father. He refused to lift his eyes from the newspaper. Eventually he said, very lightly: "Do you merely want to pass some time, or do you want to win?"

"I want to win. Tell me how."

Sergei was pleased but did not let it show. He folded the paper and wrinkled his nose. "You are not ready yet. Yesterday, when Mama was feeling ill and trying to sleep in her room, you made a dreadful racket in the passageway outside, even though I told you not to, and the two of you had a row about it. I heard every word."

"That's not fair, Papa. I already said sorry."

"The point is that you did not consider how your mother was feeling. The secret of this game is that you put yourself in the other person's shoes. You always think about what your opponent wants."

"Teach me, Papa. Please."

"Will you listen? Will you think about other people?"

"I promise."

Sergei removed all the pieces from the board except six. He set the remaining chessmen up in the corner. He moved first and had more pieces.

"This is where we begin," he said. "It is called the endgame."

Yulia was eleven, and about to walk into the kitchen of their second floor flat on a bright morning in March 1953 when an unusual sight made her stop in the doorway. Her parents were holding each other in a silent embrace. She could not see her mother's face, but Anna's shoulders were trembling. Sergei said to Yulia: "There is no school today. Look outside."

She realized that her parents were standing in a puddle of spilled milk and broken glass. As she went to the window, Sergei took his wife's face in both hands and kissed her on the lips.

Yulia could see the faces of people gathering on the football pitch between their block of flats and the one opposite. Some clustered into groups, while others stood alone, swaying slightly as if drunk. Patriotic music was being piped from the loudspeakers that stood in the four corners of the sports field. Some wept openly, but not everyone who was crying looked sad. It was hard to tell what people were feeling. No one spoke or looked each other in the eye. Someone had propped a portrait of Stalin against one of the goalposts, and people were leaving flowers and other offerings around it.

"He is dead," said Sergei. Yulia's mother let go of her husband and ran from the room.

School was closed for a week. Anna stayed at the Kremlin for three days and nights. Sergei told Yulia her mother was like a sailor, trying to steer the ship in the right direction in the middle of a storm.

A year later, Anna became the first woman to join the Politburo of the Soviet Union. Her new salary was seven times that of a factory worker.

"Only a general or marshal of the Red Army earns more," Anna announced over dinner.

"They are the only ones who can kill more people than you with a bad decision," said Sergei.

Anger clouded his wife's face, but she did not reply immediately. She chewed and swallowed three more forkfuls of food. She rinsed her mouth with brandy and said: "That is where you come in. That is why I need you."

The family moved into a house in Barvikh that was four times the size of their old flat. There was no more queuing in shops. Anna was given a driver, and soon insisted on personal bodyguards too. She was allowed to choose the men herself. They were always handsome young soldiers.

The Young Pioneers gave a presentation at Yulia's school that year. They were looking for new recruits. They talked about how children around the world were helping to build socialism. They told stories of the heroic Pioneers who had died after being sent into battle in the Great

Patriotic War. Anna thought Yulia would look very fetching in a Pioneer uniform, posing for photographs alongside her mother. Yulia didn't like the outfits of the girls who visited her school: their white blouses looked itchy and badly cut. Anna told her that such things could easily be solved by a visit to a place called the Black Market. People like them did not have to wear blouses made from scratchy polyester. Anna would have a beautiful uniform made for Yulia by hand out of imported cotton. Yulia asked what her mother meant by "people like them" but Anna could not explain and became angry.

When they played chess that evening, Sergei told Yulia that he would buy her any of the things she had been pestering him for—a new bicycle, piano lessons, a trip to a summer camp—if she made him a solemn, secret promise: that she would never join the Young Pioneers.

Yulia was fifteen in the summer of 1957, when the influenza pandemic that was sweeping the world hit the Soviet Union. Sergei fell into a long fever, his temperature spiking above forty degrees. Anna told Yulia to stay away from him. She ignored this and sat by her father's bed as he fretted and muttered to himself and looked around the room at people and things that were not there. It was the first time she heard him talk about the Zone.

The stories were disjointed and it was hard to make sense of them. He had been building a railway line. Logs rolled off a train one day and killed the men unloading them. The bodies were left out in the sun. The work schedule could not be interrupted.

The guards did not bother to watch the prisoners when they turned them out to work in the *taiga*—the endless wilderness that was more deadly than any penal regime. They knew the inmates would return at the end of their shift, preferring the cell walls to the bears and tigers outside.

A group of Kalmyks arrived late one night and were kept in a holding cell. It was an administrative error. There was no room for them in the camp. Sergei heard the head of security grumbling: "We are not made of rubber. The walls won't bend."

Guards stood around, patting their pockets for notes and coins, looking keenly at the six men in the holding cell.

The platoon commander slid a sharp pickaxe between the bars and it clattered on to the concrete floor. The Kalmyks looked down at the axe, then up at the platoon commander. He said: "I will free the one who survives."

The women grew as coarse and aggressive as the male inmates. The men gradually became animals. They would do anything to distract themselves from reality. They made vicious, blinding methyl alcohol from boot polish strained through bread. Guards and prisoners alike played dice and cards incessantly. Gambling led the *zeks* into perilous webs of obligation. Men who could not pay their debts had to sever the tips of their fingers as punishment, or prostitute themselves to other men.

There were times when Sergei talked lucidly about his life in the camp, in great detail and without passion. He spoke of the climatic conditions: the waterlogged land that bred the swarms of biting insects; the air that formed over the tundra, much colder than Arctic Sea air, which made the killing Siberian winter. Yulia realized he had lapsed into the habits of thought that had sustained him during his imprisonment. He had learned to step back from the horror of immediate experience and analyze everything like a scientist, looking for the principles and deep structures that might explain the brutal world of the Zone.

As his fever grew to its climax, Sergei began to give in to emotion and his voice weakened. It was not clear that he still knew who Yulia was as he spoke haltingly of the final phase of his prison term. Something terrible had happened in those last months, which he struggled to put into words. Sorrow and shame consumed him eventually and his voice gave out, but not before she had teased out the dark secret with gentle questions. Sergei's record of good behavior had impressed the camp authorities. Near the end of his sentence, they had made him an auxiliary guard. It was an honor reserved for the most trusted *zeks*: they became responsible for keeping order among the other inmates, in exchange for privileges, protection, and a uniform.

In the second half of 1957, the autumn of Sputnik 1, Anna became known as the hostess who threw the best parties in Moscow—raucous gatherings of great political value. The whole country seemed to be flying as high as the little satellite, and fellow members of the Politburo, their families and their courtiers flocked to the house in Barvikh every weekend. Sergei stayed away on those evenings. Yulia was allowed to attend, and her mother encouraged her to drink alcohol and dress in the latest fashions. She had always thought of the girl as a kind of attractive doll. As Yulia reached her late teens, she became an increasingly amusing companion, entertaining the adults with a wit and wisdom beyond her years.

Yulia remembered the night when her mother produced a magnum of real champagne, a gift from the French ambassador. The guests all crowded together in the kitchen. The new foreign minister, Shulgin, was given the task of prizing cork from bottle. There was a cheer when the bang came. Yulia had never tasted anything so complex and beguiling, so alive with effervescence. Everyone rolled the wine around their mouths and looked at Anna. She loyally pronounced it inferior to the Soviet answer to champagne—sweet sparkling wine from the east of Georgia. All the others dutifully agreed. Anna winked at Yulia and they smiled.

Later that night, Yulia pulled Shulgin's son Pavel into her bedroom by the tie and almost kissed him into unconsciousness. When he declared his devotion to her in a long, ungrammatical letter, she dropped him instantly. Anna was livid. The boy was said to have threatened suicide. It meant that the foreign minister would not be attending Anna's parties from now on. She slapped her daughter's face and called her a "street butterfly."

When Yulia sat opposite her father that evening, the chessboard between them, he saw what she had become: a slender beauty with a lively, mischievous face that drew all eyes to it.

"There will be men, from now on," he told her. "They are going to come creeping around here like cats. My advice is to try out as many as you can before you decide to keep one. But there is no need to be a little Baba Yaga about it when you throw them back. Treat them with kindness, and they will remember. Then you can be friends later."

After that Yulia lost interest in the house parties. She enjoyed the occasional release of a wild night out with school friends, but in truth, it was becoming increasingly obvious that she was her father's daughter. She could lose herself in study for many hours, forgetting to eat. Sergei set her a mathematical problem every morning. An English tutor was arranged. She was encouraged to read everything in the house.

One box of books had long remained unopened at the bottom of the wardrobe in her father's study. Yulia picked through it one day, rubbing the dust from her eyes. There were unlined notebooks of different sizes, full of pen sketches, and a large folder of paintings. The pictures dated from Sergei's teenage years in the 1920s. Yulia could see the early evidence of his genius for draftsmanship in all of it.

The young Sergei had seen the future. He had sat cross-legged on the floor of his bedroom and experienced visions. He had drawn lancing rockets and communications satellites and floating, enclosed worlds in bubbles where spacemen and women lived, circling the Earth. Sergei had sketched in the plants the star-dwellers grew, the pipes that carried water and oxygen for them. In one picture, a helmeted man swam through pasteled darkness, attached to his spacecraft by an umbilical tether. Four Cyrillic letters on his chest showed that he was a Soviet cosmonaut, decades before such a thing existed. There were cities sketched out on Earth too: spectacular towers as busy as hives, linked by bridges. The rooftops were gardens. Cars rumbled along underground roads. Athletes pranced on the green land above.

Sergei laughed cynically when Yulia presented him with the drawings. As the 1960s approached, he became increasingly troubled. Snatches of overheard conversations told her that he was taking a great interest in military technology, and nuclear weapons in particular. He once let slip that he had seen the plans for a new hydrogen bomb of terrifying power. A colleague had shown him secret blueprints at great personal risk. Sergei drew concentric circles on his blackboard, explaining what would happen to the people who lived inside the rings if such a monstrous device was ever used in anger.

Atomic warfare was not Sergei's field, and the consequences were not his responsibility. Yulia did not understand why he tortured himself by probing the darkness. She took some of his youthful sketches from the box in the wardrobe and attached them to the wall of the study, all around the blackboard. She wanted to remind him of the pure dreams of his boyhood. Her father laughed at the gesture. But he did not take the pictures down.

Her parents rarely argued openly, but Yulia could sense the tension between them. Anna came home noisily one night after Yulia had gone to bed. The girl heard her mother's shrill, mocking voice coming up from the living room: "You are not like a Russian man at all. Can't you at least stop moping around and have a drink? It would do you good."

"You drink enough for both of us. You are making a fool of yourself."

There was a sharp crack that could only have come from her mother's palm against Sergei's cheek. After a long pause, Anna said: "Since when have you cared about gossip?"

"Since the day you started presenting my ideas to the Politburo. I need them to listen to you."

"Very patriotic!" There was a nasty edge in Anna's voice. "Shall I tell them everything you are pondering?"

"When you start having ideas of your own you can criticize mine."

"Like running away and leaving us?" Yulia had reached the bottom of the staircase now, moving like a cat.

"You are mistaken," said her father, steadily. "I would never abandon this family, as you once tried to. That is the difference between us."

Yulia was peeping through the gap in the door now and she saw the effect of these words. Anna was doubled up, holding her stomach

as though someone had hit her there. She gasped for air. When she subsided on to her hands and knees Sergei walked over to her and scooped
his palms under both his wife's shoulders and pulled her from the floor.
Anna had let herself go limp. She looked up at him, pleading, as he led
her gently to the sofa.

Sergei went down on one knee next to where Anna lay and whispered something Yulia could not hear. When her parents kissed suddenly, it was so unexpected and strange and intimate that she retreated
from the doorway with a shudder of disgust at herself and crept back up
the dark staircase.

Chess was the constant. It was always there: a secret language that bound
father and daughter together through the years, excluding Anna and
all others.

In her earliest lessons, Yulia started from a hopeless position and
had to fight off the inevitable checkmate for as long as she could. If she
survived for ten moves, they chalked it up as a victory in the corner of
the blackboard.

Later, they added more pieces. She always moved second and was
always behind on points. Now, if she fought to a stalemate from a bad
position, it counted as a victory. Gradually, they worked their way backwards to the middle game. She was not allowed to think about winning
yet, only avoiding defeat. She ground out rearguard actions, finding
tiny opportunities to delay and frustrate her father. He was relentless
in attack, making no allowances for her age or inexperience. He always
asked her the same questions: "What do I want? What am I going to do
next?" She was never allowed to concede.

It was not until a full year had passed that they played an entire
game of chess from beginning to end.

Later, Yulia began to compete seriously. Her father's methods had
made her strongminded. Most young players could not cope when they
made a blunder or suffered a sudden reversal of fortune. If they slipped
behind, they would fall into a spiral of self-recrimination and lose their

focus. They would give up quickly. When Yulia found herself losing it was like coming home to a place of comfort. She had been on the back foot so many times that she knew how to dig in, to stop the slow slide to defeat and push back, one agonizing step at a time. Her father never watched her compete, as other parents did. Yulia played alone. She never gave up.

The endgame was her first love and her specialty. Later in her career, a favorite tactic was to take any equal exchange offered. She would trade a bishop for a bishop or a queen for a queen as soon as possible. It led to early bloodbaths—blizzards of cross-capturing that left her adversaries bewildered. The board emptied fast and space opened up. Her opponents struggled to adjust their tactics to the new angles and possibilities. Yulia loved having the space to maneuver. She rose quickly through the tournament rankings.

5
ENGLAND, 1961

"Bikini," said the woman. Michael nearly spat the tea out of his mouth.

"I'm sorry, miss?"

"Bikini Atoll, in the Pacific. They've detonated another H-bomb. That's the big story today."

She glanced down at her newspaper. "Thirty times more powerful than Nagasaki. Are you waiting for an interview?"

He was dressed smartly and there was a thick pile of handwritten notes on the seat next to him, along with a flask and sandwiches.

"Modern languages," he said, wiping his mouth with the back of his hand.

"They always ask you what's on the front page of *The Times*. Everyone knows that! Do you want to have a look at this? Or shall I shut up? I'm distracting you, aren't I?"

This was undeniably true. He was sitting outside the entrance of the dining hall where the students of King's College, Cambridge, ate. The end of the Easter vacation was approaching. Major Gagarin had recently orbited the Earth, and it was warm enough to sit outside. Ever since the woman had clicked past him and arranged herself at the other end of the wooden bench, Michael's mind had drifted away from the idiosyncratic religious beliefs of Leo Tolstoy to altogether more worldly matters.

The woman had slanting green eyes and a pantherine face. Her fine bright blonde hair was swept back from a high forehead. She was wearing leather boots, a tweed skirt and a sweater that clung to her upper body. Something about her posture radiated health and strength. He wondered if she swam—or lay on her back and pressed dumbbells, like the great Monroe.

Michael tugged at his tie and nudged his spectacles, smiling weakly. He made a valiant effort to dive back into the notes. He had a theory about Tolstoy's short stories that he had been working up for a while, but when he rehearsed it with Father Malachy, he always lost the thread halfway through.

The woman had a scuffle with her newspaper, then stretched one arm out along the top of the bench toward him. Emerald-green fingernails that matched her eyes lolled a few inches from Michael's shoulder. "Are you going to stay the night?" she asked softly.

"Sorry?"

"Are you staying overnight in Cambridge? Or are Mummy and Daddy lurking somewhere, waiting to whisk you home?"

"It's just Daddy, these days. And no, he's busy." It sounded so self-pitying that he added quickly: "My dad can't stand Cambridge, actually. He was at Trinity before the war and he says he hated every minute of it."

"Trinity College in the thirties. That must have been fascinating. But it can't have been much fun without any women around, can it?" She had a wicked smile.

"Are you here for an interview too?" he asked.

"How *sweet* of you. We both know that I'm far too old. I'm a mature student, also studying languages. I'm from Sweden. My name is Greta."

"Michael Fitzgerald." She made him say it again. She repeated the surname as though it was something exotic.

"Greta is easy to remember. Like a film star."

"Am I?"

"Like *the* film star, I mean. Like Greta Garbo."

"How kind. But you really must concentrate now. I am going to leave you to your preparation." She stood and wrestled the newspaper into submission. She squeezed his arm as she walked past. "I know you are going to do well today. Good luck and remember Bikini."

Michael spoke Russian with Professor Colin Sinclair for almost an hour without a break. He flagged toward the end and had a feeling he had made a mess of the whole interview. Eventually Sinclair said: "I think that will do, Michael, we'll leave it there. Let me have a look at your application form. What did you put for hobbies?"

There was a cavernous dark oak cupboard the size of a double wardrobe right behind the professor's desk. It was empty except for a pile of thin cardboard folders. The professor bent down to sift through them.

"Chess," Michael replied sullenly, convinced he had failed.

"I have it now. You're rather good, aren't you? Any other interests?"

"Nothing that would look good on a Cambridge application. I love music from Chicago and the Mississippi Delta. I love the cinema."

"Do you have any posters on your bedroom wall?"

Michael drew a deep breath. It probably didn't matter now anyway, so he said truthfully: "Gina Lollobrigida. A few friends of hers. Muddy Waters. Yuri Gagarin."

"I can't imagine your father would approve of the last."

Michael looked very intently at the smoke that was curling from the bowl of Sinclair's untouched pipe.

The professor said: "I know him slightly—the vice admiral. I was half expecting this form to be written in invisible ink."

There was a shout from one of the protesters out in the street and the professor got up and walked over to the big bay window to watch them. King's Parade was packed with marchers. The CND logo was everywhere. There were banners that read "Action for Life" and "End Imperialist Wars." A group of young men in duffel coats and roll-neck sweaters were doing a fair imitation of a New Orleans funeral band, led by a tall, handsome young man with a trumpet.

Michael said: "I am not my father. My politics aren't his. I'm not a Communist either. Sorry if that's a disappointment." The professor stared silently out of the window. "I don't want any favors. If I'd wanted to pull strings I would have applied to Trinity."

Professor Sinclair turned back to him. "You will find that Trinity and King's are very different." He looked at Michael with one eyebrow raised, waiting for the significance of the word *will* to sink in. He smiled when he saw Michael's face flush with gratitude. "Just one more thing. I think it's against the law for me not to ask you this: what's on the front page of today's *Times?*"

Michael could smell the sea through pine trees. A warm riviera some-where. The tree line came right up to the beach, and you crunched through pinecones to get to it. The sand was bright white. There was a girl—no, a woman—laughing, beckoning. Reaching *down* toward him. Her features were indistinct. The smell of tobacco intruded.

He awoke slowly into the cold reality of the small dormitory room he shared with three others. The funk of young men living together at close quarters hung heavy in the air. It was the middle of July, nearly three months after his Cambridge interview, past the official end of his last term at boarding school. But he was still there, in the big white mock-Gothic cube on the outskirts of Oxford, and there was a chill in the early morning air. Michael reached for his spectacles and was rewarded with a view of his gallery of poster girls: Gina Lollobrigida, Jean Seberg, Brigitte Bardot.

Craig was already awake, smoking by the open window.

"That's why it's so fucking freezing. Thanks very much," said Michael. He had the beginnings of a sore throat. "You must pay for this outrage in tea, Mr. McNichol."

"No," said Craig, peering grimly out across the broad quadrangle. "Coffee time, I think." He got up and stubbed out the cigarette franti-cally, then started flapping a towel toward the open window.

"Is it Malachy?"

"He's like a bad smell. You can't get rid of him. There's a man in uniform with him. Michael, will you for shite get up and help me?"

"Don't open the window wide. You'll blow it back in. Put the fag ends under the coffee grounds in the bin. Wash your hands and brush your teeth."

A knock came and Michael swept open the door. "Father. Always a pleasure . . . *Christ.*"

The priest was standing next to a young man in sharply creased RAF blue. Peter Deacon, the fourth resident of the room. He had left six weeks ago as a schoolboy cadet. Michael had never seen him in uniform before. The unruly hair he remembered was brutally short at the sides now and plastered down flat on top. Deacon stepped into the room and said: "Wish me luck, boys. I've taken the Queen's commission."

Tom wolf-whistled from his bed. Michael said: "Well done, Peter, congratulations."

"Load of bollocks," said Craig, then raised a hand. "Sorry, Father."

"I have heard worse. I will take a cup of Michael's excellent coffee as recompense. I don't think Pilot Officer Deacon needs any. He has enough to be nervous about."

Deacon sat on the edge of his old bed. The priest sank into the ancient leather armchair. It took him a while to settle, like a cat. The chair was directly under a poster of Bardot in fishnets, and he looked up at her doubtfully.

"Pin-ups," the priest mused. "The eternal privilege of the upper sixth. What an odd mixture of traditions we have here. But, Michael, I have it on good authority that this particular young woman is considered past her prime now."

Michael said: "I will remain loyal to Brigitte forever."

From his bed, Tom called: "You're never loyal to the real ones."

Michael grimaced. He put the beans into the grinder, then spooned the ground coffee into the Bialetti. He packed it down tight with the back of the spoon. If you put milk in the top part, the hot coffee scalded it when it bubbled up.

The priest cast a slow eye over his charges. He wasn't much older than them. Deacon had one leg thrown over the other and his Oxford shoes shone with polish. Craig was brushing his teeth. Tom hauled himself out of bed and padded over to the mirror above the wash basin. He yawned and began to fuss with his hair.

Father Malachy looked at him with great interest. "Do you remember when I had to go back to Ireland? Then I was called to Rome? I was away for a year in all. It is a strange thing, but when I left every young man in the school was combing their hair from front to back, like Elvis Presley. And when I came back, every single one was brushing it forward. I'm not complaining. It's an improvement. You ought to look like what you are: polite young English men, not American hooligans."

"Mmm, not English," said Craig, through the toothbrush.

"I never appreciated the fact, until I taught here, that boys preen and primp themselves as much as girls, if not more so. Mr. Clarke is going to wear that mirror out soon, and Michael already has the best wardrobe in the school. Michael, I propose to add to your enviable tie collection."

"Sir?"

"No joke. A new tie of your choice. Courtesy of the headmaster, if you can believe that. Peter and I have important news. A game at chess, my masters."

Instantly, the young priest had Michael's full attention. He accepted the mug of coffee gratefully and snuffed up the curling steam extravagantly. "This is an odd obsession for a boy of eighteen. Not that I am complaining."

Tom said: "Michael's father. One of his extravagant presents. He gives a fifteen-year-old boy a coffee machine. Can you imagine? Michael had to promise him two things when he came here: don't get any townie girls pregnant and never drink instant coffee."

"It's the only fatherly advice he's ever given me," said Michael. "You mentioned chess, sir?"

Deacon piped up from the bed. "I was supposed to play in the European semi-finals next week. I can't go, Mike. My squadron's had our orders."

"Where?" asked Craig. "Is it Czechoslovakia?"

"You know I can't say."

"Is it Germany?"

"Leave him alone," said Michael. "What is this thing? What did you say? European finals?"

"Semis. You're in, Mike. You've got my place. The head fixed it with the organizers."

Michael opened his mouth to protest but Deacon said: "No false modesty, Mike. Who else would we send? We both know you're better than me on a good day."

Deacon was ranked third in the country in his age group. Michael wondered what his own true ranking was. He was a temperamental chess player who performed erratically in competitions. The thought of taking on the best young players in Europe made his stomach turn over. Father Malachy raised an eyebrow archly. "The headmaster wanted me to go with you, Michael, but I think you will do very well on your own. Of course, this will be your very first night out in the great capital, so you may get dazzled by the bright lights." Craig and Tom sniggered.

Father Malachy said: "You get two nights in the Excelsior. Not far from your usual haunts in Soho. Accommodation and travel expenses paid. No need to hitchhike down this time. Thank you for the coffee. Gentlemen, I will leave you."

When the priest had gone, Craig burst out laughing. "No flies on him. He's got you figured out, Mike. *Your usual haunts.*"

"Have you been tearing up London?" asked Deacon, leaning back on the bed. "Can't say I blame you. What the fuck are you all doing hanging around here, anyway? Hasn't term finished?"

"They're letting a few of us stay for a bit because our parents are on a war footing. It's very queer. There must be three priests in the whole place. We've been running riot."

Deacon cast a critical eye around the square room, with its flaking plaster and thin, mean lead windows. The school had been built as a grand Victorian mansion, but everything had been badly done. There were cracks in the walls around the windows into which the boys could squeeze the tips of their fingers.

The other three were all eyeing Deacon curiously. He was the same age as them, but the uniform made everything different. He had moved beyond them into another world.

Craig said: "How many babies are you going to kill, then, Pete? Going to flatten Moscow?"

"That's right. I'll write your name and address on the bomb."

"We saw the film on Friday. Have you seen it? *The Firestorm*. Banned by the government. For sowing terror and despair. They showed it at Tom's brother's college. Tell, him, Tom."

"It's like a drama, but it shows you what happens after a nuclear strike. The first thing is that everyone goes blind. The flash melts your eyeballs."

"They give us goggles," said Deacon. "Next."

"Something called the Shock Front. It knocks all the houses down. If you survive that, you get the radiation. A silent, deadly cloud of poison."

"I'll be sailing above all that, men, but I'll be thinking of you all down here."

"You're a callous bastard, Deacon," snapped Craig.

Tom had begun to shave at the washbasin. "It scared the shit out of me. Michael wouldn't go. He's staying away from the Oxford colleges, though, aren't you, Fitz? He was hanging around my brother's friends, passing himself off as an undergrad. He was knocking the girls over like skittles, until they found out he was an impostor."

"It was one girl," said Michael. "And I didn't tell her any lies."

"I don't believe any of this," said Craig, bitterly.

Deacon goggled. "An older woman? The dream. You disgusting fornicator, Mike. I love it. Tell me everything."

"A gentleman doesn't," said Michael, piously, to a chorus of groans. "I don't believe a word of it," said Craig. "Older women. What has he got that I haven't?"

"Good looks," called Tom from the basin. "Manners. And they can understand what he's saying. Jesus Christ, not again."

He turned around to show them a long crimson slash along the side of his chin. Michael and Craig yelled in alarm. Tom always cut himself spectacularly when he shaved, and the bleeding took an age to stop. He was supposed to take medicine for it.

"We don't need any horror films with you around," said Michael, getting up to help him find the styptic pencil among the toiletries littered around the sink.

Michael glanced past Tom at his own reflection, seeing all the things he didn't like: the jutting ears, the angry traces of acne on the forehead. *Good looks?* The chin is all right, he thought—too strong, in fact, for the skinny frame below. He had a firm enough jawline and a rather big mouth, which a girl had once said reminded her of Jean-Paul Belmondo. Michael did not argue, although he could not see the resemblance.

Nothing like Belmondo from the mouth up, he thought. He had never had his nose broken, and he believed that his eyes were weak, watery and set too close together. The glasses magnified them and brought balance to the face. This is my best feature, he thought, running his hand through dark brown hair, which the summer sun had turned the color of straw in places. I wonder if I'll lose it one day. Dad never did.

Michael ruffled his hair. He liked to dress well but leave one element of his appearance askew: a wayward tie or collar; the fringe artfully disheveled. It was an old ploy. It made girls want to reach out and fix you.

"So none of you are going to do your bit?" Deacon was asking, looking around him with a hint of contempt. "All too busy womanizing?"

"I'm not fighting on the side of imperialism," said Craig.

"I'd bleed to death if I got a paper cut," said Tom, cheerfully. "Never mind the Shock Front."

Michael turned away from the mirror, tapping the frame of his glasses ruefully and mumbling something.

Craig said: "The Shock Front wasn't the worst bit. It was the going blind. I don't mind dying if it's like that." He snapped his fingers. "But imagine creeping round the ruins, blind . . ."

"Shut up a minute. What did you say, Mike?" asked Deacon, cupping his ear.

"I said I asked about joining the air force. My eyesight wasn't good enough."

6

Before the day he walked into the lobby of the excelsior Hotel, Michael had never seen a pack of reporters and photographers in action. The press men were there for Szekeres and the great champion posed for them gamely. He wore a bow tie and his last few strands of hair were slicked back. The photographers were clamoring for shots as Szekeres walked slowly across the thick red carpet with its bold diamond pattern toward the entrance of the hotel, and Michael had to dance away so they didn't back into him.

He saw a bank of telephones near the grand staircase at the end of the lobby and thought about ringing his father. In his jacket pocket he carried a pack of cigarette papers with a telephone number scribbled on top. His father's people changed the number every month for security and Michael threw away the top paper and wrote the new number underneath. Every wood-paneled phone booth was busy with reporters calling in their stories for newspapers and agencies around the world.

There was a sudden shower of rain outside and the girl came through the revolving door into the lobby, followed by her bodyguards. She was holding the collar of her jacket up. Her hair was wet and her face was screwed up with displeasure. She nearly stopped his heart.

She wore a simple black dress and no makeup. Her hair was the true strawberry blonde. She could have been Irish, but the eyes would have been blue, and these were dark brown. There was a spray of freckles radiating out from a point between and below the eyes, as though she had just been speeding along in an open-topped car and the onrushing wind had left an imprint of its vitality stamped on her face. She wore flat shoes and walked like a dancer, with her feet turned out a little. Michael realized he was staring openly at her. He wondered how the other men in the lobby managed not to do the same.

The two men flanking the girl looked methodically around the room as they walked. Michael had never seen a Russian tough guy before, but he knew instantly and with absolute certainty that these men were Russian and very tough. The man loping behind the girl, just off her right shoulder, was enormous. His hair was cut short at the back and sides and it stood up tall and straight like a brush on top. He was heavy all over but not fat in the stomach. His suit was shiny and boxy over the shoulders. The trousers were too long, piling up in folds on top of the shoes. The tie was unfashionably broad. The second man walked a few paces behind the other two. He was a different kind of animal altogether. He reminded Michael of the Sicilian and Maltese blades he knew by sight from the cafés and clubs they ran in Soho—the kind of men who got their fingernails manicured but would not hesitate to smash their knuckles against your head if the occasion demanded it. This man wore gray flannel trousers with a sharp crease that broke high over black square-toed shoes. He had a houndstooth sports coat and a skinny knitted tie, kept in place with a simple silver clip. His head was shaved smooth with a razor. He had very Slavic features.

As he passed Michael, the Russian saw how he was looking at the girl with frank admiration and their eyes met for a second. The man smiled, and it was an expression that contained good humor and menace in equal measure.

Everyone had three games on the first day. Michael played a very young, terrifyingly good Hungarian boy and lost quickly. Then he played a Norwegian man in his mid-twenties with film star looks, and they reached stalemate. In his final game, Michael faced another English contestant, a boy from a Jewish boarding school he had played before. He struggled to concentrate but his opponent made a catastrophic blunder in the middle game and could not recover. Eventually the boy tipped his king over in disgust, shook hands and stood up quickly.

You got a point for a win and half for a draw, so that gave Michael one and a half points out of a maximum of three at the end of the first day. They had set up a big scoreboard on a tripod near the main staircase at the back of the hotel lobby, and Michael's name was halfway down the list. He had done just enough to make the cut for the second day. It was surreal to see his name among those of famous players whose fortunes he had followed for years in the chess magazines. Some of the older competitors had given their names to strategies and positions that had become fixtures in the modern game, and which he had pored over as a boy.

Michael remembered that these were semi-finals and that he had meant to find out when and where the final round of the competition would take place. He had forgotten to ask. It felt good just to turn up and play for the hell of it, unburdened by expectation.

The Russian girl was deep in her last game of the day and Michael hovered close to her table. She was behind on points but was playing very confidently, pausing only briefly between moves. Her opponent wore a look of intense concentration, like someone who had unexpectedly been asked to take the controls of an airplane. The girl's bodyguards lounged on a bench nearby.

The young Norwegian man he had played in his second game clapped him on the shoulder.

"Michael, right? We weren't introduced properly. I'm Johannes Jensen, but friends call me Johnny. I enjoyed our game. Someone just told me you are joining us at Cambridge soon."

"Oh—I don't know yet. I'm still waiting for my A-level results. I was going to defer this year, but they put on special interviews at Easter for people whose parents are on active service."

"I'll keep my fingers crossed for you. I run the university chess society and we're always in the market for world-class players."

"I've heard about you," said Michael. "They said you were a maths lecturer, but you look too young."

The Norwegian was the kind of man people talked about. His father lived in a castle. He spoke five languages. He won medals for mathematics and roared around in a sports car. He was a spy, he was a con man, he was the illegitimate heir to the throne of Norway. His mother owned an island. When he walked across the hotel lobby, women stared.

"I'm halfway through my doctorate. I do a bit of teaching on the side. You're a mathematician too, right?"

Michael said, no, he wasn't, and the Norwegian's face fell. "I'll be reading modern languages, if I get in. Mostly Russian."

"That will come in very handy when our new masters take over. I'd better stick with you, Michael. You'd better let me buy you a drink if you're finished. Or are you waiting for someone?"

The Norwegian had noticed that Michael kept glancing over his shoulder while they were talking and he turned to see what the young man was so interested in.

"Now I get it. Other things on your mind. The red princess!"

"Do you know that girl?"

"Played her once. She tore me limb from limb. Crushed me like a steamroller. Want me to introduce you?"

"Yes, please, Johnny. I'd like that very much."

There was a drinks reception in the Excelsior's grand ballroom that night. Michael wore a tie and a blazer. Johnny Jensen was talking to Yulia, the Russian girl, on the far side of the room when he caught Michael's eye and waved him over. Her shadow with the shaved head sat in a chair at the side of the room, like a chaperone at a dance in *War and Peace*. His giant friend was nowhere to be seen.

As Michael crossed the room, a boy wearing a loud red jumper over a shirt and tie rapped his arm with his knuckles.

"Sorry," said Michael.

"Chas," said the boy, sticking out his hand. "I'm a reporter. We met at that youth thing last year." He shook Michael's hand and held on to it.

"Hello again. I can't remember who you're with."

"I'm an agency man. We put our copy out on the wires."

Michael was gazing over the boy's shoulder. He saw Yulia tug at her left earlobe with a finger and thumb.

"Struggle to get anything in at a big show like this," Chas was saying. "They can't get enough of chess in the east, can they? And the States. They're calling this the first battle of World War Three."

"Is that right?" Michael couldn't drag his eyes away from the Russian girl.

Chas nodded glumly. "Whoever wins tomorrow will be in the papers in thirty countries. They'll probably get a new tractor or something, won't they, if they're a Communist? Most of the national papers are staffing it themselves. Desks hack my copy to pieces. Never put my name on anything . . ."

Michael forced his attention back to the reporter. It was coming back to him. He had been drunk the first time they met, in a pub near Earls Court. The boy had been an apprentice at a Fleet Street newspaper then. He had shown Michael how he made notes in shorthand. He had to drain his glass suddenly and race to King's Cross to get the first editions of the next day's papers and call his news desk with all the headlines.

"I've never understood how agency reporters get paid," Michael said. "How do you know the paper used your version if everyone is covering the same story? Couldn't they say they got it from someone else?"

Now Yulia was fanning her face with her hand as if she was suddenly flushed and hot. What was in her glass? Michael couldn't quite see.

"Trade secret," said the reporter, glancing around and lowering his voice. "We put in deliberate mistakes. Nothing serious, of course—some tiny little detail. Let's say Szekeres has a green handkerchief in his pocket today and I say it's turquoise. Well, if *The Times* mentions a turquoise hanky in its write-up tomorrow, they must have based it on my copy, mustn't they?"

"You learn something new every day," said Michael. "Look—will you excuse me?"

Johnny was talking to Yulia about Russia when Michael approached them. The Norwegian was saying, "I never got to go to Leningrad . . ."

Yulia looked as though she wanted to ask him something, but Johnny caught sight of Michael and broke off so he could introduce them. Then he pretended to see someone else he knew by the drinks table so that he could leave them alone together. Michael was really starting to like him.

Michael and Yulia looked at each other for a beat. She shook her glass so that the ice cubes clinked against the side. He had been rehearsing what to say to her in Russian, but his nerve failed him at the last second and he spoke English.

"Everyone calls you the red princess. I wondered if you needed any dragons slaying?"

He could see instantly that it hadn't landed, and he cursed himself silently.

The girl said: "Drag. And sleighing?"

"Dragons. Killing. It means killing." It sounded very strange out loud and he realized he was waving a hand meaninglessly in the air. *Christ*, he thought.

"You don't look like a killer so much," the girl said. "Perhaps if you took your glasses off."

Yulia saw that he was dying inside and decided to rescue him. "Of course I am a princess. Every girl in the Soviet Union is a princess and every boy is a prince. We are a royal family of two hundred and ten millions."

"I've never been. I've heard it's lovely in Moscow this time of year."

"It is unbearably hot in summer. And winter is so cold that a pink English boy would die on the spot. It was below twenty-five degrees last Christmas."

"God almighty."

"It is all right as long as you wear your hat and gloves all the time. And if you do not get attached to anything."

He didn't quite understand what she meant, until she said: "I know a man who went drinking and lay down in the street, to make a joke. His face froze to the tram track. He could not stand up again. The others had to rip him away from the metal before he got squashed by a tram. He had a big red stripe across his face."

"Do you and your friends do a lot of drinking? I think you're going to fit in beautifully in London. You'll find it's just like home."

"This was not my friend. One of my mother's soldiers. And, no, I do not go out very often. Not at home and not on these trips. There are many places I wish to see in London, of course. But it is impossible."

She nodded toward her bodyguard, who was still sitting at the side of the room, smoking a Belomorkanal cigarette in a plastic holder.

Michael leaned in so close to the girl that he could hear her eyelashes when she blinked. Her physical presence was bewitching.

"I don't know what kind of things you like," he whispered. "There's an Italian place I go to that's not far, and a house party later on too. Johnny the Norwegian has invited everyone. Or will they think you've defected?"

"Don't make jokes about things you don't understand," said Yulia, sharply. Then she saw how stung he was, and how hard he was trying to please her. She reached out and touched his tie, which wasn't quite hanging true. "You are a handsome boy. But I cannot step outside this hotel. I have two guards. One is pig. I do not know the bald one over there very well, but he is an important man. He is unusual."

"Is he looking at us?" The man with the shaved head appeared to be singing softly to himself. They could see him tapping his fingers on his crossed leg and moving his lips.

"I don't think so. He is strange. I have never met a Soviet official who manages to travel so freely."

"Does he work at the embassy here?"

She shook her head. "Another of our government agencies. My mother said he was number three or four in this organization. But I cannot imagine Vassily ever taking orders from another man."

Upstairs, Yulia changed for dinner, because that was what English people were supposed to do, although it did not matter, because she would end up eating in silence with the two pigs in a deserted corner of the hotel dining room. Well, Oleg, at least, was a pig.

They had taken a suite of rooms, like a little flat. She had the big double bedroom with the ensuite bathroom and the balcony. The two men shared the smaller anteroom, which opened on to the hotel corridor. There was one door between the rooms with no lock on it. She couldn't go out into the corridor without getting past the bodyguards.

Yulia went into their room without knocking and the man with the shaved head was sitting cross-legged on the floor in his socks. A transistor radio was playing a news report in the Spanish language and he had the volume down low because the Pig was snoring loudly on one of the two single beds, still wearing his ill-fitting suit. The man called Vassily was working his way through a pile of newspapers: *Le Monde*, *El País*, the *International Herald Tribune*, *The Times* of London.

He said: "Our friend is feeling out of sorts. Something doesn't agree with him. The food, perhaps. The weather. The stink of capitalist excess in the air. I have given him something to help him sleep." He looked up and held her eye for a second as he said this.

"We have agreed that I am going to watch over you alone tonight while he recovers. I am going to lie across your doorway so no one can come in or out. Oleg believes that this is a fool proof plan. But he does not realize that a fire escape ladder is fitted to the side of your balcony, and that you could very easily lower this ladder, climb down it and find yourself on the service road behind the hotel. And if you left the balcony door unlocked, you could slip back in very easily later, as long as you did not make too much noise. And no one would know you were gone."

Yulia looked at Vassily the way she looked at a chess problem. She did not know him well, but she had come across many other Chekists like him—men from the same secret world. They breathed tricks and stratagems the way ordinary people breathe oxygen and nitrogen.

Vassily said: "Of course you and I, of all people, know what would happen if you came back too late." He looked over at the sleeping giant and checked his watch. "If you returned one minute after the stroke of midnight, you would never leave Russia again, and I would swap this comfortable suite for a private room on Lubyanka Square, with a sloping floor and a hole in the corner for the blood to drain away. So, Yulia Sergeiovna, you thought your life was in my hands this weekend, but really it is the other way around. Can I trust you?"

7

Night in Piccadilly. the neon burned: Coca-Cola, delicious and Refreshing; Smoke Player's; A Double Diamond Works Wonders. The air crackled with possibility. They sprinted for the statue of the winged boy god, and she balanced on one leg next to it, drawing an imaginary bowstring, posing for a picture that could not be taken, because there could be no record of these illicit moments.

Michael took her to Collini's. The boss, Santino, came over and shook their hands. He said: "This one's beautiful, Michael, not like all the others. It's a scandal, miss. Every week he's in here with a different girl." Yulia threw her head back and laughed.

As he walked away, Santino saw a customer tapping his cigarette under the table and shouted: "Hey, my friend. You let me know when the floor's full and I bring you an ashtray, okay?"

They went past the Vinyl Furlong and it was closed but Buddy was still there, counting the cash in the till, and he let them in. He was a Black American GI who had never gone home after the war.

They talked about the new releases until Yulia said: "What is this bird music?" and Buddy said: "Well, you're right. It is Bird. It's Charlie Parker. You don't like jazz?"

"I don't like this, whatever it is. It is like a flock of parrots. Do you have nothing that we can dance to?"

Buddy seemed taken aback, and Michael said: "You'd better get used to taking orders. She's from the other side of it. They'll be in charge soon."

"Oh—Russia? For real? In that case, young lady, I better fight you for control of the free world." And they arm wrestled on top of the counter and Yulia won and Buddy yelled: "God damn it, I was trying my hardest. She's as strong as a bear."

The prize was the first play of a new record straight in off the train from Liverpool. It was called "Smokestack Lightning" and it had a slapping, compulsive beat. In Moscow, the dance music was from Cuba and when Yulia danced it was all in the hips. It was the only way she knew how. It wasn't quite right for rhythm and blues, but Michael did not complain because she took his hands and they went up and down the aisle next to the listening booths, dancing very close.

In the Old Ship there was a drag act in the back room and it was three-deep at the bar. Michael bought gin and limes but a man in a seaman's uniform accused him of jumping the queue and cocked his fist at him. Two friends grabbed the man around the shoulders and pulled him away. When they left, the sailor followed them outside and got down on his knees unsteadily in the middle of the street. He slurred an apology to Michael and kissed Yulia's hand. The man's shipmates watched, so hysterical with laughter that they had to hold each other up.

Yulia bought champagne in the Deux Garçons. Every time she traveled outside Russia, she had to have the real thing. Even people like her parents could only get the stuff from Georgia. The name on the label was Tribaut and it was very cold and clean and refreshing. She looked through the windows at the crowds hurrying past. There was so much energy and variety. She thought of Gagarin's homecoming parade, and how the students had worn T-shirts with the words *Kosmos Nos*— Space Is Ours—on them. She wished she could wear something with London Is Ours emblazoned on it.

When the waiter refilled her glass a few spots of wine dripped on to the sleeve of her dress. She exploded at him, hissing oaths in Russian. The waiter recoiled, exchanging glances with Michael. Yulia's face was momentarily ugly, and a cold wave of doubt passed over Michael. He watched her dab at herself with a napkin, before crushing it in her hand. She sat in a despondent silence for a moment, then got up abruptly and walked over to the bar, where the waiter who had served them was scooping up another tray of drinks. Michael watched Yulia go up to him and touch his chest very lightly. The waiter stooped to hear over the noise of the bar and whatever she told him made him break out into a broad smile.

When she sat down again, Yulia said: "You will forgive me. I am not one of those bitches. I am on edge. This is a difficult time."

"Are you allowed to talk about it?"

She looked at Michael curiously. She saw that her changes of mood had thrown him. He had given up on the idea of seducing her, she guessed. But he had decided that he could still be a friend to her. She liked that very much.

"I've had enough of this place," she said, draining her glass. "Take me somewhere you go with your boys."

In the Endeavour they suddenly felt drunk and had their first argument. Michael said he liked America's new president because there had to be a counterweight to Communism, and Yulia said the president was a warmonger and the whole world was against Russia, and that Michael had been brainwashed, like all Catholics.

In the ladies' room, a woman was sitting peeing with the door of the cubicle wide open. "If you don't want him, I'll have him, dear. Good-looking boy like that. Or is he one of those? He could be, couldn't he?"

Yulia was still angry. "One of who? What do you mean?"

The woman made her way unsteadily to the washbasins. "The kind of boy who'll be your best friend, but not your boyfriend. There's a lot of them around here. I suppose there's only one way to find out, isn't there, darling?"

When Yulia got back to the table she reached under the duffel coat that was folded on his lap and explored between his legs with her hand. She felt his body responding eagerly and she said: "I am not a *kurva*. But we don't have much time."

He seemed to have lost the ability to move or speak. She leaned in slowly. "Are you frightened?"

"I don't want to cut myself on your cheekbones."

"You talk nicely. I like the way you talk. Keep going."

"I don't want to slip and fall into those enormous brown eyes and drown."

They kissed for the first time. Everything else ceased to exist. Olive, the landlady, hooted at them and told them they would have to go somewhere else if they couldn't behave themselves.

They looked at the time and tossed back their drinks, hailed a taxi and kissed again, seriously, in the back. No one interrupted until they got to the Golborne Road and the driver said they would have to get a bus back because none of the cabs would stop round here, not even for whites.

The party was in a basement flat. Johnny the Norwegian had a guest spot playing trumpet with the band. The style was called blue beat and Yulia had never heard music from the West Indies before, but it did not matter because it was literally irresistible: you could not listen to it and stand still.

It was an odd mixture of people. About half were white. Michael recognized some faces: a famous actor; a boy who had gone to his school and was now studying at the LSE; a young naval officer who worked for his father.

Johnny played with restraint at first, filling in the gaps left by the singers with little stabs. Then the band stretched out the same song for twenty minutes so they could all take it in turns to improvise. Michael liked the way Johnny played. He didn't just ripple up and down the scales. He put his solos together thoughtfully from clever little phrases and built to a crescendo.

A very blonde woman was dancing barefoot with an older white man right in front of the band, attracting envious glances. Michael recognized the man as a Cambridge academic who sometimes appeared as a guest on the BBC political programs. Michael was sure that he knew the woman from somewhere too and then it clicked.

"Greta," he called. Then, louder: "Hydrogen bomb." A blank look, then that lazy, sinful smile. She might have been a little drunk.

"The boy from the interview! How did you get on?"

"They made me an offer."

"How wonderful. What questions did they ask you?"

"About the newspaper. You were right. I owe you."

"You can pay me back some time. When do you arrive in Cambridge?"

"Nothing's decided yet. I'm still waiting for my exam results. This is a great party. Who do you know?"

"Me? Everyone!"

The band took a break. Johnny Jensen came over to the side of the room where Michael was standing and brought Scotch and Cokes for both of them. He slurped his drink as he followed Greta's movements with his eyes.

"All right, Michael. Time to return the favor. Who's that girl?"

"Greta from Sweden. She's a very close friend of mine and I want you to be a gentleman. She knows everyone and she's very interested in current affairs."

"Okay, Squadron Leader. Cover me. I'm going in."

Yulia had disappeared and Michael had a moment of mild panic until he heard the sound of her laughter and followed it outside. The party had swelled, spilling out on to the street. He recognized more people. Yulia was with a boy called Roosevelt and a West African man called Doctor something. Michael knew them from the clubs. There was a thick coil of smoke around their heads.

"Do you know what that is, Yulia?"

"Some kind of herbal cigarette, is what they told me. It has an unusual taste."

She waited until the look of horror had spread across the whole of his face, then roared with laughter. "You think we do not have this in Russia? I can get Indian hemp, my friend, if I want it—and better than this. We have everything you have and more. We have knives and forks, moving staircases, cosmonauts. How many English cosmonauts, please?"

"You don't have real champagne."

Yulia was trying to think of something clever when she caught sight of his watch. She grabbed his wrist so she could see it properly and cried out: "*Gavno.*"

Roosevelt had a 50cc Piaggio and the young man Michael knew from the LSE had a 150cc Innocenti. Yulia got on the back of the Vespa and Michael climbed on to the more powerful machine and they roared through Kensal Town and Maida Hill.

Yulia refused to hold on to scooter or rider. She was trying to bite the cork out of a half-empty bottle of wine that Roosevelt had swiped from the party. Michael was shouting at her to be careful and the wind was whipping her hair around. The street was empty and the two scooters were going at full throttle side by side on both sides of the road and she tossed the bottle to Michael, six feet away. It was an impossible catch but he made it, nearly overbalancing and making the scooter wobble danger-ously. She whooped with delight.

Near Paddington they went past four rows of bombed-out houses and fell silent, without knowing why. Away from the road, the rubble had not been cleared completely and you could see the wheel of a child's pram poking out from among the bricks.

They got back to the Excelsior at ten to midnight.

8

Michael and Yulia were over the road from the front entrance of the hotel. He looked at her and there were things that needed to be said and he did not have the words. She pulled him toward her and kissed him hard, dragging him several paces to the left. He was off-balance and he couldn't see where they were going and his shoulder thumped into the corner of a telephone box.

"Mmph," said Michael. "Be quiet."

"I wanted to tell you—"

"Shut up, *balvan*." She put her hand over his mouth and he realized that she was peering over his shoulder with a look of intense concentration. "Don't move and don't turn around."

"What is it?" he managed to croak.

"It's Simonov. And the ambassador. A kid called Berg. Another kid I don't know. Temir. And another big guy."

"Who are they?"

"That's about half the MGB officers who work out of Soviet Embassy in London."

"Well, what are they doing?"

"They are talking to Vassily. He is stalling them. They have come to see me! I have to get back in."

Vassily was greeting each of the men elaborately, shaking hands emphatically with the juniors. He was smiling and talking fast. The others all had serious faces. Vassily embraced Simonov and kissed him on both cheeks. The ambassador had come in a Bentley with embassy number-plates along with two other men. Three more had swept up in a black cab.

Vassily kept the whole party out on the steps for a while. He was gesturing expansively, as though he had just bought the whole street and was showing off its features.

Eventually the group moved inside. Two had the MGB desk officer look Yulia knew well: awkward, skinny, prematurely bald boy-men. Two others were muscle. They had massive necks, like Olympic weightlifters, and their heads nodded around all the compass points as they went through the revolving doors of the hotel last.

When the group crossed the threshold of the Excelsior, Yulia took Michael's face in her hands, kissed him and said, "I love you," in Russian. She paused for a second as a double-decker went by, then ran behind it when it passed the entrance of the hotel. Michael watched her disappear down the narrow alley that ran along the right side of the Excelsior. After a moment, he crossed the street and thought: This morning, I was a schoolboy. Now I'm following a group of Russian spies into a hotel. When I go through these doors, nothing will ever be the same again.

He looked into his own eyes in the mirrored glass of the revolving doors as he pushed his way in. Inside, Vassily was steering the deputy ambassador into the bar immediately to their right. Some of the other men exchanged unhappy looks, but Vassily marched the diplomat to the counter, where a bottle and a line of shot glasses were set up.

Yulia got to the end of the side alley and turned the corner into the service road that ran behind the hotel. What she saw made her heart kick against her ribs.

When she had made her escape earlier, she had left the sliding fire escape ladder that led to her first-floor balcony hanging down so that it almost touched the tarmac. Now someone had pushed it back up. The bottom rung was too high to reach from the pavement.

A laundry van was parked directly under her balcony. The engine was running and the driver was sitting behind the wheel, facing her, leafing through a sheaf of papers. Yulia cursed and patted her pockets, as if she was looking for a cigarette. The driver wore thick glasses and he had them pushed up on his forehead so he could see underneath as he read the paperwork. It made him screw up his face. She was standing right in front of him in the beam of the headlamps, but he did not look up at her.

In the bar, the Russian men threw back the shots and Simonov said: "Comrade Vassily, I hate to be rude but I'm under orders to check on the girl and ring through with an immediate report. I hope you understand." Vassily beamed at him. The art-deco clock on the wall said it was a minute past midnight.

They all swept up the grand staircase together, the thick red carpet muffling their steps. As they passed the huge portrait of the Queen on the landing, Vassily said: "Babysitting this kid has been the hardest mission of my career, gentlemen." He dragged a hand over the stubble on his head. "I had a thick head of hair before I started." The men laughed. As they reached the room, he put his forefinger to his lips theatrically. He had told them Oleg was unwell and was sleeping it off.

Vassily turned the room key and pushed the door open. Simonov was right on his shoulder and the others were crowding in behind them. Oleg was still asleep on his back in the stuffy darkness, snoring loudly. Vassily crept past his bed and went to the door that led to the adjoining room where Yulia slept. He put his fingers to the handle of the door and prepared himself for whatever he would find on the other side.

In the alleyway, the driver let his spectacles fall back on to his nose. He pushed open the door of the van and left it wide open as he walked into the back entrance of the Excelsior.

Yulia ran up and looked through the doorway after him, down a long empty passage like a hospital corridor. Double doors were swinging in the man's wake. The van was dirty yellow with a black bumper. She went to the passenger side and put one foot up on to it. The window was down completely, so she placed both hands in the frame and pulled herself up. She put the other foot on the sill, boosted herself on to the roof of the van and stood swaying in the center, dizzy from the height and suddenly feeling the alcohol in her system. The railings of her balcony were within reach.

She heard the driver shouting goodbye from inside. She flattened herself on the van's roof, wincing as she pressed her cheek into a thick layer of grime. The man got back into the driver's seat and she heard his door bang shut.

Yulia let out the breath she had been holding with a gasp. The engine was already running and she stood up quickly and gripped a square white iron balcony railing with each hand. She lifted her right leg, wedged her toes between two railings so that her foot rested awkwardly on the floor of the balcony. The other was still on the roof of the van when it pulled away. The sudden movement left her hanging ten feet above the tarmac with one leg dangling in space.

She pulled herself upright with her arms, grimacing at the effort, and planted her left foot safely on the edge of the balcony. Only then did she look down. There was no one in the alley and the van was at the end, already turning the corner. She leaned her stomach on the railing and rolled forward over it. She landed inelegantly on one foot, cursing her clumsiness. The balcony door was still unlocked.

When Vassily opened the door to Yulia's room, she screamed at him and he jumped back. Simonov switched on the light. Yulia was standing open-mouthed in the doorway of her room, wearing nothing but a towel. Oleg sat up suddenly on his bed and yelled.

All six men from the embassy were crowded into the room, like commuters in a packed train. They all flinched as the girl let fly with a string of obscenities, questioning their paternity and sexual orientation in some detail. She retreated into her room and slammed the door with all her strength.

There was a moment of silence. Then the ambassador said: "So, we can report that Miss Forsheva is in fine health and good spirits, gentlemen."

Oleg was rubbing his eyes and blinking dumbly at the other men. Then there were hushed conversations, and stilted phone calls to and from the Soviet Embassy. When the telephone rang, the junior men all trooped out of the room and lolled against the walls of the corridor. There was a protocol to be followed.

Eventually when only Simonov and the diplomat were left, Vassily poured Scotch for them. Yulia had finally fallen asleep in the next room. There was a pink film over Oleg's eyes and he did not want to drink. Simonov said: "I like a girl with spirit, but it would be wise for her to watch her language from now on."

The ambassador laughed indulgently. "She is still a child. She doesn't know what she's saying."

"But she knows who she's speaking to," said Simonov. "Or if she doesn't, she ought to find out. Things are going to be different for her and her mother from now on. They are not going to be protected from on high anymore."

He looked at Vassily for any reaction to this, but Vassily smiled warmly, raised his glass and said: "To your health."

Michael trailed the Russians up to Yulia's floor. He stayed twenty paces behind the group and did not follow them as they turned the corner into her corridor. He loitered there uselessly for a minute. You stupid boy, he thought. What in God's name are you doing?

When he heard Yulia shouting and swearing he stormed around the corner and saw two young men in suits backing out of a room on the left side of the corridor. The sound of the girl's voice came from inside. There were five rooms on this wing and hers was the third. Opposite her door, the narrow corridor opened out on the right into a square area where you could catch the lift. The corridor had been decorated with a nautical theme. There were circular mirrors that looked like portholes between the doors and a brass rail ran down the opposite wall.

He recognized the men as two of the officials he and Yulia had seen arrive at the hotel. They both looked terrified. One glanced at him briefly and said something to the other in Russian. Michael bristled for some kind of confrontation, but the men paid him no more attention.

They were transfixed by what was happening inside the room. Michael stood staring at them. He could still hear Yulia yelling in Russian. She sounded angry rather than scared. His face was burning.

When the noise subsided, he walked slowly toward the door of her room, then veered off to the right in the direction of the lifts. The Russians glanced at him as he drew near, but they were deep in a whispered conversation now. Michael stood facing the closed doors of the lift with his back to the men, trying to peek over his shoulder to see what was happening. Now Yulia's bodyguard, the one with the shaved head, had come out into the corridor and was speaking to the two men. Michael could not hear what was said but he heard all three snigger like schoolboys. When the lift came, Michael got in helplessly. He had no idea what else to do.

As the doors were sliding shut the bodyguard with the bald skull, Vassily, loomed in the doorway and jammed them open with his hands. He leaned in and slapped Michael's face sharply. "You need to disappear. She's fine. What's your room number?"

"Go to hell!" Michael had a hand to his cheek.

"Calm down. I'm your friend. I promise you the girl is fine. I will come and knock in half an hour."

Michael glowered at him until Vassily hissed: "What number?"

"Three hundred and one."

Michael sat on the edge of his bed with his head in his hands. Then he walked up and down for a while. He fished out the cigarette papers with the phone number on the top one and tried to telephone his father. No one answered.

He thought about calling the police. But what would he tell them? He picked up the receiver again and was looking at it when there was a knock on the door.

Michael kept the chain on and glared at the bald Russian bodyguard through the gap. His cheek still stung.

The man said: "You are Mikhail Stephanovich? My name is Vassily. Your new friend is asleep. I understand you had an enjoyable evening out. Now you need to forget all about her."

He started to walk away. Michael took the chain off and opened the door. "Wait."

Vassily stopped and turned. He had something red tucked under his arm. "That's the last you'll see of her, I'm afraid. It's just the way things work out sometimes."

"Is she in trouble?"

Vassily looked at him curiously. "You might say that. You will hear it sooner or later, so I may as well tell you. Her father has disappeared. He is an important man in the Soviet Union. Everyone is trying to figure out what's going on."

"Disappeared. Do you mean defected? To the West?"

"For all our sakes, I sincerely hope not."

"Is there anything I can do?"

They studied each other's faces. The Russian could appear very simple and peasant-like one moment, very serious and dangerous the next.

"Do you want to see her again?" he asked.

"More than anything. She's like . . . you know . . ."

"No, I don't know. Tell me what she's like."

"A thousand volts."

"Good. What else? What did it feel like when you first saw her?"

"Like when you slapped me just now."

The Russian was nodding thoughtfully. "That's the way it is, eh?"

"That's the way it is."

Vassily took a thick red cardboard foolscap folder from under his arm and handed it to Michael. "This is something her father was writing. There's no point in asking me about it. I don't speak chess. The girl has been translating it for him and she thinks there are strategies in here that no one outside Russia will know."

Michael thumbed through the sheaf of papers, hundreds of pages of tightly packed text broken up with chessboard diagrams.

Vassily shrugged. "She wants you to win. If you get through tomorrow, you get a ticket to the finals in Germany. You'll see her again in six weeks."

The Russian stretched out his hand toward the folder. "Or you take my advice and change your mind. I give this back to Yulia. You find another girl."

Michael wasn't listening. He was absorbed in the first diagram. It was an opening he had never seen before.

"Could be another pretty Russian girl. There's no shortage of them. We've got a big factory that turns them out, year after year . . ."

Vassily's arm was still stretched out for the red folder. Michael kept a tight hold on it, walked back into his room and closed the door without another word.

9

Michael's first game was at ten. he slept until a quarter past nine, washed quickly and pulled his clothes on. He had been up half the night reading Yulia's translation of her father's thoughts on chess strategy. The skin on his head felt as though it was one size too small for his skull. In the foyer downstairs, he checked the noticeboard again for the times of all his games, and which rooms he needed to go to. He thought about trying to telephone his father again.

As he was searching his pocket for coins the Spanish head waiter touched his arm and said: "There's coffee waiting for you on the bar."

The cup was sitting on the polished wood with a saucer on top to keep the contents warm. There was a small glass beside it with clear spirit in it. Vassily sat on a stool reading the *International Herald Tribune*. He did not look up from the newspaper or otherwise acknowledge Michael's presence.

Michael took the saucer off the cup and a breath of steam rose up. He sipped the coffee gratefully, then picked up the shot glass and held it up to the light.

Without looking at him, Vassily said: "I like these little half measures. You only need a little nip in the morning to set you up for a day in the fields. Swallow that and finish the coffee. Then eat something solid."

"That looks like a full measure to me."

"A double here is a single in Russia. Drink."

Michael slammed the glass down when he had finished. Vassily got up and left the bar.

Yulia's father had some big ideas. She translated the first as "offensive ambiguity." It sounded better in Russian.

When most chess players go on the offensive, they have one object in mind: capturing a knight or pinning down the opponent's king. They throw everything they have at the assault, and if it fails, they start again from scratch.

Yulia's father had a different philosophy. He liked ambiguous moves that could develop into attacks on two or three different fronts. A less aggressive move that creates many branching possibilities is harder for the opponent to deal with than a single bold raid.

Another of Sergei's ideas was translated as "mutual destruction." You always accepted an equal exchange of pieces: a knight for a knight, a queen for a queen. Most players shied at the cost of these exchanges and became uncomfortable. The object was to clear the board of pieces and race to the endgame.

This was Sergei's specialty, and he believed that he could teach any player how to kill off a game, as long as black and white were equal on points. Michael did not have time to absorb all the lessons, but now he put into practice the things he had read. Sergei had already given him enough for a small edge. Michael won his first two games.

The third chess game of the day—the last of the tournament—was in the hotel's grand ballroom. A single table stood in the middle with chairs all around the outside. Michael now had three and a half points out of five and needed another full point to reach the finals in Germany: he needed a win.

When Yulia came in he stood up. It was just like the first time he saw her. He could see that she had been crying and he tried to keep the concern from showing on his face. Oleg trailed behind her, with the young man called Berg, the Soviet ambassador and one of the muscle- bound men from the night before. The Russians arranged themselves on a line of elegant chairs at the edge of the room close to the door.

Yulia was white and she brought out her king's knight first. She put three pawns out in a wall, leaving the queen's bishop's pawn dangling undefended for a long time. Michael had never seen this opening before.

When the action slowed, she said in a murmur that was quieter than a whisper: "You read the book."

"How can you tell?" asked Michael. He glanced at the Russian spectators but there was no sign that they were listening. Most of them were bored, muttering to each other rather than watching the game.

"You are playing like my father," she said. "Not so pretty-pretty in the middle game. No grand plan. Just waiting for openings."

"How do you know I don't have a grand plan?"

"Do you, Dragon Hunter?"

"We'll see, won't we?"

The balance shifted subtly. She dominated the center, and her knights could move more freely than his. Suddenly he had lost both his knights and one rook. Michael could feel the game slipping away. He said: "Did you mean what you said last night?" He suddenly had the idea that the ambassador was watching them and tried not to move his lips.

"About hating jazz? Every word."

"You know what I'm talking about."

"You must listen now," she said, suddenly serious. "I am spoiled. I have foul temper. I am a lazy student. I am as jealous as Satan. I have no patience with people, and I change my mind about everything one hundred times in an hour."

"Anything else?"

Her eyes drifted toward the ceiling and she bit her lip. Michael couldn't see her hands, but he had the feeling she was counting on her fingers under the table. "I cannot cook. I sing like a donkey. I am sure there is a lot more."

"I think you're perfect."

She looked at him without sentimentality. "Is this only a game for you? Or are you a serious man? It is time to decide."

"I'm all the way in. I've been in it up to my neck ever since I saw you walk into the hotel."

She bit her lip again. "I hope you mean it. Because I have never done this before in my life."

And she moved a knight instead of her queen, leaving the queen undefended, threatened by his pawn. He stared at the board for a while because he could not take in the enormity of the blunder. Then he understood.

"You beat Szekeres today?" he murmured.

"We drew. I have four and a half points. I already have a place in the next tournament. Here is your ticket to Germany. Are you sure you want it? Last chance."

"I'm sure."

"Finish me off, then, darling."

He took her queen. She made a play of putting up some resistance and he was so nervous that he almost fluffed the endgame—then killed it with his remaining rook.

Yulia almost ran from the table and Michael heard the ambassador saying: "What the hell was that?"

Yulia shouted: "I can't concentrate. Can you blame me?" She stormed out with the Russian contingent hurrying after her.

Michael walked across the foyer in their wake and Johnny yelled triumphantly when he saw him and pounded his shoulder. "Amazing job."

"Thanks. Next stop Germany."

"That's the spirit—we'll tunnel you in. Launch you over the fence with a catapult."

Michael shot the Norwegian a questioning look. Johnny said: "You know you can't actually go, right?"

"What are you talking about? That was the whole point of today."

"There isn't enough time to get a visa. You had to apply months ago."

"Why do I need a visa for Germany?"

"Michael, for the love of God, it's not our Germany, it's theirs. It's on the other side."

10

LITHUANIA, 1941

Samogitia is the western part of Lithuania. The name simply means "lowlands." The country is all flat, so if you want to ski, you must do it in the cross-country style. When Greta was small, they skied every winter, because the snow fell so thick that it would cut off one village from the next for weeks. When she was a girl of seven, slight but with legs already strong from the skiing, it would pile up as high as her head. Winter made everything clean and fresh.

But to be indoors on a cold evening was best, in those grand old wooden houses. She would become drowsy as the fire crackled and spat, as her grandmother told stories of the Laumés: long-haired maidens, spirits of the woods. Bestowers of gifts, or snatchers of children, who reward the industrious and punish the wrongdoer. Grandmother had seen them once, when she was Greta's age, deep in the forest's dark heart, leaping over fires.

In the summer, the women swam in the Black Lake. The water was supposed to be good for the skin. A hot August and autumn rain brought wild mushrooms in abundance—the delight of every true Samogitian. The old women collected them by the armful and sold them outside the railway station in the town, squatting on the pavement in a line.

Once Greta took the girls, Vita and Riva, foraging for mushrooms in the deep woods. Just to show them which were poisonous and which were good to eat. She knew what to look out for: a blue stain in the flesh, pink gills, or a white 'skirt' halfway down the stalk. Her father used to say that with mushrooms, as with people, a skirt was a sign of impending danger.

The sisters could speak the local language by then, of course, although they always used German when they were alone together, which was often. The three had spent almost every day together from the time Greta could walk. Vita and Riva's parents had moved to Samogitia from Vienna when their daughters were toddlers.

Did the two sisters think of themselves as Lithuanian, after all those years? Were they still Viennese at heart? Above all else, were they Jews? Greta could not recall, in later life, if she had discussed this philosophical question with them.

Vita and Riva's father, Dr Klausner, was unquestionably still as Austrian as *Wiener* sausage, a dish he consumed with great enthusiasm in a rude snub to his Jewish ancestry. He was a liberal man with a great dislike for religion. The black-clad Haredi men who came to the town in great numbers in those days to study the Talmud at the rabbinical school terrified him even more than they scared the local peasants, if that were possible.

Klausner claimed not to see the sly looks from the townspeople but, then, he did not have to deal with them often. He was away in Vilnius during the week, working at the hospital. His beautiful wife spent more time at their house in Samogitia for Vita and Riva's sake, but never really warmed to the place. She claimed she could hear people whispering when she passed them on the pavement.

Many Lithuanian Jews owned businesses in the main street of the town. Some people had long said that the Jews planned to take over Samogitia and create a country for themselves. They would enslave or exile the Lithuanians. Even before the Germans came, these were the things people were known to say.

The three girls did not live in the town proper. Their families had neighboring wooden houses in a tiny hamlet outside, at the end of a long, shallow valley, the sides of which were the highest ground for miles around. The doctor's house was bigger and had better views.

That day, the mushroom hunt was not a success. Greta led them into a dense patch of pine forest near the Black Lake. The ground was boggy, and the air hummed with the pungent smell of fungi and with clouds of biting insects. Greta had told them to wrap themselves up in scarves like sheikhs' wives, leaving no flesh exposed. They had ignored her.

When they came home the two sisters' necks were alive with angry red bites that swelled like boils. Vita was horrified. Riva contorted herself to see all the bumps across her shoulders in her mother's full-length mirror.

"It's not fair," she cried. "We are covered, and Greta hasn't got one. Look at her."

"Those fucking flies are anti-Semites," said Vita.

On the evening of Greta's fifteenth birthday, in June 1941, the doorbell rang. Her father answered it. Greta knew straight away who the caller was because she saw her father fold his arms grimly and put on his most formidable face as he stood on the threshold. The teenage girl outside did not quite dare to meet his gaze. She hopped from one foot to the other until he slowly turned his head and roared: "Zofija, your Jewess is here to teach us all how to behave."

Vita looked meekly up at him and swept off her hat. "I—I heard it was the peasant girl's birthday. Is it permitted . . . ?"

Her father always cracked first. He burst out laughing and aimed a slow swipe at Vita's head as she ducked past him. She ran into the kitchen and hugged Greta passionately. Both girls started whooping like the Apache they watched in films on the town square in summer. Greta's grandmother tutted and looked helplessly at her daughter, who was busy smacking Vita's hand as it crept toward the birthday cake on the kitchen table. "They are savages," Greta's mother said to the old woman.

Vita took the seat next to Grandmother and shouted into her ear: "Mama Birute! How well you are looking! Do you remember me?" She took the old lady's arm and bellowed: "But why is no one feeding you? I will fetch you something!"

Bemused by this sudden assault, Birute turned to her daughter again. Vita made a hideous vampire face and clawed at the air with her fingers. Greta's mother stared at her imploringly. Her father had a coughing fit and had to leave the room, raising a hand to excuse himself.

Greta had made the mistake of telling Vita how her grandmother used to frighten her as a small child. When they were coming home in the dark, the old lady would clutch Greta from behind and hiss: "The Jews are going to get you!" The story left Vita and her older sister incapacitated with laughter. It became a favorite catchphrase of theirs.

Riva joined the party after she had finished her schoolwork. The three girls ate the cake and sang. When Greta's parents left to escort her grandmother home, the girls went out into the garden, wandering down to the end where the woods began. They smoked, with one eye on the back door of the house, and took it in turns to swig from a flask of brandy mixed with grape juice.

Vita said: "I can't get over how they all call you Zofija."

"It's my name, foolishness."

"Not anymore. Not since the night they showed that film outside the town hall. You've been Greta Garbo and nothing else ever since then. What was it called again?"

"*Ninotchka*," said Riva. "And she looks nothing like Garbo. I don't know why you started all that."

"It's not about the face, it's about the *spirit*. Wasn't that the night you lost your virginity to your cousin, darling?"

"For heaven's sake," said Riva, elbowing her sister.

Greta swallowed some brandy and sighed. With infinite weariness, she said: "He wasn't my cousin, and I didn't sleep with him, as you well know."

Vita said: "It was a trainee priest. That's what I heard. He was as handsome as a film star. Greta showed him the path to Heaven."

"He wasn't a priest either," said Greta.

"I saw him in the seminary one day. All the best-looking boys are in there. It's a crying shame. There they all were, flocking around me. Girls? I didn't know where to look."

"You've never been inside the seminary," said Greta. "I go to seminaries all the time, *Schatz*."

"Kosher seminaries."

When Greta went to bed, her head was a little heavy from the brandy. She awoke early the next morning to the sound of the radio screeching downstairs and her parents' raised voices. The Germans had brought a great horde of men and machines across the river Vistula and they were massing along the borders of Lithuania and down the whole of the Molotov Line. The Soviet soldiers who had been occupying Lithuania for exactly a year were not expected to put up much of a fight. Everyone was waiting for the hammer to fall.

The next week was a time of wild rumor and dizzying fear. The girls in the village were forbidden to leave their homes. On June 20, Greta was woken by men's voices in the early hours.

She came halfway down the stairs and saw her father and her uncle sitting on opposite sides of the kitchen table with a candle burning between them. Her uncle was leaning back in his chair, smoking a Russian cigarette in a plastic holder. He was in business clothes, not the Red Army uniform he had been obliged to wear for the last year. Greta's father was sitting square on to the table, both hands resting on it, screwed into fists.

Her uncle said: "Call me a dreamer if you want. Say what you like, but I'll say this. There's time for one roll of the dice—"

He broke off as the girl came heavily down the stairs, her night dress brushing the wooden floorboards.

"Little *falcon*," he said in Russian, with great emotion. He opened his arms to receive her. She hesitated, one hand resting on the balustrade. "My favorite niece! How long has it been? What a time to be young. Great and terrible events! It is for you, the children, that we—"

"All right, all right," growled her father. "Sit down with us, Zofija, if you can't sleep. I don't blame you."

"What's going on?" asked Greta, stupidly. "Have they come?" She took the empty chair and started, noticing another presence in the room: a bear of a man with a bushy mustache. He sat motionless in the corner of the kitchen in a high-backed chair that looked like a child's with all his frame crammed into it. He had a cap on low and you could not tell if his eyes were closed.

"Don't mind Viktoras," said her uncle. "Things are getting hot out there and I need a good driver."

"Are the Germans coming?"

"Soon enough," said her father. He looked at her uncle steadily the whole time and his voice shook. "And all along the border, there are young girls like you waiting with their hair in plaits and the bread and salt out, ready to greet the Germans like old friends. Your uncle is looking forward to them arriving too. Many men like him are ready to cast off those awkward, scratchy Russian uniforms they have been wearing with ill grace. They're going to swap them for ones that will fit them much better."

Greta's uncle blew out a lungful of smoke and said nothing. "Your uncle supposes," said her father, "that our friend Adolf is going to hand this country back to the Lithuanians to run, and the town squares will ring to the joyful sound of the accordion once more."

"I say it's worth a try," her uncle replied pleasantly. "No more, no less. We have been in discussions with them for a while and have been given certain assurances. The Wehrmacht will be in charge initially. They are rational men."

Her father said to Greta: "You and I are taking Vita and Riva away. Their mother is in Kaunas. She won't be able to get back in time."

"What are you talking about? Taking them where?"

"Somewhere safe. I'll bring them back when this Black Death has passed over us."

Her uncle said: "I wouldn't hold your breath. The Germans don't leave when they get their boots under the table." He chuckled, but stopped when he saw the murderous expression on Greta's father's face. "Who are these Jewish girls?" he asked quickly. "Not Klausner's daughters?"

"My neighbor. Do you know him?"

"Do I! He was on the board at the hospital when I was there. One of the main reasons I had to give up my studies." Her uncle gave another little laugh, and Greta felt the bitterness that was in him, hidden carefully under his studied air of casual indifference to the world.

"Their day closes," he said solemnly. "All that sort of thing is coming to an end. Actually, I hear that Professor Klausner is not endearing himself to the Russians. Naturally, when they leave, they'll strip the hospitals of anything they can use. Apparently, they've already started in Vilnius, and our little professor got right up in one of the officers' faces and gave him a tongue-lashing. He doesn't realize he'd be better off making friends with the Russians, and hitching a ride east with them when they go."

Greta's father said: "Klausner won't run from the Germans. And he won't let any Russian take a sticking plaster from that hospital without putting up a fight. That's why I am going to drive to Vilnius tomorrow and fetch him. I'll tie him up and put him in the boot of the car if I have to."

"Out of the question," said her uncle, raising his voice for the first time. "You stay the hell out of Vilnius."

"Klausner is an old friend. He doesn't understand the danger."

"Neither do you, you bloody fool. The Bolsheviks haven't left yet. They're rounding up everyone connected to the Rifle Club. Men like you are being shoved on to freight trains bound for Siberia. Zofija, talk some sense into him, for the love of God."

"I made a promise to Klausner's wife," said her father. He glanced at Greta. "Ivan has enough to worry about, stealing everything that isn't nailed down. They won't have time to bother with a crazy old man like me driving around the country roads."

"I'm coming too. I can speak German better than you. It will come in handy if . . ."

"If we get overtaken by events. You," he took her hand, "are the finest daughter a man could wish for. But I have important work for you here. Get Vita and Riva comfortable and wait for me. I'll tell you the place when these villains have gone."

Father and daughter were crying openly now. Greta's uncle sat between them and looked down at the tabletop with his eyes that could not cry.

"The German Army will be in charge at first," he said quietly. "They have given us assurances. They will put the Jews in well-ordered settlements and let them run their own affairs. They are reasonable men."

"It's not the Germans I'm afraid of," snapped Greta's father. "It's the Lithuanians who want to impress them."

The next morning, Greta folded her father's hunting rifle in two and placed it in the bottom of the basket that fitted over the handlebars of her bicycle. It was leaning against the telegraph pole on the grass verge outside their house. She covered the gun with a blanket, then went back inside.

Her father had left at sunrise. He had said he would get Professor Klausner to safety, then come back for Greta and the sisters. He was vague about the timing: it would take several weeks, perhaps a month or two, to arrange everything. All they had to do was stay out of sight until then. Greta's mother would resupply the girls on the first of each month. She was taking jars from the kitchen cupboards and standing them on the sideboard now: bilberry jam, smoked sprats, dry buckwheat, cured meat with lots of fat.

"It's enough," said Greta. "You'll make the bike tip over." Her mother looked at her and burst into tears.

When everything was stowed away, Greta looked down at the basket with satisfaction, then clapped a hand to her forehead and swore. She ran back into the house and stood on a chair to take the big biscuit tin down from the top of the dresser. She filled her deep pockets with bullets and ran outside again. As she was wheeling the bicycle away a voice called out: *"Grüss Gott."*

The boy had a kind, open face, with gingery hair and freckles. His friend was shorter and darker and lagged behind, unsmiling. Greta could tell that the ginger boy always did the talking. Their uniforms were spotless. Their rifles were slung on their backs.

"*Guten Tag*," Greta replied stiffly, and the boy gave a rueful grin. "I'm sorry," he said. "My friend and I are both Bavarian and we forget to speak the Hochdeutsch sometimes."

Greta was holding the handlebars tight. She tried not to look at the basket.

The boy said: "We are knocking on everyone's door. I know you have all suffered under the Russians. We want you to know that things are going to be better now. Do you . . . really have to run away, miss?"

"I'm taking some groceries to my grandmother." Greta gripped the handles even harder. "My mother is at home alone. You might give her a shock when she sees you, but I am sure she will bring coffee out."

"I promise we won't frighten her. We'll just show our faces."

The other boy said: "No more pretty girls lurking inside?"

"You like Lithuanian girls?"

"You are all angels!" said the boy, rolling his eyes.

Greta laughed, a little disapprovingly. It gave her the chance to start wheeling the bike away from them in a light-hearted show of fear, calling: "I had better go before you get down on one knee!"

As she cycled away, she heard the ginger boy saying: "Idiot."

Her father had taught her to shoot a rifle and clean it, to drive cars and farm vehicles, to understand the habits of game and lie quietly in wait for prey. She had spent nights out in the open, even in winter, under canvas or wrapped in a sleeping bag. She could skin animals and navigate her way by the stars.

She led the girls toward the hut where her father sometimes stayed overnight when he hunted boar, away south toward Varniai. Vita and Riva were not used to walking across country, but Greta drove them on. It was a hot day and they sweated and slipped, tripped on tree roots and cursed the biting flies. Halfway, Vita turned her ankle scrambling down a slope. She threw down her pack in tears. "This is hopeless. What are we doing, anyway?"

"Taking a step," said Greta, quoting the last words her father had said to her. "That's all. Then the next step, then another. That is how we beat them."

"We can't beat them. There are more of them than there are mosquitoes."

"Surviving another day is how we win. I told you not to wear those shoes. Take it off and let me see."

The hut was just a tiny wooden lean-to with three sides. The fourth wall was the edge of a hillock that hid the place from anyone who might come up from the nearest road. That was a three-hour walk away, and the ground in between was so boggy that horses and armored vehicles would not be able to pass.

At first, they started at every snap of a twig, or threw themselves undercover if they heard the distant noise of an airplane. After a while, the work took over: fishing in the lakes all around, patching up the roof of the hut, collecting firewood. Riva had the idea that they could hide the roof and sides of their new home with thick branches of pine and fir. It would insulate them when winter came on. Greta left them to it and went out looking for game with the rifle. When she came back, empty-handed, the roof was unfinished. Vita and Riva were inside, in each other's arms. Vita was sobbing.

"I'll do the last bit," mumbled Greta, leaning the rifle in the corner.

"*Schatz*," said Riva.

"We need firewood and fresh water too."

"It is our mother's birthday today, *Schatzili*."

"I'll give the bucket a good clean. We should make sure we do it every time. We're going to poison ourselves."

"Greta," said Riva gently. "Won't you sit down and talk for a little while?"

"There's too much to do."

"We have to think about our parents sometimes, darling."

"Not yet," said Greta, awkwardly. She was standing in the doorway with the metal pail in both hands. "I've got too much work to do."

* * *

They built a smokehouse from tree branches woven together, and began to build up a store of dried food. Later, they collected hazelnuts and berries. Once Greta spotted a family of boar but did not have the rifle with her. Autumn was long and golden that year. Apples were plentiful. They saw no one in the woods.

On the first day of each month, Greta's mother came to a clearing near the road with a hamper. It took Greta all morning to reach the meeting place. The first time, her mother was sitting waiting on a fallen tree trunk. She heard Greta crunching through the branches toward her and stood up. They embraced. There was more homemade jam, and pickled vegetables for vitamins. The first time, there was chocolate. After that, you could not get it.

On November 1, Greta's mother was sitting in the usual spot. By now, she could not hear Greta coming. When her daughter touched the hair on the back of her head with her fingertips she jumped.

Greta said: "You won't be able to get through when the snow comes. We'll be all right though. We'll barricade ourselves in, eat chocolate and sing songs all winter."

"But not Christian songs. At Christmas."

Greta was about to say something sharp but stopped herself when she saw the pain in her mother's eyes.

"You can't stay out here all winter," her mother said. "Come home."

"What are you talking about?"

"Don't you think you've done as much as you can for those girls? What is the point in all of you freezing out there?" Greta bit her lip and said nothing. "The Bavarian boy keeps asking after you."

"He comes to the house?"

"They like to talk and play the piano. I make them dinner sometimes. He can't understand why you are never at home."

"He's suspicious?"

"It's starting to get awkward. Things are not as friendly now. There are patrols out on the roads. They stop you and ask for papers."

"Well, don't come any more if you don't want to. You sit at home by the fire. Entertain your Bavarian friends."

Her mother said: "And is it a terrible idea to have friends at times like these? Who else do I have?"

"He will come back," said Greta, quickly. When she saw the expression on her mother's face the violins began to swoon tunelessly in her head.

Her mother swallowed. "Your father . . . has been taken—"

"Stop. Don't say it."

"Your uncle knows what happened. He said—"

"Be quiet. I'm not listening." Greta clapped her palms over her ears. Her mother took her hands out of her pockets and gently pulled her daughter's away from her head. "We need friends now. Come back. He's a nice boy. It won't hurt to have someone to protect you.

To protect all of us."

Greta said: "Don't come here again. I'll look in on you and Grandmother in the spring."

On the way back she got within a quarter of a mile of the hut and saw three men standing under an ancient tree that people called the Grand Duke's Oak. They were Lithuanians, not Germans, men in rough country clothes and flat caps, with grim, hard faces. They all had shotguns. One was gesticulating to the others. He stalked off in the direction from which Greta had come. The other two went north, following a line that would take them close to the hut.

After that, the girls did not dare light the fire. They took it in turns to stand guard at lookout points around the hut, watching the paths that any intruder would have to take to reach them. Days later, the snow came and they wrapped themselves in as many layers as would fit while they did sentry duty, shivering, in hollowed-out trees or in narrow spaces they burrowed out under the gorse.

Vita sickened first. She tried to keep it from them, but the coughing fits became longer and more frequent. As Christmas approached, it was clear that she could no longer be outside. Riva had been feeling feverish for weeks before she mentioned anything to Greta. They were down to their last scraps of dried fish.

On Christmas Eve Greta awoke from a troubled sleep. Vita was dozing fitfully on the floor next to her. Riva was on sentry duty outside. They had not eaten protein or fat for weeks now. Only a few wrinkled apples were left. Greta got up and took down the rifle from the hooks above the fireplace. When she passed Riva at the sentry post, she saw that the snow had piled on top of the girl's head and shoulders where she sat. Greta reached out and touched her face as she went by. There was only a flicker of recognition. She did not have the strength to talk. Greta went past the lake, walking with difficulty. In some places the snow had piled up as tall as a man. It changed everything and made familiar places hard to recognize.

"Come to me," she whispered, "my beautiful boy. Antlers so heavy, how can you even lift your great head? Come closer. That's it. Now show me that mighty flank. Turn your head toward home. Think of the harem waiting for you. Ah, the eyes under the long lashes! Show me a little more. *Now.*"

The stag darted when the shot rang out, but his front legs caved and it was as though he drove himself into the ground with the force from his hindquarters. She imagined the points of the antlers catching on the ground and the beast breaking his own neck as he ran and fell at the same time, but when she came near him, he was still alive, sitting low with his legs tucked under, like a cat, panting hard. Greta was so close that she could have reached out and touched his nose with the tips of her fingers. He was big and bull-like around the head and neck. She had never been so close to so much twitching animal muscle before.

She did not want the noise of another shot, or to waste another precious round, so she crouched next to him and spoke soothingly, calling him the prince of the woods and her beautiful boy, until the life went out of his eyes and his head sank into the snow. The birds were still wheeling, and she listened for any rumor of men or dogs or machines. None came.

She cut open his belly with her father's hunting knife. It had a bone handle with an engraving of St. Michael the Archangel on one side and the words *Defend Us In Battle* in Lithuanian on the other. The blade was carbon steel and the lower third was serrated, like a saw. Her father had taught her to spike the intestines on a branch for the carrion birds, but there was no time now to honor the ancient woodman's code. Greta had dreamed of this moment and imagined draping a whole stag across her shoulders and carrying it triumphantly home through the forest. But when she tugged at its hind leg, it sapped her strength to move the dead weight even a few inches.

Greta sawed into the joint at the top of the leg with the jagged lower section of the knife blade. It took some minutes before the steel bit into the tendon properly. It was awkward at first but then the blade naturally followed the curve of the joint and at length she pulled the limb free from the rest of the carcass, dripping and steaming. She knew she would have to leave the rest and the awful sense of waste hit her like a punch. "I'm *sorry*," she shouted.

All the steam from the body had gone now and frost was starting to form on the wiry fur. How wonderful it would be to skin the deer and warm themselves under its hide. Not tonight, she thought.

The three of us can come back tomorrow, if the wolves have left anything.

She picked up the haunch and put it on her shoulder, like a workman carrying a plank. Then she saw how much blood was dripping from the exposed flesh. It stained the snow all around her feet. I am going to leave a bright red trail all the way to our door for every enemy in the area to follow, she told herself bitterly.

It had taken a while for that thought to form and she realized, with a shudder, how tired she was and how dangerously stupid it was making her. If she held the bloody end of the haunch right against her shoulder, all the gore would soak into the wool of the coat first and it would not drip on to the ground. It would make the coat repulsive, but she could clean it later. It was the best option. She set off.

When she reached the sentry tree there was no sign of Riva, and her stomach turned over. But she could see that the door of the hut was closed and there were no signs of a disturbance. She opened the door slowly and saw both girls' heads under their blankets. They had reached the end of their strength. She put the haunch of venison on to the grill in the fire and went to feel Riva's forehead with her hand. The girl stirred and opened her eyes. She smiled and it was the first lucid expression Greta had seen on her face for days.

"Forgive me, *Schatz*."

"It's all right, my darling. All is well."

"Any Germans? Tell them to wipe their feet."

"There's no one out there tonight. This is the real winter. This is what will finish Hitler."

"You really think so?" said Riva. She had woken, and was propping herself on her elbows.

"Of course. And we are going to celebrate with a fire and a feast. We are going to be warm tonight. Let them come, if they want to."

Both girls were awake now. They were looking at the haunch of meat in the fire.

Vita said: "Am I dreaming? What the hell is that?"

"A leg, my darling. It will feed us for a week. I had to hack it off him. Look at the state of my coat."

"Was he German or Lithuanian?

"You fool. A giant of a stag. Like the god of all deer. And he has saved our lives."

Waiting until the meat was cooked properly was one of the hardest things they ever did. It was delicious beyond description and they ate like savages, blood and juice dripping down their chins.

"Wait." Vita yanked at her sister's arm, her mouth full. "I can't remember if venison is kosher. We'd better not have any more until we find out."

"One more crack," said Riva, "and you'll go on the fire next."

11
MOSCOW, 1961

Maxim Karpov sucked the tips of his fingers. "More boys," he observed, as two waiters cleared the table. "Tripping over their cocks." Oleg—the huge man Yulia had christened the Pig in London—raised his eyebrows. His boss had been subdued on the ride over. Then Karpov had disappeared to the bathroom and come out rubbing his hands with a manic look on his face. He drank quickly after that, and his manners deserted him. He talked loudly and rapidly in a careless, vulgar way. Cocaine again, thought Oleg. It did not bode well for the rest of the evening.

The waiters muttered apologies. One dinged a plate against the neck of the brandy bottle, almost knocking it over. The other boy caught it in time but let a dirty fork slide on to the white tablecloth with a thump as he did so. He gave his colleague a murderous look. The staff at Saroyan's always lost their composure when they served Maxim Karpov. He had that effect on people.

In his presence, people referred to him exclusively as the chief administrator. Karpov's attendance at meetings of the Politburo was never reported in the official channels. His name was never printed in state newspapers, and no photographs of his face were ever published. But whenever he and Oleg dined at Saroyan's or the Metropole or Café Prague, a curious thing happened.

Karpov always ordered beer for Oleg, sweet Georgian sparkling wine for himself and at least one bottle of the best brandy the house had to offer. As the two men drank, their voices became louder and people started to hear them above the music. After a while, diners began to turn their heads with irritation. But when they saw who was making the noise, they paled and generally studied their plates very intently for the rest of the meal, which was always a brief affair.

Appetites were lost, waiters summoned, desserts scorned, wives and mistresses chivvied, complaining, into their fur coats and squired away.

It usually took about half an hour for whichever dining room the pair were in to empty completely. It gave Oleg enormous satisfaction to watch these people—the kind who would sneer at a man of his background and appearance if they passed him on the Moscow metro—cowering in fear at the sight of his tubby little master.

The first two waiters did not have the courage to return and another appeared, bearing more beer.

"An army of young men in here," Karpov mused, "but I already have one."

Oleg had finished the bean soup and was working his way through the dumplings. It was two nights after the mysterious dizzy spell had forced him into an early bed at the Excelsior in London. He was feeling better now, although his suspicion about what had triggered the sudden illness remained. His appetite had returned.

Karpov said: "So. Has Sergei really jumped over the fence without warning that dried-up old hag of a wife? God knows I wouldn't blame him. Or is Anna in on it? Is this a British plot? Is it the Yankees? Could it be the Yugoslavs? We're not short of enemies capable of constructing a *konspiratsia*."

Oleg shrugged his shoulders.

"It can't be the British," said Karpov, "because the King would know about it."

Oleg tensed as though someone had kicked him under the table. He had feared something like this, but it was still a shock to him how drink and stimulants could loosen Karpov's tongue these days. Five years ago, even two, his boss would never have made even the most oblique reference in public to the King. The greatest agent in the history of the MGB. Their man inside the British establishment. Karpov's oldest, deepest source.

The chief administrator's eyes were bright and he was talking fast. "It can't be the West Germans because they tell the Brits everything. The French are buried up to their necks in North Africa. *Unless . . .* it *is* the Brits—or the Yankees—and they think the Imperial Crown Jewels have just fallen into their lap. Perhaps they are treating Sergei like I treat the King. Maybe they've got him wrapped up in cotton wool somewhere."

Oleg winced openly when he heard *King* for the second time. The chief administrator alone knew the origin of the workname. The rumor was that it had been chosen to give the impression of a wide network of agents, all named after chessmen, so that if the British got wind of one Judas in their ranks, they would tie themselves up in knots looking for others who did not exist.

The waiter passed close by, bearing cutlets for the last remaining diners on the far side of the room.

"You know what Sergei was working on?" asked Karpov, when the boy was out of earshot.

"Computers," said Oleg, eagerly, grateful for the change of subject.

"More than that, *mudak.* Artificial intelligence. Don't pretend you know what it means. It's the new big thing. Invented by an American. We're having to catch up, as always, but Sergei thought it was the future. Do you remember his assistant, the Karelian? I made him explain it to me."

Oleg raised his eyebrows.

"Right—that snooty bastard. He looked down his nose at me like this. Said it was impossible to explain to a layman. Do you know what I told him?"

Oleg shook his head.

"The King told me a story once about Churchill's chief scientist, professor something—like a Jew name. He's like the British equivalent of Sergei. And Churchill says to him, "What's all this quantum theory? You know, Einstein." And the guy says, "It's complicated." And Churchill says, "Well, you've got five minutes to explain it to me and there's one catch: you can only use words of one syllable!" That's what I said to the Karelian!"

Oleg smiled weakly.

"I mean, I had to liven it up a bit," Karpov went on. "I told him I'd shoot his wife in front of him if he couldn't do it. And then I'd shoot him and *adopt* their daughter!" He roared with laughter. The wine and the drug were really getting to him now. "I said I'd make myself her legal guardian!" He was almost crying.

Oleg laughed his deep laugh, through a mouthful of dumpling and sour cream.

"Computers I know all about," said Karpov, suddenly serious again. "This artificial *intellekt* is different. You don't just feed information into a machine. You teach it to teach itself. It starts to think like a person, but a hundred times smarter. Always logical, never makes mistakes. Sergei had taught a computer chess and it was starting to beat him. Even an expert . . . you know . . ."

"Grandmaster."

"Even a *grandmaster* can only think so many moves ahead. A machine sees all the way through to the end. All the different possibilities." He was fluttering his fingers in the air and his eyes had a faraway look. Suddenly he noticed his shot glass was empty, and he motioned at Oleg to refill it.

"If Sergei had something big and he's taken it to one of the capitalist countries, we've got a problem. Like suddenly the machine isn't playing with chess pieces, it's playing with Germany and Poland. Figuring out all the moves. What chance would our senile generals have against that?" He tossed back the shot. How many was that now?

"I have to do everything for them. Cherkezishvili and the rest of the clown show," Karpov muttered, looking off into the distance and apparently talking to himself. "The Red Army couldn't plan a coordinated attack on a gypsy camp, let alone something on the scale of *Rhinemaiden*."

At this word, Oleg felt another lurch of horror. A curious, obscure name, not even Russian. People were not supposed to know it. A drunk who shouted it in the street could be arrested. Oleg gripped the edge of the table. This was too much. He had to do something. He brandished an empty bottle and shouted for a waiter. Oleg's voice seemed to shake Karpov out of his reverie.

"Only I understand the scale of the risk," the chief administrator said, speaking slowly so that he would not slur the words. "This is why we need to move fast against Anna. The Devil's Mother. She must know more than she is letting on. Or there's something in the house we missed."

Oleg grimaced. "Difficult."

"I know, damn it. Of course, it has to be the chairman's pet. Anyone else would get a bag over the head and a shot of pentothal in the arm."

Oleg looked past him, and Karpov turned to see a very tall, thin young man in a trench coat appear at the far end of the dining room. The visitor stood hesitantly, holding a fedora over his crotch with both hands. Karpov waved to him with an air of irritation.

There was no one else in the room now, but the young man leaned in close to whisper to them.

Karpov said: "Anna's still at the police station? With the deputy chief? Who else do we have in play? All right—go back quickly and get ready. We're going to press her." He raised a warning finger. "Within reason. Go now—like one leg is already there. Beat it."

He wagged the same finger at Oleg. "You. Don't get involved in harassing Anna. I want you standing back and watching all of them—like bugs under a microscope. Her and Vassily. I don't trust that bald bastard. If he takes a leak behind a tree, I want a full report."

"What about Yulia?"

"How was she in London?"

"Rude."

Karpov pursed his lips. "She is still a child," he said, with a chuckle, sounding so jarringly benign that the fork paused halfway to Oleg's mouth and he raised his eyebrows sharply.

"I don't think we need to worry about full surveillance," said Karpov. "What harm can a youngster do? I may . . . check on her myself from time to time."

They had drunk two-thirds of the bottle of brandy, but a man like Maxim Karpov did not bother to take the remainder of bottles home with him when he dined out. He made his way unsteadily to the cash desk, although there was, of course, no question of payment.

Saroyan waited for them with an exaggerated, obsequious smile. The host's wife bawled at someone offstage for Karpov and Oleg's coats, then stood next to her husband to wish them goodnight. Her head was bowed respectfully. These Armenians aren't really Europeans like us, thought Oleg. They are more like the Chinese or something. This part of the restaurant was screened off from the main dining room and the rumors of Karpov's presence had not reached the people, mostly couples, eating in there. The conversation died away as he walked past.

"Tell me something," Karpov asked the restaurateur, a little too loudly. "Where is that splendid girl with the deep waist who served me last time?"

Saroyan laughed heartily. "It is her night off, Comrade Chief Administrator. Her night off tonight!"

"What a pity. I will have to get you to send me her timetable before I make my next booking!"

The Armenian man laughed again, with even more enthusiasm.

As he was helped into his coat, Karpov said: "What about the other girl? I've seen another fine dark-haired girl hanging around on other occasions, although she never waits on tables—or, at least, not when I'm around." He said it so everyone in the room could hear it.

Saroyan guffawed again, giving it everything he had. His wife continued to smile brightly, tension visible in the muscles around her mouth and jaw.

"The thought occurred to me that she might be your daughter, Saroyan."

The restaurateur made a wretched circular movement of his head that was neither confirmation nor denial. He was visibly sweating.

Karpov turned his head to the side, like a stage actor, as he spoke, so that his words rang out over the heads of the other diners, who had fallen completely silent.

"It will be easy for me to find out. Everyone is registered and their details can be viewed by people with the right security clearance. Daughters, wives, sisters: there is no hiding anyone from me!" He was staring at a young woman sitting at a nearby table when he spoke these words, and it gave him satisfaction to see her openly shaking. He looked slowly from table to table and found that no one could meet his gaze.

"Perhaps I will be luckier with the girls next time!" Karpov boomed jovially. Oleg was holding the door open for him, and he swept out, his long coat swirling around his heels.

12

When Anna Vladimirovna Forsheva left the headquarters of the Moscow police in Petrovka Street late on the evening of July 24, 1961, the official car that had brought her was gone and her bodyguards nowhere to be seen.

She stood on the pavement, looking in vain for a taxi. A man leaning against the wall on the opposite side of the street was staring at her with an odd intensity. He spat loudly when she started walking. It was all part of the theater of the thing, Anna knew. There would be more of this to come. Karpov would pressure and humiliate her in the coming days and weeks. But he would not move openly against her yet.

It had been years since she had used a train or a tram, still less walked the streets of Moscow alone at night. Nevertheless, she did not have to think about where she was going. Her feet took her automatically down past the Bolshoi, past the fountain in Revolution Square, to the metro station where the soldier crouched with his dog. She rubbed the animal's nose for luck as she passed. Neither pet nor owner reacted. They were both made of bronze.

There were only a few people waiting on the platform, and the green line train, when it came, was almost empty. A couple got on behind her—a thin blade of a man in a fedora and a very plain little sparrow of a girl wearing a headscarf and thick spectacles. The girl had a line of dark down across her upper lip. She stood close to the man but they did not quite fit together.

Anna faced the doors, trying not to catch anyone's eye. An old man rose to offer her his seat and she waved it away. He swept off his mariner's cap with an exclamation. She tried to whisper at him to be quiet but he insisted on taking her hand and kissing it. He had been in the line at Khimki in '41 when she'd come out to inspect the troops. He was not young then—the other men called him Grandfather. She had been so brave to come out and see them, the German swine within shouting distance, curse them in their graves. It was the second time in his life he had been called upon to defend the Motherland from those beasts. Did she remember him? *Of course*, Anna lied.

She got off at Belorusskaya station to catch the last train out to Barvikh and the young woman in the headscarf and glasses leaned in close as she passed and hissed a single word into her ear: "Whore."

There were no soldiers at the checkpoint halfway up the hill. The old man in the cabin wanted to tell her something. He tapped on the plastic with his fingers. Anna shook her head and carried on, breathing heavily from the walk up the slope. A car was parked on the opposite side of the road just before their house: a Gaz M23 V8 in French racing blue, an impressive model even for this neighborhood. Two men sat in the front. They eyeballed Anna—boldly but not maliciously—as she passed them.

The noise of the door closing behind her reverberated around the empty house. Anna leaned back against it in the darkness. The house was unusually cold. She had forgotten that the maid would be gone. When Anna walked into the lounge, she saw from across the room that the fish were floating dead in their tank next to the window. The water around them was discolored. There was an arrogant cigarette burn in the dead center of the carpet, directly under the ceiling light. It was the size of a small coin, black around the edge. It looked as if the tip of an infernal thumb had been pressed into the fabric as a sign of Satanic disapproval.

Karpov's men had left her a gift in the toilet bowl upstairs and she flushed it away, gagging. Someone had rifled through Yulia's underwear drawer and left the contents strewn around her room. Anna could almost hear the mocking laughter of the men who had invaded her house, and this was the thought that stung her to tears.

She went down to the kitchen, fetched a bottle of brandy from the dresser and took it up to her bedroom, her head bowed as she climbed the stairs.

* * *

Yulia came in the blue hour before dawn, squashed into the back of Vassily's car with an enormous pile of sweets and toys he had brought back from London for his sister and her children. He drove her to the same checkpoint Anna had passed and watched her until she disappeared up the hill. The same two men were sitting in the parked car and they shook themselves awake as Yulia went by. They tried to summon the hard stares of officialdom but could not help blinking and yawning. We are all newborn babies at this time of the morning, thought Yulia, even thugs and spies.

Anna was asleep, still rouged and fully clothed. She had left the curtains open. Her face looked very old and lined as the first light fell across it. Yulia lay down next to her mother and curled an arm around her.

She was already awake at six, when Anna stirred. She watched her mother's eyes dart around the room. It took a while for the world to swim back into focus.

"Do you know where he is?" asked Yulia, studying her mother's face closely and speaking very softly.

Anna blinked several times. Her face cracked slowly and she began to cry. "Even you. My own daughter."

Anna tried to sit up in bed, gave a long moan and flopped down, kneading her temples with her fingertips. "God help me." She looked sharply at Yulia. "What about you? You two were always plotting. Leaving me out of everything. You thought I was stupid. Do you know where your father is?" Suspicion possessed her and she took hold of one of Yulia's wrists and squeezed it viciously. "Is this one of your chess games? Have you cooked all this up between you?"

Yulia yanked her wrist away. "You don't know what you're saying. Where is Masha anyway?"

"I sent her away. I don't trust her. Always watching at the keyholes. She can go to Germany to get the dacha ready. I don't want her hanging around here."

"You don't know what you're saying. How much did you drink last night?"

Anna tried to shake her head but quickly stopped. She clamped both her hands on to the top of her skull. "Go downstairs," she said carefully. "Get the book by the telephone. Call the number on the inside back cover with the red circle around it."

"Vassily said it's no telephones from now—"

"He doesn't give me orders! Do it!"

The doctor was there in forty minutes. He offered a very specific service to clients who moved in the highest circles of Moscow society and speed was always of the essence. He put Anna on a saline drip. Then he injected her with a low dose of morphine and gave her a new kind of tranquilizer called Phenibut, which was not available to most Soviet citizens. By half past seven Anna was out of bed and changing her clothes.

At eight, a car came for them from the Kremlin and at nine o'clock sharp Anna was standing on a podium in Manezhnaya Square, saluting the newly commissioned officers of the Moscow Regiment as they paraded past. She was its patron and it was a great day for the young men and their families, who gathered in a crowd around a small section of the square roped off for the ceremony. Tourists milling around the national museum snapped pictures. They liked to watch the soldiers performing their strange, slow goosestep.

Yulia stood with the relatives of the new officers, watching her mother from a distance and marveling at her powers of recuperation. She was shaking her head with disbelief when she felt a light touch on the upper arm.

"Andrey." She smiled. He held his cap in both hands. He looked smart in his dark blue dress uniform. He stared at the ground and swallowed.

"Yulia Sergeiovna! You are looking well." The last time they had met, they had both been drunk and the evening ended with his mouth pressed against hers. He had been too scared to take her to bed. He was on duty at the time, supposed to be guarding her. The details of that night were coming back to Yulia now and she realized that the episode in London with Michael had obliterated any feelings she might have had for this young man. She had simply forgotten about him. She felt vaguely guilty. They both said, "I'm sorry," at exactly the same time. She laughed. He did not.

"What is the matter with you? This is supposed to be a happy day. You look like you're at a funeral."

He took a deep breath. "There is no longer any possibility of a romantic attachment between us. I am sorry if I led you on. I am older than you and it was a dishonorable thing to do. You are the last person in the world I would want to anger."

He was very serious. She had to bite her lip to stifle a laugh.

"You didn't lead me on. I walked willingly into damnation. Now, for God's sake, put your hat back on and cheer up."

The young soldier looked at her properly for the first time. "I have to tell you that there is another girl. She is expecting a baby. I am praying that you will forgive me."

It took Yulia a while to process this. She felt anger stirring somewhere in her. Then she said "baby" to herself, unconsciously making the shape of the word with her lips. The warmth and joy of everything it promised made her smile.

"There is nothing to forgive. Who is the lucky girl?"

"Xenia is here now."

Yulia looked over his shoulder and saw a very slight girl in a headscarf standing alone twenty yards away, staring hard at them. When she caught Yulia's eye she hung her head. The girl was thin, almost malnourished, but pretty. She wasn't showing yet.

"Bring her over here," said Yulia. An unpleasant thought had begun to form in her head. When Andrey returned with the girl, the expressions on their faces confirmed it: both of them were mortally afraid—of Yulia.

Andrey seemed to read her thoughts: "They could send us all away at any moment. Czechoslovakia, Germany, Poland. God knows what will happen. The uncertainty is killing Xenia already." He lowered his voice. "Yulia, one word from you about what happened between us, and it's Siberia for me. My son will grow up without a father." The girl stifled a sob as he spoke. She looked pale and weak.

Yulia felt it properly for the first time: the power that people of her rank held over the lives of others. It was exhilarating and sickening at the same time. She shrank away from it with a shiver of horror.

She reached out and drew Andrey and Xenia close to her. The three young people stood in a huddle, their foreheads almost touching. Yulia said: "Never. I would never do anything to hurt either of you or your child. I swear this on my mother's life."

The girl sobbed again and slumped down. For a moment Yulia thought she was going to kneel and kiss her hand in the middle of Manezhnaya Square.

"For God's sake, stand up straight. We're not living in the time of the Tsars. Andrey—take her somewhere out of this heat immediately. Both of you, go and be happy. There is nothing to fear. Go!"

Xenia smiled tearfully at Yulia, and Andrey gave her a look of intense gratitude as he led the girl away by the arm.

13

Maxim Karpov sat in the MGB's offices on the second floor of the Kremlin, watching Oleg eat and wondering how long he could stand it. They were waiting to be called to the third floor for an audience with the most powerful man in the world.

Oleg's wife had made "little pigeons" with a sauce of tomato and sour cream. She always used a mixture of pork, veal and beef mince. Every morning before he drove into the Kremlin, Oleg put a deep bowl of her homemade food on the passenger seat next to him with a plate domed over the top. He handed the covered bowl to the women in the cafeteria in the morning and they kept it in the big refrigerator for him, ready to reheat. He could never last until lunchtime.

The telephone on the desk between them rang. It was Madame Sorokina, private secretary to the chairman of the Politburo, asking them to come up. Oleg wolfed the last few mouthfuls that remained in the bowl, bending over it so that he would not splash sauce on to his shirt and tie. Karpov's face bore a look of intense disgust.

Upstairs, they were still made to wait. Karpov paced, the thick green carpets swallowing the sound of his footsteps. They were refurbishing the palace, bit by bit, and they had replaced the dark wooden panels along the corridor that led to the chairman's office. Karpov ran his hands over the grain. After five minutes he was muttering under his breath.

"That simpleton," he hissed. "Who is he to keep me hanging around like a gypsy pedlar at his door? That weak fool. A shambling farmer's boy from Ukraine." Well, Karpov would never make it back home by noon now. What would she be doing, the Uzbek girl? He felt a jolt of excitement. Putting on the clothes I have prepared? No, he thought. Eating the food laid out for her. Well, that would do her no harm. The girl was very young, spindly and emaciated, exactly how he liked them.

Her bright green eyes were very Central Asian. They had made her stand out from the other girls offered to him by the deputy chief of the Moscow police department. They brought back strange, anxious, stirring memories.

The girl had taken well to her training so far. He had left her alone to rest on the first night. On the second he had explained exactly what was expected of her and she had complied, with a reluctance he found deeply exciting. He photographed her in various poses but did not touch her. She had been extremely frightened, but no harm had come to her. That was the key to it. She would be less scared next time. Karpov had struggled to restrain himself when he was alone with her, but his patience would be rewarded in the end.

After he had finished with the girl, he would experience a deep inner peace that nothing else could replicate. He would stretch out in glorious solitude on the carpet in his study, legs bent, knees pointing at the ceiling, head resting on a cushion right next to the gramophone, surrounded by his mother's books and records. She was a cultured woman who had read literature and taught languages, until marriage to a Cossack ape had killed all her ambition and potential. Karpov would take out one of his mother's Debussy records. He was returning more and more to the composer's piano pieces lately. They were soothing and dreamlike. The time immediately after he sated himself with a girl was like the cool, clear spell that follows an afternoon thunderstorm over the steppe in late summer. He knew his lust would build again soon, as the heat and humidity build in the summer air in an endless cycle.

Oleg was standing against the paneled wall. Every couple of minutes, he transferred a caramel from the paper bag in his jacket pocket to his mouth. He chewed continuously.

When Karpov saw Vassily and Anna approaching at the far end of the corridor, he broke into a broad grin and spread his arms wide.

"El Catalan himself!" he cried, in an exaggerated Spanish accent. "Gallivanting around the capitalist countries suits you, Vassily. You look like that Egyptian—what was his name, Oleg? I can't remember but he ran the biggest cathouse in Cairo. That fine tie must have cost a month's salary. And this is a whole new kind of shirt collar. An American design?"

Vassily said: "You are looking very well yourself, Comrade Maxim Georgevich." Karpov flinched. He did not like people saying his first name out loud and he disliked being reminded of his father's.

Vassily came up close to Karpov—too close. He looked down at him insolently, allowing his eyes to drift across to the right side of Karpov's neck. Oleg took a step away from the wall toward them. Vassily's eyes hovered around the throat of Karpov, who appeared to be bracing himself for some outrage.

"If I may say so, Comrade Chief Administrator," said Vassily, mildly, "that high style of collar suits you."

Karpov colored and chewed his lip. His hand rose as if to reach for the spot on his neck where Vassily's eyes had rested, but he mastered himself and forced it back to his side. He scowled at Vassily but said nothing.

Oleg was two paces away, still chewing slowly. Vassily jerked a thumb at him. "How come he's always eating, but he doesn't get fat? Is there a trick to it? I've always wondered."

"He gets a lot of exercise beating the shit out of people I don't like."

"Is this really necessary, gentlemen?" asked Anna.

Oleg walked right up to Vassily and stood there without expression. Their faces were inches apart, like those of boxers squaring up to each other at the weigh-in.

"For God's sake!" said Anna.

The two men stood toe to toe for a moment, searching each other's face for signs of weakness. Neither detected any. Vassily sniffed theatrically and said: "Too much garlic." A smirk played at the corners of Oleg's mouth.

Madame Sorokina threw open the door and said: "Good morning to you all. The comrade Chief Administrator is kindly invited in first."

The chairman of the Central Committee of the Soviet Union had a headache that morning. He had been obliged to drink heavily for three evenings in a row, against the specific advice of his personal physician. Saturday was a national holiday in honor of socialist agriculture. Guests from all the Soviet republics and foreign trade representatives had been invited to the grandest hall in the palace and the chairman had put in a classic performance, expending his impressive stock of jokes and stories and leading the party in endless toasts. On Sunday night he had spent a tense three hours with a group of senior military officials from East Germany discussing a document with a single long word printed on the front in bold type. Relations between the two allies were frosty and the chairman had relied on liberal amounts of good brandy as well as his considerable charm to lubricate the conversation.

On Monday there was an annual dinner to celebrate the defense of Moscow from the Nazis. This year was the twentieth anniversary of the siege. Anna should have been there. She had been his deputy then, when he was the chairman of the local party in the capital's darkest days. The guests were a mixture of officials, military officers and ordinary people from the city who had stayed to defend it, when the Germans had reached Khimki and were looking at the spires of St Basil's Cathedral through their field binoculars. Many others had tried to flee, choking the roads that led east, but that was not mentioned now.

In a normal year Anna would have sat on the chairman's right, laughing and joking and squeezing his arm while he called her "daughter." If he got lost in an anecdote and forgot the name of a comrade or the date of an incident, she would remind him gently. Last year, the main course had been a magnificent whole trout stuffed with pomegranate and sour apricots, which the waiters had placed in front of him with a flourish.

Only Anna noticed the strange, fixed expression that had come over the leader's face, and she had swiftly had the plate moved. It was not widely known that the chairman, who regularly weighed decisions that might lead to the destruction of millions of lives, could not bear to contemplate death and suffering in the smallest of everyday things. He could not endure the sight of blood, be it from man or animal, and it was his wife who had to dispatch the live carp that she brought home for special occasions.

He wanted Anna at the feast, but the shadow that had suddenly fallen upon her family made it impossible. They would be cast out of the circle of light until the mystery of Sergei's disappearance was solved.

There was a grand desk in the chairman's private office with a highbacked chair, but he never sat behind it. It was covered with books and plastic scale models of Soviet airplanes and satellites. There was a small coffee table immediately in front of the desk with two soft leather chairs on either side. This was where the chairman entertained visitors. He lolled in one of the chairs now, a hand pressed to his temple. His secretary, Madame Sorokina, walked in with a glass of water fizzing with painkillers. She watched with great sympathy as he took a long sip.

"Are they both here?"

"Comrade Karpov has been waiting for a while now, Comrade Chairman, with his assistant. Anna Vladimirovna has just arrived."

"Let's get this over with. Send the MGB delegation in first, please."

Karpov left the chairman's office and walked past Anna, jamming his trilby down hard on his head and grinning his hunting dog grin. Oleg loped behind. The leader of the Soviet Union put a finger to his lips as Anna came in through the open door of the office. He gestured for her to sit opposite him. Vassily followed Anna into the room, walked over to the wireless set in the corner and stooped in front of it. He opened a panel at the back and fiddled with something. Then he moved the dial on the front up and down the spectrum. No radio stations could be heard, only static.

When Vassily had finished, he turned to the chairman. "Nothing." He got up on a chair and looked at the light fitting in the center of the ceiling. He ran a finger over the light switches, and the bank of controls for the intercom system. He shrugged. "Nothing new."

The chairman smiled warmly. "Thank you, my friend. I will not keep Anna for long." Vassily nodded and left the room.

Anna looked at the chairman in amazement. He said: "There is a signal generator hidden in the radio to disrupt any devices. I want us to be able to talk freely."

"You think Karpov would dare to bug this office?"

"He has done so before."

She screwed her hands into fists and almost shouted the word *pederast*. The chairman winced. His head still ached. "Why in God's name do you tolerate him?" she said. "He is like a nightmare we cannot wake up from."

"Do you know what my wife calls him? The long shadow that lingers all year round to remind us of the winter. For me, Maxim is my penance—the price I pay for everything I did back then."

"I won't let you talk that way. You were the springtime. You gave us hope again."

The chairman shook his head. "I wasn't brave enough to make a move against the Boss."

They sat and looked at each other for a while. She had been crying but had done her best to conceal it with makeup. She was fifty and he was sixty-seven, but they might have been the same age. Drink and worry had aged her.

"You did the right thing by raising the alarm," the chairman said at last. "If you had left it to Karpov to discover the news, things would be harder now. When did you report Sergei missing?"

"The night before last. We haven't seen or heard from him." She swallowed. "For four days now."

"And Ivanov interviewed you last night at police headquarters?"

"The little deputy. Ivanov doesn't want any part of this."

"Very sensible. What did you tell him?"

"Everything I know. I told him he could search the house. I told them about our place in East Germany. There is nowhere else Sergei could have gone. Nowhere that I know of."

The chairman considered this. "There was a panic about Yulia that night, of course. I was in here, watching the embassy wires. Karpov wanted to drag her home immediately. Vassily insisted she continue with the second day of the chess tournament. He got his way. The honor of Soviet sports was at stake, and there was no point in creating a scandal in the foreign press."

"Are you sure we can trust Vassily?"

The chairman raised an eyebrow. "I was under the impression that he was a friend of yours."

"Of mine? Certainly not!" she snapped. "What has he said to you?"

"Nothing, daughter. I understood that you and Sergei knew Vassily well, that is all."

"I might have bumped into him once in the war. I do not remember him clearly. They are all the same, that type of man. I believe Sergei was acquainted with him. And, of course, I have heard stories."

"Not all of them, I think. Your hair would have turned white." He chuckled to himself.

Anna did not return his smile. "Vassily always reports to you directly?"

"Absolutely not. When you employ a man like that, it is of the utmost importance that you have no idea what he is doing half the time. The truth would give me nightmares." She was still not amused. The chairman said: "In so far as there is any certainty in this world, I believe that Vassily Andreyevich can be trusted. He is a rare man: one who thinks for himself and is prepared to take risks. Our system does not excel at producing people with these qualities. Do you remember Cuba? That was all him. I could not have found the place on a map and the name Fidel Castro was unknown to any of us. Vassily went absent without leave and ran the whole show alone. I have taken great pains to avoid finding out any of the details.

"And now we have our little opera box a hundred miles off the coast of Florida. I could have shot him for insubordination. Naturally, I am going to make him a Hero of the Soviet Union instead . . . when the time is right. It was for Vassily's sake, among other things, that I have fought to keep the Fourth Directorate out of Karpov's fat little hands for all these years."

Anna's face flushed: "You have *fought?* You, the leader of our country, must haggle with this hangman, this pervert? Please explain to me why."

"Because we tried dictatorship," said the chairman, patiently. "And look what happened. Now we have a chairman in charge, not a marshal. And, yes, everything is a negotiation. It is exhausting sometimes, but both of us know what the alternative is."

"Karpov would make himself dictator in a heartbeat," said Anna. "He would outdo Stalin in viciousness."

"No," said the chairman, firmly. "This analysis is incorrect. He is more cautious than you think. And he is always gnawed by doubt. Karpov had his chance on the day of the Boss's death and did not take it. When the crown was rolling around the floorboards of the dacha, and the rest of us were scrabbling around, trying to pick it up and place it on our own heads, Karpov drew aside. He helped me become chairman then. His survival was the price. And then he set about making himself indispensable. He designed the nuclear weapons program and it would be hard to make it work without him now. There is, of course, the small matter of the files."

"Now we are getting somewhere!" said Anna, bitterly. "He has a file on you."

"He does, of course." the chairman replied pleasantly. "And on you, and on your husband, without a doubt, and on many, many other people. Those flimsy little folders, finally, are the source of Karpov's power."

Anna's control over herself slackened and she wept openly. "You have no idea what this is like. No one trusts me. They whisper poison when I walk past. My own daughter does not believe me when I tell her I had nothing to do with her father's disappearance. And I am forced to tolerate that repulsive man, when part of me is convinced that he has murdered my husband. All my guards are gone, on his orders, no doubt. Tell me what to do. I have no one left."

The chairman got up with a wince, came around the little table and put his arms around Anna's shaking shoulders. He said: "Of course it was Karpov's idea to take your soldiers, my daughter. But matters of internal security like that are technically within his remit, and he chose his moment well. Every last armed man is being mobilized. I signed that order, and I cannot be seen to make exceptions for my friends, even my dearest ones. There is only one thing I can give you now: Vassily. Lean on him. If I cannot spare a dozen men to look over you and Yulia, I can give you the next best thing: a man who has lived a dozen lives."

14

The air hostess had a flat on the seventeenth floor of a gleaming white tower block in Novye Cheryomushki. There was hot water all day in these new places. Vassily sipped coffee and shaved and washed his face and neck, trying not to wake her.

When he had finished in the bathroom, he took the coffee into the kitchen and closed the door behind him carefully. He switched on the Astrad and rolled the volume down. He was just in time for the Kremlin chimes. The wheat harvest forecasts were in. Every automobile worker had been promised a new apartment within three years. Armed robbers had held up the Metropole Hotel in Moscow in a daring raid.

Vassily swirled the dark grounds around the bottom of the cup as he listened, and ran a hand over his chin, feeling for rough patches. The girl had left a carton of duty-free Camels out for him on the sideboard: the Turkish blend, not the American. He switched off the radio when the bulletin finished.

When he padded back in to retrieve his clothes, she was moaning and stretching.

"Is that a new lamp?" he asked her. "In the kitchen? Next to my cigarettes?"

"Mmm. Present."

"Got another boyfriend?"

"Lots. All more handsome than you."

"That wouldn't be difficult." He kissed one of her bare shoulders.

"It's from my friend at Air France. The Italian girl. You met her."

"The one with the big mouth."

"The one who's so pretty it's like you're dreaming." She laughed. "Don't pretend you didn't notice."

There was a mattress on the floor, a full-length mirror propped against the wall and nothing else. The air hostess slept at home about four nights in the average month. She watched him while he did up his tie in a complicated knot.

Every few years, Vassily flew to Paris, staying one night in a room above a Spanish bar in Belleville. Then he caught a flight to Naples. He had at least one suit and several sports coats made with the natural soft shoulder line for which the city was famous. He had shirts made too, the cuffs cut looser on the left sleeve so they would fit over the top of his Strela chronograph. He bought knitted silk ties, Acqua di Parma cologne and English-made shoes. He unstitched all the labels with nail scissors before he returned to Russia. He did not want to give ammunition to Customs officials or colleagues in the intelligence world who might be curious about his disposable income.

The girl had been looking at him for a while, her chin propped on one hand. "My friends all think you're a peacock. But it's not vanity, is it? It's control. The way you look at the start of the day is one thing you can control."

He glanced over at her. Clever, he thought. And exquisite. He'd have to be careful.

The girl smiled. She knew she had scored a point. "Do you really have to go now?" she drawled. "I'm not flying until this evening."

"I need to go to Moscow."

"Why don't you keep more of your things here? Then at least you'd have a clean shirt in the morning. I'll give you a key if you like." She tried to make it sound casual but he gave her a searching look, then came over and kissed the back of her neck and shoulders. She had opened a magazine and was pretending to read it.

"*Statuettochka*," he said. "What is the attraction? I'm not surprised your friends don't understand it. I am old enough to be your father."

"I don't care. Make love to me again."

"I have to go to Moscow."

"You keep saying that. We're in Moscow, you lunatic. Do you think we're on the moon? Get in the lift and go seventeen stories down."

Vassily put his jacket on, smoothing the front with his hands and pausing to check the overall effect in the mirror. "The Moscow I need is eighteen stories down."

He pulled his car over by a phone box next to Neskuchny Garden and dialed the news desk at TASS. The man at the end of the line called him *batya,* the name Red Army soldiers reserve for a loved and trusted superior officer.

"This robbery at the Metropole," said Vassily. "What's the real story?"

"It happened exactly as broadcast this morning." The voice sounded hurt. "My scripts are always accurate."

"What did they make you leave out?"

There was a swear word, then the sound of a hand scrabbling through piles of paper.

"Two guys. They go into the reception and demand the manager opens the safe, which he does. All right, here's what we couldn't say: they're dressed as police and the uniforms look authentic."

"There are plenty of witnesses, then?"

"The manager. The security guard. He doesn't like the look of them and he comes over. They start waving pistols around and he backs off. The guns aren't police issue. Czechoslovakian, the guard thinks. The old nine-millimeter ones. They get outside and a police detective sees what's happening. There's a shootout. The cop gets one of these slimes in the shoulder. They miss him and hit an old lady walking past the entrance of the hotel."

"Christ."

"Sweet little *babuchka,* just finished her cleaning job. Right behind the eyes. No one knows who she is. No name, no papers. Family haven't come forward."

"The uniform thing is interesting. Ever heard of it before?"

"Not in Moscow. Down south, maybe. It makes perfect sense. People see a police uniform, they do as they're told. It's the Soviet mentality," the journalist added bitterly.

"It's human nature. Did they take much?"

"I mean, they hit the jackpot. The place is full of foreign *biznesmen*, for the agricultural fair. Stacks of overseas currency in the safe, jewelry, the lot. It's getting picked up by the Western press now. Ivanov has egg all over his face. He doesn't know where to start."

Vassily thought furiously, until the voice at the end of the line said: "*Batya*, I hate to hurry you, but I'm up against it."

"What? Oh, of course."

"I'm sorry, Vassily Andreyevich. There's nothing else I can tell you."

"All right. You've been a big help. There's smokes coming your way."

"Russian?"

"Capitalist cigarettes, of unbelievable decadence."

"*Batya*. Call any time."

In a room above a shop at the north end of Gorky Street, Vassily met an Armenian man and exchanged a quantity of gold for three brand new Czech-made firearms. The gold came from a heavy chain bracelet, which he fished from the inside pocket of his jacket and placed on the fine Alexander I table between them. He had taken the bracelet, with menaces, from his opposite number in American intelligence in Santa Clara, Cuba, in 1958. Each link contained exactly one-eighth of a troy ounce of pure gold.

The Armenian prized open the links with a pair of needle pliers, then weighed each one on a set of antique brass scales. After he had finished, they proceeded to haggle. Anyone eavesdropping would have believed that the two men were locked in an argument so bitter they might come to blows at any second. But when the price was agreed, they sat back in their chairs and beamed at each other. They drank black tea from twenty-sided glasses and Vassily enquired with great interest about the health and prospects of the Armenian's children.

When they had drained their glasses, Vassily seemed in no hurry to leave. He held one of the pistols up to the light to peer at it, then gave it an extravagant sniff. The Armenian grinned. "No fingerprints. No chemical wash. These have never been fired. They are straight from the factory, as fresh as new laid eggs."

"This is why people come to you! I suppose . . . the only drawback is that these Czechoslovakian beauties stand out, don't they? You know that robbery everyone is talking about? I'm told the guns they used were very similar to these."

The Armenian shook his head apologetically to indicate that he had not been keeping up with the news.

"I'm just trying to be a good neighbor," said Vassily. "Even the Moscow police will make the connection eventually. God forbid that rabble should come and disturb you."

The Armenian put both his elbows on the table, wrapped a fist in the palm of his other hand and inclined his head politely.

"The old woman they shot was Armenian," said Vassily. "Did you know that? I'm surprised you hadn't heard. Four grandchildren. Now, I would be willing to make a bet that if the Moscow police had something to go on—and I mean anything at all—they would be too busy to pester you."

The Armenian took him down to the front entrance and opened the four heavy locks. The Gorky Street traffic drowned out their farewells. But Vassily heard one word, whispered sharply in his ear: "Chechens."

At Turgenevskaya, Vassily opened the front door of a residential block, ducked into the mail room just inside and unlocked a box for a flat that did not exist. All the letters inside were addressed to a fictitious company that purported to export natural gas to Western Europe. None of the letters had the French or Spanish postmarks he was looking for, and he threw them back in disgust.

At Taganskaya Hospital, Vassily lounged in a chair in the corridor. The doctor called him in ahead of the other patients, and they glowered at Vassily as he passed them all—the amputees, the antique women as wrinkled as raisins, the men who wheezed incessantly through lungs scarred by prison camp or factory.

The doctor had been a well-known dissident in his student days. He had acquired a conviction for hooliganism, which Vassily had scrubbed from his official record before it could hurt his career. He motioned Vassily into his office and indicated a large brown paper bag on the desk. The two men did not exchange pleasantries. The bag contained cocaine hydrochloride, Benzedrine tablets, phenobarbital and ampoules of morphine with military markings. There was a small bottle containing red and white capsules with no label. Vassily questioned the doctor closely about the contents of this unmarked bottle. When he rose to leave, he did not thank him.

He paused just before he opened the door. "I nearly forgot. I'm told you still do private work from time to time. Getting rid of hangovers for special clients? Stitching up gunshot wounds?"

The doctor's back stiffened visibly. He was pretending to read something on his desk.

"A police bullet in the shoulder. You would remember."

"I might do the occasional job off the books," the doctor said carefully. "A hunting accident, let's say. I would still be bound by confidentiality."

"No need to say a word. Just nod." Vassily reeled off a string of Chechen names. At the fourth, the doctor's head dipped, very stiffly.

In Taganka, Vassily walked gingerly down an alley behind a parade of shops, trying to spare his good shoes from the muddy puddles and the cracked edges of the paving stones. The passageway smelt of cooking fat and the detritus of restaurants stuffed into industrial bins. Emaciated cats stalked around.

He paused at the back door of a grocery shop. There was a string curtain to keep the flies out. He could hear a radio blaring. It was the fourth quarter and Torpedo were heading for a famous victory over Kryla Sovetov on the ice. For a second, the noise took him back to the Moscow of the beginning of the war, when radios were banned in private homes but could be heard shrieking from every street corner, proclaiming an endless false message of victory over the advancing Germans. Vassily parted the curtain and walked into the back room of the shop—into the Thieves' World.

Two men sat together at a table, sharing a bottle of *kvass*. One was wearing a vest, and his upper arms, chest and back were almost entirely covered with black ink. He had a big drooping mustache, like a caricature of a Prussian army officer from the previous century.

The other man was younger and wore a smart shirt with an open neck. He was bald on top, like a tonsured monk, and had a knotted leather prayer rope in his right hand. This man greeted Vassily warmly and offered him a drink. The tattooed man stared into the middle distance in silence.

The ink all over his torso was made from the melted rubber soles of prison boots, mixed with urine. The designs were applied with the sharp end of a guitar string over several torturous days. The Latin phrase *Non serviam*—"I will not serve"—ran below the man's collar bone. A splendid clipper floated on his right biceps, each sail representing a prison sentence. When the Thief scratched his side, his white vest rode up slightly and Vassily saw the upper half of a familiar face poking above the waistband. It signified that the wearer had been incarcerated at the end of the 1920s, when prisoners had the faces of Lenin and Stalin inked over their vital organs in the belief that the guards would not beat those sacred images. The three letters of the Russian word for "peace" were incongruously stamped between the knuckles of the Thief's right hand. Vassily knew the joke: it was an acronym for *Only a bullet can reform me.*

"He is not being rude," said the younger man. "He's not allowed to talk to anyone from the police or the government. He can't even acknowledge that you exist."

"I know all that stuff." Vassily sighed. "Is this really still necessary in 1961? Is he really going to say everything through you?"

"This man is a legitimate Thief," said the bald man, proudly. "Unsullied by any contact with the Bolshevik state. He is an authority on our Code and on all the traditions. A word from him settles disputes from one end of the Zone to the other."

"This is what my mother used to do to the old man when they were fighting," grumbled Vassily. "All right. Tell him I need four passports. One for me. Germany—theirs, I mean. And three more for a young woman and her parents. Swiss, if you can get them." He patted his breast pocket. "I have photographs and all the other details here. I need them soon and I don't have cash. One does not owe money to a Thief, so I am offering a trade. I have guns, pharmaceuticals . . ."

The tattooed man understood Russian perfectly but insisted on having all of this translated into Georgian. He gave a laconic reply which contained only one word that Vassily understood—the Russian word *Tsar*.

"He says German is easy but getting a Swiss passport is like finding the lost jewels of the Romanovs."

Vassily sighed with impatience. "Tell him Austrian, then."

There was a sharp exchange and the tattooed man shook his head emphatically, at no one in particular. He slurped noisily at his glass of *kvass*. That appeared to be the end of the matter. Vassily stood up to leave, but the Thief smacked the glass down and raised a hand. He began to speak Georgian, slowly and very formally.

The young man looked at Vassily with curiosity as he listened. When the tattooed man had finished, he said: "You were in the Zone."

Vassily made a slight movement of his head. "I was a political *zek*, of course, not—"

"I didn't think you were one of us! Unless you have some tattoos hidden away."

"Only in here." Vassily thumped his chest with his fist. "Where they can't be cut out."

The Georgian men exchanged a look and the younger said: "These were his words. You can see the stars drawn above his heart. Also, there are stars on his knees. This means he kneels before no one—neither God nor Devil. But he knows who you are. He remembers that you were kind to his people once in Kazakhstan. For this reason, there will be no charge for the service, neither in cash nor in kind. The passports will be ready tomorrow night. Consider it the settling of a historical debt."

"Tell him . . ." said Vassily ". . . tell him I value his word, knowing him to be a good and honorable Thief."

Vassily was driving west along the north bank of the Moscow River when he felt a pang in his midsection and realized he hadn't eaten for almost twenty-four hours. He glanced at the Strela and parked near the public gardens at Zaryadye. The teenage boy selling buns at the kiosk was Kazakh or Uzbek. This is what people think the average day is like in the capitalist countries, thought Vassily, as he queued. You start with a donkey. You trade it for a bicycle. You swap the bike for a car, the car for a house. By the end of the day, you're a millionaire. Vassily was chuckling to himself as the boy racked up his order on the wooden abacus and took the kopecks from him.

"You're having fun today," said the teenager. "I'm living the American dream."

When Vassily arrived at the Kremlin, he went straight up to the third-floor office of Madame Sorokina, private secretary to the chairman of the Politburo. He knocked and called: "Grandfather Frost is here!" He had bought her a long powder-blue cashmere scarf in London. It took a while to unwrap. She hugged him with tears in her eyes.

Vassily went down to the second floor, near the suite of rooms that were used to accommodate MGB personnel when they visited the palace. Oleg was not in his usual seat. Vassily walked to the toilets at the far end of the main corridor. This corner of the building had not been refurbished yet and few people visited.

He pushed the door open silently and heard someone gagging. He slid in, walking toe to heel. A man in one of the cubicles was trying to make himself sick. Vassily held the door open for a moment then gave it a hard push so that it smacked loudly against the frame. The noise from the cubicle stopped instantly. Vassily clumped heavily over to one of the washbasins and turned on the tap full blast. He let the door bang again on his way out, then leaned against the wall of the corridor ten feet down from the toilets, reading a copy of *Paris Match*.

Oleg came out and stopped when he saw Vassily. He wiped his hands on the front of his trousers. Without raising his eyes from the magazine, Vassily said: "You'll lose all your teeth if you keep that up." He could feel Oleg's eyes boring into him. There was silence.

Oleg cracked first. "Do you have it or not?"

Vassily reached into the outside pocket of his sports coat, plucked out a bottle of cocaine solution, and gave it a shake. Oleg peered at the label, which bore the insignia of the Merck pharmaceutical company, then stretched his hand toward the bottle. Vassily snatched it out of reach.

"Child," growled Oleg.

"He can't keep guzzling all these stimulants as well as morphine. It's a bad combination. It will weaken his heart. And his sanity." Vassily shook his head. "How did he get a taste for this stuff anyway? It's not easy to find. Even for me."

"Fuck you. In the mouth."

Vassily beamed. "If you want me to play doctor and hand out the sweets, I'm going to ask a few questions. I don't want Maxim Georgevich dropping dead on me." He clicked his fingers suddenly, as though a good idea had sprung to mind. "Why don't I ask him myself? Presumably you tell him who is supplying you?"

Oleg colored and cleared his throat. "He's been taking it on and off since the war. A doctor started prescribing it for fatigue. He has an illness that saps his energy. There are days when he can't get out of bed."

"A Red Army doctor prescribed him cocaine?" said Vassily, doubtfully.

Oleg coughed again. "German."

"*Now* I understand. One of the Fritzis you scooped up in '45? If it was good enough for Hitler, it's good enough for Karpov, eh? That fatigue you describe isn't a medical condition, you know. It's his soul weighing him down like a millstone."

"Fuck you. Talking like a doctor. What are you really? A bourgeois drug pedlar."

Vassily smiled like a happy child. "*Pedlar* is a little unfair. I never ask you for a kopeck. I just like to help comrades in distress."

Oleg's massive hand was still stretched out. Vassily placed the bottle upright in the middle of his palm.

"Make him go easy with that. I won't be able to get more for a couple of weeks."

Oleg grunted, turned on his heels and strode away. Vassily shouted after him: "He'll drag you down with him."

One of Oleg's hands was closed tightly around the bottle and the other was clenched into a fist.

Vassily was supposed to be at Strastnoy Park at three o'clock sharp. He was almost ten minutes late. Ivanov, the chief of the Moscow police department, was not hard to spot, even with his back turned.

He was an enormously fat man who wore an unconvincing hairpiece and an air of permanent anxiety. Ivanov was filling a glass with crushed ice and strawberry juice from a vending machine on the south side of the park when Vassily stuck his fingers into his back like a pistol barrel and said: "Aslanbekov."

The police chief turned slowly with an expression of wounded dignity. "What, Comrade?"

"Who. Mahmud Aslanbekov. A resident of Urus-Martan, Chechnya. Currently holed up in Moscow, taking strong painkillers and antibiotics after having a police round removed from his right shoulder."

It gave Vassily pleasure to watch Ivanov's eyes slowly become very wide. "Give me another day and I'll have an address in Moscow."

Ivanov's mouth opened but no sound came out. "*Rhinemaiden*," said Vassily. "Any more arrests?"

The policeman glanced around nervously, then drank the strawberry juice in one gulp and dabbed at his mouth with a handkerchief. You were supposed to wash the glass and replace it when you were finished. Ivanov studied it as though he could not understand how it had come to be in his hand.

"Any more *Rhinemaiden* arrests?"

"Not so loud! I'm trying to think, curse you. One police arrest that I know of, in the last week. The MGB might have done more. We picked up a shortwave radio enthusiast who used the word several times while talking to a friend in Germany. They were obviously discussing opera. Who is it again?"

"Wagner."

"Indeed. The man was clearly innocent. Karpov wanted us to sweat him, but I let him go and told him to be careful, if he wanted to keep his radio license. It's academic anyway. We're jamming all the Western shortwave frequencies from this week."

"That sounds ominous."

"Read into it what you will," said Ivanov. He added irritably: "That is a top-level military secret by the way, Comrade."

"All right. What about the other thing we talked about?"

Ivanov put the glass back without washing it. His hands were sticky and he rubbed them on the crotch of his trousers. He waddled off into the middle of the grass where there were the fewest people, beckoning at Vassily to follow.

"My little deputy is the problem. Always peeping through my keyhole. He belongs to the chief administrator."

"Then he will get washed away too when Karpov falls."

"For Christ's sake, be careful what you say, you fool!"

"Missing girls," said Vassily. "Bones buried under the rose bushes."

Ivanov exhaled deeply. "The deputy takes Karpov round to the cowsheds at night. He puts all the young street butterflies in the same cell block. Railway station whores with no papers, no family in Moscow. He parades them up and down in front of Karpov. If Comrade Maxim likes one of the girls, the deputy tells her she can have her freedom if she goes home with the important gentleman and does what she was born to do for a week."

"A week. Alone in Maxim Karpov's house?"

"Three square meals a day and a few rubles at the end of it. And no more police trouble."

"And what really happens to them?"

"God knows."

"For the love of Jesus," snarled Vassily.

"I need evidence before I can do anything. I've never received a single complaint of any wrongdoing. No missing person reports. Now calm down. Don't get agitated."

Vassily was beating the air with both hands. "Detectives who won't investigate," he shouted. "Soldiers who won't fight. Workers who won't work. Do you know what the joke is in the factories? *They pretend to pay us, we pretend to work.*"

"I need evidence. Think about who we're discussing here. I need Eisenstein filming the crime from three angles while it happens. I need a sworn statement from Christ himself."

"When Karpov falls," Vassily told him, "it will happen all of a sudden, like when a tree goes. You'd better be ready."

"Evidence. Come back when you have some, not before. Write that Chechen's name down for me before you fuck off."

He reached the biggest of the new housing estates down by the river and parked at the water's edge. The afternoon had warmed up as it wore on. A gang of children were paddling in a shallow section that lapped against the end of the half-finished road next to the estate.

Vassily stood looking at the tall white buildings, the children's shouts and cries in his ears. A hydrofoil was slicing down the middle of the river and the boys and girls cheered, waving when it drew abreast of them.

Yulia's father Sergei had designed every detail of the estate. Identical versions of it existed across the Soviet Union. Sergei called them "vertical villages." He had shown Vassily the original drawings in his study one drunken evening. What a strange night that was, thought Vassily, not for the first time. Two men who could not have been more different coming together and finding that they saw the world in a very similar way. Two old *zeks*, drinking and remembering.

Every estate had its own school, playground, laundry, sports stadium. And, most importantly of all, according to Sergei, a polyclinic. "I can't stop those missiles raining down," he told Vassily, with a sudden depth of feeling, "but I can give the people below a chance. When the war comes, every neighborhood will be cut off from the center. No help will come from Moscow. My villages will have to pull together to survive. It will be a new world of autonomous communities."

"That's what they said about the collective villages when I was a small boy," said Vassily, looking over the blueprints and scratching the back of his head. "It didn't last. Moscow couldn't keep its fingers to itself."

"American bombs," said Sergei, "will bring real socialism to Russia at last."

Andrey, the young army officer who had once kissed Yulia, lived on the first floor in a flat that looked out over the running track. His mother answered the door. Vassily wasn't prepared for her strong, bright, false smile. Her headscarf and gold teeth. She stood with her feet apart, resting her fists easily on her hips. She did not invite him in.

"Is Andrey at home?" Vassily felt momentarily ridiculous. He produced a box of cherries in chocolate from the shopping bag in his hand. "For the beautiful young mother-to-be!"

Andrey yelled, "Who is it, Ma?" from the dark flat behind her.

"A Chekist is my guess." The woman did not quite spit on the concrete.

"Let's go for a walk, Andrey," said Vassily.

"I'm getting changed out of my uniform," the boy shouted from the darkness.

"You can take your duchess out too if you're going for a stroll," said his mother. "Exercise will do her good. Sitting around with her feet up all day long."

"Xenia is under the weather today, Ma." Andrey was just behind her now, putting on a casual white jacket.

"She is suffering from a mystery illness called pregnancy," said his mother. "The first woman who's ever had it." She stepped aside to let her son pass. Her eyes were still fixed on Vassily and the exaggerated smile on her face did not waver for a second. "Will I ever see my son again if he goes with you, Chekist?"

"Ma!" shouted Andrey.

They walked around the outside of the running track while the ladies' team from the cement factory warmed up in the middle.

"I wasn't sure if it was really you," Vassily told him. "You look different when you haven't got your tongue halfway down some girl's throat." Andrey shut his eyes and muttered a curse.

Vassily's voice dropped. "Your two best boys: Ilya and the Ukrainian."

"What about them?"

"They like you and they listen to you. You are a good officer, as all the world knows."

"What do you want with my lads, *Batya?*"

"They are on secondment from the unit for a month. Shut up. You don't know where they are, but I do. They are guarding Maxim Karpov's house."

"Christ."

"Indeed. I want them to pay special attention to the beautiful garden that lies to the rear of that property."

"Karpov's back garden."

"It is a security risk. A burglar could scale the back fence one night if no one is on patrol. Or tunnel underneath it. Imagine that. We don't want any tunnelers disturbing the chief administrator's slumbers."

They stopped. Andrey was looking all around distractedly with one hand pressed to the back of his neck. The women from the factory team were jogging on the spot and windmilling their arms.

Vassily said: "So, tell those boys to keep an eye open for patches of freshly dug earth. Any unusual gardening activity. Suitcases buried under the rose bushes. They report to you, you report to me."

"*Batya*, this is too much. Think about what you're asking. Those boys are teenagers."

"Did you ever see the crowds pulling down statues of the Boss after he died? No, you're too young. It was quite a thing to see. They seemed to sway forever. Then suddenly—bang!" He clapped his hands. "They fall. It happens faster than you would believe. The important thing is to be ready."

"*Batya*. All I'm saying is that those two are still kids. And I have a son on the way. Not everyone can be a Hero of the Soviet Union."

"Your father would not have hesitated to help me with this," said Vassily, with casual brutality. He watched Andrey turn red.

"That's all very well," said the young soldier, "but other people are relying on me. What if something goes wrong? What if we get caught?"

Vassily put both his hands on the boy's shoulders. "You know that I never let them take anyone. I might shoot you myself, but I never give anyone up to them." Andrey did not want to meet his gaze.

"The statue is swaying," Vassily told him. "It is coming. Be ready."

15
ENGLAND

Greta had a suite of rooms in Caius College, Cambridge, for the summer. It was the loveliest place she had ever lived, with views of lawns as smooth as card tables, honey-colored stone walls and a pale blue sundial looking down over everything.

The cleaning staff came in and out as they pleased, so she had to be extremely careful about what she left lying around. The arrangement was due to end in September, before the undergraduates came back. Then she would have to find lodgings somewhere else in the city, or retreat to the camp bed that was always waiting for her at the townhouse in West Kensington. She spent her days shuttling between London and Cambridge, her life ruled by two columns of men's names.

One was a long list, written in a red-and-black notebook by several hands. Most of the names were German. She carried the other list in her head. There were only five names on this one. All were men with links to British intelligence who had been at Trinity College in the middle of the 1930s, the time of the Spanish war. The Soviets were fighting the Fascists there and idealistic young people from around the world were drawn to their cause.

She went to a peace rally in Trafalgar Square on August 10. The philosopher Bertrand Russell was the big attraction, a month before his arrest for breach of the peace. Professor Colin Sinclair was speaking too, further down the bill. He aroused Greta's interest, but she did not have time to wait for him to take to the stage.

Her cashmere sweater, heels and pinned-up hair made her stand out from the female students in the audience. That was all right. She wanted to be seen. So far, she had spotted one man who might be interested in her. As she drifted eastward around the back of the crowd, her eyes on the stage, the man tracked her at a respectable distance.

She was careful not to turn her head in his direction, but she sneaked a look at him over her shoulder in the mirror in her powder compact. He could have been Greek, or from the northern Balkans. He wore an open-necked shirt and had a bulky camera around his neck with a large flash diffuser.

Greta did not like to get too close to people who carried cameras or walking sticks or umbrellas or bicycle pumps in the street. She did not like it when men held out cigarette lighters for her. Soviet ingenuity meant that all these implements might contain a nasty surprise.

It was unlikely that the Russians would try any thuggery in a busy London thoroughfare in broad daylight, but you never knew. In the mid-1950s two agents from what was then the Ministry of Internal Affairs had attempted to snatch her in Paris while she was walking down a shopping street much like this one. Be bold again if you want to, my little friends, she thought. I splashed your blood all over the white paving stones that day, and I will do it again.

Greta walked out of the southeast corner of Trafalgar Square and headed up the Strand, purposefully but not too quickly. The street was thick with pedestrians, so she was careful not to turn. If the man was mingling with a group of people behind her, she would not spot him instantly, and it would be obvious that she was looking for him. She stopped abruptly at the jewelers on the corner, as if something in the display had caught her eye. A man who had been coming up the Strand behind her stopped suddenly too, right at the edge of her peripheral vision. She did not turn to look at him, but she had the impression that something was slung around his neck.

Greta wheeled left around the corner into Bedford Street at an easy pace. When she was out of sight of the Strand, she pelted forward fifteen yards, then pressed herself into the deep doorway of an office building on the left. She heard footsteps approaching. There was no one else in the side street. Greta had a small folding knife pressed against her left wrist, under the sleeve of the sweater, secured with an elastic band. She pulled it out, opened it and held it behind her back. When the man breasted the alcove she was hiding in, Greta swung out her left leg and kicked him just below the knee. He stumbled forward and she caught him by the windpipe with her left hand. She was ready to bury the knife in him up to the hilt when she saw that the thing around his neck was not a camera but a small brown leather satchel. Her eyes met his and she released him instantly and swore in Lithuanian.

"*Bled*. Creeping up on me! You were supposed to stay in the square." Mindaugas had gone down on one knee, but he rose quickly, massaging his throat.

"I'm sorry, my old friend," she said. "I'm jumpy."

"You're right to be. There were two of them."

"I made one. With a camera."

He nodded but they did not speak until they were around the corner in Maiden Lane, looking back anxiously. They saw no one.

Mindaugas said: "I was sitting on the ground like a tramp next to one of the fountains. I could see everyone. It was the strangest thing. Two men. The guy with the camera and an older fellow. Very well dressed. Their eyes met—and they jumped out of their skins! It couldn't have been more obvious that they knew each other. I saw the photographer go bright red. They hurried away in opposite directions. They were almost running. What do you think it means?"

Greta chewed a thumbnail. "It could be someone from the British side, spotting an enemy agent. Could be friends of mine trying to keep an eye on me. I will find out later." She was thinking of Yakuv and what he had told her in the café about the MGB and the Fourth Directorate. "The wolf hunting with the bear," she muttered. Mindaugas shot her a questioning look. "Never mind."

They split up and she hailed a black cab, directing the driver to a tailor's shop on Whitechapel Road. She kept the man waiting outside for nearly ten minutes on yellow lines, then ordered him south of the river, cutting off his grumbling with a sharp word.

There was a personal errand she had been planning for a while. Today's events had brought it back to mind. Flashes of her past life had been resurfacing recently. She thought about the Russians she had killed in Paris. The fight played out in her head like film footage, but she could remember no detail of the men's faces. How many others like them had there been over the years? Twenty? More? She began to count.

The service had already begun when Greta slipped into the back of the church on the Isle of Dogs. Saturday evenings were always well-attended. The priest told her later that many of his congregation were Irish and liked to get mass out of the way so they could drink freely afterward and sleep in late on a Sunday.

Greta knew the prayer to the Virgin and fragments of others in English but could not follow the whole service. She had to read along from the paper sheets they scattered along the pews: "May the Lord accept the sacrifice at your hands, for the praise and glory of his name, for our good, and the good of all his Holy Church."

The young priest waited by the door to shake people's hands as they filed out. Greta stood close by, waiting as he bent almost double to talk to an ancient woman in black. When he glanced at Greta she called, "*Labas vakaras,*" and he returned the Lithuanian greeting with a jolt of surprise. He and the old woman whose hand he was holding looked Greta up and down. She was decades younger than the average parishioner and her skirt was cut short.

Ignoring the old woman, Greta gave the priest her full-beam smile, making her eyes very big. "They told me about you," she said in English. "You're the kind of man I've been dreaming about." The old lady started with horror, let go of the priest's hand and backed away, muttering good-bye. When she had gone, he shot Greta a reproachful look and said in Lithuanian: "Come with me. You can turn off those headlamps. I'm immune."

He came from a family with resistance in the blood. His grandfather had smuggled books written in the forbidden Lithuanian language across the border in the days when the Russian Tsars ruled the Baltic nations with a knotted whip.

They liked and understood each other immediately. After the service, he took Greta into the living room of the little house that backed on to the graveyard. He began the Sacrament of Penance immediately. She did not need to explain that she could talk only under the seal of confession. It had been years since she had been able to trust anyone enough to unburden herself like this and she told the priest everything. It took a quarter of an hour and he paused for a long while after he had heard it all. She thought she had shocked him, but it appeared that he was just taking time to calculate the right prescription in his head.

In the end she got off with a light dose of Hail Marys. He left her alone while she prayed, then came back with tea. He had been living in England long enough to know how to make it properly. She sipped it gratefully. Her body felt lighter.

"Finished?" he asked.

"Yes. Thank you. Is that really all?"

"You sound disappointed. What were you expecting?"

"I don't know, but didn't you hear all the things I told you? About . . ." she swallowed ". . . torturing men?" She was aware that her face was becoming very hot. "Killing them?"

"Nobody's perfect."

"I don't believe this. How many murderers do you get dropping in for—"

"No," he said, suddenly very serious. He wagged a finger. "No. A soldier is not a murderer. God loves soldiers who fight in a just cause." Greta struggled to speak. She had been expecting a lecture on the theme of damnation. She was not prepared for kindness. "I cannot . . .

I do not sense . . . I do not have the feeling that I walk . . . in the grace of God." The spoon she was holding was rattling against the saucer.

He sat beside her and put a hand on her shoulder. "You have work to do. You must stay strong. We will pray now, together, to your patron saint. His protection is powerful. Say the words after me . . . *Holy Michael, archangel, defend us in battle, and against the wickedness and snares of the Devil, be our protection.*"

16

Michael finally left school a few days after the chess tournament. His father did not collect him but sent his driver, Joe, instead. Michael went to stay with his beloved aunt Valerie in the suburbs of north London. Joe slapped a wad of notes into Michael's hand and told him to stay out of trouble. He wrote down a new telephone number on the uppermost cigarette paper and said Michael's father would be in touch soon.

He received his A-level results by post five days later and looked at the piece of paper alone in his room, reading it several times with quiet satisfaction. He went to the library at the bottom of Charing Cross Road and came back with a pile of books he was supposed to read before he started at Cambridge. He worked through them for six hours a day in blocks of two hours: *The Queen of Spades*, *A Sportsman's Sketches*, *Anna Karenina*. Aunt Valerie made him sandwiches and told him he was going to hurt his eyes.

In the evenings Michael went with his old school friends to blues clubs and parties in the basements of houses, and on an island in the Thames they danced to the music of Jimmy Reed and Freddie King. All women who were not Yulia were ugly to him now. Tom and Craig had always relied on Michael to take the lead with girls when they went out together. They were disgusted by his sudden lack of interest.

"What's it like, then?" asked Tom. "You know what I mean. Don't make me say the word. How does it feel, though?"

The best Michael could do was to tap his skull and say: "It's like she's just taken up residence in here. There are times when I can't exactly picture her face, but the image of her is always in here. And when I think about the future, she's always part of it."

He met the Norwegian man, Johnny Jensen, for drinks several times. Johnny was older and had friends who would have excited Michael enormously only a few months earlier. But he had other things on his mind. He was beginning to form a plan.

Late on the morning of August 15, Michael knocked at the flat Johnny's mother had bought for him above a bookmaker in Covent Garden. The Norwegian had a house in Cambridge too. He kept the London flat for weekends and holidays. There was no answer.

It was raining so Michael bought a *Mirror* and went to Café Napoli on Parker Street. He ordered a cappuccino and *spaghetti alla carbonara*. He sat right next to the coffee machine and it coughed in his ear, spat and steamed up the windows.

The paper had splashed on Berlin. The Soviets were starting to build a wall around the Western part. There was a picture of a Communist border guard leaping over a roll of barbed wire to defect. The next fifteen pages were devoted to the crisis. Troops were massing on the borders of Hungary, Czechoslovakia and East Germany.

The American president said he would resume the testing of atomic warheads if Russian provocation continued. The Americans had a new missile called a Minuteman. Sidebar articles asked how the Soviets would invade. Would the Reds strike through the Fulda Gap into Germany? Would NATO respond with a nuclear attack? How many people would survive a counterstrike on Britain? None of the stories actually answered the questions posed in the headlines. There was a full-page diagram showing concentric circles of destruction radiating across southern England.

When the rain stopped, Michael went to Cecil Gee on Charing Cross Road and ran his fingers along a rack of jackets. He cut through Seven Dials to Buddy's shop and bought a record titled *Spoonful*.

He knocked on Johnny's door again in the afternoon and this time the Norwegian answered with a trumpet in his hand. In the living room, a tall girl was sitting on the sofa, her long legs folded underneath her, wearing a crisp white blouse, a pair of black knickers and nothing else. She had a clarinet in her hands and she smiled at Michael with her wide mouth. There was a metronome on the coffee table with sheet music spread around it. Michael looked at them in disbelief and the girl said: "You've never seen a music lesson before?" She burst into a gale of laughter.

"Mine weren't like this," said Michael. "Not with the vicar's mother."

"This is jazz," said the girl. "This is how we do it."

She was called Margherita and came from Sardinia. Her English was excellent, but when you spoke to her, she studied you with intense concentration, as if she needed to hang on to every syllable to keep up. She laughed often and with complete abandon.

The girl put on an airline uniform and did up the tie. She kissed and embraced Johnny and Michael in turn, as though both men were her lovers. When the door closed behind her, they looked at each other in a daze. Michael said: "She is a goddess."

Johnny nodded grimly. "That is a very soulful girl. She's Italian but she works for Air France. She's going to Moscow tonight."

"That's how you do it? Keep one in the air while the other lands."

Johnny's eyes twinkled and he gave a triumphant blast on the trumpet.

"What happened with Greta from Sweden the other night?" asked Michael. He had the English dislike of getting down to serious business quickly.

"Who? At the party? She's not Swedish. My mother was Swedish. That girl speaks it well but with an accent. If I had to make a guess, I would say she is from somewhere in the godless East."

Johnny said all this over his shoulder as he walked into the bathroom swinging the trumpet in one hand. Michael heard the tap come on. He took off his jacket, folded it carefully over the end of the sofa and placed himself next to it.

"It didn't go well." Johnny called. "She was a tough one. Apparently, she is only interested in gray-haired old Cambridge dons."

"You crashed and burned."

"I went down, baby. Into the *soup*. Like a, you know . . ."

"Messerschmitt."

"Right."

Michael was glancing over the sheet music, drumming on the table with his knuckles. The tap went off and another peal of trumpet notes came from the bathroom.

"So, can you help me with that thing?" Michael called, trying to sound offhand.

Johnny came back, the trumpet at his lips. His fingers were rippling on the keys silently. "The visa? Sure thing, baby." He played another loud line as he sat down on the other end of the sofa.

"You said you knew someone. Johnny, concentrate."

"Here's what you do, baby. There's a lecture tonight at the LSE. The speaker is a man I know from Cambridge. A big anti-nuclear guy. I'm going to introduce you and get him to write you a letter of recommendation." He made the "OK" shape with thumb and forefinger. "This guy is the best, right? I went to Moscow last year on an exchange. He wrote me the reference. Worked like a magic spell. He runs an East–West friendship thing: academics reaching out across the Iron Curtain. Exchanging knowledge. Peace and progress. Get the idea?"

"Got it. Then what?"

"Then you do the other thing we talked about. If you're really sure . . ."

"We've been through this. I'm sure."

"It's going to be a big black mark against you if you ever want to work . . ."

"I know. It doesn't matter. What do I do?"

"Go to number sixteen King Street tomorrow morning. It's just around the corner from here. Not too early, they don't keep capitalist hours."

"Sixteen King Street. Got it. And then?"

Johnny shrugged. "Then you're in. You've joined the party. Provisionally. A man called O'Dowd will write you another letter, and then you take a tube to Victoria and you tell the officials at the East German consulate all about the chess tournament. You pay the fee and ask them to process your visa application as a priority, and you give them the two letters."

"And they'll give me a visa in time?"

"I don't know. That's the best I can do. I'm passing on what I've been told."

Michael sat back with a scowl, muttering to himself.

"Relax. My man is good. Very well respected. Professor Colin Sinclair."

Michael laughed out loud. "I know him. He interviewed me."

"Well, all right. That is . . . a happy coincidence."

"More than that. It's a sign from the gods. Sinclair must be my lucky charm. It's going to happen, Johnny. This was meant to happen."

He smiled for the first time. He looked around Johnny's flat. The building was Georgian and the walls bowed in slightly on both sides. The coffee table and the drinks cabinet looked like they were made from solid rosewood. Everything had a careless, unshowy beauty that spoke of real money. The door of Johnny's bedroom was open. The girl had left a white camisole lying on the floor. "What time's this thing at the LSE?" asked Michael.

"Soon. We can walk over there now. We'll swing by the bar first. I'll introduce you to a couple of people. I'm not staying for the lecture, though. I'm allergic to dialectical materialism."

It was almost dark the following evening when Michael left the consulate of the German Democratic Republic in Belgrave Square. He had expected rudeness and bureaucracy. Instead, a middle-aged Berliner made him tea and talked to him with great enthusiasm about chess strategy while they filled in the forms.

You had to declare that you did not have a criminal record and had never been a member of the armed forces. They wanted a list of all the foreign trips you had been on in the last five years. They seemed very preoccupied with the health and medical history of prospective visitors.

Michael was turning the conversation over in his mind when he passed a small white painter's van in Eaton Square Gardens. A man in overalls was leaning against the railings and, as Michael passed, he said: "Can you spark me up, matey?" As Michael fished in the pockets of his sports coat for matches a hand gripped his shoulder and turned him round forcefully. He had not seen a second man approach him from behind and he did not have time to brace himself before the man punched him in the belly with a short, sharp right hook.

Michael doubled up in agony and nearly went sprawling on to the pavement, but the man in the overalls took him under the armpits and pulled him upright. He held Michael up while the other man hit him again, in the liver this time.

That was all Michael knew for a while. Then he became aware that he was in the back of a van, and that there was a coarsely woven sack over his head. He could smell coal when he breathed in. He was lying on the floor and rolled around as the driver took the corners quickly. The air was stale with the smell of men who had sat, smoked and stewed for days on end.

The van stopped and he felt fresh air on his face. Hands grabbed him again and he thought about screaming for help, but something told him not to. They marched him along with his hands cuffed behind him and his arms forced up high so that he had to stoop. His shoulders burned with pain. A Midlands accent came through the sack, right next to Michael's ear: "He doesn't even know how much shagging trouble he's in."

Another voice, from Northern Ireland, said: "A fucking ton of bricks just fell on him, so it did."

They sat him down and took the sack off. He winced at the light from the single bulb. The two men didn't hit him anymore and he knew that it was because they wanted to show that they were in complete control of everything, even their own tempers. Threats, commands and questions rained down instead of blows.

"Do you know where this man comes from? He hates Fenian bastards like you. He'll rip your fucking head off."

"Listening . . ."

"Are you eyeballing me? Is he eyeballing me?"

"Pay attention to every member of staff. Follow all our instructions."

"Start. Shagging. Listening."

They put the sack back on him and left him alone for almost ten minutes. When they came back in, they took it off and put a cup of tea on the table in front of him. Michael reached out to take it, but the man with the Midlands accent knocked it away and the bag went back on roughly. When they took the hood off again, there was a pen and a reporter's pad on the table, open on the first page.

The Ulsterman said: "Look at me. Why did you join the Communist Party today?"

Michael said: "Where am I? Am I under arrest?"

The man from the Midlands put his lips next to Michael's ear and screamed: "If you ask one more shagging question, I'll leave you in here with him, and the last Catholic boy I left in here with him lost all his cunting teeth."

Belfast said: "In a hole is where you are, Michael. You got dropped down a deep, dark well. And it's up to you if you ever come back up into the light again. We can arrest without charge and hold suspects indefinitely under emergency powers. It is entirely within the remit of the law. No lawyer or anyone else is going to come and rescue you. So stop bleating like a fucking little girl, stop answering back, and start using your intelligence."

"It's a funny thing," said Michael, "because when we were walking in, I could see out of the bottom of the hood and there was a parking slip on the floor that said Paddington Green Police Station on it. But you're not police, are you?"

Ulster was sitting opposite him and Black Country was pacing up and down behind and he saw them exchange a glance. He closed his eyes and braced himself for a blow.

Instead, a voice from the open door of the cell behind him said: "They belong to the Royal Navy, Michael. Just like me." It was an educated, mellifluous voice, built on a hard standing of flat Lincoln-shire vowels.

Michael shook his head in disbelief. Then he began to laugh. All the fear and pain of the last hour throbbed through him and he laughed oddly in a voice that was not his normal one. When he got himself under control, he opened his eyes and there were tears in them. He said: "Hullo, Dad. It's been a while."

17
LITHUANIA, 2004

The café near the castle in Vilnius was quiet, in the lull between breakfast and lunch. Indrė Žukauskienė had filled one reporter's pad with notes and was about to start a second. She had written the year at the top of the first page: 1942. She wished she had brought the portable computer with her from the office. The map of Lithuania was spread out between them and she had scribbled some arrows on it.

Greta took a sip of tea and ran a hand through her short white hair. "You must not think," she said, "we set out to become heroines. We had no thoughts about roaming around the place righting wrongs. We simply wanted to survive. That was the way we would win. We didn't go looking for trouble. But it found us."

Indrė sat poised, pencil in hand.

"We were stronger after that awful Christmas. It was the beginning of '42. We took it in turns to hunt, and Riva turned out to be a fair shot with a rifle. I am afraid my Vita was hopeless, and she struggled with skinning animals, and the entrails and all that. I do not recall her objecting to doing any of the eating. We had lost our fear of discovery now—we lit a fire every night, and we shot game when we could find it. All the country around seemed deserted. I was out with Riva one afternoon when I saw a doe looking down at us from the top of a ridge . . ."

It took them half an hour to slog up to the spot. They could see no prints. Then they heard something heavy moving in the undergrowth down in the steep gully next to them.

Greta whispered: "I'll circle around to the other end and work my way back up. Stay here in case I drive her out in front of me. You'll be able to see where she goes."

The fog was thick at the bottom of the ravine. Greta picked her way along as quietly as she could. She could hear her heavy woolen clothes rustling. When she heard what sounded like the hoofs of a running deer ahead, she froze. It was hard to tell where the sound had come from. Then she heard a man shouting.

The German soldier was stout, with broad shoulders and a big belly. He had tethered his gray mare to a peeling silver birch and left his rifle tied to the saddle. His face reminded Greta of her late grandfather— ruddy and full from good living. Perhaps this man was a drinker too.

He had Riva by the collar of her coat. She was crying piteously as he slapped her across the face. He was barking single words of Lithuanian. When he saw Greta striding toward him, he switched to German.

Incredulously, as though speaking to himself, he said: "Another little girl, playing out in the woods." His eyes widened with indignation when he saw the rifle in Greta's hands, and he let Riva go. He reached out his hand to Greta and said: "Give that to me."

She was very close to him now. He had the face of a schoolmaster, bristling with outrage at a show of bad behavior. The man said: "Silly little girls, playing with guns."

Greta raised the rifle and shot him in the chest.

Riva ran to her and Greta held on to the girl. It took her a long time to calm down. When she stopped crying, she said: "He was slapping me."

"Not anymore," Greta replied.

She looked down at the soldier, the big dead beast, and bent over to scream into his face: "Not anymore."

They scrambled back and stuffed everything they could carry into their satchels. Greta had formed the notion, from what her father had told her, that any organized resistance to the German occupation would be centered in the forests around Kaunas. He had talked about friends from the Rifle Club stockpiling guns in that area before the invasion. It was the vaguest of plans, but the girls headed south. They did not want to waste any time, expecting at any moment to hear the shouts of men and the barking of dogs at their back. They would cross the main east–west road to Kaunas quickly and drive due south, sticking to the thick forest, before wheeling to the east.

The Germans had cut back all the trees and bushes along the main road for thirty yards or more on either side. The road followed an ancient ridgeway that rose slightly from the surrounding fields, so that the traffic appeared to skim along the horizon. The three girls could see a long way in either direction. A farm vehicle or motorcar passed every few minutes. They did not see any sign of Germans.

When the sun was highest in the sky, there was a long lull, and they decided to make a dash for it. There was no cover so they would have to clear the road and the bare ground on the other side in one sprint. They stood up, looked left and right for the last time, and ran as one.

Halfway to the road, they heard the hum of a vehicle from the right. They saw it coming around a slight bend in the road, far off to the west but approaching fast—a big car with a noisy engine. What to do? If they turned tail, could they make it back to the trees? Greta saw a pile of pine logs in a dip in the ground ahead and to the left.

They raced for it and threw themselves down, trying to squash themselves against the timber. It offered little protection—just ten or twelve thin trunks in a stack. The top of the pile was less than three feet off the ground.

They heard the note of the engine change. The car was slowing. Through a crack between the logs, Greta saw it pull over to the side of the road and stop very close to them. There was no other traffic.

The car was an exquisite Mercedes-Benz 770. A man in civilian clothes got out and they were close enough to hear him say, in German: "Don't laugh at me, you rogue—I'm an old man. This will be you one day." Now he was walking straight toward the log pile, picking his way carefully through the many tree roots that poked through the rough grass. She could see the enamel badge on the lapel of his suit: a black swastika on white, inside a red ring. It was a good suit.

She had the rifle in her hands and she was fingering it and Riva clutched her arm and shook her head pleadingly. On the other side of Riva, Vita had her face pressed against the log and was biting into the bark.

The man stopped on the other side of the pile of logs and made a groaning sound, like he was performing some tedious labor. His crotch was a yard from the girls' faces. He began to unfasten the buttons of his trouser flies. Greta realized what was about to happen, and the idea of the man exposing himself to her was so unbearable that she popped up and shot him neatly through the throat.

Before his back had hit the ground, she had vaulted the logs and was running past him, straight at the car. She didn't have to think about any of it. The driver had his window down. He blinked at Greta, took his hands off the wheel and stuck them in the air. Greta shot him from two yards away.

"Pow!" the old lady shouted, making a sudden movement with both hands that almost scattered the plates and cups on the café table. The waiter glanced over at them. "And that was the end of both of them." There was a fierce gleam in her eyes.

Indrė Žukauskienė looked seasick. "How did you feel?"

"Honestly?" Greta leaned forward and whispered: "Like a *goddess*. I didn't give a second thought to those swine. They would have shot us without hesitation. Later I felt differently about killing . . ." She shook her head to dislodge the thought and made a leveling motion with her hand. "There was no time for weakness then. Although . . ." she smiled, ". . . we were not as tough then, at the beginning, as we became later. We flapped like chickens! Vita started running back in the direction we had come and Riva had to go after her and grab her. She kept saying: 'You fool! Greta can drive!'

"We left the bodies by the side of the road and jumped in. I cannot describe the fear and the exhilaration. If any other German vehicle had been on the road for miles around, we would have been finished. We roared away east, desperately looking for any track that would get us off the main road. We passed a couple of farmers but the girls were lying on the back seat and I had my hat over my face. No one looked closely at me as they passed. I must have been driving well enough, thanks to my poor patient father. God bless him!

"The traffic was coming thicker in the opposite direction, and we became almost mad with terror. And then we saw a narrow country road branching off to the south. Those back roads were quiet, and we had half a tank of petrol. We crossed the river Neman late that afternoon. We were close to the deep forest to the west of Kaunas when the fuel ran out. We bumped along farmers' tracks, going in as deep as we could, until the car failed. It was a magnificent machine. We rolled it into a patch of brambles, the three of us heaving at it from behind, and we thought that would have to do. I remember standing there covered with sweat, panting from the effort. We were about to walk away when Riva said: 'We haven't looked in the boot.'

"It was wrapped up in a sheet, spotlessly clean and oiled, with ammunition clips in a little leather wrap. I don't think it had ever been used."

"You always call it a Schmeisser," said Indrė Žukauskienė. "I thought it was called something else really."

"I think you are right. It had a different name. I cannot recall it now. But I remember my first look. It was the most beautiful thing I had ever seen. There was a coat folded up in the boot next to the gun with a wallet inside. German money. And there was more currency in an envelope in the glove compartment: about a month's wages for the average soldier. There were letters too. The driver had written them, I think, not his passenger. They were simple letters to a woman—his wife, I suppose. He talked about how things were quiet in the west of Lithuania, but partisans were causing trouble near Kaunas and over toward Vilnius.

That made us all laugh. We felt we had done the right thing by heading east, more from luck than judgement. We would happily throw in our lot with anyone causing trouble for the Germans."

The waiter came over and cleared away the crockery. He was becoming grumpy. They would have to buy lunch soon if they wanted to stay.

"We were in good spirits," said Greta. "We would have to sleep out in the open, but we had money, and that meant we could buy food, if we could manage it safely. It was a strange thought—being around people after months and months alone out in the wild woods. What would the locals do if we strolled into a town for a shopping trip? God knows what we looked like by then. I don't think we would have won any beauty competitions! That was when the girls remembered a place they had been to with friends before the war."

The shop had been famous as a meeting place for teenagers. It was on the outskirts of a village close to the main Kaunas road. It stood out on its own, surrounded by forest: a big wooden building that had been built as a place for motorists to stop and eat.

The owner had specialized in importing goods from America before the war—vinyl records, picture-magazines, cosmetics and real blue denim jeans. The craze for riding motorcycles had begun to take off in Lithuania and young men from the motorcycle clubs came from across the country to meet there.

He had decorated the place so that it looked like a frontier trading post in a Western movie. There was an Indian chief carved from wood, a machine that dispensed chewing gum and a real Wurlitzer with instructions in English: "Select program—one or more numbers."

"Do him," said Riva. They had been trudging along all morning and had stopped to breathe and set down their packs, an hour's march from the store. "The owner. I'm bored of Hitler." Vita laughed, trying to remember the man who owned the shop and his mannerisms. She had a gift for mimicry. She always did Hitler as a campy window-dresser in a Vienna department store, flapping his hands and winking coyly at men who passed by.

"All right," said Vita, puffing herself up pompously. She sidled over to where Greta was sitting on a fallen beech and put one foot up on it, thrusting her crotch in Greta's direction. "My dear girl," she said, in an oily drawl. "What a *pleasure* it is to have such fine young people around the place. All the hopes of our fledgling nation rest on you, the future generation. Such fine youngsters. So . . . young. So *firm*." She reached out and squeezed Greta's thigh, then jumped back suddenly, pretending to be startled, and called over her shoulder: "What's that, my love? Yes, of course, my angel. I am just dealing with a query from a customer."

The other two were in tears. "Not bad," said Riva. "Except that the wife was always too timid to say anything, wasn't she? She used to drift past like a ghost and give him an icy blast whenever he was talking to the young girls. Which he always was. Dealing with their queries."

Their high spirits faded as they got closer to the shop. It had a dismal air about it now. They watched for a long time from the tree line. It was dim inside, but they could see bundles of firewood heaped on the porch by the front door as though for sale, and there were handwritten signs in the window advertising bread and cheese. They could not hear music playing.

They watched an elderly woman climb the steps on to the porch with difficulty, eye one of the bales of firewood, and shuffle through the door. She came out again presently with a sour look on her face. Well, the shop is open, thought Greta. But who knows if there's anything left on the shelves?

Riva was judged to be the least unkempt and was sent in first. A little bell above the door rang as she opened it. She recognized the owner immediately, even though his back was turned to her as he reached up to place an item on a high shelf. He had lost almost all his hair now. His wife appeared at a side door behind the counter as the bell tinkled—the same nervous little sparrow.

The man took his time turning around. He looked at Riva with an expression she could not read. He did not say, "Can I help you?" or offer any other pleasantry.

"*Laba diena*," said Riva, quietly. There was no reply. The man rested his palms on the counter. The wife was rubbing one hand against the other.

"Do you have bread today?" asked Riva. He did not reply. "I would like sausages too," she said.

"Would you now?" The man snorted. "How about some smoked salmon? A case of champagne?" His wife looked at him and chewed her lip.

"Why don't you tell me what you do have," said Riva, "and we'll take it from there?"

"The menu changes, depending on who is doing the buying."

She felt the blood rising in her. Her anger pushed her fear to one side. "I wouldn't have thought you could afford to be so choosy in these times. Isn't everyone's money the same?"

"No. Will you pay in Reichsmarks or shekels?"

Ah, thought Riva. Now I understand. That's how it is.

The shopkeeper beamed at her, as if he had scored a great victory. "I have this memory for faces," he announced. "I know exactly who you are. I have to say I didn't expect to see any of you coming through my door again. But you're like cockroaches, aren't you? You'll survive anything!"

The woman stood in the doorway, her eyes fixed on her husband's face, throughout the whole exchange. Riva saw that the nails of one of her hands were working furiously at the other forearm. The girl stepped back several paces, keeping her eyes on the shopkeeper the whole time. When her back was at the door, she pushed it half open and showed her head outside. She didn't need to call. Then she came just inside the door and stood silently.

The self-satisfaction drained from the shopkeeper's face as Vita and Greta came in. It was obvious that they had guns under their coats. The three girls formed a line in front of the counter.

He looked at them with a mournful expression. Then his face cracked into a slow, broad smile. "What can I do for you fine young ladies?"

He made a fuss of fetching sausages from a secret stash reserved for the most valued customers—strings of fat smoked ones made from venison and boar meat. He had dried figs stowed away too, and buckwheat, and good aged cheese. He tried to wave away payment but Greta ignored his twittering, laying out the notes on the counter and smoothing them flat with exaggerated care. She made the man count out the change coin by coin, and she checked it laboriously. By now there were beads of perspiration all over his face.

She took her time stowing the goods in her pack. At last they were ready to go, but they made no move to leave. The man said to Greta: "Come back any time. You are always welcome! I am afraid I mistook your friend here for someone completely different when she came in alone."

Greta reached up and shifted her hat slightly so it sat back on her head, suddenly aware of her unwashed hair and grimy face. She stuck out her bottom lip so she could blow away the stray hairs hanging down over her forehead. She said: "What will he do now?"

The man's wife did not react until Greta glanced at her. Then she gave a little jolt, and a hand flew up to her throat.

"What will he do?" asked Greta again. "He will go to the Germans."

Greta nodded. "Is that who you keep the firewood for?"

"Yes. They pay more."

"If he goes to them now, I will hear about it. I will come back and visit you again. And when I leave, I will take both your heads with me."

The woman nodded. Her face was creased and she was trying not to cry. The man stood with his head bowed, his eyes fixed on a spot on the counter.

When the girls reached the trees, they heard a shout from behind. The shopkeeper's wife was running awkwardly toward them. She was not wearing a jacket. They stopped. She came to a halt five yards away.

"Take me with you," she said. She was still chewing her lip.

Greta looked her up and down slowly. Too skinny. And was she lame?

"He won't go to the Germans now," said the shopkeeper's wife. "He's too afraid. But he hates himself for it! He will take it out on me later. He will hurt me."

Greta frowned. "What's wrong with your leg?"

"It's nothing. I've had it since childhood."

"You won't last out here," said Greta.

Riva said something at the same time and the woman looked at her and said: "What?"

"I said you made your bed. Now go back and lie in it." When the woman did not move, Riva crouched down and picked up a stone—a flat piece of flint, the kind that would be good for skimming on water. The woman showed the palms of her hands and backed away from the girls. Her eyes were very wide. "Go back!" Riva shouted, and made as if to throw the stone, as though she were driving away a stray dog. The woman broke and ran.

As they walked away, Riva scratched the back of her head and said: "What did he mean—*I didn't expect to see any of you again*?"

"Ignore that bastard," said Greta. "*Any* of you?"

18

LONDON, 1961

Vice Admiral Sir Stephen Fitzgerald took the slim Longines watch from his wrist and laid it on the table in the cell so that his son could see the dial.

He said: "You have five minutes to tell us everything. Look straight up. See that hoop in the ceiling? That's where they hang you if you don't cooperate. Upside-down. They beat your kidneys first. I will happily sit here and watch if I have to. You'd better get started."

"I can't tell if you're being serious or not, Dad. What does that say about you and me?"

Michael's father tapped the watch with his forefinger. "I wouldn't waste time with any of that rot if I were you, old man. There's a war on."

"The Russians have already won it, if we've turned into them."

"Why did you visit King Street today? Then the East German Embassy?"

"I wanted to borrow a bag of sugar. The local Communists didn't have any so—"

Sir Stephen said: "Gentlemen."

The Ulsterman came around the table and took hold of Michael's wrists. The other man smacked the left side of his head on to the top of the table and kept it pressed down while he wormed the tip of an index finger into Michael's right ear. The finger went down into the ear canal as deep as Michael thought it could possibly go. Then it went a little further. He did not think he would cry out so soon. He filled the cell with screams. The man was reaching into his head. It went on for as long as he thought he could bear it. Then it went on longer. He was looking at his father the whole time, sideways on. The vice admiral's face remained completely impassive.

The man with the Belfast accent went back to his chair and smoothed his hair down with his hands. He said: "The sooner you tell us the truth, the sooner we can all go home."

"I haven't had a real home since my mother died." Michael was sobbing like a child, hating himself for sounding so weak.

His father said: "These men are not social workers. They are not interested in my failings as a father. They are killers. I have more important people for them to kill. You have ninety seconds left."

Michael fought to get himself under control. He looked at each of the three men in turn: the granite stares of the interrogators; his father's undertaker's face, solemn and unreadable. He said: "There's a girl. A Russian girl. I think I'm in love."

The men all blinked at the same time as though a camera had gone off in their faces. They kept looking at him to see if it was a joke. They saw that it wasn't.

Belfast groaned and rolled his eyes, bringing both hands up to his temples. Midlands gave a low whistle and said: "Good Christ." Then he elbowed the man next to him and said: "Well, that's me, mate. I owe you a quid." He grinned at Michael. "I could have sworn you were a shirt lifter."

Michael smiled and felt relief flooding through him. It will be all right now, he thought. They never really hated you.

"Well, you're the experts," he replied. "You're the sailors."

Michael had never seen his father in military uniform. The vice admiral favored double-breasted suits with a chalk stripe, and long coats with velvet collars. He looked like a city gent on his way from Threadneedle Street to a Pall Mall club, not a man who spent his days poring over maps of Central Europe in underground rooms behind concrete walls ten feet thick. He was proud of his hair and never wore a hat.

When Michael was young, Sir Stephen told him he had been burned badly as a boy in the First World War and had always been self-conscious around girls as a result. That was how he had got into the habit of buying the best clothes he could afford, he said. "Women like a man who takes pride in his appearance. A good suit always makes them look twice."

Years later Michael relayed this conversation to his father's driver, Joe. An anguished look came over Joe's face. Eventually he told Michael the truth. Sir Stephen had not sustained the ugly burns to his lower body in the Great War, but in 1942, when a German incendiary bomb destroyed the house he was renting for his wife and newborn son in York. He had gone into the burning wreck to pull Michael's mother out. He could not save her. The child was unhurt. Sir Stephen languished in hospital in the weeks that followed, neglecting his injuries and refusing treatment. He did not want the boy brought to him. He told the doctors he did not want to recover.

"Who is the girl?"

"Yulia Forsheva."

"The surname again."

"Forsheva."

"Do you know her middle name? They use it as a sign of affection."

"I know all about Russian names," said Michael. "I'm going up to Cambridge in October to read Russian." He gave his father an accusing stare as he said this.

The vice admiral said: "Well. What is it?"

"It's Sergeiovna. Her father's name is Sergei. He writes about chess."

"Does he indeed? And did she tell you who her mother is?"

"Someone important, I think. They've got money." He started to doubt himself as he said it. Yulia had hinted about her parents' privileged lives but had carefully steered the conversation away from any details. He realized he had missed something important.

His father said: "The habit of reading a decent newspaper would have served you well here." Sir Stephen took a folded sheet of newsprint from his inside pocket and smoothed it out on the table in front of Michael. The text at the top said it was page four of *The Times*, a fortnight old.

The piece was arranged as a gallery of faces—five of them in grainy monochrome, with a few paragraphs of copy underneath each headshot. The vice admiral's index finger lingered on the first: the only woman.

"Allow me to introduce your mother-in-law. Anna Vladimirovna Forsheva. The most powerful woman in the Soviet Union and the only one who has ever served in the Politburo, if that word means anything to you. Mrs. Forsheva is the leader of a modernizing faction who are trying to drag that country into the twentieth century without killing half the population. She is the kind of moderate Her Majesty's Government would like to do business with, before we are all—"

"Reduced to ashes," said Michael, immediately regretting the phrase.

"You ought to know the other faces here. Shulgin is the foreign minister, probably an ally of Anna, but not brave enough to declare himself for fear of angering the old Stalinists. This is Marshal Cherkezishvili, head of the Workers' and Peasants' Red Army. A hero of the Patriotic War who rises above factional politics. And even you will recognize this affable gentleman: the leader of the world's biggest country."

"Which faction does he belong to?"

"Who knows what goes on behind that smile? There are others, more powerful than some of these—more powerful than the leader himself, perhaps—who manage to keep themselves out of the newspapers. Yulia's father, Sergei, is never photographed, but he is hardly less important than his wife. He is a mathematician, an architect, an engineer. A polymath, who has changed Russia in subtle and profound ways, from safeguarding the wheat harvest to putting a man into space."

"What do you need me for if you know all these people already?" asked Michael.

"Oh, I make it my business to know all about my enemies—down to the shoe size. You can be sure they are paying us the same courtesy. Did you meet any other Russians apart from Anna Forsheva's daughter?"

"A man called Vassily. I didn't get his surname. Or his *otchestvo*." He enunciated the word with a little flourish.

Michael's father might have breathed in a little more sharply than usual. He exchanged the briefest of glances with the Northern Irish man next to him. "A military officer?"

"I'm not sure. He was guarding Yulia. I took her out for the evening. Then a lot of men from the Russian Embassy rolled up and Vassily stalled them so she could sneak back into the Excelsior."

"How could she come out with you if he was guarding her?"

"She just slipped past him, I think," said Michael lamely. He had not really thought about it at the time.

"Nothing slips past this man, if it's who I think it is. Did he know who you were?"

Michael had to think hard about this. "He knew my name. He called me Mikhail Stephanovich. I suppose Yulia told him."

"She told him your father was called Stephen?"

"No," said Michael, after a pause. "I never told her your name. I don't know how Vassily knew that."

The admiral looked hard at the other men on his side of the table. Then he picked up the pen and wrote a single long word in his elegant cursive grammar-school hand. He ripped out the sheet of paper and slid it across the table as the two others leaned back in their chairs and looked away.

"Study that word," he told Michael. "Don't say it out loud. Did any of the Russians use this word in your presence? Take a moment."

"I don't . . . think so. I mean, no, I've never heard it before. I'd remember, wouldn't I? It's unusual. What is it? Sort of Wagnerian?"

"That's exactly what it is. I want you to commit it to memory now." He watched Michael's eyes flicker from left to right two or three times, then reached out and snatched back the sheet of paper. He began ripping it into thin strips with his long, strong fingers. The wardrobe of a banker, thought Michael. The hands of a panel beater. When the admiral had shredded the paper, he gathered the pieces and squeezed them into a tight ball in the center of his fist. Then he ripped out the next two or three blank sheets from the pad—the pages that had been underneath the word he had written and might carry an impression of it. He crumpled these up, too, wrapped them around the ball of shredded paper strips and dropped the whole fistful of wastepaper into his coat pocket.

He stood up abruptly. "We'll get you something to eat and drink, then go to my office. I need to talk to these gentlemen outside for a moment first. Do you smoke these days? There's no need to look sheepish. It's too late for secrets between us."

The vice admiral offered him an open packet of untipped Senior Service cigarettes as the two other men stood up. Michael said, with dignity: "Those are too strong for me. They make my head spin."

"Shirt-lifter," said the man with the Midlands accent.

The car crawled along the Marylebone Road for a while, then plunged down into Fitzrovia. His father liked to use a black cab when he was in London. Joe always did the driving. It was the first time Michael had been alone with his father for a long time. The vice admiral was not the kind of man who could kiss or hug his son. He squeezed Michael's leg for a second, just above the knee, as they looked out of the windows in opposite directions. He had the grip of a man who had spent his teenage years climbing ropes on training ships built in the days of Nelson.

"How is your aunt Valerie?"

"All right. A bit worried about that thing. They think it's got into the foundations now."

"She should never have bought that bloody wreck of a place."

The taxi nudged its way through heavy traffic around the back streets before breaking out on to Tottenham Court Road. The admiral ran his fingers around the edges of the sliding plastic screen that separated driver from passengers, as though feeling for a gap.

"Colin Sinclair got a message through after you saw him yesterday. Your visa application would have been flagged to me anyway, but the professor gave me an early warning. He's an old colleague of mine."

"Really? *Really?* I thought he was a dyed-in-the-wool left . . . Oh . . ."

His father chuckled. "I can practically hear the cogs spinning, Michael."

"Is that what they call 'cover'?"

"Never mind all that rot. Sinclair worked for me years ago. He is a perfectly respectable civilian now, as far as I know. He pretends to be sympathetic to the East, and he goes to drinks parties at embassies, but I doubt he has the kind of contacts these days who can get you into East Berlin in a hurry. I do. Assuming you still want to go?"

"What's in it for you?"

"I want you to keep your ears open, that's all. Listen out for that magic word I showed you."

"What am I listening for?"

"Someone might use you to make an approach to me. An offer of service. A piece of information. We think that word has some significance, but we're not sure what it is yet. There's no point in looking at me like that. I don't know any more, and if I did, I wouldn't tell you. Then no one could beat it out of you. It's a professional habit that has served me well."

They were crawling past the Fitzroy Tavern and the usual crowd of late drinkers had spilled out on to the pavement. A man staggered into the road in front of them and Joe jammed his hand on to the horn. Michael swore and looked out of the window.

"I meant what I said at the police station," the vice admiral said quietly. "About letting them hang me from the ceiling?"

"Yes. Also . . . the bit about failing as a father."

"I shouldn't have said it."

"It's the truth, after all. No. Wait. It is true that I failed you. Things have been hard for you. It's tough, growing up without a mother. But no one has time to feel sorry for themselves now. The clock is ticking."

Sir Stephen had a drinks cabinet in his office in Admiralty Arch. He poured Scotch for both of them and equal amounts of soda water, then got the fire going. Joe was supposed to be out hunting for fish and chips.

The vice admiral squatted by the grate. Michael saw him take the ball of paper from his coat pocket and throw it on to the coals.

Michael said: "You and Colin Sinclair were at Trinity at the same time, weren't you, Dad?"

His father stood up with a grunt and wiped his hands on the front of his trousers. "Before the war, yes. We both had that misfortune."

"So, did you fix up my interview with him?"

"Ha! You flatter yourself. I haven't seen Colin for years. And I'd forgotten about your interview. I've had more important matters to worry about than the many ups and downs of your education."

Michael took a slurp at the tumbler and kept the glass in front of his face for longer than was necessary. He was hurt but didn't want to let it show. "Are things really as serious as everyone says?" he asked.

"Well, now. I've been spending my nights out in the middle of nowhere for a while. Every morning, my alarm goes off and I lean over to the radio and turn it on. It takes about five seconds for the valves to warm up and in those five seconds I don't know if the Home Service is still broadcasting. If the airwaves are silent, it means London is in ruins and everything I value has been turned to powder. And all we have left are the *Dreadnought* and the *Valiant*, cruising around somewhere in the deep water, ready to strike back."

"I never understood the point of that," said Michael. His father gave him a sharp look. "The dead hand hanging on the trigger," Michael added, with a touch of defiance. "More pointless destruction."

The vice admiral came and sat opposite him, scooping up his own tumbler. "Do you remember me talking about the eastern front in '45? You know that I was an observer, attached to the Red Army? I didn't tell you everything I saw out there. When Soviet soldiers got captured by the Germans, they did a queer thing. When they were waiting for the firing squad they raised their fists and shouted: "Stalin will avenge us!" At first the Germans mocked them. By the end they'd stopped laughing. They knew it was the simple truth."

"Those men still died. What difference did it make to them?"

"Revenge can be a powerful thing. You may say that it doesn't achieve anything. But people need to believe in the possibility of wrongs being righted, even after they are gone. The thought that Stalin would avenge their deaths helped keep those poor devils throwing themselves at the enemy day after day."

Michael yawned and stretched himself out on the sofa. The warmth from the fire and the Scotch in his belly were dulling the sharp edges of the day.

His father was leaning back and finishing his second drink, one leg resting on the other. "You're not really a Commie, I suppose? Not having us all on?"

"I'm not that clever," said Michael, sleepily. "I just wanted to find a way to get to Germany and see the girl again. I can't say I've ever thought about politics very deeply. Are the Soviets evil? I don't know. I've heard the stories about Stalin. What do you want me to say? That I hate the Reds and sing "God Save The Queen" every night before I go to bed?"

His father chuckled and drained his glass: "I was with those Red devils when they crossed into East Prussia at the end. We'd given them an enormous amount of money and guns and about a thousand Spitfires. I was part of the deal: they had to let me ride along and see what they were up to. A young officer babysat me, a charming man who tried to keep me away from the worst of it. He couldn't hide everything, though. We went into a village just after his comrades had left. There was a cart blocking the road and a lot of bodies and the man looking after me desperately tried to obstruct my view but I shook him off. His friends had nailed a woman to the cart."

Michael rubbed his eyes dumbly. "What do you mean, *nailed?*"

"They had bent her over the back of the cart, spreadeagled her and driven nails through her palms, like the crucified Christ. So that all the men could line up and take it in turns with her. That is the world I am throwing you into now. Those are the kind of men you may come across. If something happens, you'll be a long way away and I won't be able to protect you. If you have any misgivings, now is the time to say so."

"She needs me," said Michael. "Someone needs me, for the first time in my life. I have to go to her."

A little later he woke up but kept his eyes closed. He was lying on the sofa with his father's coat spread over him like a blanket. He did not remember falling asleep.

Joe came back into the room, took a jacket hanging from the hat-stand by the door and folded it carefully. He carried it into the adjoining room and left the door ajar behind him. He was packing the vice admiral's things. Michael kept very still and listened.

Sir Stephen said: "We're not talking about a tip for the two-fifteen at Aintree, Joseph." You could hear the whisky in his voice. Either Joe made no reply, or it was too low to hear.

The vice admiral said: "Their entire order of battle, man. The disposition of every Warsaw Pact unit, down to company level."

"He is so young," said Joe.

"It's his turn to go into bat, and he'd better take his chance, that's all."

"Go in there and look at him. He's only a boy."

"Rot. He's older than I was when I first saw action. He's about the same age you were."

"Kids are different now."

"I was sixteen. Ever seen two dreadnoughts slugging it out, Joe, with the eighteen-inchers hammering? Trading punches like giants?" There was an odd edge to his voice. "I wouldn't have missed it for the world. My father was dead, but if he had been around then, and if he'd tried to stop me going, I would have *cursed* that man."

"I remember those big shells landing on the sand beside me."

"Of course you do. I'm sorry." Neither of them spoke for a while. Michael could hear wardrobes and drawers opening and closing. Then Sir Stephen said: "You were nineteen, weren't you? Just older than Mike."

"I was, aye."

"And what did your father say about it?"

There was another pause. Michael strained to hear Joe. "We were all ashamed when we came back from France. My forehead was touching the pavement in front of me when I reached our street. I was expecting the neighbors to throw rotten fruit, but they got up a cheer when they saw me coming. The governor had our lot lined up by the door— Maddie and the twins and our Frank. Mother ushered me into the front room. A couple of months before, she would have boxed my ears for setting foot in there."

"The best room."

"Aye. And the best service laid out. She wanted to give me tea, but my father flicked her hand away. He poured beer for both of us. Filled my glass first. He wasn't a great talker, but he showed me the Bible with my name written in the front, after all the others. Passchendaele for him. Dunkirk for me. I knew what it meant."

Sir Stephen said: "I'll never be able to write down what Michael is doing. But I will pour him that beer one day, and he will know. Like you knew."

19

Joe was ruffling his hair. his father's coat covered him. It was very early.

"You look shattered, lad."

"I'll be all right. Dad gone?"

"He doesn't stay overnight in London, these days. I've written the new number down for you on the fag paper."

"Couldn't . . ." Michael yawned uncontrollably ". . . couldn't get him to answer last time."

"He will now. He always looks after people who are doing a job of work for him. When's your run?"

"Next month. East Germany."

"Now, there wasn't any need to tell me that, Michael."

"Oh, Christ. I'm not cut out for this."

Joe laughed and clapped a hand beneath Michael's shoulders. "No one is—at first. Just put one foot in front of the other and learn from your mistakes. How are you getting back to Belsize Park?"

"Bus, I suppose."

"I think Her Majesty can stretch to a taxi. A real one, I mean. Take this." He held out a note. "Take it."

Michael crossed Trafalgar Square stiffly and headed for the line of black taxis waiting in the rank at the bottom of Charing Cross Road. The square was almost deserted except for the street cleaners. A toothless old woman he recognized was combing the pavement for cigarette ends. As he came close, she flashed a gummy smile and said: "Won't you take me home to bed?"

"I can't right now, Mary." He touched her gently on the arm.

A wine-red Rover pulled up in front of him as he reached the edge of the pavement, a middle-aged man in a flat cap at the wheel. He did not turn his head to look at Michael. Two younger men got out quickly.

He knew what was going to happen and he couldn't stop it. The men gripped him tightly by the upper arms, one on each side. Michael swore loudly and the gaggle of pigeons around them shuffled itself in fright.

One of the men stabbed a fist into the same spot where the sailor from the Midlands had punched him twelve hours earlier. Blood roared in his head and he felt his feet leaving the ground as the men took his weight. The black interior of the car yawned open to receive him. The world went sideways.

Another hood, softer this time, with no scent of coal. When it came off, he was in a room with high ceilings and thick carpets. A huge map of Europe hung on the wall to his right. He was on a high- backed chair. A heavy desk stood ten paces in front of him, with three people sitting behind it like a panel of magistrates.

The woman he knew as Greta from Sweden was on the left. Michael gaped at her. The man who had been driving the Rover in Trafalgar Square was on the right, still wearing the flat cap. A well- dressed gentleman of about sixty sat in the middle. He had thinning hair, a mustache and a very thick, prominent skull with a strong jaw and cheekbones.

The man said: "You are in an unusual position. In two places at once. In West Kensington, and on the sovereign territory of the Republic of Lithuania. In different circumstances, I would bid you a warm welcome to our country."

Michael could not take his eyes from Greta. She returned his stare without expression. "Lithuania?" he said stupidly.

"Quite so. The Soviet occupation of the Baltic states is, of course, illegal. So all three are still recognized as independent countries by the Western powers. All maintain a diplomatic presence in London. I am Lithuania's envoy to the United Kingdom. We do not call ourselves a government in exile. We do not deceive ourselves with grandiose titles. Nevertheless, you are technically outside the jurisdiction of the Metropolitan Police while you are in this room. Please remember this when you speak to my colleague here. I believe you have already met."

"Bikini," said Michael, weakly.

The man ignored this. "It is very important that you are completely truthful with us now. Your life depends on it."

"Is this what diplomatic missions usually do? Kidnap people and threaten them?"

The man looked at Michael regretfully. He got up from his chair and walked over to the wall on the right. The map covered most of it. Someone tall could have touched the north edge of the Scandinavian peninsula with their outstretched fingertips.

The diplomat stopped in the center of the map. "I wonder if you even know the location of the Baltic nations, let alone anything of our history. I don't blame you, Michael. Geography was not my strong suit when I was your age. There is nothing like a war to make one appreciate maps. They become all-important."

He raised his right hand to the Gulf of Finland, then brought it down slowly. "As in real life, we are on the bottom floor of this building, with the Latvians above us, and the Estonians up in the attic. I don't know if it was planned that way as a joke."

His palm hovered over Lithuania. "It is my country's fate ever to be the corn trapped between two millstones. Observe. Here on one side, the warlike Prussians." The fingers drifted westward to indicate the central mass of Germany, colored deep red on the map.

"You are British. You need no introduction to Germans and their wicked ways. Your history books are full of these stories, yes?"

"I think I remember something about a couple of wars," said Michael.

"Quite so. And here, on the other side, the Slavic host. Now we come to recent history, and we give this old enemy a new name: the Bolshevik horde." The envoy moved his hand to the right, out into the white emptiness of eastern Russia.

"It was my misfortune to witness the Bolsheviks invade my country twice. They came for the first time in June 1940. It must be conceded that they did not cause too much trouble at first. They tried to make our army Russian, without much success. Most of the time, they lurked behind the razor wire in their military bases and looked nervously westward, toward Germany. You have heard that the Soviet Union signed a peace deal with Adolf Hitler?"

"Vaguely."

"A deal with the devil. Designed to buy both sides some time before the storm broke. The arrangement left the Soviets in control of Lithuania for exactly one year. In June 1941, Hitler finally invaded from the west and booted the Red Army out, as had been long expected. The Russians fled in their undergarments. They had time to cause a little mischief at the end. They rounded up anyone who had been a thorn in their side and transported them to Siberia. And so it came to be that many Lithuanians hated the Russians and rejoiced at the arrival of the swastika."

"People were *happy?* To see the Nazis?"

The envoy looked at Michael keenly. "Some people, I am afraid. Do you find that shocking? You have never been occupied by the forces of the Soviet Union. Perhaps you will understand one day. Not everyone, of course, was pleased when the Germans came. I do not need to tell you what happened to the Jews of Lithuania after Hitler's forces took over."

"No," said Michael, quietly.

"Your history textbooks stretch as far as these events?"

"They do."

The envoy went back to his seat. He opened a silver box on the desk and lit a short cigarette that reminded Michael of his father. The syrupy smell of Virginia tobacco began to fill the room. The Lithuanian held his cigarette as prisoners do, cupping it inside the palm with the thumb on one side and all the other fingers in a line on the other. He smoked right down to the very end while he talked.

"We will not dwell on the fate of those poor Jews now," said the envoy. "Let us take comfort in the fact that a terrible vengeance was visited on their persecutors. The Red Army swept back into Lithuania from the east in 1944, raining death upon the retreating Germans. I suppose the last remaining Jews rejoiced at their deliverance. For the rest of us, the Bolsheviks brought the same two gifts they always bring: the murder of men and the rape of women."

Michael looked at Greta. Her face was impassive.

The envoy blew out smoke. "The second Soviet occupation was infinitely worse. Stalin believed that the Lithuanians had collaborated eagerly with the Hitlerites during the German occupation. He thought we were all waiting to rise up and cut the throats of the Russians as they slept. How I wish that were the case! The truth was that, by then, most people were too tired to fight. There were a few exceptions—*forest brothers*, as we call them. Some people who had fought the Germans in the forest chose to stay out there, refusing all rest and comfort. The war did not end for them. They tightened their belts and turned the sights of their rifles on the new invaders. Imagine what caliber of person we are talking about now."

He wagged the cigarette in Greta's direction. "Please do not underestimate this young woman. Her fury is a terrible thing. We are a weak people, scattered and few in number, but resolute and determined, especially in the matter of the payment of debts."

Michael said: "What does any of this have to do with me?"

The diplomat inhaled sharply and said: "You know this woman as Greta. If you knew her real name, you would not leave this room alive. She is one of the few survivors of a Baltic resistance network— brave men and women who fought against the German occupiers, then stayed out in the cold to fight Stalin's invaders too. The network was assisted for a while by friends here in Britain. Help was not always given when we asked for it, but a beggar has few choices. We took weapons and other equipment when we could get them, and we passed on intelligence to our contacts here in return. We worked with the British Secret Intelligence Service . . . and with your Naval Intelligence Division."

Michael went rigid when he heard that.

The Lithuanian envoy went on: "After 1947, it became increasingly difficult for the partisans to operate. The Soviet reaction was pitiless. Serious armed resistance gradually ground to a halt. We suffered a catastrophe in 1951, when the key members of our network were arrested on the same night. It was obviously an operation that had been carefully planned, and rested on excellent intelligence. It has taken us years to piece together what led to the events of that evening. It is increasingly clear that we were betrayed by someone on the British side."

He paused to let that sink in.

After a few moments Greta spoke for the first time, and it was a completely different voice from the flirtatious one Michael remembered. "A Judas. Someone secretly sympathetic to the Bolsheviks. A man probably still working within the British system. He would be very senior by now." She let the words hang in the air.

The envoy said: "There are scraps of intelligence about who the traitor might be: a student or a junior academic at Cambridge, probably Trinity College."

"When?" snapped Michael.

Greta glanced at the others and said: "In the middle of the 1930s."

Michael had been shaking his head. "It's not possible. You may as well say that the Pope is secretly working for the devil. He has many faults, but I know my father. This can't be him. It must be someone else."

The strength of his words seemed to impress them, and the diplomat nodded.

Greta said: "It's just a question of time, Michael. It's running out for everyone. I need to speak to your father and hear the truth from him. He is a hard man to track down at the moment."

"I don't know where he is. If you were thinking about holding me hostage, I wouldn't bother. He won't try to rescue me."

The envoy raised a hand. "Things will not come to that. We are not going to harm you in any way, Michael. In a short while, you will walk out of here quite free." He stubbed out the cigarette. "You are going to do a job for us, that's all."

"A job."

Greta said: "We know that you are going to Germany. We know who the girl is. Yulia's mother is one of the few people who regularly finds herself in the same room as a Soviet official called Maxim Karpov. Say the name out loud now so I know you remember it."

"Maxim Karpov."

"Is this name known to you?"

"Of course," said Michael. He watched their eyes widen in unison. "He plays in goal for Bolton Wanderers."

It took Greta a second to process this and then she got up out of her seat, came around the desk and walked toward Michael. He flinched and shut his eyes. When she came up close his nerve broke and he stammered the words: "I'm sorry. Please." Later, when he told people about the events of this day, he always left this moment out of the story.

Greta was on one knee next to him. "You will listen out for any piece of information that might establish the whereabouts of this man. An address in Moscow, a description of his daily routine, the names of the people who guard him. You will report back to me. Do you understand? Nod if you do . . . Excellent."

"Who is he?"

"Never mind that. It is a simple trade, Michael. Your father's life for information that leads me to Maxim Georgevich. Say it."

"Karpov," said Michael. "Good boy."

Greta opened the door for Michael. The two men who had snatched him in Trafalgar Square were waiting out in the corridor. They were tall, strong men with baby faces. They were both very blond. They could have been brothers.

She said something to them in Lithuanian and they did not follow as she led Michael by the arm down the long corridor. As they turned at the end, she squeezed his arm and whispered: "Bolton Wanderers!"

There was a short flight of stairs around the corner. She led him down to the bottom, to a square entrance area next to a heavy door to the street, with notices pinned on it in several languages and a cage to catch the letters. Greta held Michael's arm the whole way down. There was a mischievous smile on her face. Just before the door he turned to her and started to say something but she pushed him against the wall hard and pressed herself to him, forcing her mouth against his. Despite himself Michael kissed her back, and when she moved his hand down over her hip, he squeezed it instinctively.

Her face was in his and they had their eyes closed. He could not see the shut folding knife in her hand. He did not sense that she was setting herself to swing the hand. She hit him hard with the end of the knife handle right on the peroneal nerve, about a hand's span above the left knee.

The leg spasmed and Michael collapsed. As he fell, she dropped one knee on to his belly, dumping all her weight on to him through that one sharp point. She tapped his right temple with the end of the knife handle and his right hand shot straight out, as she had known it would, trying to find her face to push her off him.

She made a swiping motion, using both of her arms against his right arm, shoving it sideways and down so that his right shoulder was turned tight into his neck.

Greta straddled him, sitting on his thorax with one foot on either side of him. Her left elbow turned his face to the left, so that he was staring at the peeling wallpaper at the bottom of the corridor wall, crushing pressure pinning him down. Her weight was jamming his right shoulder into his throat, locking the head in place and making the arm useless.

Michael gasped and flexed his body, trying to use abdominal strength to buck her off him, but he was just exhausting himself, unable to generate any leverage. The black object in her hand loomed into his view. She flicked the switch and the blade jumped out, the point quivering an inch from his eyeball. Michael yelled and gave a final spasm of struggle, which shifted her balance but did not unseat her. With the palm of her left hand still pressing his face to the floor, she used her fingers to peel back the lids of his uppermost eye. The point of the stiletto shivered closer to the eyeball. Half an inch. Every muscle and sinew in his body was straining, to no effect.

The knife point hovered within touching distance of his eyelashes. The merest movement would see the sharp tip dive straight into the heart of his dilated pupil. The blade was so close that it was fuzzy and indistinct.

Greta said: "This is where I live. Do you think you can live with me out here? What about your aging father?" He wheezed and grunted. "This is the sea I swim in. Cheat me in any way, and I will find both of you. I will eat his heart in front of you."

Michael was trying to say something. The blade snicked back. She sat back on her hips and let him catch his breath.

"I know," said Michael. "I know."

20

MOSCOW

Yulia did not give in to despair after her father disappeared. She tried to fall back into the normal rhythm of her life in Moscow, but she found that few people wanted to associate with her now. One of her school friends was celebrating an important birthday that week—the last full week of August. But no call came to confirm the time and place of the party.

She saw another classmate she had thought of as a close ally in the Gum department store, and the girl actually broke into a run to avoid having to stop and talk. Yulia watched her in disbelief. The girl was the daughter of a scientist who worked closely with her father. He was a haughty, rather nervous man, but Yulia liked the daughter. They were from Karelia, the region of Russia that bordered Finland, and they had an unpronounceable surname. Her father sometimes said they considered themselves more Scandinavian than Russian.

A security guard in a rust-brown suit stood at the bottom of the staircase on the ground floor. Yulia touched his arm and pointed out the girl to him as she scampered for the exit. "I think she's a shoplifter."

On the Tuesday evening Yulia decided, with a flash of defiance, that she would attend her usual music lesson, as arranged, and let the teacher slam the door in her face if she wanted to.

In the end, the woman invited Yulia into her little flat in Butirsky with a broad smile of welcome. There was always tea from the samovar before they began.

Yulia said: "You have probably heard some rumors about my family."

"I don't care. And neither does Schubert. Shall we?"

The woman had arranged the song for piano. Yulia began strongly and the teacher hummed the words as she played: "'Pass by, ah pass by! Away, cruel Death!'"

Yulia stumbled over the first tricky passage and they hammered away at it for a while before she slammed both hands down on the keys. "I'm so sorry, I don't know what's wrong with me."

"I think you're trying to play too quickly. Let's slow it right down. You can always add speed later."

When they had finished, the teacher helped her into her coat and Yulia embraced her impulsively. She opened the front door and let herself out. Maxim Karpov was standing on the landing, four feet away from her. His pupils were very small. He was carrying an enormous bouquet of peonies.

Yulia stepped out and closed the door firmly behind her. She stood there, barring the doorway. Whatever happened to her, she would not let him pass over the threshold.

Karpov spread both his arms wide, and the head of a peony fell on to the uneven concrete floor. The flats were comfortable inside, but everything was rough and unfinished in the communal areas.

Karpov said: "I happened to be passing. I heard the music. It led me here, like a mermaid calling to a sailor. I didn't want to interrupt you two."

Yulia kept her eyes fixed on his, trying to appear confident without offering aggression. She kept her breathing steady. She had been introduced to Karpov twice before, at official functions. She had treated him with cold, disdainful politeness on both occasions, taking her lead from her mother. She remembered the second time, the grand dinner on October Revolution Day. The alcohol on Karpov's breath had made her recoil from him.

He had leaned close to try to talk to her that night, his eyes trained all the time on her neck and the top of her breasts. Yulia's father had seen what was happening. Sergei took her arm, steered her away hurriedly and started looking for someone to drive them home. He hardly spoke on the journey back.

Yulia had laughed at Karpov then. He seemed a clownish little figure. It was different when you were alone with him in a badly lit stairwell in Butirsky.

He said: "This is a time when you need friends. Believe me, life is nothing without them. They are like the muscles in the back that keep us upright. And there is no reason why you and I should not get along. I know your mother disapproves of me, but what is that? Politics! See? I have beautiful flowers for you."

He sniffed them extravagantly, like an actor, then thrust the heads of the peonies toward Yulia's face.

The door of the neighboring flat opened, and an old woman's head appeared. The neighbor took in the scene and glowered at Karpov. He gave no sign that he had noticed her. His eyes appeared to be fixed on a spot just under Yulia's chin. The strangeness of his expression and his tone made her shrink back against the door.

Karpov said: "Take the bouquet, Yulia Sergeiovna. It will become a symbol of our new friendship. Women who become my friends always accept it. Those who do not . . ."

He took half a step forward and the old lady who was watching them opened her door wider and muttered an oath under her breath. But Karpov's eyes did not move from Yulia's white, exposed throat.

"Take it from me," he said, in a strange, low, cracking voice. He was reaching out toward her now with both arms. A tiny trail of spittle was running down from the corner of his mouth. As he lurched toward Yulia, the woman who lived next door crossed the gap between them and kicked him hard in the left shin.

Karpov gave an astonishing howl of animal pain and the noise made Yulia cry out with fright. She heard footsteps from inside the flat behind her and felt the door at her back tremble. She flattened the palm of her hand against it.

Karpov was hopping on one foot ridiculously, bending down to clutch at his shinbone. The old woman had darted back to her own doorway and was peering out at him, half shielded by the door. He looked over at her and his pupils were pinpricks. One hand still gripped the flowers, like a club. The fingers of the other were stretched wide, as if he were imagining them closing around the old woman's throat.

"Vassily!" shouted Yulia, and Karpov jumped. He actually looked back over the banister instinctively to see if someone was coming up the stairs. It was almost comical.

"What about him?" Karpov barked, annoyed.

"He always comes to fetch me around this time. He'll be waiting now. I'd better go down."

Karpov blinked at her several times, then turned his head slowly back to the old woman. Yulia sensed his hesitation and stole away from him, sliding her back along the dirty yellow plaster walls. She reached the top step and turned slightly. She was staring hard at the neighbor and nodding, silently imploring the old woman to go back inside.

Yulia picked her way carefully down the stairs until she reached the landing below. Her eyes were on Karpov the whole time. Then she broke into a run and clattered noisily down the remaining steps to the entrance of the tower block.

She saw Oleg, the Pig, sitting in the driver's seat of a black Volga. The lights were on and the wipers were going. His head turned as Yulia pelted past him and the other parked cars and crossed the grassy area in front of the flats, heading for a pedestrian walkway that arched out over the arterial road running past the blocks. There were streetlights there, and people: a man on a bike, a couple walking arm in arm. She cried out in relief as she reached the circle of light from the first lamp.

Upstairs, Karpov was taking deep breaths. He brought out a dirty hand-kerchief and dabbed his face and neck with it. His anger was subsiding. The old woman was still watching him from behind her front door. Her feet were set square and her fists rested on her hips. Karpov looked over at her, gave a great belly laugh and held out the bunch of flowers. "They had better not go to waste!" he said jovially.

"Save them for your funeral, you son of a bitch," said the woman, stepping back into her flat and slamming the door.

Oleg was chewing sunflower seeds while the engine idled. He had the window down so he could spit out the shells. A little pile of them had formed next to the car. Karpov was still chuckling when he dumped himself on to the passenger seat. He still held the battered flowers.

Oleg looked at him quizzically. "Trouble?"

Karpov creased with laughter. "Trouble! The worst kind. That's what I ran into, all right. The toughest kind of customer there is." He slapped his thigh, next to the flower stems. "Old Russian ladies. Never fuck with them."

Karpov was still chuckling when Oleg saw him to the door of his residence. The big man walked away quickly. He knew there was a girl inside and Karpov sensed his disapproval. Oleg had once gladly supplied his master with women, but in recent years he had become reluctant to play the role of procurer. Maybe he thinks he is too good for me now, thought Karpov. Perhaps a lesson is in order soon.

He put Oleg to the back of his mind as he walked through the rooms on the ground floor. The housekeeper had left everything spotless and had laid out a cold supper on the dining table for Karpov. A plate of pancakes with jam and cream lay on the top shelf of the Zil Moscow refrigerator for the Uzbek girl.

The chief administrator had freed his housekeeper's son from captivity in 1953, but the young man had the kind of conviction that meant he could be recalled at any time. His mother kept Karpov's house immaculate and never asked questions about the girls who came and went.

Karpov had selected the Uzbek from six young women in police custody for prostitution and vagrancy. The deputy chief of the Moscow police department had delivered her personally to his home, marching her to the back door and muttering in her ear. Karpov stood on the doorstep with his arms folded as they approached. The girl was so thin that her head and hands looked too big for the rest of her. That was what he liked. He heard the deputy say: "Don't play the innocent. Do what comes naturally. It's one week of your life. I have been talking you up. *Do not embarrass me.*"

Karpov had worked out the schedule in advance. On the first night, he spoke to the girl like a father. "You look exhausted. You need a hot meal and a rest." He stayed away from her while she slept in the single bed the housekeeper had prepared.

On the second night he spoke to her in a frank, businesslike way. "I know that you're scared. People talk a lot of rubbish about me. I want you to forget everything you have heard and think of me as a friend. The truth is that I like to take photographs of beautiful girls. That is all. I never show them to anyone else."

He led her down to the basement. He had laid out all the clothes for her. She swapped from one outfit to the next as he snapped away with a Zorki camera. Sometimes he said: "Slow down." She kept looking up at the noose that hung from the strong point in the center of the white ceiling. He said: "Don't worry about that. It's not real. It's a prop."

The poses were tame, and he did not touch her at all that night. She was trembling when they started, but she had calmed herself by the end. Her relief was obvious when Karpov told her that was all for the evening. He said: "See how you and I are getting along?" The girl managed a smile.

He went harder on the third night, as planned. The poses were more explicit and he tied her hands and feet with rope. She began to cry and he liked the way it distorted the thick makeup she was caked in. He put a gag in her mouth and took closeups of her tear-stained face.

At the end of the session, he slid a chair under the noose and asked her to stand on it. It was perfectly safe, he said. He would never bind her hands in this position. She was shaking and he had to coax her into putting the noose around her neck and placing her hands behind her back. He kept his distance from her and took photographs from every angle. She swayed a little and cried out, reaching up to grab the rope with both hands. Karpov darted forward and held her hips carefully to steady her while she slipped her head out of the noose. He helped her down gently from the chair and patted her back. "You did well tonight," he said. "There is a beautiful dinner waiting in your room."

The fourth night was another evening off. Tonight was the fifth. As before, there were neat piles of clothes all around the basement. It was a square room, 16 × 16 feet, bare white brick. A low wooden bench ran around three sides like the seats in a *banya*.

Karpov pointed up at the noose and said: "Let's start over here and get it out of the way. The shots didn't come out well last time. There will be a bit of dressing up afterward, but nothing too strenuous."

Her face wrinkled with distaste as she got up on the chair, but she was calmer than before. He stepped back several paces and waited until she had steadied herself, the camera swinging from his neck.

"Ready?" She nodded stoically. She slipped the noose over her head and under her chin. She put her hands behind her back, fingers gripping a sticklike wrist. The veins in her forearms stood out and there was a fine down all over the skin. Karpov breathed in and out slowly as he circled her, the camera clicking and whirring.

When he was directly behind the girl on the chair, Karpov gently let the camera rest on its leather straps again. Without snatching, he went to her and took both her wrists firmly in each of his hands. He put his shoulder against the girl's hip and pushed her off the chair. He pushed rather than shoved. He did not want her neck to break.

He kicked the fallen chair to the side of the room with a flourish, then jumped back so that he would be out of the way of the flailing legs. There is strength in her, he thought, as she kicked out savagely. She puts her whole spine into it. There were times when he thought the girl's toes would touch the ceiling. Perhaps she was a dancer or a gymnast in childhood.

It took her a long time to succumb. She revolved slowly in the air, clockwise, as she jerked and contorted. He walked in a slow circle, keeping pace with the turning girl so that he could see the changing expressions on her face. As the kicking weakened, he moved in closer. The panes of his glasses were right up against her green Asiatic eyes, as they finally glazed over.

He looked at the camera doubtfully afterward. He had probably not got the shutter speed right, he reflected, given the violence of the movements he was trying to capture. Karpov was a clumsy man with no talent for gadgets. He had no illusions about that. Next time, he would get Simonov or one of the others to adjust the settings properly in advance.

21

"Just tell me one thing," The minister of foreign affairs of the Soviet Union asked thickly. "How many people are we going to kill?"

Everyone in the newly refurbished meeting room on the third floor of the Kremlin looked at each other. No one answered the question. Marshal Cherkezishvili stopped mid-sentence and shot the chairman of the Politburo a dark look from below his unruly black eyebrows.

You are right, thought the chairman, silently agreeing with Cherkezishvili's unspoken complaint. Shulgin is drunk. He is embarrassing us in front of our guests. And, yes, it is unacceptable. The leader of the Soviet Union did not outwardly betray any hint of annoyance.

Both he and the head of the Soviet military knew very well that Foreign Minister Shulgin had never been able to tolerate alcohol. The three men were very old friends. Shulgin had been an ambitious young Party man before the war, when the chairman was head of the governing council in Moscow and Cherkezishvili was a captain of artillery. It was a time when all the great political questions were decided in the early hours of the morning around tables that groaned with bottles.

The normally affable Shulgin became cruel and sharp-tongued when he drank. He picked arguments and insulted people unrestrainedly. At the court of Joseph Stalin, this was a flaw that could shorten not only your odds of rising to high office but also your life. One morning, in the grip of a hangover that brought him to the edge of tears, Shulgin confessed his problem to his two comrades. It was a serious weakness of character for a Russian man of their generation to disclose.

"You'd better try your luck in one of our new desert republics," Cherkezishvili had sneered. "With the Mustafas and the Abdullahs. You'll fit right in."

The chairman saw the misery etched on Shulgin's face and started listing all the tricks he had picked up over dozens of dinners in the terrifying presence of Stalin.

The dictator liked to see empty glasses around the table filled swiftly with what he called a "man's measure"—one hundred milliliters of strong drink. If you could do so safely, you watered the nearest pot plant with your share.

If all eyes were on you, you drained the glass with a flourish, then tried to distract everyone. You might balance the empty glass on top of your head, dash it into a fireplace or gesticulate for applause. The important thing was not to swallow. You kept the spirit in your mouth. Then, when the attention turned to the next victim, you appeared to take a sip of cherry or plum juice or whatever soft drink was to hand. Someone would have to be looking very closely to notice that you were not really drinking from this second glass at all, but stealthily depositing a tepid mouthful of vodka or brandy *into* it. You made a waiter take it away before anyone realized the level of liquid was rising, not falling, as the dinner wore on.

When Shulgin was invited to a meeting where spirits would flow, the chairman was always careful to make sure plenty of soft drinks were on hand, and to brief the waiting staff on what to do. Tonight, Shulgin had ignored this courtesy and demolished shot after shot in earnest. In all fairness, thought the chairman, the horrors they were discussing were enough to drive any sane man to drink.

The guests had been asked at short notice to attend. The chairman and his secretary, Madame Sorokina, stood while the others filed in and took their seats. The deputy foreign ministers of Hungary and Poland were in attendance, with high-ranking army officers from those countries and from the Soviet Union, with Marshal Cherkezishvili presiding over all the military men with his great drooping gray jowls and heavy hooded eyelids.

It was the second meeting of its kind that the chairman had overseen in as many weeks. On the last occasion, the guests had been from East

Germany. There would be one more meeting next week. No official record would be made of any of them.

There was no stenographer to take notes, and the newly installed microphones and recording devices were not plugged in. The hulking brute who trailed around after Maxim Karpov came in briefly and stood by the door with his arms folded, watching Madame Sorokina unlock the safe and hand out copies of a thick document to everyone. A single word was written on the front cover in capitals: *RHINEMAIDEN*.

Madame Sorokina asked for attention and said that the documents must not leave the room at any time. She would return at the end to collect the copies, count them and lock them away. She swept out of the door with Karpov's ogre in her wake.

Cherkezishvili cracked open the first bottle of spirits and made a florid toast to world socialism, then began reading the document aloud from beginning to end. If the chairman had heard it all before, he showed no signs of boredom. Shulgin, on the other hand, visibly struggled to concentrate as the briefing wore on, punctuated by noisy toasts. His expressions ranged from helpless incomprehension to frank distaste.

The foreign minister snorted with frustration when the military men lapsed into the impenetrable jargon of atomic warfare: *integrated structure, weak-to-strong deterrence, counter-value strategy*. He interrupted with facetious questions. It became obvious to everyone that Shulgin's grasp of European geography was embarrassingly poor, given his post in the Politburo. He was clearly struggling to recognize many of the cities being discussed.

"Where is this Eggsberg?" he blurted out, interrupting Cherkezishvili while the marshal was in full, monotonous flow.

"Esbjerg," said the chairman pleasantly. "A small city close to Copenhagen."

"What is the strategic value?"

"It has great historical and cultural significance. It would be demoralizing for the Danes to lose it. It's similar to the logic of hitting Nuremberg and Verona."

"Verona," said Shulgin, laboriously. *"Romeo and Juliet . . ."*

"A work of fiction," said the chairman. "They have a place they call Juliet's Balcony, but clearly it's a fantasy, as she never existed."

"They'll have to build a new one when we're finished," said Cherkez-ishvili, gruffly. He did not seem at all pleased with all the interruptions. "What do our modernists think about all this?" said Shulgin. "Anna? Borokin? How will they vote?"

The generals looked at each other miserably. They did not like this kind of talk. No good could come from being in a room like this when high politics was discussed. The chairman sympathized.

He said: "The policy is decided, Foreign Minister. I am briefing all of you individually so there are no surprises when it comes to the vote. It will be passed unanimously without debate, so that every soldier, sailor and airman in the Warsaw Pact knows he is carrying out a plan in which his leaders have absolute, unwavering confidence."

"This is all Karpov's work, presumably?" asked Shulgin.

Cherkezishvili cleared his throat loudly.

Enough, decided the chairman. "We should all take a short break, gentlemen. I for one have had too much brandy. I am going to send for some water and get some fresh air for five minutes."

He ushered Shulgin out on to the balcony. The foreign minister smoked.

"This has Karpov's hoof-prints all over it," he said. "I can practically smell the sulfur. What does Anna say about it?"

"It's not clear whether Anna Vladimirovna will cast a vote," said the chairman. "Given her personal circumstances at present. There is a protocol to be followed. Ultimately, nuclear policy is strictly Maxim Georgevich's remit."

"That's how you carved it up when he put you on the throne. Very nice! What exactly was the point of me backing you as leader if he has a gun to your head the whole time?"

"It is the Americans who are pointing the guns at the moment. You might have seen one or two stories about it in the newspapers."

Suddenly, the chairman's patience and calm appeared to annoy Shulgin immensely. "Why can't you answer the question?" he asked. "How many? I mean all this: *Rhinemaiden*. How many people?"

"You are thinking about it the wrong way. The plan is purely defensive. It assumes a first strike by NATO against the cities of the Vistula. You should be asking the Americans how many lives they are prepared to sacrifice."

"Don't bullshit me. How many?"

The chairman shrugged. "Ten. Maybe twenty."

"Ten or twenty, okay. What did Hitler do? Six? No, that was just the Jews, wasn't it? Ten? So you might get more? You might get the record?"

The chairman said: "What are you talking about Hitler for? How many did the oss kill? I don't recall you doing anything about that."

"Did you do anything? You bastard!" They suddenly had each other by the lapels. Two men with more than a hundred and twenty years between them.

The door of the meeting room opened, and a young Hungarian adjutant came in with a sheaf of papers. The chairman and Shulgin let go of each other quickly. The foreign minister smoothed his hair back into place. He had dropped his cigarette. He squatted down to look for it. He nearly lost his balance. Both men burst out laughing.

Shulgin carried on laughing a little longer than was necessary. When he straightened up, there were tears in his eyes. "Imagine what would have happened to me if I had clapped hands on the Boss! Look how far we've come." He shook his head. Suddenly he sounded desperate. "I can't go back to those days."

The chairman's voice was very low. "Listen to me, you old fool. Things are in train. I can't say any more, but timing is everything. For now, Karpov's great scheme is the plan of the moment and everyone is four-square behind it."

"For now?" Shulgin's eyes shone, in the darkness of the balcony.

"Sober up," said the chairman. "When we go back into that room, fucking pay attention. Keep your mouth shut outside it. When it goes to a vote next week, you smile and stick your hand in the air. You can bang on the table if you want, like in the old days."

Shulgin's eyes were flickering backward and forward.

The chairman could tell his mind was racing. "I mean it, Comrade Foreign Minister," he said. "Sober up and behave. Don't fuck this up. Remember that I can still send you to Siberia."

Shulgin grunted with bitter laughter. Then he noticed the chairman's expression and the corners of his mouth dropped. He was suddenly looking at a very different man from the cheerful, avuncular one every Soviet citizen thought they knew. The leader of the nation always made sure he was wearing a genial smile whenever he was photographed. Now it was impossible to detect even the slightest trace of humor on his face.

22
LONDON

There was an anti-war demonstration every Saturday now, at the foot of Nelson's Column. Afterward Colin Sinclair always held court in the Tom Cribb off Leicester Square. Michael saw him through the window, standing at the bar, surrounded by a gaggle of smiling graduate students.

The young men all seemed to be wearing shapeless fishermen's sweaters and duffel coats. Some were still carrying placards from the protest. They wore their hair long and shaggy. The crowd Michael ran with were younger: they cut their hair shorter and dressed sharper. As he pushed his way into the crowded pub, he was wearing a very dark blue Italian shirt with a button-down collar and a dark brown sports coat, blue jeans and desert boots.

The professor beamed when he saw Michael and slipped away from his admirers, clutching a pint of bitter. He was an ageing man with a young, lively face and a solid build.

"Sorry I'm not wearing a duffel coat," said Michael, as they shook hands.

Sinclair grimaced. "I must admit I've always found it a bit odd that these young men who hate militarism end up wearing their own uniform."

Michael said: "I wanted to say thank you for your letter. I got the visa."

"That is wonderful news—I presume? You're still going to East Germany? With your father's blessing?"

The question was so quick and innocent and natural that Michael had to catch himself before he blurted out something close to the truth. He stammered a noncommittal phrase, aware that his face was turning red.

They talked about the Russian novels Michael needed to get through before the start of term. They talked about the critics who were worth reading and the ones who set you on the wrong path.

After five minutes, Michael said: "I mustn't keep you all afternoon. I just have a small favor to ask. I'm afraid this will sound strange, but I have an unusual medical condition." He caught the sudden look of worry on Sinclair's face and said hurriedly: "It's nothing serious. A very mild form of hemophilia, except that sounds more dramatic than it is. I don't usually mention it to anyone. It's more of a bore than anything else. But whenever I travel, I try to learn the name in the local language in case I need to go to a doctor. And the name of my blood type and things like that. My German doesn't stretch to medical vocabulary. Would you mind?"

He was reaching inside his jacket pocket for a pen. The professor was nodding and leaning in close, his brow furrowed. Over Sinclair's shoulder, Michael could see people pressing up to the bar for last orders. It was getting close to three in the afternoon.

23
CAMBRIDGESHIRE

Greta took out her flick knife and opened it right in front of his face so he would hear the noise.

She said: "I have sliced men's noses off before now." The Russian man's eyelids flickered.

"Cut the skin out of both cheeks too," said Greta. "Have you seen it done? It looks like you've got three mouths. You can still talk, but it doesn't look too pretty in a mirror."

A muscle spasm passed over his face, beneath the layer of dried sweat and blood. She yanked the white rag out of his mouth and his head began to nod. He was coming out of it. It would take a couple of minutes.

The man was tied to a chair in the center of a long, low, empty cattle shed that had just been whitewashed. He was a black smear in the middle of a white canvas. His suit was conspicuously better than the usual Russian stuff. The shoes were made from that shiny leather whose name Greta could not remember, either in English or Lithuanian. Ričardas and Antanas were a hulking presence at the side of the room.

The man in the chair tilted his head to look at Greta and she saw the black pupils focusing. She put her face close to his. She heard the soles of his feet rattle against the white concrete floor, making a noise like a drum roll, as he tried to say "please" in Russian: *pazhalsta*. He ould not get the word out properly. Greta stepped back suddenly with a curse.

The man was pissing himself, a stream of urine mixed with blood curling down the pale gap between the bottom of his hiked-up trouser leg and the top of the sock. A dark stain spread around the chair.

* * *

Mindaugas was on look-out duty outside, scanning the flat Cambridgeshire fields, watching the fat rooks that haunted them. When Greta slid open the vast rusting iron door behind him, he looked back into the shed and saw the prisoner, the pool forming under him, and grinned at her.

"It's not fear," she said. "They've smashed his kidneys."

"They've been working on him all night. He only cracked an hour ago. He's given us a workname. I ran it through the embassy."

"And?"

"Fourth Directorate."

"Christ. They must be losing their touch."

"They are in a hurry," said Mindaugas. "So are we."

The farm building belonged to the husband of a Latvian woman who liked to help the group. Inspectors from some local branch of government were expected to call at the farm at any moment. Something about a breach of planning laws. Jealous neighbors had informed on her husband to the authorities out of spite, the Latvian woman had said. All the Lithuanians nodded when they heard this. They understood perfectly. The woman's warning had come early that morning—too late for them to change their plans. The prisoner was still there and Greta was already on her way.

She heaved the door open again and went back in. Ričardas indicated the puddle of urine with a villainous grin. "He knows who you are, anyway. That ought to save time."

"Out," snapped Greta. "Both of you."

"You're not one of Karpov's, at least," she told the prisoner. "That's why you're still alive."

"I am a distant neighbor," said the Russian. He was tired but lucid. He nodded gingerly, wincing at the effort. He had thick graying hair cropped short and a pleasant, tanned face.

"I thought so. Your lot dress better. What are you doing here, Comrade?"

She had to say it three times. His left ear was full of blood. She moved to the other side of the chair.

"We heard that Karpov sent a lot of new people over here. The embassy in London was suddenly full of MGB. There was a lot of noise about a woman popping up all over the place. You haven't been very discreet." He looked at her keenly. "I guessed it was you. I remembered the stories. I've been around for a while."

"Too long. Someone on our side recognized you from the old days." He smiled painfully. "I was in a rush. We have less than a week left. The Soviet Union is going to throw out all the Western diplomats the day after tomorrow. Then the NATO countries will follow suit."

"It's another war, then?"

He shrugged. "The dominoes are starting to fall."

Greta took a step back and looked at him with her chin on one hand. "You missed your chance to get a famous scalp, Comrade. You didn't get the drop on me."

The Russian shook his head slightly. "It wasn't an offensive operation. We just wanted to find out what Karpov's people were up to."

She snorted. "It's always the same. You spend more time spying on each other than on Russia's enemies."

He chuckled at this, but it turned into a wheezing cough. When he had finished, he said: "I swear on my mother's life we had no orders to go after you."

"I believe you." She glanced at her watch. "But I'm going to need some names. You're not going to make me hurt you, are you, Comrade?"

"Alas, I can give you only one name: Karalauskas."

Greta snorted with laughter, baring her teeth. "That is an old game, Comrade. You give me the name of a friend, not an enemy. You want us to kill each other for you and spare you the trouble?"

"Viktoras Karalauskas," said the man, "is the MGB's source on you. I regret that I cannot give you any names from my side of the business. You will have to cut me into pieces with that letter-opener, alas."

"A big gorilla with a mustache. This is their source?"

"I have no idea what the man looks like. I have seen the neatly typed reports he submits to the Soviet Embassy four times a year, with his name at the bottom. It was the price of his early release from prison. The reports contain intelligence on you and other Lithuanians operating in Britain."

"Liar. The man we are talking about can understand Russian but can barely write in his own language. And he has hands like shovels. The idea of Viktoras *typing* . . ."

"His daughter translates his words into English and types up the reports. She delivers them by hand to the Soviet Embassy. She works in a lawyer's office in the center of London. Father and daughter share a house with her two children in the west of the city. The address is number fifteen . . ."

"All right," said Greta. "All right. What else can you give me?"

"I told you I cannot provide the names of my colleagues. You will have to kill me. Begin."

She thumbed the knife thoughtfully, but did not open it again. "There's a way I can get you out of this." His eyes sparked with a flash of childlike hope. They narrowed as professional cynicism took over.

"We might be able to do an exchange," Greta told him. "I have people in Russian prisons. I would be willing to hang on to you and arrange a trade."

The conflict on the man's face was intense. She knew that he would be thinking about his family.

"The problem is that Karpov has someone working on the British side. I would have to broker a prisoner exchange through their diplomats here. I can't deal with them if they have a Judas." She crouched again and put her face very near his. "Give me his name," she said. "And I can get you off the hook."

Suddenly the Russian looked intensely tired. His eyelids were heavy with it. His skin was very yellow, and she wondered if Antanas and Ričardas had burst his liver.

He said: "I believe you are right about the Judas here. That's always been the rumor. No one knows the name, I am afraid, except Maxim Karpov. All I can tell you is that the man is supposed to be an *ucheny* at Cambridge."

"*Is?* You mean he is still working there now?"

"I believe so. I'm not sure what his field would be. It cannot be anything too technical because there is a protocol for scientific sources. They would have subcommittees and expert panels and God knows what. Karpov keeps this source entirely to himself."

"So, a professor of humanities."

The man swallowed. "Something like that. I hope you see that I am telling you everything I know and no more. Most men in my position would say anything to save themselves. Please weigh that in the balance."

The man closed his eyes. He must have known it was almost certainly over for him the minute she had told him she knew about the existence of a Soviet agent in England. No one in her position could reveal that knowledge to him and let him live.

Greta paid the Russian a professional courtesy. She was standing behind him and he did not see her nod. She began shouting loudly in Lithuanian for Ričardas and Antanas to come back in. Something about moving the prisoner. The grinding noise of the opening door covered the sound of the knife blade sliding out of its handle.

She was still shouting when she pushed the point of the stiletto into the back of his neck, just under the occipital bone. The Russian made a flapping, gurgling noise with his tongue. The Lithuanian men stared at him, stunned. They were both framed in the open doorway with the strong sunlight coming in behind them.

The man sat with the knife sticking into him for a second, wriggling horribly like an enormous pinned insect. Then Greta drove her palm against the handle of the knife, slamming it home up to the hilt. The Russian's head snapped forward and hung down at an oddly sharp angle, his chin resting against his collarbone.

Ričardas ducked out of the doorway and vomited loudly outside. Greta said: "I'll wait until you have finished."

When he came back in, wiping his mouth with a handkerchief, she said: "Come over here please, both of you." Neither of them could look at the face.

"We don't beat prisoners around the head. They get concussion, which means they can't think properly. Or they get blood in the ears, so they don't hear the questions. Understood?"

"Yes, Greta," the men said at the same time.

"And this. Look at the feet. We always put men up on their toes. You see? We tie the ankle here. If the feet are flat, they can still get some leverage. They might try to stand up, turn the chair over. Put the heels up in the air and it takes away their strength. And if you have a chair like this with a bar—use it. Loop the rope through it like that. Do you see?"

"Yes, Greta."

"Good. Let's get him out of here before those officials arrive. This kind of thing is probably against the local byelaws."

Boys, she thought, as she walked out. I need men and all we have left are boys.

24

EAST GERMANY

The little Air France heron's wheels were almost going sideways when they hit the asphalt at Schönefeld. A storm was blowing itself out and the delegation that had formed up to welcome the chess players were having their hair and clothes whipped around.

There was only one other British contestant, a Jewish schoolboy in a *yarmulke*, whom Michael recognized from the Excelsior. Few Westerners were taking part in the tournament. Some countries, including France and Iceland, had formally boycotted the event in response to recent acts of Warsaw Pact aggression. Many other players would not risk a journey to the East at this time of tension.

Michael had never been treated so deferentially before in his life. The air hostess insisted on taking his suitcase from his hands and said the porters would bring it through for him. The state officials waited stoically in a small phalanx, holding bouquets of flowers with both hands, trying to shield the petals from the wind. A border guard checked Michael's papers. Another brought his case back and returned it to him stiffly. The man did not reply when Michael said: "*Danke.*" Apart from that, the East Germans seemed friendly enough.

It took an hour to get to Lake Werbellin, up Autobahn Eleven. It was clear and calm now. Adolf Hitler had built the road in 1936, said the driver. He said it without pride or shame. The man's name was Horst and he was tall and thin, with prematurely gray hair. He had a bone-dry sense of humor that was hard to tune into at first. Michael liked him immediately.

Horst said: "You'll love this place. It's copy of Artek. You know Artek?"

"I'm afraid not."

"Whoa! Artek is . . . oh, my God." The man shook his head. "Like the mouse, your mouse. In America."

"I'm sorry?"

"Mr. Mouse. My God."

"Mickey? Mickey Mouse?"

"Sure. Like his castle."

"It's like Walt Disney Land for young Communists?"

"Exactly."

"Sounds interesting."

"Everything here. Fishing, swimming, all kinds of sportive. You like the sportive?"

"Oh, yes," said Michael. "Boxing, weightlifting, that kind of thing." He flexed an unimpressive arm. "We're all very strong in England."

Horst looked at him doubtfully. "Most of the kids are gone now, after the summer. But there is technical school. Few kids all year round. Later they will perform. Flags, torches, more flags. There's a song about peace all over the world. We know how to enjoy ourselves here."

The parade went on for nearly two hours and Michael could see the back of Yulia's head from his seat, but no one was allowed to move. The children chanted the names of Ulbricht, Ernst Thaelmann and the current chairman of the Politburo of the Soviet Union. There was an excruciating speech in English, welcoming Michael and the other contestants.

The youngsters applauded warmly. Both girls and boys wore caps, like wartime RAF pilots, and many of the girls wore trousers. They sang and paraded with very serious expressions without a break. The thought occurred to Michael that the Warsaw Pact nations would surely beat the capitalist countries if the two sides sent their respective children into battle.

The adults were free to mingle afterward but there was no alcohol. Michael was looking around for Yulia when Vassily touched his arm.

"How is the dragon slayer?"

"I'm well, thank you. It's good to get a handshake and not a slap in the face. I don't think we were introduced properly last time."

"I can never remember which name I'm supposed to be using on which day. "Comrade" will generally be a safe option with most people you meet on this trip."

"Is your big colleague here this time?"

"Him? No. They couldn't afford the catering bill. It's just me. No need to bring an army—we should be in safe hands with the East Germans. Also, don't shout about it, but this is a time of slight political sensitivity between our two great nations. It would not do for half of Moscow to descend on a children's camp."

Vassily's eyes were twinkling and Michael had the distinct impression that he was fighting the urge to wink. The Russian said: "I think you will find that things are a little more . . . *relaxed* than they were in London—" He cut himself short when he saw that Yulia was approaching them. Michael's heartbeat lurched into double time.

It was not correct for two young people to be alone with each other in one of the bedrooms, but Vassily invited them both to his suite to get ready for the dinner so everyone could see that he was chaperoning them. He walked a few yards ahead. Yulia was behind Michael's shoulder.

"Tell me about the other girls," she whispered. "There are no others."

"Tell me the truth. I will find out. How many pretty girls have you had?"

"Not a single one."

"I believe you. There are none in London. It's better for you if you don't chase girls, my boy. I am as jealous as the Devil." She punched him in the small of the back, making him exhale sharply. Vassily glanced at them.

They could all relax when they got to Vassily's rooms. He went out on to the balcony to smoke. Michael opened his bag for a clean shirt and pulled out a copy of *The Times*, unfolding the newspaper with an exclamation.

Yulia was applying mascara in the bathroom. She called: "What is it?"

"I must be going mad. I don't remember packing this. Don't remember buying it."

She poked her head around the door while he was still putting on the shirt and saw the deep blue bruises on his stomach. She gasped and ran to him.

"It's been a strange couple of days," said Michael. "I'll explain later. Let's go to dinner and not sit together." His voice sank to a whisper. "Will you meet me afterward?"

As the sun went down, people wandered along a wide path that ran in a circle around the lake. Michael and Yulia sauntered along, keeping a respectable distance from each other.

"What have you been reading?"

"Pushkin. Umm . . . Turgenev."

"No," she said. "Read Chekhov. He is the one who understands the Russians. Are you still in love with the president of the United States?"

"Please, God. Let's not start that again."

"I have changed my mind about him. I have formed the opinion that the president is a great and a true Communist."

"You are making a joke," said Michael.

"No. The American president wants to take on the Soviet Union in the battle for the cosmos. He will have to use all the resources of the state to do it. It will be greatest ever triumph for socialist economics. To compete with us, they must turn into us."

"So Russia wins the moral victory."

"Absolutely not. Our own space program relies on individual genius of the American kind."

"So you both succeed when you become the opposite of what you pretend to be."

"We need both sides to make the coin. Sooner or later, world will realize this."

"The world doesn't have much time left."

"Then work quicker!" She thumped him again. They were on the far side of the lake now, and no one else could see them.

Michael took Yulia's hand and said: "I've just spotted a rare species of butterfly." They plunged off the path into waist-high bracken. A thick beech tree hid them from the path. She stepped back toward it slowly, her arms reaching out behind her. When her splayed fingers touched the bark, she arched her back and put her neck and shoulders against the trunk. Her hips were pointing toward him. Michael wove an arm into the space behind her lower back. He tried to pull her upright but she resisted.

"Nature lover," she said. "Do you see any butterflies you like?"

"Only one. A big, beautiful one."

She shook her head. "No. That is hopeless. I am *big* butterfly? No. A woman is never big."

"I am dying to go to bed with you." Her back was flat against the tree trunk now and his lips were against the side of her neck.

"Better. That is much better. That is the way to talk."

"You once said I was a good talker."

"That was foolish of me. You are without hope, like all men. When a girl tells you that she loves you, you gape at her."

"Oh, God." He took a step back and looked at her at arm's length, holding her shoulders.

"Exactly. Exactly like that. Catching the flies."

"I don't know what I was thinking."

"You stood there like a piece of wood."

"I love you, of course."

"*Dubina!* You cannot say *of course!* It ruins it."

"I love you, Yulia. How else can I say it?"

"In Russian."

"*Ya lyublyu,*" he began. "*I am in love with you. You are the only one. I adore you absolutely.*"

"That is better. That makes it real." Her eyes were almost closed. He heard the eyelashes batting against each other as he kissed her neck reverently. "You have been practicing your Russian."

* * *

There was a large wooden building on the edge of the water, like a boat-house. It rested partly on stilts. A side door was open and they slunk in like burglars. The ground floor was one big hall and there were tables folded up and hundreds of chairs stacked on top of one another.

There was a kind of attic room upstairs and the keys were in the lock. It was like the back room of a junk shop and they picked their way around the furniture. There were filing cabinets and an enormous alu-minum bust of Stalin covered with a white bedsheet, a new Rus projector loaded with a reel of film and an old sofa with cleaning materials on top of it, a bucket and a mop beside it.

They heard no voices and Yulia locked the door behind them qui-etly. It looked like the kind of place where someone might stash a bottle and Michael searched every cupboard and cabinet for hidden contra-band. Yulia tried to start up the projector. While her back was turned, he furtively moved the cleaner's things off the sofa. He hoped it would not be too cracked or stained underneath. Perhaps something could be done with Stalin's sheet. Sorry, Yosip, old boy, Michael thought, but my need is greater.

No sound came from the projector, but Yulia pushed the heavy device around with her foot so that film footage was suddenly sprayed against one white wall—a grainy print, saturated with color. There was Gagarin in his orange overalls, climbing the stairs. Then Vostok 1 began to rise magisterially in an absolutely straight line. The glare from the rockets filled the screen. Yulia took her dress off.

He tried to draw her to him but she danced out of reach. "Not until I say." She stood proudly in her underwear, her knuckles resting on her hips. She did a slow pirouette, lit up by the film. He was trembling with desire.

She said: "I am torturing you, yes?" Michael tried to say something witty but all that came out was a whimper of agreement. "No. I don't torture you. I am not one of those *suki*." She tossed her head, beckoning him forward.

When he pulled her close her skin was cold. There was no heating in the room. He kneaded her back as they kissed and tried to undo her bra fastening, cursing himself silently as he fiddled clumsily with the strange design. They were standing in the beam of the projector and the pictures lit her up. He let his hands fall to her hips. He glanced down and the flame of Vostok's ascent blazed across Yulia's naked torso.

Later they showed their faces in the common room on the ground floor of the hostel, where the other young contestants had gathered. It was decorated like a hunter's lodge, with antlers on the walls and wood paneling everywhere. The wood was cheap new pine, stained to look older.

The front door faced a grand staircase, and there was one long corridor at the top with eight rooms coming off it. Horst, and a woman he introduced as his wife, had rooms downstairs. She was a handsome blonde woman of around thirty-five. She had sat next to Vassily during the dinner. Vassily told Michael she was married to Horst in name only. It was a professional arrangement designed to make it easier for them to live abroad under diplomatic cover. The couple were supposed to be looking after all the young guests, like house parents in an English boarding school.

Michael settled himself in a comfortable chair in the common room, but he did not want to talk to any of the other competitors. Yulia had begun a chess game with the Jewish boy. Michael could not see her face from where she was sitting. He glowered at her from across the room, wanting her again.

Horst came in twice and peered around the door at the young people. Michael felt he was searching for Yulia. He had an exaggerated smile on his face that did not disturb the muscles around his eyes.

Michael made a big performance out of saying goodnight to everyone and going to bed alone. As he left the common room he saw Horst and his wife at the end of the corridor that faced the room. They were speaking quickly in low voices. They glanced up at him when he passed the opening of the corridor and fell silent.

Before midnight, Michael padded down the corridor to Yulia's room. They kept the lights off and tried not to make any noise. It was better the second time, and the moment of crisis was unlike anything he had ever experienced. He felt as if something was ripping itself out of him, as though his soul was leaving his body. He had the selfish urge to fall asleep immediately afterward, but she took his hand and put it between her legs and showed him how she wanted to be touched.

He was aroused again when it was over and she straddled him and pressed her hands hard against his upper arms and chest to keep him pinned down while she did what she wanted to do on top of him. Neither of them had managed to maintain their silence for a while now.

Yulia subsided on the mattress next to him, uttering a last blasphemy. Michael said: "I didn't think you were religious." That earned him a sharp dig in the ribs.

She came up on one elbow and studied his face. "Look at you. Celebrating another conquest, my boy? How many beads on the abacus now?" He was about to say something, but she put her fingers over his lips and said: "Don't tell me. I don't want to know."

"I was going to say that this is different. With you. It's like starting all over again."

Yulia's eyes flashed with pleasure. She wiggled her head like someone weighing their next words carefully. He had the feeling that she was on the edge of revealing something very intimate, but she wrinkled her nose and said: "Enough of your lines."

It was cramped in her single bed. Her head rested on his shoulder and the muscle was going dead. The discomfort woke him, but he did not want to move her. When Michael saw the door of the room opening very slowly, a crack of light spreading across the floor, he wasn't sure if he was dreaming, and he lay there in a kind of paralysis. A shape loomed in the doorway.

Michael was pressed up against the cold plaster of the wall and Yulia was right on the edge of the bed with one arm hanging off. With painful slowness, the reality dawned on Michael that a man in a suit and a Homburg hat had crept into the room and was looking down at Yulia's face as the light from the open door fell across it. The man had a rag balled up in his left hand.

Michael sat up suddenly. The man jumped back and swore. Everyone started shouting. Later, Michael could not recreate exactly how he had ended up fighting the man in the bathroom. He remembered jumping out of bed, and they must have grabbed each other's wrists. The man in the suit was bigger and he forced Michael across the carpet.

Michael must have backed into the bathroom door and the impact shoved it open. Yulia had left the light on in there and everything was suddenly lit up in ghoulish white. The man's face was a horrible rictus as they wrestled with each other.

His hat had fallen off. He was in his thirties, with a beard and thinning curly hair stiff with pomade. Michael got a whiff of something sweet and chemical as the rag in the man's hand came close to his face, and he had the feeling that his strength would not last much longer, when he saw through the doorway that Yulia was out of bed and a second man, older than the first, also dressed in a business suit and tie but no hat, had grabbed her from behind with his arms around her middle.

The second intruder's hands were clasped together, and he was squeezing Yulia tight under the ribs, making her short nightdress ride up, exposing her bare thighs. She was trying to prize open his grip and kicking back with her bare feet. She could not cry out.

Michael looked at his opponent and let go of the hand that was holding the rag. He put the heel of his palm under the edge of the man's chin and snapped his head back with a savage upward thrust. The crown cracked the bathroom mirror behind him and he gave a sharp grunt of pain.

There was a glass next to the mirror, with Yulia's toothbrush standing in it. Michael plucked it out of the glass with the bristles in his fist and the handle sticking out. He stabbed the sharp end of the brush into the corner of the man's eye, as deep as it would go.

The man went down on to the floor and curled his knees up to his chest, covering his face with both hands. That was the end of him for a while.

When Michael came out of the bathroom, the second man let go of Yulia and was chattering very quickly. It was not Russian but some of the words sounded like Russian.

The light in the main room was off but the door was half open. Michael could see that the intruder was a square-built man and considerably bigger in height and frame than himself. But the man backed away, dabbing one hand in the air in a calming motion.

He backed out of the room into the corridor, talking unintelligibly, Michael matching him step for step. It occurred to him afterward that the man could see he was holding a weapon of some kind—but could not make out that it was a plastic toothbrush.

Yulia ran out after Michael in her nightdress and flattened herself against the wall on the far side, like a cat, as the man slowly backed away from them. Michael was in his underwear but felt completely naked.

Up and down the landing, doors were opening and heads were appearing. German words were being shouted and voices were calling in answer. From downstairs, Michael heard the noise of a door opening and slamming somewhere, and footsteps drumming over the flagstones of the ground floor.

The man in the suit gave Michael a pleading look, and Michael could see that his red drinker's face was slick with sweat. Then the man turned and sprinted down the stairs toward the front door.

Michael did not know, afterward, how he could have forgotten about the first intruder—the one he had stabbed in the eye. A kind of tunnel vision came over him, which blocked out everything that was not immediately in front of him.

He was still looking down the empty staircase at the open front door when the first man—the one he had left half blind on the bathroom floor—stormed out of Yulia's room and barged past Michael from behind as he stood in the middle of the corridor.

Yulia screamed at the top of her voice and Michael turned to her, confused. He watched the second fellow race away in the same direction as the first. He watched the man go out of the front door and heard shoes crunching on the gravel outside. He heard a car or motorbike engine snarling into life.

He realized his hand was pressed to his stomach, and when he looked down at it, he saw that it was covered with blood. The lower half of his vest was a solid rectangle of red. The man Michael had poked in the eye had slashed him across the belly with a straight razor when he pushed past him.

Later, Michael thought he heard gunshots outside, but he wasn't sure afterward if that was real. Everything was like a dream again. He was lying on his back now. It would be pleasant to rest for a while and gather his strength, he thought. God knew he deserved it.

Then he saw Vassily's face and heard the Russian yelling at the house mother in broken German. A surge of panic swept over him. Michael tried to sit up. He said: "Vassily, don't let them give me any drugs. Or a blood transfusion."

"Okay, okay, easy. Just lie back." Yulia said something and Vassily replied in Russian: "He doesn't know what he's saying."

"Listen," Michael shouted. He had Vassily by the jacket collar now. "Are they talking about giving me something to stop the bleeding?"

"She's got your medication downstairs. You're a hemophiliac?"

"No! There's nothing wrong with me. If they give me drugs, or the wrong type of blood, they'll kill me. You must listen."

"All right, all right. You're a good soldier. Rest now. I'm going to treat you myself. No drugs, no blood."

Horst's head loomed into view. He was cresting the stairs with a white paper bag held triumphantly in one hand. Vassily barked something at him. The bag was sealed with a white label. Horst went down on one knee and ripped it open.

Vassily shouted a Russian obscenity at him, put a hand against his shoulder and shoved. Horst went sprawling on his back. Yulia picked up the bag and screamed an even more filthy word into the German's face, so loudly that the windows rattled in their frames.

25

Michael opened his eyes and saw Neptune and dolphins in gold livery pulling the king's chariot across the ceiling. Fish with human faces were in the corners, blowing the four winds. On the walls around the bed, knights in armor were performing deeds of valor.

He rose from the bed and went to look in the mirror. That maneuver took about half an hour. The maid came in and shrieked when she saw him sitting on the end of the bed, panting like a distance runner. He asked her who the knights were but she didn't understand so he pointed and she thought he was hallucinating. Then she understood and said, "*Bogatyr*," and he said, "*Bagateer*," and she wiggled her hand to show that it was close enough. He looked at himself in the mirror and he had two more days of stubble than the last time he'd checked. Yulia and Vassily ran in and made him lie down again.

Later, there was a gramophone in the drawing room downstairs, and they found some ancient jazz records for him. The French windows were open for the air, and the garden outside was wet with rain.

He could hear gulls, and a faint white noise in the distance that could have been breakers.

Yulia said: "We're in northern Germany, on the Baltic coast. This place belongs to my mother. It's a kind of dacha. But I don't know what the German word is. Vassily?"

"My German's rusty. Maybe they don't have one. How do you say it in English, Mischa?"

"We don't really have dachas. Only a few people. The prime minister has one. I think this one might be bigger than his."

The Russian smiled sheepishly. Then he looked at the carpet. He made an expansive gesture with both hands and said: "Well, I will never forgive myself, anyway."

"Vassily Andreyevich!" cried Yulia. "We have talked this out a hundred times."

"I underestimated Maxim Karpov. I got outwitted by a German harpy."

"You don't know that for sure."

"Why else would she invite me for a nightcap at exactly the moment when our Bulgarian friends drop in?" Vassily lamented.

"Are you sure they were Bulgarian?" Yulia asked.

He nodded. "Karpov's favorites. This job was always going to be too risky for Russians. I'm guessing those two clowns were supposed to drag you off somewhere, and if I went tearing after you, that would leave Michael alone with the East Germans. He surprised them, I think. They didn't expect to find him in your . . ."

Yulia looked at him, blushing.

". . . immediate vicinity." Vassily shot a look of theatrical disapproval at their English guest, who wore an air of concentration. Michael had started, twice, when he heard the name Karpov, and he was determined not to do it again.

"Our charming friend Horst is one of the most feared interrogators in East Germany," Vassily went on. "A shot of something nice and relaxing in Michael's upper arm, I am guessing, was the plan. Then a friendly chat. He probably wouldn't remember anything when he woke up."

He looked at Michael carefully and added: "It is possible they had something rougher in mind. They didn't want you to bleed to death before they got what they wanted."

"Please," said Yulia. "I can't talk about it anymore."

Michael leaned over to her, rubbed her shoulder and said: "All's well that ends well. I'm on the mend now." Vassily looked at him with great curiosity.

Michael indeed appeared to be feeling better and they managed a slow dance later, him in an outsized dressing gown and pajamas, her in a black rollneck and tan corduroy skirt.

* * *

When Vassily came back in, his arms were full of bottles and he was smiling like a schoolboy. "I performed a reconnaissance operation earlier and located what would, in a bourgeois society, be known as the cocktail cabinet."

They got Masha, the maid, to bring lemons, sugar and hot water from the samovar for sugar syrup. Yulia sat close beside Michael while Vassily mixed the drinks.

He said: "I am creating a new cocktail in Yulia's honor. Michael, your personal physician has prescribed for you a small dose of dilute alcohol solution in effervescent form."

"And who is my personal physician?"

"Me."

Yulia elbowed Michael. "You trained as a doctor, didn't you? But I've never heard you call yourself one."

"I never finished my training. Later I discovered that the world was full of people pretending to be doctors and did not need another one."

"I heard that you worked as a battlefield medic in Spain."

He was doing something tricky with crushed ice that apparently required so much concentration that he could not answer her.

Yulia looked at Michael and made her eyes go very wide. "Vassily Andreyevich? When I mentioned your name for the first time, my mother said she didn't know you. But I asked her again when she was drunk and she told me that you saved her life in the Battle of Moscow. Which is it?"

"Now, something like that, I really can't talk about. A doctor is like a priest in that respect. Not that you young people know about priests."

"I do," said Michael. "Vassily? Is it true that you were in the war in Spain? I'm not fishing for classified information. I'm just interested."

Vassily winced at the taste of the drink as though it had too much lemon in it. "Who is the state official here? And who is the one on enemy territory? This should be me interrogating you."

He poured drinks for them and made a toast in Spanish: *"Arriba, Abajo, al dentro, al centro."* He moved his glass up, down and across, like a priest blessing them. Yulia tried to copy him but she couldn't pronounce the lisping sounds properly.

When they had finished laughing, Vassily said: "It is true that I went to fight in Spain in the 1930s. It wasn't a secret. They gave me a medal and did a big article with a picture. They mentioned my name on the radio and everyone from Leningrad to Vladivostok heard it. But then I had to come back to Russia in '38. And that was a bad time to come back."

"I thought the worst was over by then," said Yulia, gently.

He shook his head. "It was still bad. I was sent to Kazakhstan for nearly three years. The place I was in was supposed to be better than Siberia. I don't know. There were shops and a school and a barber. It was like they made a little town in Hell. They used to beat the women for picking the children up and holding them in their arms. It wasn't like the place where your father went. That was a special compound for scientists. They had little flats and the men lived with their wives. I mean, it was still tough. No offense, Yulia Sergeiovna."

"None taken. My father knew he was lucky, and he always said many other people had it worse."

"Sergei said the same thing to me. The strange thing about my country, Mischa, is that you get a whole new history along with a prison sentence. It turned out that I never really received that medal in the first place. If you look in the archives of *Pravda* now, you won't find that article. And if you ask me about Spain and we are speaking in front of other Soviet officials, I will tell you I was never there."

He saw the confusion on Michael's face and raised his glass in the air. "In the Soviet Union, if you get tired of reality, a new one will come along and replace it. Every new leader ushers in a glorious new past. *Na zdrovye!*"

Night was falling. The newspaper Michael had found in his luggage was on the sofa. Vassily picked it up, then threw it down in disgust when he saw that it was three days old. Yulia closed the French windows and slid the bolts. She rubbed her arms as if to warm them. She looked around the corners of the ceiling.

"Are you sure the MGB aren't listening to all of this?"

Vassily said: "The man you may have seen loitering outside the front gate is called Wolf. He is my right hand in East Germany. He drove hell for leather from Berlin to put your stitches in, Michael, and pump you full of antibiotics. Then he and I swept this place for devices."

He shook his head. "I was complacent. I did not think Karpov's tentacles would reach this far West. I should have known something was wrong when he agreed to let you leave Russia again without a whimper of protest. I never guessed he would try a kidnap attempt on East German soil. It can't have been easy to arrange. Relations between Moscow and Berlin are tense, and Karpov isn't good at building alliances. That's what happens when you're an evil, repulsive little fucking gargoyle."

Yulia snorted with laughter. "You are the only person I've ever met who dares to talk about him like that. You are not afraid of him!"

"Everyone who is not insane is afraid of Maxim Karpov," said Vassily. "But he and I have an . . . unusual history that makes it harder for him to hurt me." He looked at them uncomfortably. "It's a long story. And not at all suitable for impressionable young people."

She shot Michael another look. "My mother said that something happened between you and Karpov in Latvia but she never found out the details."

"Close. Lithuania." Vassily drank again. He looked at Michael doubtfully through his eyebrows.

Yulia said: "Vassily Andreyevich! He has shed blood for us. Doesn't he deserve a bedtime story?"

She was sitting opposite him on the sofa with her legs crossed under her and a cushion clutched to her belly. Michael was next to her. Both of them were looking at him with the expectant, hopeful faces of small children waiting for a gift. Vassily rolled his eyes and gave a long sigh. "We had all better have another drink first."

After he had settled himself back on the carpet, in his socks and with his legs crossed, Vassily said: "I told you that I was in prison for nearly three years. Then the war began and they had to let us all out again. Our obscure political crimes suddenly didn't seem so unforgivable with the Germans pounding on the front door!

"I made it all the way to Berlin and by the time it was over, I was worn away to a shadow. I dreamed of a peaceful, simple life after the war, but an unpleasant surprise was waiting for me, along with a few other officers who had proved their worth in the fighting. Our prison sentences had been deferred, not quashed. Either we stayed in uniform and took over new commands, or we returned to the camps. Can you imagine? Another cell for me—a man who had been promoted twice and decorated. What a world that was! Mischa, when did the Great Patriotic War begin?"

"'Thirty-nine," said Michael, before he could stop himself.

Vassily shook his head. "Not for Russia. You are forgetting we came in later. And when did it end—'45? Wrong again. For men like me, the war never ended. Stalin had found new enemies everywhere—in Ukraine, in the Baltic States. Fascist sympathizers and reactionaries, enemies of the revolution, financed by the capitalist powers. You would call them guerrillas and partisans. People who would not accept the kind attentions of Uncle Yosip. That is how I came to be in the pleasant land of Lithuania in the glorious summer of 1946, and how the shadow of Maxim Georgevich Karpov first fell across my path."

Yulia could not help shuddering at the name. She was remembering the stairwell in Butirsky. She held out a hand as if to fend something off. Michael looked at her quizzically but she shook her head.

"Maxim Karpov does not rule by fear alone," said Vassily. "No one can forever. He is loyal to people close to him. Oleg, whom you have both met, has been Karpov's man since the war."

"The Pig," said Yulia.

"Indeed!" Vassily showed his canines. "A swine at the trough, as you say, although he purges himself like a ballerina afterward." He shook his head. "I cannot bring myself to hate that one, knowing all that I know. He is simply a damaged model—a baby that got dropped on its head. Like me, it was Oleg's great misfortune to get pulled into the orbit of Maxim Georgevich.

"You can be sure that Karpov kept himself and Oleg well out of harm's way throughout the war—no medals for those two! When the Germans were beaten, he found something more to his liking: counter-insurgency work in Ukraine. That meant what it always means: paying sons to inform on their fathers. Terrifying mothers into giving up their children. Karpov had the mass of the Red Army behind him if something went wrong, and those are the kind of odds he likes.

"It was supposed to have been a big success and by the summer of '46 things were quieter in Ukraine. So, they sent Karpov to Lithuania to repeat the trick. I was stationed there at the time, and things were hot. Many of the Baltic people carried on fighting us, their new masters, the same way they had fought the Fascists. They couldn't tell the difference.

"When Karpov arrived, the Red Army were taking heavy casualties in the forests of Lithuania. I was in charge of army operations in the western part. The partisans had just killed a local mayor—a big beast in the Lithuanian Party and someone personally known to Stalin. I just about kept my head but they sent Karpov to oversee a joint military and intelligence operation, run by the NKVD—or whatever the hell they were calling themselves that month.

"And so it turned into the usual fight between the village dogs. Me and my men on one side, supposed to be working closely with Karpov and obeying his commands, but straining at the leash and snarling every time he gave us an order. They kept changing their name, but these were the same NKVD commissars who had been machine-gunning my soldiers from behind a few years earlier when they didn't advance quickly enough."

He glanced at Michael to see if he understood "commissars" and Michael nodded quickly.

"The Lithuanians did not always help themselves. They liked to shoot people who betrayed them to us, which spooked the villagers. And do you know who helped us? The British!"

He grinned at Michael and raised his glass. Michael said: "Cheers. But I don't understand."

"The Western countries had begun to pay some small attention to the Baltic states. They always maintained that the Soviet occupation was illegal, and they loved to stir up trouble for us—if it didn't cost too much. London parachuted in the odd man—invariably some desperate villain—and of course we always caught them and made the most of it. It proved that the whole partisan movement was a Fascist reactionary coup orchestrated by foreign enemies, and so on.

"Karpov never wanted to go out into the woods and trade punches with the rebels. Of course not! He dreamed up the most incredible scheme where a bunch of actors working for us pretended to attack a police station, and we pretended to fight them off, and then the survivors ran into the woods, where we knew the partisan bands were waiting, and some of our people were welcomed into their arms as heroic patriots. Within a year, some of the biggest bands were being led by Soviet agents. Karpov had a genius for deceit. Another of his ideas was to pretend that the partisans were plotting to assassinate Stalin."

Yulia groaned loudly.

"I know!" said Vassily. "Can you imagine anything more ludicrous? These miserable creatures, buried up to their eyes in snow in the pine forests, were supposed to be able to spirit themselves to Moscow and take a pot shot at the Boss. It was the purest nonsense but Karpov staged the whole thing like a theater production. He got prisoners to write elaborate confessions, and there was supposed to be secret intelligence from a source in Britain that stood the story up. Anyway, Stalin swallowed it. Maxim Karpov was his golden boy for a while. That meant he lost all need to act with restraint. Some of the partisans we captured found themselves decorating the village squares—" He broke off and gave Yulia a hard look.

"It's all right," she said. "Go on."

Vassily shrugged. "We were teaching them civilization. So we put the corpses out on display. Strung up, castrated, eyes poked out with wires. If the families came out to take the bodies in, the NKVD would be watching and waiting to see who they were. We burned villages. We sent women and children to the far east. And Karpov . . ." He shook his head.

"Yes?" said Yulia.

"Well, I didn't know it at the beginning, but the favor of Stalin gave Maxim Georgevich a license to indulge his personal vices to the full. He desperately wanted to go back to Moscow after Ukraine. He was terrified of flying and he hated being away from Russia. He took over a grand, sprawling house in Telšiai to make himself feel better. It was the best address in the town, on a private road up by the lake.

"The army were already using a big mansion up there as our headquarters. Karpov took the place next door—even more aristocratic—for himself and Oleg. It was sheer stupidity. He should have been keeping a low profile. Instead, everyone in the west of Lithuania knew where Maxim Karpov was living, so we had to waste resources surrounding him with armed men. But he insisted on living like an Ottoman pasha—complete with the harem. He would point his finger at a girl passing on the street, or working in a field, and Oleg or one of the others brought them to him. His men fed him with women, the way you feed a furnace with wood. Most—" He broke off again and gave Yulia a very doubtful look.

"Please go on. I'm a big girl."

Vassily took a pull at his drink. "I believe it is well known that most sexual perverts have a particular type they fixate on. Karpov was different. He would prey on schoolgirls and grandmothers. I know of one occasion when he inflicted fatal injuries on a girl of thirteen. The best thing I can say in his defense is that if his victims did not put up a fight and kept their mouths shut afterward then most of them—most—survived."

They all fell silent and Michael was surprised to hear the hard quiver in Yulia's voice when she said: "You seem to know an awful lot about it, Comrade. Couldn't you have put a stop to any of this?"

"Easy for you to say!" Vassily snapped. He was gazing at her darkly through his eyebrows. "What do you know about those times? About men like that? A child like you, who has never spent a night out of a soft bed!"

They held each other's gaze for a few moments. Then Vassily passed a hand slowly over his face. "What am I saying? Of course you will judge me. That is what children always do: pass judgement on the ones who came before them. Very well. I will tell you the whole story and at the end, you will deliver your verdict." Michael and Yulia shifted in their seats to get more comfortable.

"I was busy at that time," Vassily began. "We were still being ambushed out under the trees almost every day. I had heard rumors from my men about Karpov's singular habits, but this was a man my soldiers hated so I assumed that the stories were exaggerated. It suited me to worry about my own problems and stay out of Karpov's way—until a day came when I could no longer ignore what was happening."

Vassily put his glass down and kneaded his temples with his fingers.

"A Russian tax official was driving along with an NKVD escort and a troupe of partisans shot up the car. They hanged the tax inspector from a tree by the side of the road. They were learning civilization from us. Karpov was furious. We received intelligence linking the assassins to a small village just outside Telšiai, a place where people were already known to be sympathetic to the partisans. We had searched houses there for hidden weapons the year before and found nothing. Karpov often grumbled about it.

"Now he got twenty NKVD men together and headed straight for that village without waiting for me. It was right on the edge of the deep woods, a place where there was a lot of activity at the time, where it was hard for us to operate in safety. The partisans could have had hundreds on the spot within an hour. They had mortars and heavy machineguns at that time. A little army.

"Karpov was behaving very foolishly. Someone came by motorbike and told me what was happening. I got a dozen soldiers together and we raced over to the village. It was at the far end of a little valley, and as we came into it we could hear the shots. By the time we got there, everything was on fire.

"They had killed all the men and a few women and they were pouring diesel on the bodies. They had lined up the women and girls who were left and announced that they were going to shoot them too. Karpov got a translator to give them a countdown in Lithuanian. *In two minutes you will be executed. In one minute you will be executed.*"

Vassily worked at his forehead with his fingertips. "I smacked the interpreter around the side of the head and stood down the firing squad at gunpoint. There were men lying all around us where they had been shot. One moved his hand, like this, and groaned!

"I couldn't believe it. I finished him off myself. I was furious. Karpov's fools hadn't even checked the bodies to see if the men were really dead. I remember screaming in the face of the NKVD captain. Karpov was screaming at me. He couldn't gun those survivors down now!

"The women and girls stood in silence the whole time, looking straight ahead, listening to us squabbling. I will never forget their dead eyes. Karpov told the translator to make an announcement to the women. He said that the Soviets were doing Lithuania a great service by ridding them of the menace of Fascism. The next day, he expected a girl from that village to visit him with a bouquet of wildflowers picked from the fields, to thank him personally for his efforts on behalf of the local people.

"He put his hand on the head of a sweet, curly-haired lass of about twelve. She looked up at him and I swore . . . I swore to myself that, one day, I would see Maxim Karpov dead."

Vassily looked at Yulia gravely. "I said those words to your father once. I have never uttered them to anyone else. They must stay in this room."

"Was that what you were talking about on that strange evening when you both got roaring drunk together?"

"I hope you were not eavesdropping that night, Yulia Sergeiovna?"

"Of course not! But you kept waking me up, the pair of you. Yelling at each other into the early hours."

Vassily smiled. "Your father invited me in for a drink as a courtesy. I thought I would stay for one. I did not think I would still be there when your mother came home three hours later! It turned out that Sergei and I had more in common than anyone would have guessed."

Yulia raised her eyebrows.

"Shared interests," said Vassily. "Shared concerns."

"I know my father hates Maxim Karpov as much as you do. There is no need to be coy."

"He loathes the man. And the fear and terror that walk always by Karpov's side. He hates the thought of what Karpov might do to the whole world with his missiles. And he hates the system that keeps producing men like that and allowing them to flourish. He hates the whole political philosophy that—"

"For the love of God!" shouted Michael. "What happened next? Did the girl come to Karpov's house the next day with the flowers?"

Vassily shook his head. "The girl did *not* come. Another girl came in her place. A girl Karpov was not expecting."

26
LITHUANIA, 1946

The partisans came down into the eastern end of the valley in a long, loose line. They did not bunch up into little groups. They were from the Green Devils band—experienced and disciplined.

Greta took the lead and was the first to see the bodies. Her mother was lying on her back outside her house and the front door was wide open. Her mother's arms were down by her sides and someone had lifted the white apron she was wearing up over her face. Greta's grandmother's body had been burned.

As the men checked the corpses, Greta wandered away, and the thought came to Mindaugas that she might go off under the trees and shove her pistol into her mouth. Instead, he found her talking very gently to an elderly woman who was sitting on a stool outside another house.

They gathered the survivors around the fire in the kitchen of Greta's childhood home while the men worked outside. The children sat in a circle in a room upstairs. The older girls automatically cared for the younger ones, soothing them and stroking their hair.

Greta sat with her legs crossed among the children. Through the open door, Mindaugas heard her asking: "Did he have a little bit of hair left, or none at all? Do you think he was the same age as Uncle Mindaugas? Older? And you are sure that he was wearing glasses?"

When she came outside again, the men had their shirts off and were digging a communal grave. Greta said to Mindaugas: "I need you to bury my mother for me. Then I have to go. Here." She had taken bars of chocolate from her rucksack. "Give these to the little ones. I'm not coming back. I won't be needing this either." She took a single grenade from her coat pocket—the last one they saved for themselves—and gave it to him carefully. He cupped it in both hands.

"You're not going anywhere," Mindaugas said. "You're not in your right mind."

"Bury them for me," said Greta. "Don't stay too long. Twenty minutes."

She walked due south, cresting the side of the valley and trudging down into another, shallower, one that ran alongside it in parallel. She timed her breaths to the beat of her steps. One and two were in- breaths and then she breathed out in two parts. If she kept exactly the same pace, the rhythm took over and she did not have to think. She crossed a railway track and began the slow ascent of the far side of the valley.

There was a firebreak in the trees and she walked up the middle of it, using it as a broad road. The steepness of the climb made her breathe heavily and disturbed the rhythm of her walking. At the very top of the ridge, it was as though the wires that were holding her up snapped, and she collapsed on to the forest floor. It was covered with pine needles and cones, fragrant and burnished by the early summer sun.

She rolled around like a small child having a tantrum, losing her sense of where the sky and the horizon and the earth were. She lost track of time. After a while, she sat up and hugged her knees tight, rocking backwards and forwards. She could not cry yet. She had taken out her pistol and it lay next to her in the thick needles. The solidity of it, its heavy realness, calmed her. She picked it up and ran her hands over it, feeling its coolness and the patina in the steel. She got to her feet.

Greta could see lights twinkling below and a long way off in the dusk. She walked down a lane that was as straight as a Roman road for two miles, meeting no one. At the end of the track there was a farmhouse on its own. A spindly boy of about sixteen was in the yard.

"Something I can help you with?" said the boy. He looked her up and down with frank interest.

"I need to see the schoolmistress."

"Well, I'm the man of the house, so you can tell me your business first," said the boy, sticking one of his thumbs into the belt of his trousers.

"I don't have time for this. Go and get your mother now."

The two women had never met but they were both partisans and knew each other by reputation. They shook hands formally over the threshold. Greta spoke to her very rapidly and candidly.

There was a hunter's stew in a pot on the range and she ate hungrily. It was the biggest meal she had eaten for a long time and she had to force herself not to bolt it. After the meal, the teacher took down a suitcase stuffed with new school uniforms from above the dresser in the kitchen.

The items sized for a sixteen-year-old fitted Greta perfectly, although she was almost twenty. Greta said: "Too big." The blouse one size smaller was uncomfortably tight across her chest, and the skirt was indecently short. Greta hitched it up higher and looked at herself critically in the full-length mirror at the foot of the stairs. "That's better," she said.

After the fitting, she bathed in an old metal tub in the bathroom upstairs. She shaved her legs and the hair between them. She rubbed good shampoo into her scalp. She dried herself and brushed her hair for almost half an hour and tied it in a single long plait.

When the boy had gone to bed, Greta climbed through a trapdoor into an attic room and helped the schoolmistress correct proofs for the nationalist newspaper she published. They worked by the light of a single weak electric bulb. The woman checked Greta's work afterward. She had to correct some of the corrections.

Greta said: "I am ashamed of my grammar. I missed years of school."

The schoolmistress said: "You learned other things."

Greta spent the night in a soft bed for the first time in months. She slept for nearly fourteen hours and was awoken by shouts from the boy. A horse-drawn cart was waiting outside and a man was standing with his hat held in both hands. The women made him wait while they applied makeup liberally to Greta's face.

The horse and cart arrived at Karpov's house at half past eleven. Oleg came outside and frowned. The girl was older than the one his master had selected. He recognized the man with her: a shifty Lithuanian the Russians employed as an interpreter. The man climbed out and helped Greta down from the back of the cart. She had a light gray coat on and school clothes underneath.

She was carrying a bouquet of poppies, cornflowers and yellow rue. Her suppleness and prettiness were obvious, even from a distance, and as she walked slowly toward Oleg the eyes of the soldiers and the NKVD men who loitered around the house followed her closely. She looked straight ahead with her mouth shut tight and her jaw jutting defiantly.

The interpreter took his hat off and held it with both hands when they reached Oleg. He said: "The family apologizes, Comrade. The younger girl has the chickenpox. They have sent her sister in her place. But this girl is more, ah, friendly. She will be, ah, less shy around a man. Alas, she has no Russian."

Oleg took Greta by the arm and led her around the side of the property and into the large back garden. Two soldiers looked at her keenly as they passed. He paused under a balcony at the back of the house. The doors were flung open up there and long curtains swayed. A pudgy, balding man with thick-rimmed black glasses emerged in his shirt-sleeves. He squinted down at the girl and barked something unintelligible in Russian.

Oleg steered Greta back to the front of the house. The palm of his hand was at the small of her back the whole time and he made her walk quickly. The front door was open and a very young NKVD man with straw-blond hair sat on a chair next to it with his rifle across his knees.

Oleg made Greta stop and he helped her take the coat off, revealing the school uniform and her long legs. There was a ripple of whistles and catcalls from some of the men who were watching. A smattering of applause broke out. Oleg silenced it with a murderous look.

The young sentry stood his gun against the wall and began to search Greta. He took his time, letting his hands linger on her hips and waist. He reached under the short skirt with both hands and slid his fingers up her legs, beginning at the ankles, then ran them around the elastic lining of her knickers. She looked straight ahead and said nothing. Her legs were bare and she wore rubber-soled tennis shoes with no socks. "It's not the worst job of the day," the young man said, and Oleg growled at him. He jumped back to let the big man and the girl go past.

They crossed the threshold and stopped at the foot of the staircase. The house had once been glorious. There was a grandfather clock in the corner and a fine wooden dresser, now stripped of valuables. The black-and-white tiles on the floor were badly cracked. At the top of the stairs there was a large landing and she could see a closed door immediately opposite.

In a crude approximation of Lithuanian, Oleg said: "Go up. Do everything what he says. Everything. Afterward we go home. Home." He squeezed her arm. Greta walked up the stairs. There was a sway in her walk. At the top she paused outside the door and looked back down. Oleg mimed a knock. She rapped on the door twice.

Karpov was still in shirtsleeves when Greta went into the room. His breath smelt of alcohol and there was a film of sweat on his forehead. He locked the door behind her quickly, trying to make it seem casual.

The balcony doors were still open and the room was light and cool. There was an old chintz sofa next to the balcony, very worn and stained. In the corner a door led into an adjoining room. To her right a heavy oak dining table had been pushed up against a wall.

Karpov said: "You don't speak Russian?" She shook her head emphatically. He reached out and took her chin between one thumb and forefinger. "Or are you just shy?" he asked.

She wiggled her head ambiguously. Her features softened into what might have been the ghost of a coquettish smile.

"You young devil," Karpov said. He tried to make it jovial but his voice cracked. She had a pretty, feline face and a hint of Central Asia in her green eyes. Her breasts were small and firm and their shape showed frankly through the tight blouse.

He let his hand fall down and slowly undid the top button. Karpov could see dazzlingly white underwear beneath and her young skin was soft and unblemished. He realized he was salivating and it reminded him of the food on the dining table at the edge of the room.

He turned to the table and said: "Eat something. I have beautiful cakes for you. And that poppy drink you all love here." He waved his hand grandly. "When you are with me, you eat like a princess. Afterward we will drink a toast together."

But when he turned back, he saw that she had walked away from him and arranged herself on the sofa. She put her feet up on the cushions and reclined back along its length. Her skirt had ridden up and he could see her long, smooth thighs. She was looking away from him, gazing into the middle distance. There was a sense of self-awareness about her, like a model posing for a portrait. Her right arm hung down, and her fingers were extended, like a ballerina's.

Time seemed to slow for Karpov and he breathed very heavily as he paced over to her. He went down on one knee next to the sofa and buried his face in her chest, inhaling deeply. The girl did not react. He undid three more buttons, parted the blouse and kissed the space between her breasts.

The intensity of his lust made him groan long and low, like an animal, and she stroked the back of his head with her left hand, as if to soothe him. She could see big white flakes in his hair. Folds of pale, flabby skin gathered at the nape of his neck. He turned his head to the right to rest his cheek on the bare skin of her chest. He was facing the wall, his eyes closed in rapture.

Looking down at him, Greta opened her mouth, hesitantly at first, then very wide, like a child opening up for a doctor's examination. Laid flat on her tongue was a new blade for a double-edged razor. She took it out carefully with the thumb and forefinger of her right hand, making sure to hold the small, flexible blade by the blunt ends.

She used the palm of her left hand to press Karpov's head tight against her breast. When she felt his body stiffen, she dug the corner of the razor blade into his skin just below the right ear and cut deep and wide.

* * *

Vassily was standing next to a broken-down troop carrier outside the house the army used for its operational headquarters when he heard whistles and jeering and looked toward the mansion next door.

He saw Greta standing with Oleg and the NKVD man posted there. When he looked again, she was gone. Vassily put down the spanner he had been holding, wiped his hands carefully on a rag, then walked over to the blond man. "Where did that girl go?" He tried to push past the man but Oleg loomed in the doorway, barring his way. Vassily said: "Is this a whorehouse now? Have you changed profession?"

Oleg slapped him contemptuously with an open hand and Vassily punched him hard in the mouth. The big man rocked back on his heels.

They had each other by the lapels when they heard a scream that rattled the windows of the house. They looked at each other and there was a heavy thud. Vassily was first up the stairs and found the door locked.

When she cut him, Karpov jumped to his feet and screamed. She had seen the thing done twice before and on both occasions the blood had erupted from the wound, like a fountain. When this did not happen now, she feared she had not cut deep enough.

But then she saw that the blood was pulsing strongly between the fingers Karpov held to the wound, and that it was very red arterial blood. He lurched toward her suddenly and she kicked out desperately, catching him on the left shin. She tensed herself for an attack, but the color drained from his face and he fell on to his back.

She ran into the other room. There was a bed, a writing desk and a bedside cabinet with two drawers. Nothing was locked. The top drawer contained contraceptives, boxes of pills and a bottle of scent with an atomizer attached. The bottom drawer was stuffed with scraps of women's underwear. They were all different sizes and some had been torn. All looked unwashed.

Greta threw the pillows from the bed, then felt under the mattress and between the sheets. Then she saw a heavy overcoat on the back of the chair by the desk and found a gun in the pocket. When she went next door, Karpov was on his back with his legs bent and his feet flat on the floor. Outside, there were shouts and banging on the door. She put her foot on Karpov's upper chest, aimed the gun at the center of his face and tried to pull the trigger. Nothing happened.

She wrapped both hands around the pistol and squeezed the trigger again with all her strength. The gun would not fire. A fist came through one of the thin door panels, sending chips of wood flying into the room.

She looked at the pistol properly and scowled. It was a clumsy old Korovin, practically an antique. There were spots of rust all over the nickel and the slider was jammed.

Vassily's boot kicked out the whole door panel and she saw his face poking through the hole. Their eyes met and, for a second, she felt like a small child caught red-handed in some misdemeanor. Then anger flared in her and she roared, *"Ateik tada"*—"Come on, then"—and threw the useless lump of metal at him.

He ducked back as it turned end over end and hit the door six inches from where his nose had been. She went out through the swaying curtains on to the balcony.

Vassily broke the lock with his shoulder and fell sprawling into the room. Oleg was almost on top of him. He saw the girl plant both hands on the rail of the balcony and vault over it. She seemed to hang in the air for a second, ten feet up, her hair out behind her in a long thick cable. Vassily gazed after her. From the carpet, Karpov gave a terrible groan and extended an arm toward him.

The old stager Vadim and the new recruit Nikolai were loitering at the back of the house. Vadim was about to light a cigarette when they both heard the thump of the girl landing on the grass behind them. She bent her legs, went forward and rolled over. When she got up her legs wobbled but she recovered and went into a hard sprint, pumping the air with her arms.

The cigarette fell from Vadim's open mouth. He looked at Nikolai and they both had the same thought at the same time: that the girl had leaped from Maxim Karpov's bedroom window. They burst out laughing. Then they heard shouting and saw Oleg emerge on to the balcony with a rifle in his hands.

Vadim swung his own Mosin down from his shoulder and ran after the girl. Thirty yards away, there was a four-foot evergreen hedge and the girl did not slow down but took it like a hurdler. She crashed through the top part where the branches were thinner.

By the time Vadim got to the hedge, she was belting along through a meadow toward the thick woodland that lined the edge of the grounds. The NKVD were supposed to be patrolling the tree line but there was no one in sight. The girl glanced back and Vadim saw that she might have been the same age as his daughter so he took careful aim and fired deliberately high and wide. Another rifle shot came from the house as she reached the first tree. The girl did not look back again. She did not stumble or fall. The forest swallowed her.

27

EAST GERMANY, 1961

"A young girl," said Vassily. "Running like a deer. I will never forget that face. Like an angel of vengeance."

"But you saved Karpov's life?" Yulia cried, and for the first time since he had begun the story, Vassily's face creased with real pain.

"God help me. I could have let the life drain out of him in that room. But I did what I was trained to do. I got my fingers right inside the wound, pressed the artery against the bone and staunched the bleeding. Karpov lived. He went back to Moscow and had plastic surgery on his neck. Later, he made a solemn vow that he would never leave Russian soil again."

All three were thinking it, but only Yulia said it. "I wonder if the girl made any vows."

Vassily got up to refill his glass. Yulia picked up the copy of *The Times* from Michael's bag and turned the pages idly. Michael had been trying not to yawn but, at last, he could not hold it back.

"What are we doing," exclaimed Vassily, "torturing this young man? He needs rest."

Michael put his hand up. "I'm not physically tired. It's just a lot to take in. It's all so . . ." He shrugged helplessly, failing to find a word to sum up the vastness and bleakness of the history of the East. "I feel hopelessly out of my depth when I listen to you talking about . . . being in camps and things like that. Things I just can't imagine." Vassily smiled at him graciously.

"Here's the big thing I don't understand," Michael went on. "How can someone like you, or Yulia's father, have gone back to work for Stalin after you came out of prison? After he had done those things to you. Couldn't you have escaped from Russia?"

"I considered it," said Vassily, "but I had family. Responsibilities." He glanced at Yulia and frowned, but she was ignoring both of them.

Michael had taken off his glasses and was polishing them on the lapel of the dressing gown. He was shaking his head.

With a wink, Vassily said: "Things aren't all bad in Russia, you know. The women are phenomenal."

"Shut up," said Yulia, poring over the newspaper.

"I mean, some of them are temperamental," added Vassily.

"Shut up!" She raised her hand as if to push him away. She was reading with furious concentration. "Shut the hell up, both of you, in the name of *Christ*."

The sound of breaking crockery came from the kitchen. Masha had dropped something. Michael and Vassily looked at each other with wide eyes. Yulia still had one hand in the air. The other was jabbing at something printed in the newspaper. Her gaze was fixed on it.

Michael went over to her and looked down at the page. Her finger was resting on the little black-and-white grids of the chess column.

She looked up at him and her face was pale.

"What is it?" said Michael.

"It's my father. He is sending me a message."

Vassily left them for a while. He wanted to check in on Wolf, the man on guard duty outside the house. Then he made tea in the samovar. When he came back, he said: "Tell me again."

Yulia said: "It's a chess problem I have been working on with my father for months. No one else in the world knows about it. Look at the diagrams."

"You know I don't understand this."

"You don't have to be an expert. Look at where the pieces are. White drives deep into the center. Throws its pawns forward. Black doesn't contest the middle of the board. It withdraws, then exploits the attacker's weaknesses. These four squares are the important ones. There's a high-risk attack where you sacrifice your queen but you get checkmate in a few moves. Only a world-class player would see it coming." Vassily was straining to see what Yulia was talking about.

"This diagram shows a stage in what we call the middle game," she said. "We were still working on the endgame. There are three variations."

Michael said: "I don't remember this from the book you gave me."

"It's not in there. My father and I were still playing it out." She caught herself. "We *are* still playing it out." Michael touched her arm and she blinked at him. "He is still alive," she said distractedly. "I need to call my mother."

"No telephones!" shouted Vassily. Then, more quietly: "Later, all right? Yulia. Look at me. Concentrate. Your father is a genius and so are you. But what the fuck is he trying to communicate here?"

"He hasn't given me much to go on . . ."

"Of course not," Vassily muttered. "Just enough and no more."

Yulia's brow creased. "I think the final line of the column is the important bit: *Next week, we shall decide which endgame to play.* Only I would know what that meant."

"The end of the game?" said Vassily.

"It will be one of three variations. He named them after places: the Paris, the Valencia and the Geneva."

"What? Why?"

"It's very common. The Sicilian Defense, the Scandinavian Defense . . ." She glanced at Michael. "The English Opening. I didn't think anything about it at the time. I didn't realize there was a hidden meaning."

Vassily grabbed the newspaper from her. "*Next week . . . we shall decide which endgame to play.* So, we get the name of one of those three cities in next week's newspaper? And then something happens in that place the week after. But what?"

"The endgame plays out," said Yulia.

"What kind of ending does he have in mind? I wish to Christ I knew." Vassily was shaking his head with a mixture of admiration and disbelief.

"This column is printed once a week?" he asked Michael. "We have to wait to get the name of the city?"

"It comes out every Friday. It's the longest-running newspaper column in the world. If there was a nuclear war, it would still come out."

"We are about to test that theory, I think. But hang on!" Vassily laughed out loud. "What are we talking about? This is absurd! Surely the column is always written by the same correspondent. Isn't that how they do it? How could Sergei get something like this planted in a Western newspaper?"

They all peered at the page again, crowding around it. The byline read: *Guest columnist: Sieger.*

"That's an anagram of Sergei isn't it, if you spell it out in English?" Vassily had to close his eyes to see the Cyrillic letters in his head. "*Sieger* is German . . ."

"Like *Sieg heil,*" said Michael. "The victor."

"Jesus." said Vassily. "What is tonight? Monday? We've got four days until the next column comes out."

"Three, I think," said Michael, remembering what Chas the reporter had once told him. "The first editions of the newspapers always hit the stands in central London the night before. You can pick up Friday's *Times* at King's Cross from about ten o'clock on Thursday evening."

"Then I need to start getting the word out to my people. We need to be ready for Thursday. Start preparing for the endgame!" He announced it with a dramatic flourish, then laughed darkly. "I'd better try to find out what is going on at *The Times* first of all. Has the newspaper been taken over by wandering Russians? Or are we all going out of our fucking minds here?"

Vassily walked toward the door, kneading his temples with his fingertips. "I am going to break the habit of a lifetime and make some phone calls. I'll need Wolf for a while. It's safe, though. Both of you ought to get some rest now. Especially you, Patient." He shot Yulia a black look. "Did you hear me? The boy needs rest."

"What on Earth do you mean by looking at me like that?"

"I'm saying the young man needs to recover his strength. When a man is convalescing . . ."

"Yes, Comrade?"

"There are certain things that are conducive to rest, and others that . . . drain the vital energy."

"Enlighten me."

"Well, when I boxed in the army, we always had a rule. Two weeks before a fight . . ."

"Shut up and get the hell out of here." She reached behind her to snatch up one of the sofa cushions and throw it at him as he left the room.

When Yulia slipped into bed beside Michael, he felt a fever coming on, but her skin was cool to the touch and it soothed him. She stroked his chest then moved downwards.

"Where are those stitches? Here?"

"Yes. You'll have to be delicate with me."

The hand drifted further down. "How about here?"

"I think that's the right sort of area."

Later, the sound of low knocking on the bedroom door woke him. Yulia had left him alone to sleep. His throat was sore and his forehead felt clammy. He struggled to find his glasses next to the bed. He didn't know what time it was. The knocking came again and he said: "Yulia?"

"Not this time. Your luck has run out."

Vassily walked over to the bed on stockinged feet as Michael swung his legs out from under the covers. Light came into the room through the half-open door. The Russian sat next to him on the bed in the semi-darkness. It had been a long time since they were alone together. Neither spoke for a while, until Vassily said, "Do you want to tell me what that was all about with the blood and the medication?"

"I can't."

Vassily nodded sympathetically, then studied Michael's face. "There is more to you than meets the eye, Stephanovich. You are tougher than you look. Most soft capitalists would be in a state of acute distress after a close shave with the East German secret police, then a nasty injury like that. But you accept it all without blinking. It's almost as if you were expecting something bad to happen to you."

Michael said: "It's funny. I thought the same thing about you that night in London when Sergei went missing. Everyone else was flapping. Grim faces all around. And you were making jokes. As if you weren't surprised by the news."

They held each other's gaze steadily until Vassily's face cracked into a smile. He looked Michael up and down, like an army doctor assessing a new conscript. "How are you feeling? Tell me the truth."

"Like a champion," Michael lied, acutely aware of his outsize borrowed pajamas and the tape that was holding his spectacles together. "Ready to go another fifteen rounds."

"It took me a while to figure out this business with the newspaper. Then all at once it seemed very simple. I wait for the international edition of *The Times* to arrive in Moscow, then make arrangements for a trip to the place Sergei names in the column."

"Paris, Geneva or Valencia."

"I am hoping for Paris. I have friends there. It is not going to be all that easy. One of my colleagues has found last Friday's *Times* in our archive. We get the international edition. It is not the same newspaper as the one you brought here in your luggage."

"Not the same?"

"The chess column is entirely different. No Sieger. No endgame variations. No Paris-Geneva-Valencia. Do you see the problem? The next column will almost certainly not appear in the edition we get in Moscow. I cannot sit around at home and wait for the name of that city to fall into my lap. I need someone in England to get hold of the domestic edition for me."

He passed the palm of his hand over his face. "It should have been straightforward. I had a man in London. A very experienced, reliable man. He has just been found curled up in a storm drain at the edge of a farmer's field close to Cambridge with a knife buried in the back of his skull."

"Christ. I'm sorry. I don't know what to say. That's . . ."

"Let us call it war and leave it at that. But it presents me with a practical difficulty."

Michael didn't miss a beat. "I can get it, of course. I'll grab the first edition as soon as it's on the stands on Thursday night. I'll ring you straight away with the name of the city."

"Ring me? All international calls to the Soviet Union go through the same exchange. Every conversation is monitored night and day by the same people who sent the Bulgarians to pay you a courtesy call. That is why I like to avoid the telephone."

Vassily stood up suddenly and sucked the knuckles of his right hand. "Sergei is killing me," he said. "I really have no idea what he is planning."

He ran his hands over the stubble on top of his head. "I don't think we can use the phone, Michael. We could come up with some kind of code to confuse anyone listening—red is Geneva, blue is Paris, but what if there is more to it than one word? What is that writing called again, under the chess diagrams? BXQ?"

"Bishop captures queen. It's called algebraic notation. It's the language of chess."

"My people at home think there might be more information hidden in there. Time, map coordinates. It could be a simple cipher. It's hard to say unless the cryptographers can see the whole thing. You won't be able to read all that out over a crackling phone line."

"Say no more. I'll bring the paper to Moscow."

"*Moscow?*" Vassily looked at him in amazement.

"Wherever you want. I'll fly the newspaper to Russia."

"After the events of the last few days? You'd put your head into the tiger's mouth for me?"

"No. For her."

"Truly, appearances can be deceptive. It is not very often that I am lost for words." Vassily actually reached out and placed a hand on Michael's forehead, as if to check whether he was delirious. He sensed the raised temperature and frowned.

"You are a brave soldier. But I do not need heroics. I need you to buy a newspaper for me in London, then catch a flight to a neutral country, and stay very calm. I will get out of Moscow and meet you halfway, in no man's land—Zürich or Vienna. It's only a few hours away. We will make the handover and I will be back at my desk before anyone notices I'm missing."

"Done. Just tell me where."

"I don't know yet. You will need to go home on the first flight tomorrow. Young love will have to wait. On Thursday you grab that newspaper and cradle it like a baby. You run to Heathrow and there will be a ticket waiting for you. Look at me and understand this. You are on Maxim Karpov's radar now. You are taking a risk. Say now if it is too much."

"I'll be there."

The Russian pulled Michael to him in a crushing embrace. "I will wake you at seven. That means you have five hours to get some sleep now. No one sleeps as soundly as a good soldier."

Michael woke at six and walked out with Yulia at first light. She was worried about the stitches across his stomach, but he insisted that they climb the ridge of sand dunes that rose steeply behind the dacha.

Michael looked back as they plodded up and saw how handsome it was: a grand three-story house clad in dark brown wood with cheerful flashes of bright blue along the edges of the roof. There was fine decorative work on the gable that faced them, and the year of construction was carved there: 1896. When they crested the dune, they looked north away from the house and watched the shallow gray waves of the Baltic Sea hitting the coast of Germany.

Yulia said: "What is your plan for us?"

He took a deep breath. "I thought we'd go to England at first. You and me. Your father, depending on what happens. Perhaps your mother can join us later."

"She will never agree to that."

"All right. We'll have to think of something else then. But I need to get a university degree, if I'm going to support us."

She wrinkled her nose. "How long do these studies take?"

"Three years."

"So I will be cooking your breakfast and pressing your shirts in Cambridge for three years like a little English wife."

"Of course not. You can find some translation work. You can go to classes."

"What else?"

"Dazzle everyone. Fight off all the other boys. Beat them all—" He bit off the words, too late.

"I will never play chess again. I do not play if I cannot compete."

She sat down on the sand. It was a dull morning and the horizon was lost in the haze over the sea. Michael wondered where they were exactly. Lithuania, the place where Vassily had saved the life of Maxim Karpov, was out there somewhere in the mist. He could not picture any of it on a map.

Yulia was sobbing silently. He sat next to her, lowering himself slowly and painfully, and put his arm around her.

"Everything will be all right."

"I am not crying about *everything*. I am not crying for my ridiculous father, or my English husband. I am crying for myself. A woman who could have been a world champion. If you just wait two minutes and shut the hell up, it will pass."

"We don't have to go to England. We can go wherever you want. I will be by your side for as long as you want me."

She punched him on the shoulder, without much conviction. "Always trying to sound brave."

"I'm not feeling brave. I'm absolutely terrified. But I try not to show it."

"No. You must not put on a face for me. You must always tell me how you feel. You and I must hide nothing from each other. Do you understand?"

"Yes, I think so. It has to be perfect, doesn't it? Otherwise there's no point."

"We must not be lazy like others. We cannot have any compromises. For us, it is all or nothing."

Voices came up from the south and they turned their faces back to the house. Vassily was at the door, calling and waving. He was dressed immaculately in an inky black suit and tie. They could see his German friend Wolf carrying their bags from the house, his beard poking out of a military green parka. A car was waiting for them.

28

LONDON

Greta was waiting for Michael at Heathrow on Tuesday afternoon, as arranged. She pushed open the passenger door. "Time's up. What do you have for me?"

"The name of the Judas."

She drove with her brow knitted. Michael talked about blood groups and blood thinners and blood transfusions. She raised her eyebrows. "Your father's idea?"

"Mine."

"Are you telling me the truth, or are you sacrificing someone to save him?"

"It's the truth."

"I hope so. Get the map out of the glove compartment. I need to drop in on a friend first. He lives close by, but I have never driven there."

Michael directed her to Ruislip Gardens Underground station and she knew the way from there. She parked at the bottom of the allotments, giving him strict orders to stay in the car, and walked uphill toward the house. Viktoras was nowhere to be seen. It was three in the afternoon. His daughter was a typist in a lawyer's office in Holborn and worked until five.

Greta heard the music from a long way off. It resonated through the glass of the back door. There were no other signs of life. She slid er switchblade into the crack between the door and the jamb and lifted the hook out of the eye of the latch.

When the door swung open the roar of the music hit her. *Croce e delizia, croce e delizia.* Maria Callas drew her through the kitchen. Sliced black bread on the side and dirty crockery in the sink. A child's bicycle spread out in pieces for repair on the dining table. The corridor that led from the kitchen to the front door was very dark. Light and loud music spilled out into it from an open doorway on the left. The barrel of Greta's Baby Browning edged across the threshold of the sitting room.

Viktoras was in the only armchair, facing the front windows. His bulk made the chair look like a toy. He had a glass in his right hand. The shutters were closed. The record was spinning in the corner. The blast from the speakers was overpowering. *Croce e delizia*, sang Callas. A torment and a delight. A torment and a delight to the heart. Viktoras looked up at Greta and his body went rigid. She saw the trapezius muscles at the top of his shoulders bulging against the cloth of his shirt. He had heaved wounded men on to those shoulders and carried them to safety in the teeth of the Russian rocket barrage. He had won the Iron Cross, first class. She saw his left hand grip the armrest with terrible strength, then relax. He nodded at her. Greta nodded in reply. He closed his eyes.

After it was done, she walked in a wide circle around the body and lifted the needle from the whirling vinyl with her little finger. Viktoras's head was snapped back and his eyes were pointing at the ceiling. The hole in the temple behind them was small and neat. Greta looked around the room, grateful for the silence. She saw something on a shelf in the corner alcove. A Lithuanian–English dictionary. *The daughter translates for him and types up the reports.* Greta left the dictionary on Viktoras's lap for his daughter to find.

She stood close behind Michael while he rang Professor Colin Sinclair's desk number from a public callbox on King's Parade, Cambridge, with syrupy golden light falling around them.

Michael spoke into the receiver. "I'm so sorry to drag you down. The porters won't let me in without a note or a chaperone."

Greta couldn't hear Sinclair's reply. She looked at Michael, her hand shielding her eyes from the low sun. She heard him say: "Can we talk somewhere private? Your rooms?"

When he gave her the thumbs-up, she ran south in the direction of King's Lane, toward the side entrance of the college.

Sinclair had a set on the third floor of the neoclassical centerpiece of King's. He ushered Michael through two doors. He hadn't bothered to lock them behind him when he went down to collect the boy. The big bay window was open.

Michael was still apologizing. The professor said: "I wasn't working. I was just standing by the window, looking out at all this splendor."

The sun was setting slowly in the broad East Anglian sky, reflected from ancient stone. Down below, people were lolling against the walls and basking in the light. They wanted to reach out and gather it up with their hands. The sky over the Backs was lit up with shades of violet, rose pink and purple, like the ceiling of a baroque cathedral.

Sinclair said: "It's like watching an Old Master doing a sunset in front of you. Except these colors are too extreme for any painter."

Michael sat, unprompted, in the chair in front of Sinclair's desk. The professor raised an eyebrow, walked around the desk and took the seat behind it. He had his back to the big dark cupboard in the corner. It was a more formal arrangement than at Michael's interview.

"How was your . . . trip? A success?"

"It's hard to say."

Sinclair nodded and began to search for his pipe. "Certainty is the first thing we relinquish. We are tiny bit-part players in a vast drama. We never know if we have performed well. There's no applause."

"How do people stand it?" asked Michael, really wanting to know.

"There is a clever quotation from a great Indian epic that I am trying to remember."

Sinclair shook his head. "I'm not going to get it. The gist is that you must play the hand you are dealt and not think about the consequences. It's not for us to decide how the thing turns out."

Michael looked at him doubtfully.

"I imagine it sounds better in Sanskrit," said the professor.

Michael's fingers were knitted together and he was leaning forward, looking at Sinclair very intently. He cracked his knuckles and sat back in the chair. "I didn't thank you properly for teaching me those German words."

"You're welcome," said Sinclair, through the pipe stem.

"The funny thing is," said Michael, tugging at his earlobe, "I don't really have hemophilia, mild or serious. And my blood group is O, like most people's."

Sinclair shook out the long match and placed it very carefully in the glass ashtray so that only the smoldering tip touched the heavy base and the end was balanced on the side.

"You told me a lie," he said easily.

"A deliberate mistake. The East German police thought I was AB negative, and that I would need special medication if . . ." He tailed off. "In the event of an accident, let's say. There is only one person who could possibly have supplied them with that piece of false information. You are the only one I gave it to."

Sinclair wasn't happy with the match. He took the end again between thumb and forefinger and adjusted the angle at which it was tilted against the side of the ashtray. "I suppose it was your father's idea," he said eventually.

"Mine, as it happens."

"I don't believe you."

Michael shrugged. "It wasn't personal. You were at Trinity in the thirties. You ended up in the same line of work as my dad. You fitted the bill. When I told you about my trip to Germany, I could see that you were interested, but were trying to hide it. I thought the East Germans would be jumpy about a medical condition like that. I didn't know they were planning any rough stuff, of course. I was going to pretend to slash my hand on a glass or cut myself shaving or something, just to see how they reacted. To see if what I told you had filtered through to them. If they started talking about hemophilia, I was going to feign ignorance and say it was all a mix-up. My brilliant plan got overtaken by events. Someone gave me a swipe with a straight razor."

Sinclair's back stiffened.

"The Germans nearly pumped me full of blood thickener," Michael went on, "and a dose of the wrong blood type when I was on the edge of passing out. They had it all waiting for me, thanks to you. Either would have killed me."

"That was a dangerous game for a boy like you to play, by Christ. What did you think you were doing?"

"Trying to get some information for a friend."

Sinclair ran a flat hand from his forehead to the back of his skull. He pulled at the pipe hungrily. Michael sat back in the chair and let him think.

Eventually the professor said: "I suppose I don't have much time?"

Michael inclined his head.

"Of course I was bloody well *interested* when you told me you wanted to travel to East Germany alone! I couldn't work out whether you were having an adventure off your own bat, or if that splendid war hero of a father of yours would actually use his own child as pawn in one of his little intrigues. You didn't give much away."

"And you passed my name to *them?*"

"They would have found out who you were anyway, you fool! I passed on my doubts about you too. I said I didn't think you were a player in this game. You certainly don't look the type. They will not be sure about you, even now. But you ought to tread carefully."

"I can look after myself," said Michael, trying to sound tough.

Sinclair said: "The West can't *win*, you know, in the end. I've seen the numbers, the technology they have."

"I need to go."

"That thing with the blood. I thought I was keeping you safe by telling them. If I had known it would put you in danger . . ."

It sounded heartfelt, and a look of sympathy briefly crossed Michael's face. Then he recited some lines he remembered from the Lithuanian

Embassy: "*We were betrayed by someone on the British side. The Soviet reaction was pitiless.*"

Sinclair shook his head uncomprehendingly.

Michael said: "*We put the bodies on display. Strung up, castrated, eyes poked out with wires.*"

"I don't know what you're talking about."

Michael stood up abruptly and said: "No, I don't suppose you do."

"How much time do I have left?"

"I can't say. I'm sorry."

"What are you going to do now?"

"Me, personally? Nothing."

"That is a gnomic answer."

"I'm sorry. It's out of my hands now." Suddenly he didn't want to look at Sinclair, or even in his direction.

The outer door of the set clicked shut, and Michael's footsteps could be heard on the two-hundred-year-old staircase. The heavy front door of the building creaked open and snapped shut three floors down.

Sinclair rested his pipe on the edge of the ashtray, exactly parallel with the match. He picked up the telephone and dialed a number. Someone answered but did not speak. Sinclair said: "This is Mr. King. I need to talk to someone in personnel." The line clicked and there was a different dialing tone. Sinclair had the receiver pressed tight against his ear and he was breathing heavily. He did not hear the faint creak from the great oak cupboard behind him.

Greta pushed the doors open silently from the inside with the knuckles of both hands. The crack widened and she could see more of the man now. He had pulled his chair close up to the desk and was gripping the receiver in his right hand. His left hand held a framed black-and-white photograph.

One of Greta's stockinged toes touched the thick carpet directly behind the professor's chair. She could see the photograph over his shoulder. He had his arm around a woman. Both of them were young. The line clicked and a muffled, accented voice said a word that sounded like: "Please?"

Professor Sinclair said: "King. This is King. Stand by to take a message."

More words came from the receiver, but he did not reply. He had gone very still. Greta realized that she could see herself clearly over his shoulder, reflected in the glass of the picture frame he was holding, emerging from the darkness of the cupboard. A mirror image of her own face, split down the middle with shadow, was floating next to the woman in the photograph. Both she and Sinclair were looking at the green eyes that shone out of the glass. There was a glint of light from the coil of wire, as fine as a guitar string, that hung between Greta's hands.

The cupboard door creaked again, loudly, and broke the spell. Sinclair's head jerked around. He dropped the receiver and the photograph with a clatter and tried to jump up. But the armrests of his chair were jammed under the edge of the desk. When his hands flew to his sides to free the chair Greta lunged out of the cupboard and threw the loop of wire over his head.

29

MOSCOW

Vassily always had the boys train in pairs. he stood them against the far wall and counted them off. The evens went first, heaving the odds up on their backs and laboring across to the opposite wall, where they swapped places. They exercised without a break for three minutes, the same length as a round.

Vassily shouted over the panting and grunting: "We fight as individuals, but we train as a team."

Simonov came in while he was refereeing the older boys, who were taking it in turns to spar in the single ring. Vassily ignored him. When two fighters lost their temper and started swinging wildly at each other, he jumped between them and held them apart until they calmed down. He made them return to the center of the ring, apologize and touch gloves. "You are here to help each other improve, not take each other's heads off," he said. "As iron sharpens iron, so one man sharpens another."

After the final stretching exercises, he sat next to Simonov on the bench. Simonov passed him a towel and Vassily sat breathing heavily, his head leaning forward and the towel hanging down from the back of his neck. Simonov said: "Nice speech. I liked the bit about the iron. Who said it?"

"Marx. Lenin. Someone like that. What do you want?"

"You're still supposed to be in East Germany—you and the girl. You came back to Moscow a day early."

"German hospitality wasn't up to much. That's why you're here, is it? The teams have the night off—the long-lens guys?"

Simonov smirked. "You made them. Of course."

"I trained some of them. What do you want?"

"Karpov wants to see Yulia immediately."

"Not a chance in hell."

"He wants to see you too," said Simonov.

"Sure. I'll stroll over to the Lubyanka tomorrow with a bunch of flowers. Box of chocolates for Oleg. I can bring my own noose too, if you like."

"One of your old hands found in a field near Cambridge with a knife in the back of his head. Another dead body, which even I am not supposed to know about. Then there's you. Gadding about with British spies in East Germany? All kinds of stories are flying around. Karpov is losing his mind. He wants to know what the hell is going on."

"Maxim Georgevich can request a copy of the report I will submit to the chief of the Fourth Directorate and the chairman of the Politburo. They are the men I report to. What is it you wanted, Comrade?"

Simonov made his eyes go wide with mock innocence. "Who says I want something?"

Vassily straightened, breathing in and out slowly and deeply. Simonov could feel the waves of heat coming from his upper body. Vassily said: "You have telephoned me, I think, three times over the last month. On every occasion, it was to make some kind of complaint about the work of the Fourth Directorate. I always got the feeling you were reading from a script. Now all of a sudden you don't want to use the telephone. What does this tell me?"

Simonov made no reply.

"It tells me you need a favor, and that my office phone is being bugged."

The last boys were leaving. They saluted Vassily and shouted good-byes as they went through the door. Simonov fished a soft packet of cigarettes from his coat pocket and Vassily said, with a sudden spasm of irritation: "You can't do that in here. Tell me what you want quickly, then get out."

"There's a Lithuanian girl Karpov is obsessed with. He wants every-thing I have on her. Do you know what I have on her?"

"Nothing," said Vassily. "And you want me to save your hide. And you would rather die than admit it over the phone."

"I've heard rumors about this girl. I mean, she would be a woman now. There's a big hole where her file should be. This is Karpov himself asking me. I'm standing here with my trousers down."

Vassily folded the towel into a small square and placed it fastidiously on the bench next to him.

"Are they bugging me at home?"

Simonov blew out some breath. "You. Your air hostess. That nurse whose sheets you were dirtying."

"She was a trainee doctor and I haven't seen her for months," said Vassily, shaking his head with disgust.

"Your sister's place," Simonov said. "Even the office upstairs here. I don't know what you've done but Karpov is as hard as a rock for you."

Vassily said: "So, we're talking about a Lithuanian partisan, possibly still active, historical connection to Karpov, something of that order?"

"Don't be a prick-teaser. You know who I'm talking about. Is there a file or not?"

Vassily stood up suddenly and pulled his T-shirt over his head to reveal a compact, hard torso cross-hatched with silvery scars. "If the Fourth Directorate has information that will assist you in a matter of state security, Comrade, rest assured that I will share it with you imme-diately. You can see yourself out."

Simonov rose to his feet too, reaching for the cigarettes again. "I owe you. Here's a down payment. Know who else Karpov is sniffing around? Masha."

"Who in God's name is Masha?"

Simonov grinned. "It's always the ones you don't notice, isn't it? Drivers, waiters, servants. Masha is Anna Vladimirovna's housemaid. It seems the girl has had enough of being bullied by that old harpy of yours. She has stories to tell."

Simonov put a cigarette in his mouth but did not light it. He walked away, wrinkling his nose in distaste at the smell of sweat and leather and muscle rub.

Oleg unlocked the door of the reading room. When Karpov sat down, followed by Simonov, he went out and closed the door behind him. Simonov heard the lock click. He slid an olive-green cardboard folder to Karpov. He had an identical copy in front of him. These words were printed on the cover: "GRETA query surname query workname hostile active." Neither man spoke for almost ten minutes.

Eventually, Karpov said: "Weak. Thin fare."

"It is true that the picture is disappointingly incomplete, Comrade Chief Administrator."

"There are unacceptable factual errors in here. Look at this. Trained by Special Operations Executive in . . . I can't pronounce it, somewhere in Scotland. In 1947! They had disbanded SOE by then!"

Simonov coughed. "Only officially, Comrade Chief Administrator." Karpov pretended not to hear him. "What's this about a legal case in Sweden? We have contacts there, don't we? They might have fingerprints . . . a color photograph. Have we followed it up?"

"It was a civil case, alas. She married a Swedish man in 1948. He died of tuberculosis a year later. His children prevented her from inheriting the estate."

"Well, what happens next? "France"—and not much more detail. For all those years? What was she doing?"

"I regret that I cannot answer that, Comrade. She appears to have tramped around the French Republic like a gypsy for some time. It's not clear how she supported herself during this period."

"France isn't Russia. Surely we can piece together her movements."

Simonov had been posted to Paris before London. Before he could stop himself, he said: "France is big enough. Big enough to lose yourself in."

He cursed himself silently and kept his eyes fixed on the words in front of him as Karpov's gaze drilled into him. Fool, he thought. Never contradict him.

"Algeria?" said Karpov, contemptuously. "I mean, is any of this section remotely credible?"

"I believe it is all graded 'low confidence,'" said Simonov, wetting a finger and searching for the page with elaborate fastidiousness.

"I can fucking read!" snapped Karpov. Simonov felt sweat collecting in a patch on the small of his back. Karpov was muttering to himself, his fingers scrabbling backwards and forwards through the sheets of paper. "Only once. What does it mean? She visits Lithuania once, what, three years ago? What brings her back?"

30
LITHUANIA, 1958

The young woman who answered the door had the figure of a Paris model and a sour peasant face. She must have been twenty years younger than him. When Greta introduced herself as his niece, the woman seemed bemused rather than scared. He hasn't told her much about his past, Greta thought. Her uncle was in the kitchen, looking out over the lake. The Soviets had been in Lithuania for more than a decade now. There were more brutal beige tower blocks on the other shore, like the one they were in.

"It's not too bad," Greta told him. "You can see the lake. Do you still fish?"

"The Russians poisoned it. They diverted the sewers."

"Do you see any of the boys from the old days? How is Viktoras?"

"In England. I have no friends here."

She looked at him as he sat in profile. His cheeks were sunken and his arms were as slender and pale as a woman's. "I have a cancer," he said, still looking out of the window, in answer to her unspoken question.

She slid a red-and-white notebook across the table to him. "Do you remember all those Christmas presents? All those money orders you used to send me on my birthdays?"

"No."

"Neither do I. Now's your chance to make up for it. I want names."

He looked at her properly for the first time. "I can't remember my own name anymore. I'm someone else now."

"Let's see if you can recall any of your SS colleagues. The Einsatzgruppen are the priority, then those heroes who wore the skull and crossbones. I want Germans first, then Latvians and whoever else. I'll keep the Lithuanians out of it for as long as I can."

He picked up the book and peered down at the first few entries. His face was unreadable. "Making friends with Jews again," he said. "You never learn."

"I represent clients who have an interest in investigating historical crimes. It doesn't matter who they are. They pay well for good information."

He glanced at the open door. They could both hear a small child babbling in the next room. "I don't have a lot of time left," he said, without emotion.

"I can forward money to . . . her. Later. If you earn it."

He picked up the book again as if he had forgotten what he read the first time. He patted the pockets of his cardigan, looking for glasses.

31
MOSCOW, 1961

"Now, who is *this* rogue?" asked Karpov. "It could be Trotsky's brother, couldn't it, by God! But this one is a doer, not a thinker, I believe. Yes. A man of his hands."

The man in the photograph was a small, trim, smiling brigand with thick black Byronic curls and the goatee of a Spanish nobleman.

"YAKOV query YAKUV query surname," said Simonov. "Former Soviet partisan. Now an Israeli official. We place him in France at the same time as the woman. There's a tentative connection."

Karpov was reading. "He's their man in Paris. Then he has to leave in his pajamas with his whole outfit? Is that right? I thought the Jews had cozied up to the French by then?"

"He carried out an unauthorized operation on French soil. A Nazi collaborator who became an important civil servant after the war. It's not clear whether our girl was involved but she leaves for London very soon after the first press reports come out."

32

LONDON, 1958

When Greta walked into the shop, the tailor gave her a long look up and down, his eyes resting briefly on her bust and hips. He was guessing her measurements, but she sensed that it was from professional, rather than carnal, interest.

She said: "I'm a friend of Mr. Blancheflower. He gave me your address."

"I'm always interested to meet friends of Mr. Blancheflower. Are there are any other names that you can give me, Miss?"

"I knew Mr. Samuel is in Paris."

His face betrayed no reaction to these names. He said: "Come into the back room with me, Miss."

It was like a small factory. Men cut cloth and women worked at sewing machines. The tailor's office in the corner was a box with two glass sides so that he could watch everything that was happening out on the floor.

Greta put the notebook on the desk and slid it across to him. It was divided into sections with large headings: Kaunas, Bialystok, Treblinka. The longest sections were headed Paneriai and Vilna. Each page was divided into two columns. On the left were names: German, Russian, Polish and Lithuanian, listed alphabetically. In the right-hand column were notes, sometimes the name of a town, sometimes a full address or more information. Many of the addresses were in Spain and South America.

The tailor read quickly from beginning to end, then went back to look up two names he clearly had in his head. He read the notes that corresponded with those entries with great interest. Then he closed the book and pushed it into the center of the table. "So, what are we talking about here? Is this a gift you are bringing me?"

"I thought you might know people who could make use of this kind of information."

"And are you seeking some kind of reward, Miss?" He looked her up and down again. She was thin and her teeth were in poor condition. The dress had once been white.

"I don't want a handout. I'm looking for employment. I was hoping you might be able to recommend me for a position."

He looked confused. "Do you mean in the tailoring business? Have you had any training?"

"That's the opposite of what I mean. I'm not a seamstress. I take men apart at the seams—the kind of men in this book. I knock the stuffing out of them. I did my training in the forests of Lithuania."

He picked up the telephone and spoke for some minutes in a language she did not understand. There were moments when he lapsed into a grand old Yiddish that was close to Viennese German—*shnayder* for "tailor," *shiksa* "for girl." He glanced at her to see if she could follow it. He smiled when he saw that she could.

The tailor put down the phone, steepled his fingers and looked at her over them. "I want you to stay with me and my wife for two nights. A plane ticket is going to be arranged and there will be a formal interview in another country." He got up, opened the door of the office and yelled above the noise of the machines. "Miss Green? Come here, please. I want you to take this lady out to the changing rooms and measure her. Can we dig out a couple of dresses for her? And you know the Harris Tweed that wasn't collected? I think it's about her size. If not, we'll knock it into shape now."

He turned back to Greta. "A lady who wanders up and down the Whitechapel Road in the middle of winter needs a full-length Harris Tweed coat. It's like a suit of armor. It can stop bullets."

"We will see about that."

33
AUSTRIA, 1961

Vienna Airport was all glass on one side. Vassily leaned on the balcony, watching the jets nosing around outside, like sharks, and cursing the name Sergei Forshev.

He has shoved me out of a plane without a parachute, Vassily thought bitterly, as he scanned the faces of the people around him for the hundredth time.

"Things will be difficult for you," Sergei had told him, before he disappeared. "It is like a play, where all the actors have lines to remember. But no one knows who the other players are. That is a security precaution."

The message in the chess column of *The Times* had thrown Vassily into confusion. He was expecting some kind of showdown outside Russia, but it was impossible to figure out exactly what Sergei was trying to engineer.

Vassily relied on a small network of airline workers and commercial travelers to relay messages to his friends in the West. All of these lines of communication had failed him that night in the dacha in Germany. Emergency contacts he had telephoned as a last resort did not answer.

Vassily's memory for details and faces was excellent, but he had no high opinion of his own intellect. There were too many variables here for a normal man to calculate, too many branching possibilities. A chess column in a newspaper read by millions. How could it not come to the attention of someone in Karpov's camp? The anagram *Sieger* would not hold them off for long. Sergei was almost goading them. Perhaps that was the idea.

Then there was the question of Masha, the maid. She was talking to the MGB now, Simonov had said. Vassily had stayed in the gymnasium for almost an hour after Simonov left, frantically replaying the conversation he had had with Michael and Yulia in Germany. He had paid no attention to the maid at the time. *It's always the ones you don't notice.*

He was sure that the three of them had spoken English for most of that evening. It was inconceivable that the housemaid would have been able to follow everything that Vassily had said. But she would have heard the name Maxim Karpov. Was Masha's eye at the keyhole when they were poring over the newspaper? She could not have failed to notice its significance. Then again, perhaps she had stayed in the kitchen the whole time. Perhaps Simonov was lying, or mistaken.

Everything will be all right, he told himself. You're starting at shadows. Be rational. We're talking about the MGB here, not some group of geniuses. *No. You're lost. They're all around you now.* Listen to yourself! Vassily is vacillating. That is a joke in English. But the word is much nicer in Russian: *koleblyushchiysya.* How do you say it in Spanish? Concentrate, you fool!

To leave the Kremlin, he had been folded into the boot of a car with military markings. Andrey, the young officer who had kissed Yulia one winter night and now bitterly regretted it, drove him through three checkpoints to Kubinka.

Army contacts got Vassily on a transport plane to Uzyn in Ukraine, no passenger list, no papers, no questions asked. He took a civilian taxi up to Kiev and caught a scheduled passenger flight to Vienna, flashing a passport he had never used before.

It was a pristine West German document he had obtained weeks earlier from the tattooed Thieves-in-Law in Taganka—a lifetime ago. He had gone to those princes of the underworld because he knew they would never betray him to Maxim Karpov. Those men were obliged as a matter of honor to live entirely outside Soviet law. Their code stated that they could never earn a kopeck from honest work or speak a word directly to any officer of the state. Vassily had seen camp guards force tools into the hands of Thieves, only for the men to plunge the blades into their own bellies rather than serve the regime.

The passport was good enough for the Austrian border guards. So far so good, he thought. But what are the chances of making a smooth return trip to Moscow? MGB surveillance teams had been watching him with suffocating intensity over the previous week. An image loomed in his mind: the façade of the Lubyanka.

That's enough of that, he told himself. Calm down and think. Imagine this is just an exercise. You are training new recruits. What do you tell them to do?

There were eight people close to him on the mezzanine floor and he didn't like most of them. The young couple with the pram were the ones he liked least. They were not Russian but they might have been Slavic. The young man was very young and rather good-looking. She might have been a little older. Her hair was dyed dark red.

Who would Karpov use? he thought. Czechs, East Germans? Bulgarians again? The couple were sitting quite close to him and he looked at them steadily for a long time. Neither made eye contact with him.

It was an infallible law of surveillance that if you looked at someone hard—even at the back of their head—for long enough, they would feel your eyes on them and meet your gaze. The teams always love prams and pushchairs, he thought. Sometimes they put real children into them.

He looked back out over the balcony and scanned the people on the floor below. A professorial man with a long beard had been sit- ting in various places for two hours, always positioned so that he could see the main entrances and exits. There were two baggage handlers in blue overalls who kept strolling around the ground floor of the airport but never handled any baggage.

He looked at the arrivals board. It was six o'clock in the morning on Friday, 22 September 1961, and the first plane from London had just landed. The passengers would come through soon. There was a cold sickness in Vassily's stomach.

Michael was dressed very casually in Levi's, a polo shirt and a short khaki golfing jacket. There was no sign of the newspaper. He looked very cool and he saw Vassily a long way off, squinting through his glasses. Michael did not make any gesture of recognition and did not speed up from a slow walking pace. The kid is doing all right, thought Vassily. Well, it's in his blood, after all.

The Russian walked diagonally across Michael's path, heading for the check-in desks, then changed direction slightly at the last minute and brushed past him. Michael opened the jacket, slid out the newspaper discreetly and let Vassily take it.

He pushed it into the waistband of his trousers on the left side, so that his suit jacket would hang over it. Neither had to slow down. They were downstairs in the middle of the open floor, heading in opposite directions. Vassily could feel the ventricles of his heart beating like pistons.

One of the men in blue overalls wandered across his path, walking backwards as he looked up at the big departures board, scratching his head. The man had a stubby pencil behind one ear.

As Vassily came close the man spun toward him and grabbed him by both lapels. Vassily shoved him away. He felt two more arms gripping him around the middle from behind. The other man in the blue jumpsuit. This one was strong like a wrestler.

He wheeled Vassily around, and he saw that the young couple with the pram were blocking Michael's path. Michael was trying to pull away from them but the red-haired woman was holding on to his upper arms and hanging her weight from him.

Vassily saw a door open in the silver fiberglass wall behind the Aeroflot check-in desks and a line of men in suits sprinted out on to the concourse with Oleg in the lead, huffing and glaring. It reminded him of the start of a bullfight, when the wooden gates that hold back the bull swing open and all the snorting, stamping force bursts out into the ring.

The other Russians had been waiting around all morning just like him, crammed behind a locked door. It had not done much for their mood.

A man Vassily knew, with curly hair and a scar on his face, caught him in a crushing headlock. Blood filled his face as they strained against each other.

He was bent almost double but his eyes were open, and he saw how the people all around them were reacting. A mother had pulled her two children close. An elderly man was pointing at Vassily and yelling. A woman in very large dark glasses and a headscarf was sitting forward in her seat, her hand gripping the strap of the satchel around her neck.

Vassily heard Michael shouting. He found some strength and stamped on the foot of the man who had him in a headlock. The heel of his elegant shoe stabbed down on to the man's instep and he loosened his grip. Vassily slipped out.

The red-haired woman was still hanging on to Michael. Vassily heard himself roaring the word: "No."

The curly-haired man was squaring up to him. It was a hopeless mismatch. He had four inches on Vassily and about thirty pounds. Vassily shouted: "You don't take the boy."

The man reached out to him with his wrestler's hands and Vassily smashed a jab into the side of his jaw, knocking him back. Over the man's shoulder, he could see two policemen running toward them from the main entrance of the airport. One of the officers had a whistle in his mouth.

Vassily hit the big man again and again, his arms pumping. Both of them were wearing leather-soled shoes and they could not get the right purchase on the polished concrete floor. They slapped and scuffed and smacked at each other for ten furious seconds, until the policemen got between them.

Vassily dropped his hands instantly and showed his open palms. "Easy," Vassily said, to the man he had been punching. "We are all friends here." He grinned like a farm boy. Their ties were askew. Oleg was standing close by. Everyone relaxed visibly.

Vassily was looking at the curly-haired man and laughing when he suddenly kicked out to the side, catching Oleg between the legs. Oleg clutched himself in agony. A woman's voice screamed. Everyone started fighting again. Police whistles shrieked.

When the brawl subsided, Vassily laughed loudly and merrily. He appeared to be the only one who could speak German and he started to talk fast to the Austrian policemen. "Officers, I am ashamed and embarrassed. The truth is that my friends and I have had a little too much to drink and we were horsing around. My apologies."

"You are friends?" said one of the policemen. His uniform reminded Vassily of the German SS in the war. He was clean-shaven and he had a weak chin, like Himmler.

Vassily said: "Good friends. Crazy Russians! Drinking all night, I'm sorry to say. But we're all going home now, on the same flight. Well, we've managed to make complete fools of ourselves. I don't know what to say to you."

He looked at Oleg and saw that the big man had straightened and was holding on to the pain from his groin with a tremendous effort of will. Oleg's eyes were filled with tears and they darted backwards and forwards helplessly as he tried to follow the conversation in German.

Vassily held Oleg's gaze and repeated what he had said in Russian: "We are friends. We are all going home on the same flight." He added, first in German and then in Russian: "This young man has nothing to do with us. He got caught up in the middle of someone else's row."

Michael looked very flustered and Vassily could see the gratitude in his eyes when one of the policemen put a hand on his shoulder.

"Are you all right?" the officer asked him.

"I am. I do not know who these people are," Michael said, in stiff German. "I thought they were trying to prevent me from leaving. Perhaps it was all a misunderstanding."

"That's exactly what it was!" exclaimed Vassily. "I hope no harm has been done. In an instant, all these other Russian lunatics and I will be out of your hair and on our flight back to Moscow. Officers, I hope you will accept my sincere apologies for the disturbance."

The policeman was looking very doubtfully at Oleg, but the big man managed a wretched approximation of a smile. The Austrian shook his head, as if it was all beyond his comprehension and he would never get to the bottom of it. That was when Vassily knew they did not want to arrest anyone.

The other officer had taken Michael off to one side and was questioning him. The man and woman were wheeling their pram away, their heads bowed. The Russians grasped the opportunity to sidle away in ones and twos, watching the policemen carefully. Nobody stopped them.

Oleg came and stood next to Vassily. Vassily wanted to say something to Michael. He wanted to speak German, not English, and he was trying to translate it in his head. The phrase he was attempting to form was: *Tell the Lithuanian woman to kill him for me, if I don't get out of this.*

Oleg started to steer Vassily away toward the departure gates, taking the newspaper from him. Vassily was peering back, trying to get Michael's attention. But the boy was looking toward the door behind the Aeroflot desk, where the Russians had sprung from.

Vassily followed his gaze and saw two men standing next to the open door. Both were tough-looking characters with broad shoulders tapering to slender waists. They wore training shoes and tracksuits with white medical coats over the top. The taller of the two had a tiny bag in his hands, like a toy suitcase for a small child. The second man, half a head shorter but very stocky, was standing behind an empty wheelchair.

They were staring at Michael without animosity but with great professional interest, and he was looking back at them with an expression of horror. The boy appeared to have realized that the wheelchair was for him. It had leather straps with buckles that fitted around the shins and the forearms.

There would have been a syringe full of something in that bag for Michael too, thought Vassily. He was too far away to call out to the boy now. Oleg was gripping Vassily's upper arm and propelling him toward the gates at the far end of the hall. He had the newspaper rolled up tightly in one of his massive fists.

The last thing Vassily saw was the Austrian policeman closing his notebook and Michael walking away from him toward the escalators, free and unhurt.

Vassily took a deep breath as he walked. His ribs ached, he had sprained his left wrist and he felt as if all the blood vessels in his face had burst from the headlock. I didn't let them take him, he thought. Whatever happens to me now, that's one thing people can never say. I never gave anyone up to them.

When all the people involved in the fracas had left the ground floor of the airport, a tall, dark woman with a wide mouth came out from behind the Air France check-in desk where she had been standing and observing. She walked quickly to the main entrance, her heels echoing on the polished concrete floor.

She crossed the service road outside, passing a queue of dirty yellow Mercedes taxis. She walked across the patch of grass, studded with flowers, and came to the broad avenue that led back into the city. There were two lanes of traffic going each way and she had to wait a while for a gap. She took her chance and ran across. She was obviously used to running in heels.

A man was waiting for her in a Volkswagen Karmann Ghia. The window was down and she spoke to him for several minutes, quietly but with an agitated expression. Then she leaned in and they kissed for a long time, ignoring the looks from passers-by on the pavement and the satirical blast of a horn from a passing truck driver.

They exchanged a few more words, kissed again, and the young woman skipped back across the road. The driver sat for a while, watching her retreating silhouette with the appraising eye of a connoisseur. He was a strikingly handsome young man.

At the moment he turned the ignition key, the rear door on the passenger side opened quietly and another woman slipped into the back of the car. The driver pulled up the handbrake and put both his hands on top of the steering wheel where she could see them. He looked at her steadily in the driver's mirror.

Greta slumped low in the back seat. She took off her sunglasses and headscarf with one hand. The other was in her jacket pocket. She did not make a big show of having a gun but they both knew it was there.

"Take it easy," Johnny said. "We're on the same side here, right? Approximately."

"I'm surprised you can talk," Greta replied. "Are you sure you're not going to faint from lack of oxygen?"

"Margherita was shaken up," he said. "We didn't think they would try to snatch the boy. She managed to grab a couple of policemen and send them over."

"I saw that. She moved fast. It saved me a lot of trouble. Those air hostesses are really coming in handy, aren't they? Breaking up fights, delivering messages. Slipping newspapers into people's bags. Was that your idea?"

The Norwegian turned his head to glare at her, keeping his hands on the wheel. "Were you going to help Michael or were you just going to sit there? Maybe you want him to get caught. You want Karpov to know you're coming after him, right? Is that the idea? Force his hand?"

"Calm yourself, my little friend. Let's just wind the tape back. The first time I met you, you told me you were a jazz trumpeter. It turns out that you are actually a mathematician."

"I always tell women I'm a musician. It sounds sexier. Did you think you'd get a shot at Karpov today? Did you think he would leave Russia and fly here for this? That's why you're here, right?"

Greta said: "You are an expert in something called artificial intelligence, which I am not going to pretend to understand. You traveled to Russia recently to teach a course as part of an exchange program. What knowledge did you share with friends in Moscow?"

Johnny was very careful to keep his hands still. "It's not what you think. I'm not a trumpeter or a mathematician today. I'm an actor."

"Go on."

"I've been given stage directions. So have others. But no one knows who the other actors are."

"How intriguing. And who is giving everyone their directions?"

"I became good friends with a Russian man while I was in Moscow. An academic and a chess player. We kept in touch afterward. He has a daughter who is even better than him. I didn't believe it until I saw her play. He asked me to keep an eye on her when she came to London for a tournament."

"And now you're keeping an eye on Michael."

"They come as a pair, right? Him and the girl."

"So he tells me. And what's in it for you?"

Johnny looked at her as though he didn't understand the question. "Do you know what we were doing in Moscow, me and my Russian friend—when we weren't trying to reinvent the middle game? Bayesian analysis."

Greta shook her head impatiently.

"Working out the probability of humanity surviving a global thermonuclear war," he said. "We came up with a model. There were a lot of risk factors I hadn't thought of. The politics in Russia at the moment. He knew a lot about it."

She raised her eyebrows.

"The results of the analysis were not encouraging," said Johnny. "I like my eyes. I don't want them melting in a Shock Front."

He lifted one hand off the steering wheel but the bulge in her jacket pocket changed shape slightly and he put it back hastily.

"You know that we have a mutual enemy. Just listen to what I have to say."

Not a single muscle moved on Greta's face.

Johnny said: "It will take more than a boy in an airport to flush Karpov out. But there might be a way we can do it together."

Greta kept him sitting for a little while, watching the tension in his face, neck and shoulders with a hint of sadistic pleasure. Then she took her hand out of the pocket and rested it on the back of his seat. "I know you're not one of them," she said. "That's why you're still alive. I can see them coming from the other end of the street by now. You're a different kind of man altogether."

Her eyes were following his hairline and the day's worth of stubble on the side of his jaw. "All right," she said. "Let's go somewhere. I'll buy you a Scotch and Coke. Unless you're seeing your model later."

"Margherita is flying straight back out."

"Is that really her name? Presumably she was conceived after a night out at a pizzeria?"

"It could be the cocktail, couldn't it? Exotic, intoxicating . . ."

"Shut up."

Their mouths were inching close. Neither had blinked for a long time. When he came in for the kiss, she let his lips brush against hers then slapped him hard. Johnny's hand came up to his cheek and he gave her a wounded look.

Greta said: "You need something stronger than a Margherita."

34
MADRID, 1936-38

In 1936, when he was halfway through his medical studies, Vassily went to the war in Spain. His father had died and no one else could prevent him from going.

Getting permission to travel was hard, but he asked his father's friends from the regiment to lobby the government for him. He did not have to enlist in the Red Army, as other volunteers did, but he was obliged to join the Communist Party. He signed the papers cheerfully. It meant nothing to him. He was nineteen.

When he arrived in Madrid, he avoided all other international volunteers, Russians in particular. He wanted to be among Spanish people, using the language all the time for the small things and the big things. That was how you learned fast.

They put him on the line next to a boy of around the same age from the country near Valencia. His name was Manolito and his face was badly scarred from acne. They told Vassily to watch the boy and copy everything he did.

It was at the time when the Army of Africa was very close to the center of Madrid and there was fierce fighting in and around the area called the University City. Vassily's first job was to carry armfuls of books out of the libraries on the campus and help stack them to form barricades. A wall of books packed tightly together proved to be wonderfully bulletproof. When the firing started it brought him to the very edge of panic, but he did not abandon his post or disgrace himself publicly.

That was the day Manolito, the boy Vassily was supposed to be following like a dog, saw the Moors moving around on the top floor of the main university building, and noticed that the lights were still on, so the power must have been connected.

He ran across the quadrangle with a bag of dynamite, under fire from the Moroccans, put the dynamite into the lift, lit a couple of the fuses and sent the lift all the way to the top floor. You could still see the hole in the wall at the top of the building from the explosion, and afterward people clapped Manolito on the back and pointed up at it.

The oldest and toughest men in the line—the ones who had been officers in the army and navy and refused to join the Fascist rebellion—called him "the kid with the *cojones*," and everyone knew who they were talking about. Manolito said nothing, but brushed the hair out of his eyes and winked. He wore it long to cover his pockmarked face.

Manolito was a legend in the Republican ranks before he was twenty. One day, he was supposed to have been fighting next to a bombed-out house, a shell of a building with only the outer walls and a few wooden roof beams intact. He was said to have pulled himself up into the roof, and run along the main beam that went down the spine of the house like a tightrope walker—run, not walked—with a pistol in each hand, then jumped off the far end, dropping fifteen feet to the ground, without knowing how many of the enemy were waiting. There could have been a hundred. There were four: he stuck them up with the pistols and took them all prisoner.

Two people who did not know each other had given Vassily exactly the same account of these events, but a third man who had been close to Manolito's position during the attack roared with laughter when he heard the story, calling it ridiculous, and shaking his head at Vassily's credulity.

The Russian had only one Manolito story that he could tell from his own experience. At the height of the fighting in the university, they were in a position that was so close to the Fascist troops—a mixture of Spanish Carlists, Italians and Moroccans—that they could call to the enemy.

Vassily believed the Fascists were pulling back, and that the time was right for a bold attack, but the officers above him dithered and orders did not come for hours. Manolito peered over the barricade at the enemy line—a high, thick stone wall—and cursed incessantly at the delay. One of the enemy soldiers put an empty bottle on top of the wall and Manolito angrily whipped out his revolver and shattered it. He always closed one eye when he fired. It must have been thirty-five yards away. Another two bottles appeared and he destroyed them both without wasting a shot. There was a loud round of applause from the Fascists.

At the beginning Vassily was in the line for ten days. Then his section was rotated out. He went straight to the famous café that had never closed for a day during the whole of the siege of Madrid and ordered brandy and coffee for everyone. It was the sort of thing that one did. Vassily's hands shook so badly that he could not drink from glass or cup. He sat with Manolito and his cousin Nuria. Both of them saw the shaking, but did not comment on it. They had the Spanish manners.

The boy raised his glass and said: "Thank you, brother, but you know that we are POUM, don't you?"

Vassily blinked at him stupidly and the girl laughed. "We are both Trotskyists," Nuria said.

"What are you?"

"I don't know," said Vassily, and she burst out laughing again. "You have to be something," she said merrily.

"We're all on the same side, aren't we?" said Vassily, with a touch of anger. Both of them howled and slapped their thighs.

Vassily felt his face burning. "Well, what made you decide to become a follower of Trotsky? Come on, tell me some of his wisdom."

Manolito and Nuria looked at each other, then fell about again, only this time they were laughing at themselves.

Nuria said: "I don't know politics. I'm as dumb as a rock. We are from the same place: a village near Valencia. Everyone I grew up with is with Trotsky. It's like a football team. Don't you have a team?"

Manolito wiped his mouth with his sleeve and said: "He is a Stalin lover, like all the other Russians."

Vassily cried: "No!" He shuddered so violently at the thought that they really believed him.

"Well, what are you doing risking your neck here if you don't know which team you're on?" cried Nuria. They jeered and nagged at him and poked him in the ribs and repeated, "Why?" until he yelled: "I didn't want to end up being a mediocrity, like everyone else in my hometown!"

He said it so angrily that it could only have been the truth. Nuria gaped at him.

"You had better watch out," said Manolito. "All the Russians I know spit and cross the street when they see us coming. It's not good for you to be seen with Trotskyists."

"Just keep shooting the way you did today," said Vassily. "I don't care whether you follow Trotsky or Stalin or Lucifer himself."

The shaking did not stop, and Vassily worried that other comrades would see his trembling hands and consider him weak and unreliable, but they never did—or if they did, they never commented.

He found that he could still shoot and reload, strip and clean a rifle, and he still had the command of his legs, even if they felt weak and oddly weightless when he was under fire. Months later at Jarama, Vassily looked down at his hands during a pause in the fighting—which had been a business of stabbing, strangling and the clubbing of men with rifle butts—and he realized that they no longer shook. He studied the lines on his palms with great interest. They seemed the hands of an entirely different man.

The three of them went to the café that never closed after Jarama. They did everything together now. Vassily was spending so much time with Nuria and Manolito that he had begun to pick up their Valencian dialect and other volunteers called him "the Catalan." They sat in the square outside, watching the waiters gliding around the tables in their spotless white jackets. It was not exactly a celebration. The Republicans had not won the battle, but they had not lost. Madrid was almost encircled, but it had not fallen yet, and the friends were still alive.

Vassily was leaning in close to say something to Manolito when a man hailed him loudly in Russian from across the square. People at the tables around them turned their heads. The stranger was a stocky little fellow who walked like a boxer, leaning forward with his fists clenched. His head was too big for the rest of him. Vassily stood up slowly and the man went to him and embraced him passionately.

"Vassily Andreyevich! You are making quite the name for yourself. Recommended for a medal, I hear." People all around were looking in their direction, and the man said it again, louder and in Spanish: "He has been recommended for a medal for bravery!" There was a ripple of applause from the other tables.

The man pulled Vassily close and patted his back affectionately and whispered in his ear in Russian: "What the fuck are you? POUM, anarcho-syndicalist, union man? I know you're not one of us."

"I'm my own man, I hope."

"You should have checked in with me when you arrived, my individualist. Russian boys don't win medals here without checking with me first. They don't piss against a wall without checking with me."

People were still watching when the man gripped Vassily's head with both hands and kissed him hard on the mouth. It was a common gesture between men in the Soviet Union, but it was unknown in Spain. People stared.

"A medal," the Russian man said, looking at Vassily. "It's a good story. I might even write it myself."

When he left, Vassily sat down and wiped his mouth with the back of his hand. He saw that Manolito's face was very grave.

The Russian's name was Orlov and he described himself as a journalist. Everyone else described him as Joseph Stalin's eyes and ears in Madrid.

The hug and kiss in the square had a curious effect on Vassily's reputation. The officers above him in the Republican chain of command began to treat him with deference, assuming that he, like Orlov, had a direct line to the Kremlin.

At first, Vassily did his best to protest. He was an independent volunteer, he insisted, with no connection to the Soviet government. His friends knew this to be the truth but no one else believed him. Later he formed the idea that the myth of his powerful connections in Moscow might come in useful.

At the beginning of 1938, there was talk of a great anarchist column of thousands coming to relieve the besieged city, but nobody knew when they would arrive, or how it would be managed.

The leaders of the main anarchist and Communist groups had an unfortunate habit: they liked to assassinate one another. This had led to a certain amount of bad blood, and the current truce between the factions was an uneasy one.

There was a famous Ukrainian anarchist, once a lieutenant of the great Makhno, who went by the Spanish pseudonym Campon, and fought in Madrid under the black flag. He was supposed to be close to the anarchists in Barcelona and Navarra. The idea was that Campon would relay messages from the Republican leadership in Madrid to the commanders of the anarchist column as it approached the city.

By now Vassily's superiors were convinced that he was an important Soviet agent and protégé of Orlov, and out of a mixture of vanity, foolishness and a youthful desire to do good in the world, he did not contradict them. Vassily believed that Madrid would fall without the anarchist reinforcements and he had no time for the constant feuding between leftists who were supposed to be on the same side.

At the end of January, a message came down the line from the hotel where Orlov lived. The journalist was laid up with appendicitis. No other Russian speaker was available. Would Vassily meet the Ukrainian and relay any messages to the Republican commanders from the anarchist side?

Vassily believed that he had been given a small part in the great play of history, so he agreed to meet Campon in the café that never closed, where the waiters still wore white jackets and bow ties, at noon the following day.

Manolito said: "I don't like it. Why do you have to be alone?"

"It's a sign of trust. You don't have to come."

"There are a hundred other Russian speakers. I don't like it."

"Don't come, then. No one asked you to."

When Vassily walked through the doors of the café, as the bells of Almudena Cathedral were ringing for midday, Manolito was sitting at a table on the far side behind a bottle of Coca-Cola.

He had his cap on low over his eyes and both his hands were stuck in his jacket pockets. He had a surly expression on his lean, pitted face, like a teenage delinquent. Nuria was perched on a high stool at the bar, trying to get the barman's attention. Campon was already there, a large framed man with a thick black beard, sitting alone at a table for two in front of the bar.

The anarchist looked like a sea captain but there was no machismo about him. He had the mannerisms of a very quiet and cautious man and his eyes sagged from worry. He spoke educated Russian with only a hint of a Ukrainian accent.

Campon said: "Welcome, Comrade. I hope I can call you that?"

"Why not?" said Vassily.

"Your people have made things very difficult for us. Now we are all supposed to get together to save Madrid? The whole village pulling the calf out of the river?"

Nuria was trying to signal to the barman for a drink, but he was ignoring her. He wasn't one of the regular waiters and Nuria noticed that the white jacket fitted him badly.

Vassily said: "If by *my people*, you mean Moscow, I don't speak for them. I don't speak for Stalin. All I can tell you is what is happening on the Republican lines here in the city, where men from many countries are fighting together. And right now, no one cares if the bullets are Communist bullets or Trotskyist bullets or anarchist bullets, as long as we get more of them from somewhere, and we send them all flying in the right direction."

Campon narrowed his eyes and said: "Where is Orlov, anyway?"

"He's sick. I'm just here to listen, and pass on any messages. That's all."

"I have certain female acquaintances who tell me that Orlov has plenty of energy at the moment, yet he sends a boy like you to a meeting like this."

Campon looked at Vassily with great curiosity and an emotion that he could not read at the time but later identified as sadness.

The Ukrainian had been drinking a glass of beer. He suddenly drained it, and pushed his chair away from the table. He looked at Vassily for the last time and said: "This is the message."

He tossed the glass away from him and crouched under the table as it shattered. He moved quickly for a big man. The barman with the too-tight jacket grabbed a shotgun that was lying on a low shelf behind the bar and swung it up with both hands over the top of the bar and into the face of Nuria. She got a hand to the side of the barrel and it went off next to her right ear.

At the edge of the room, Manolito stood up and shot the barman in the temple with one hand from fifteen yards away. The hand that was not holding the pistol was still in his jacket pocket. One of his eyes was screwed shut. The shotgun hit the floor with a clatter but the barman seemed to stay on his feet swaying for a long time, a small red hole drilled in his temple.

Before the man hit the floor, Campon was up and heading for the door. Manolito shot him twice in the upper back, sending him sprawling out on to the pavement.

He reached out to try to grab something, but all that was within his grasp was a corner of the cloth from one of the tables set up outside for the lunchtime service. He yanked it toward him, pulling plates and cutlery and glasses on to his head.

Manolito walked over to Campon and looked back at Vassily, who shrugged. Manolito shot Campon in the nape of the neck.

They pelted across the square and kept their pistols in their hands so that no one would dare try to stop them.

When they got back to the room they shared, Vassily shoved the metal frame of his bed to the side and started to prize up one of the floorboards. Manolito went to the window and drew back the curtain an inch with his forefinger. Nuria sat on his bed with her head between her knees and both hands pressed to her right ear.

Manolito said: "It's all over. We are dead."

Nuria said: "You saved us. Come away from the window."

"I saved us and killed us at the same time. This neighborhood is already crawling with anarchists. They will come out like bees when the news spreads. There will be shooting all over this city tonight."

"We won't be here to see it," said Vassily. He took out a wooden cigar box from under the floorboard and tipped the contents out on to his mattress.

Nuria said: "Where? France, Mexico, North Africa?"

"I am writing a cheque," said Vassily. "Does your ear hurt?" Manolito went over, sat next to her on the bed and rubbed her back.

She tapped the ear. "I can't hear anything on this side but there is no pain now. Where are we going?"

Vassily said: "You go wherever you want. I am heading home. But I am writing a cheque first."

Nuria said: "What?" She turned her good ear to him.

Manolito said gently: "You can't go back to Russia now, brother. They already thought you were a Trotskyist. Now they will be sure that you are with us. Half of Madrid saw what happened."

Vassily said: "In fact, I am going to write two identical cheques. You can only cash one. I am giving you one each in case . . . you lose one."

When he finished writing the second cheque, he showed it to them with a flourish and they squinted to read his writing, then looked at him helplessly. He read the figure out loud, but it was in rubles, and they shrugged again. He clapped his hand against his forehead and tried to convert it into French francs. When he produced the number, Nuria inclined her head and blew out a breath. Manolito said: "Not bad."

"It's all the money my father left me. I won't be finishing my studies now. This will set you up in Marseille or Paris or wherever you want to go."

"Paris," said Manolito. "A friend of mine has a bar in Belleville. He can find us work. All of us."

"Head for the border now. Don't try to cash the cheque for three weeks. It has to be at the Bank of France. Nowhere else will accept it. If it doesn't work in three weeks' time, wait another week and try again."

Nuria spoke to him the way you speak to a child who is delirious with a fever. "Listen to me, Russian. You can cash this yourself when we get there. You are coming with us."

"I have to go home now to transfer the money. It will take a fortnight to get there, with a fair wind. I'll need another week to move the money into the account."

"Vassily," said Manolito, gently. "You cannot go back. One of Stalin's friends just tried to push you in front of a bullet that was meant for him. If this is the way they behave in Madrid, what do you think they are going to do to you in Moscow, in their back yard?"

"I can straighten things out. I will find someone who will listen to reason. I have a clean record. The Spanish Republic gave me a medal." He said it confidently, but he looked at the floor and not at their faces.

Nuria was cupping her ear and straining to hear. She exchanged a glance with her cousin.

Manolito shifted his weight forward on the bed. "Brother. You are not the only Russian on the line. They talk about how things are at home. Everyone is going to prison, even the ones who have done nothing. And now you have been corrupted by us, by the wicked Trotskyists. They will have a file on you anyway. After today, your Russian boyfriend will want you gone even more. He doesn't want you making trouble for him about this."

"Just cash the cheque," said Vassily, sadly. "They will confiscate it all anyway."

"Enough of this," said Nuria. "We are not going to let you go back to a firing squad."

"My sister is still there!" Vassily roared. His voice was so loud that it surprised all three of them.

Manolito went back to the window. He had the pistol in his hand and he mimed a shot, aiming at the distant spire of the cathedral.

"*Cabron*," he said quietly. "Bastard."

"That's how they do it," said Nuria. "Your mother, your sister . . ."

"That bastard Stalin," said Manolito.

Vassily stood up and went to him with the cheque. "You bought me," he said. "Back in that café. It's you and me now. It's forever." His voice was shaking and he was losing his Spanish.

Manolito still had the gun in his hand and the pommel bruised Vassily between the shoulder blades where it pressed against him as they embraced.

Nuria said: "Kiss him on the lips if you want to, Russian. I won't tell anyone."

Manolito told him: "We keep that money safe. Later on, you find us and you collect. With interest."

"Our love is forever, my brother!" sighed Nuria, fluttering her eyelashes and clasping her hands together.

Vassily said: "I thought you couldn't hear."

"It is coming back now," she said. "I think it is coming back."

35
MOSCOW, 1961

"Madrid," murmured Vassily. "Madrid." he moaned it like a woman's name. "Thank God I wasn't there at the end." Had he said this out loud?

There was something over his face, but he could feel a breeze from an open window. He heard someone ask a question. He heard Oleg say in reply: "Spanish." Oleg's voice came from the front of the car, on the right.

It took Vassily a few minutes to come round properly. They gave me a good slug of something, he thought. But not pentothal. His hands were in cuffs on his lap. His ribs hurt but were not broken.

He heard the rasp of traffic through the open window and felt the car inch forward in little lurches, then speed up suddenly. He could hear horns in the distance.

Vassily said: "Take the hood off. It's stupid. I know where we are. I know where we're going."

Light suddenly flooded in and stung his eyes. They were crossing the vast junction where Karetny Ryad met the ring road around Moscow, just as he had thought. They were in an official Volga, and there was another in front, going very slowly. The other motorists gave them a wide berth. No one dared sound their horn.

Vassily didn't know the driver but he knew the man next to him from the airport and from the night in the hotel in London before that. His name was Temir. He was so muscular he threatened to burst out of his suit and shirt collar. He had a scar that ran from the corner of his left eye almost down to his mouth. His hair was black and very curly, like a Turk or a Sicilian, and he used coconut-scented pomade.

As they slowed to go around the bend at Theatre Square, Vassily's cuffed hands instinctively edged toward the door handle.

"Locked," said Oleg.

The man with the curly hair peered at Vassily's hands then hit him just under the heart. Seated, it was hard to throw a proper punch, so it was more of a dig with the knuckles, a stiff poke in the top of the ribcage. Vassily still winced and saw squibs of light dance at the top of his eyes. He returned his hands to the middle of his body and tried to breathe deeply.

They were putting up a statue of Gagarin on the square, pulling it upright with steel wires hanging from a crane.

Vassily said: "I met him once. The chief space guy." Oleg's brow furrowed. "Gagarin?" he said.

"No." Vassily began to laugh but it hurt too much. "Of course not Gagarin. The designer. The guy who came up with the whole thing: Sputnik, then the dog. It was his dog. Did you know that?"

"Laika."

"She was a stray he picked up. They couldn't find another as smart as her so they had to send her. Everyone said they put her down with poison, but that was a lie. She burned alive in there. You know what he told me?"

Temir snarled at the word "lie" and balled his hand into a fist again, presumably planning to take revenge over this slur on Soviet honor, but Oleg stopped him with a raised hand.

They were crawling along Teatralny Proyezd and Vassily saw it for the first time: the northeast corner of the Lubyanka.

His voice was strained but he carried on: "He told me he wished he'd never sent the dog! He said it wasn't worth it!"

They were approaching the pavement on the side of Lubyanka Square and the cars slowed to a crawl, like hearses.

"Can you imagine, Oleg? The engineer who masterminded all the glories of the Soviet space program. The guy who put mankind into orbit . . ."

The car stopped. The driver and the man with the curly hair exited. They came around to Vassily's door and opened it. Temir reached in and helped him out. He stretched his hand over the top of Vassily's skull and steered his head under the edge of the doorframe with massive, wrenching strength.

Vassily was shouting now: "Oleg—he said none of it was worth it in the end. All that glory and progress. It wasn't worth the life of a single stray—"

Temir punched him in the solar plexus. It blew all the wind out of him and his legs buckled. Temir and the driver took his arms and held him upright.

They were standing right in front of the Lubyanka and Vassily remembered how ordinary it looked from the outside—just another grand office block in a city full of them. All the horror happened on the top floor, where none of the rooms had windows. Prisoners always believed they were in the basement. The vertigo of fear rushed through him.

Karpov had got out of the Volga in front and he walked toward Vassily now, grinning from ear to ear. He looked like a peasant getting ready to watch his daughter marry the landlord's son.

"Vassily Andreyevich! How are you feeling?" He touched a streak of dried blood on Vassily's forehead, then ran his fingers down his chest. "One of your fine shirts has been ripped, I am afraid. No matter. We have everything you need at this facility: new clothes, free of charge. But I am forgetting that you have been here before."

Karpov's eyes rolled from side to side theatrically and he leaned toward Vassily and said, in a stage whisper: "Do you remember that Estonian bastard?"

"Yes," said Vassily.

"You were a big help in that interrogation, if I remember correctly. A most enthusiastic assistant."

"No!" Vassily cried. He wriggled in his captors' grip and they tightened their hold on his arms.

Karpov pouted. "No need to get agitated. We've got your room ready for you. Nice new clothes, like I said. Three meals a day too. Oh—and medicine, of course!" He laughed. "Now what was the name of that thing we used to give them?"

"Haloperidol," said Vassily. He felt an intense, crushing tiredness. "Something like that. I will trust your medical knowledge. Do you know what it is, Oleg? It's a drug they give to crazy people to calm them down. But if you give it to someone who isn't crazy . . ." he inhaled sharply with a little whistle ". . . they worry, and fret, and start pacing up and down. They scratch themselves to death with their own fingernails!" He threw back his head and laughed uproariously.

Suddenly, Karpov decided it was enough. The smile died on his face and he spun around and jerked a hand at the guards who manned the gates. The shadow of the Lubyanka covered them all now and Vassily saw the gates begin to open to receive and swallow him.

He let his body go limp and the men holding him had to pull him. His feet, shod in their fine English shoes, dragged along the pavement like those of a crippled man.

In the end, the feeling that overwhelmed him was not fear, but sadness and shame at the things he had done to people on the windowless top floor of this very building, on the orders of men he had not been brave enough to disobey.

Someone shouted: "Stop."

They were almost inside the gates now and they heard the word again. A loud, shrill voice was shouting: "Stop. On the orders of the Supreme Soviet."

All their heads turned and they saw the curious sight of Madame Sorokina, the chairman's secretary, in a long pony skin coat and fur hat, made up dramatically as though she were heading out to the ballet.

She was running along the pavement toward them with Andrey. Two other soldiers with rifles jogged along behind them. Karpov looked at her in amazement, squinting horribly through his thick glasses. He motioned to the guard to keep going and the old woman shouted again.

"Comrade Chief Administrator. I am giving you a direct order from the chairman of the Politburo. You are to attend a meeting at the Kremlin at once. Comrade Vassily Andreyevich will come with me."

Karpov's face was purple and he was chewing his lip. The driver and the man with the curly hair had stopped, but they still held Vassily tightly. Oleg stood behind him with a hand resting on his shoulder.

"I beg you to stop and think, gentlemen," said Madame Sorokina. "This is a direct order. There is no possibility of disobeying it. Comrade Oleg Ilyich, if you do not release that prisoner, we will have to shoot it out in the street. It would not be the first time for me. I don't know about all of you."

She turned her gaze slowly from each man to the next. At last, her eyes rested on Karpov, somewhat contemptuously. He was chewing his lip and rubbing his hands together furiously, like a surgeon scrubbing up before theater.

Madame Sorokina stepped forward and took Vassily by the arm. The men standing on either side let him go without protest. She led Vassily a few yards away, then turned back to Karpov and the others. "The palace immediately, please, gentlemen. There is important news." Her coat was open, and as she turned, Vassily saw that she had pinned her battle honors to the sweater underneath. The brass medal in the center hung from an olive-green ribbon with a red stripe. It signified that Madame Sorokina—all five-foot-nothing of her—was a "graduate," as Russian soldiers say, of the "university" of Stalingrad.

Karpov marched into the meeting room first, brandishing the copy of *The Times* they had taken from Vassily in Vienna. "Comrade Chairman!" he announced. "I bring news. Grave and dramatic events—"

"Take a seat, please," said the chairman of the Politburo from the head of the conference table.

"A criminal plot," said Karpov. "Unprecedented. Vast in scope and ambition. It is only thanks to the men and women of the MGB—"

"Sit down, Maxim."

The others filed into the room. Vassily pulled a chair out for Anna. Madame Sorokina was about to close the double doors, shutting Yulia out, when Vassily darted over and whispered something in her ear. Madame Sorokina looked at the chairman, who made an impatient beckoning gesture. His secretary ushered Yulia inside and directed her to the long bench that ran along the back wall of the room as the others took their seats around the table.

"This man," said Karpov, pointing the newspaper at Vassily like a gun, "should be in handcuffs—if he is to be allowed into your presence at all. A traitor. Colluding with British spies for God knows how long. We are only now uncovering the roots of this *konspiratsia*, and beginning to understand how far it has spread through—"

"Sit down and shut up! Not another word!" The chairman slammed a fist like a ham hock on the table, making the glasses jump. He was a broad-shouldered man who had ploughed fields by hand as a boy. He weighed more than two hundred pounds. Everyone stared as the sound of his voice echoed around the room. No one had ever heard him raise it before.

When he had mastered himself, the chairman said: "You are in a state of ignorance, Maxim. You are behind the curve of events. I will bring you up to speed. Several days ago, Anna Vladimirovna came to me to inform me that she believed Sergei was attempting to communicate with his family via the chess column in a capitalist newspaper."

Yulia's anguished gasp of shock was audible from the back of the room.

"Naturally," the chairman went on, "this was a painful thing for Sergei's wife to divulge. It was also, I may say frankly, a story I found difficult to believe. I asked Vassily Andreyevich to investigate. He traveled, on my orders, to Vienna, in search of information being dangled in front of us by a young man connected to capitalist spies. The suggestion is that Sergei is attempting to arrange a meeting with his daughter in the city of Valencia. Naturally, there is a strong suspicion that our enemies are attempting to draw us into a trap.

"Nevertheless, my decision is that Anna Vladimirovna will travel to Fascist Spain with their daughter the day after tomorrow, accompanied by Vassily Andreyevich and whatever operational strength we can muster. We are going to see how this little game plays out. If Sergei shows himself, he will be reunited with his family and will return to Russian soil. If there is a threat from a foreign power lurking behind this, we will meet it head on."

Karpov exploded: "You cannot seriously consider entrusting this matter to the Fourth Directorate. There are more questions hanging over Vassily's conduct than I can count on my fingers. He is a criminal, a threat to national security . . ."

He trailed off. His voice had taken on a shrill edge and he had garbled the last words, as though he expected to be interrupted at any moment by another explosion of rage from the chairman. But none came.

The leader of the Soviet Union sat with his eyebrows slightly raised, his elbows on the arms of his chair, the left fist wrapped in the right palm.

"It is inconceivable," said Karpov, "that such a man should be allowed . . . to undertake an operation on foreign soil. Er . . . without . . ."

"Yes, Comrade?"

"Without . . . without . . ."

"Without supervision?" Karpov lapsed into silence. "I quite agree," said the chairman. "You have persuaded me, Maxim. Here is my order: you will assume personal oversight of the Spanish operation."

"Personal?"

"You will travel to Valencia yourself, Maxim. This matter falls squarely within your remit. The gravity of the situation demands nothing less than your personal attention."

They stared at each other. No one breathed. Vassily looked at the face of Karpov, then over at Madame Sorokina. She gave him a tiny nod that signified: *It is coming—get ready.*

When Karpov spoke at last, his voice was weak and wheedling. "Comrade Chairman! An old man like me . . ."

"Still draws a salary, paid by the Soviet worker. You are to liaise closely with Vassily Andreyevich now. That is my will. It is time we stopped squabbling between ourselves and learned to work together like Communists. Good morning to you all."

They lingered outside. Anna approached Yulia but the girl recoiled from her, with a shudder of horror. "Yulia," said her mother, extending her arms. The girl darted away, muttering something about the bathroom. She could not look Anna in the eye.

Karpov stood apart from everyone, staring into the middle distance.

Vassily caught his eye and winked at him. "Flying isn't too bad these days. You know what they have now? *Hostesses* . . ."

Karpov looked at Vassily absently. Then he launched himself at him. "Son of a bitch!" he screamed. "I'll send you back to Kazakhstan! This time I'll break your back."

Oleg got between them and Karpov hammered his pudgy fists against Oleg's chest. "You gluttonous swine," he gasped. It was like watching a tiny toy dog attacking a bemused Dobermann.

Karpov screamed again in animal frustration and staggered away down the long wood-paneled corridor. Oleg, Vassily and Anna watched him go. Oleg's mouth hung open.

Vassily whistled and adjusted the knot of his tie as he watched Karpov's lopsided progress.

"Kazakhstan, eh?" he said to Oleg. "Do you remember those days, old friend?"

"Don't," said Oleg, with a forced smile.

"Oleg and I were in the same camp for a while," said Vassily, glancing at Anna. "I remember you asking me once why he's always eating. Do you want to tell her?"

"Don't push me," said Oleg. His voice sounded strange and his whole body quivered. Anna felt all the destructive force that was bunched up in his massive arms and shoulders and she shivered with fear. It was like standing next to a landmine.

"It's a funny story," said Vassily, with a chuckle. "They had a tiny little cell under the main staircase. You couldn't lie down properly, and you got the marching feet above you all day long, so loud it could almost shake your brains out of your head. You could scream all day and no one would hear. They threw Oleg in there for something—or for nothing, more likely. Didn't they, old friend? He was supposed to stay in over the weekend, but Soviet bureaucracy being what it is, the guards didn't bother to write it up in the handover when they went off shift. They forgot all about him. How long were you in there for, licking the condensation off the windowsills? Could it really have been a fortnight? Ask him, Anna Vladimirovna."

Oleg was trembling violently now. At the mention of Anna's name, he glanced down at her, as though he had forgotten she was there. He was more than a foot taller than her.

She looked deep into Oleg's eyes, it seemed for the first time. She saw now that the thing inside him—the thing he was fighting to keep dammed up—was not anger after all, but a great frozen glacier of unshed tears.

"Thirteen days and nights," Oleg said to her. "They didn't feed me," he added in a very quiet voice. "They didn't feed me."

Yulia ran down to the first floor and went along the corridor that faced the rear of the palace, trying every door. The last opened. There was no furniture in the room, only dirty white sheets all over the floor, and a painter's ladder set up in the middle.

She went to the windows, parted the curtains and slid back the heavy square black bolts. One would not budge. She had to grip it with both hands and give it a shove, putting her bodyweight behind it. It made a clanking noise that seemed to reverberate, in her imagination, around the whole of the Kremlin and into the streets of Moscow, making every soldier and policeman and security guard for miles around turn his head toward her with a snap.

Yulia climbed out on to the ledge and the cold night air hit her, like a slap. She peered out over the balustrade and felt her stomach tighten. If you hang by your fingers from the bottom row of bricks, she told herself, the drop cannot be more than five feet.

She was lowering herself out of the window when a hand took hold of one of her wrists and yanked her back inside. She looked into Vassily's eyes. There was kindness in them, not anger.

"You overdid it with the sighing and the bowed head," he told her. "I knew you would have something up your sleeve."

Yulia looked back out through the window, scanning the grounds of the palace below.

"Andrey is not coming for you," said Vassily, quietly. "He is a friend of mine too."

She nodded several times. She looked defeated. But when he let go of her wrist she tried to rake him with her fingernails and he had to parry the blow with his forearm. She flew at him, snarling and spitting. "Snake. Chekist son of a bitch. Mother's c—"

He whirled her round and held her close to him, her back against him, his hand over her mouth. "I can't have you running off now. I need to keep you in my pocket for a little while. Let's go back before you're missed. If you promise to calm down, I will explain."

Anna was looking anxious when they got back to the landing outside the chairman's office. She was about to say something to Yulia, but Vassily shook his head and raised a finger to his lips. Oleg was sitting on a chair next to the paneled wall, still visibly stunned by his master's explosion. He had his head in his hands and his elbows were resting on his thighs. As the others were leaving, Vassily bent down and whispered an apology in Oleg's ear. His supply of pharmaceuticals had dried up unexpectedly, he said. There would be no more medicine for Maxim Karpov.

36

The house was empty when they got back, and cold. Yulia ran to her room and slammed the door behind her. Anna took a strong sedative as she crawled into the bed that was too big for her.

After fifteen minutes she felt a tug as it began to pull her down into unconsciousness. She kicked out in the bed and her head came off the pillow. It reminded her of times she had lain drugged in other beds—in hospital waiting for Yulia to arrive, or in a strange house in Khimki, with pictures from magazines glued to the bedroom walls.

Faces swam in and out of focus as the current took her down. A girl who had called her a whore on a metro train. An old man who had taken her hands in his and asked if she remembered him from the barricades in '41. She had not recognized him, but his words had set off a kind of drumbeat in her head, which she had not been able to shake off for days. It was the memory of the percussion of artillery fire, creeping closer.

Anna was supposed to be in Khimki on that day in the winter of 1941 to boost the men's morale. Sergei had fled to the east, like many others in the Soviet government, taking Yulia with him. Anna would not leave Moscow. She kissed the newborn baby's head dutifully but felt nothing when she watched them go.

She lurched through a breakdown in the weeks that followed, and she feared that her nerves would snap again as she flinched at the sound of falling shells. But Anna rallied on that morning in late October, as she always did when she had to perform in front of a crowd.

The men gathered round and removed their headgear while she stood on an ammunition crate and addressed them. "We are your mothers," Anna told them, "Your wives and daughters. Defend us from this evil. Do not abandon us to Them."

Afterward, a young cavalryman who had been promoted to the rank of major that very morning squired her around the defenses. The artillery fire was unrelenting and snatches of the "Horst Wessel Lied" had been heard from the west. The Germans could see the spire of St. Basil's Cathedral from their positions.

Anna watched the major address his men before a counterattack. His way of speaking was very different from hers. "Now they suffer, as we have suffered," he said, reaching out to take a battered Mosin rifle from the fretting hands of a boy not yet old enough to shave. The officer slammed the cartridge into its place and said: "Make them hurt." That was all.

He had the eyes of a man decades older. They had sunk deep into his face and were framed by cobwebs of fine lines. He had been in the line for thirty-three days without a break, refusing all leave.

There was a rumor of an imminent German attack and you could see the fear ripple through the men. The major touched Anna's arm gently and steered her out of the complex of shallow trenches and tank traps. She was astonished to see a commissar crossing himself and muttering a prayer. Her escort noticed her expression and smiled grimly. "There are no atheists here."

By late afternoon, none of the boys he had sent out on the sortie had returned. The major took Anna to a nearby house they were using as a communications post. It had been a pleasant family home once. They sat in the kitchen and he offered her brandy and a glass of tea. The shells were landing closer. They pounded the earth, like a petulant child. The young man sat in the corner with one leg thrown over the other and smoked as Anna sipped her tea.

"You are not afraid," she said. It had been a long time since either of them had spoken so he had to rouse himself and stir the gears of his brain into action. He was clearly very tired. He ran a hand through his thinning hair.

"People talk about conquering fear," he said. "It can't be done. Fear is as strong as a bull. All you can do is dodge it like a *toreador*. That's all I do. Try to keep dodging it. I've got my tricks."

There was supposed to be a ride back to the city for her, but it was too dangerous to drive now. Shells were landing on the main road. The thought of being stranded close to the front line should have terrified her, but all she felt was blankness.

In the evening, the major sat at the kitchen table to fill in the official forms for the families of men he had sent to their deaths. He attached a handwritten note to each. Anna excused herself and went into one of the bedrooms, taking the brandy with her. She guessed from the decorations that a teenage girl had once slept there.

She took a slim box out of the breast pocket of her overcoat and laid out the tablets carefully. It's a shame that young soldier will have to find me, she thought. But there is nothing to be done. I have reached my limit. That is all. She had the idea that the pills would work instantly and that she might lapse into oblivion before she could take the entire box. Of course, it did not happen like that.

Anna felt quite wide awake as she swallowed the last tablet with the last of the brandy. She lay down and let her arms flop back above her shoulders on either side of the pillow, like someone throwing up their hands in front of a gunman. It will be a sleep, she thought, and the end of all anxiety. Why don't I feel anything yet? It would be the final irony if the petty corruption that saturated daily life in Moscow meant that she had been supplied with sugar pills instead of barbiturates.

She did not feel unconsciousness stealing over her, but what seemed like a century later, something was pulling at her arms, and a strange image formed in her head: she was lying limp at the bottom of the swimming bath. A lifeguard was trying to tug her back toward the surface. Sounds came, but they were distorted by the weight of the water all around.

A man's voice. Strong arms raising her to her feet. She recognized the young major. He held her face tenderly, like a lover, with one hand. With the other he punched her hard in the pit of the stomach. There was an insane car journey through the northwest of Moscow, like a fairground ride. She looked out of the window through half-shut eyes. The major swerved around the rubble and the people in the streets. She could not understand why they were lying down.

In another house, an anxious young woman waited for them. Anna could not get out of the car seat, but planted her feet wide and bent forward low to vomit copiously between her shoes. The position of her feet and the nausea brought her back to the hospital where she had pushed Yulia out of her body. But these shivering waves were the opposite of birthing pangs.

There was salt and warm water and more spewing, until nothing came out but black bile. Later—she did not know if it was hours or days—she opened her eyes to see him standing over her in civilian clothes, very smart ones. He looked as if he had slept. He had a habit of running his hands through his remaining hair. The broken nose.

"I know what you're thinking." he said. "No, I'm not an angel. This isn't Heaven."

"Major . . ." she began.

"Please call me Vassily."

The young woman was his sister. When Anna could stomach it, she brought soup. The artillery fire was more distant now. Anna got up and walked around the tiny garden. Vassily came back one evening, and they talked. Anna pulled him down next to her on to the bed and fell asleep with his arm curled over her shoulder. He was gone in the morning.

The following week when he came again, she had been awake for most of that day and was eating solid food again. They talked for a long time and again fell asleep together. He was still lying next to her in the early morning when she woke up and they made love.

He was in the line for three days after that. When he returned, he was so broken that she had to kneel in front of him and take off his boots before he subsided on to the bed, drawing his knees toward his chest. Vassily woke with a start every few hours. He cried out once. He could not talk about what had happened, but now it was he who did not want to be left alone. They were facing in the same direction on the bed and her arm rested on his side.

When he could not get back to sleep, Anna talked to him soothingly. She tried to think of every piece of good news she had heard. Russia had nothing to fear from the Japanese, she said. The classified reports were clear on that. And she knew for a fact that the United States would enter the war soon. It was only a matter of time. The thought tormented Hitler, Anna said casually, as though she knew the German dictator personally. She had access to top-secret intelligence. Vassily listened in awe.

They made love again late that night and he spoke to her with great urgency and passion. Afterward, he was able to sleep without waking. When he got up to dress in the morning, she said: "They have given you another day's leave today. I arranged it. You have pressing official duties here." He was smoothing the front of his uniform in the full-length mirror next to the door, and turned to her sharply.

"I have good contacts," Anna said, watching his face carefully. "It is one day," she added gently, coming up on to her side and letting the top leg slide forward so that the knee touched the mattress. It exaggerated the curve of the line that ran to her waist and back to the hip. She saw his eyes take in the effect. "Please stay with me."

Anna fell asleep that afternoon, without meaning to, and when she came round in the evening, Vassily was sitting in the chair watching her. He had shaved and his sister had sponged and pressed his uniform.

He said: "I need something from you."

"Of course. Come to me."

"Not that. I need you to go to the East."

"We talked about that. It is my burden to carry. Yulia and Sergei are not your concern."

"I have never given them a moment's thought," he lied. "I am thinking about me and my men. You are sending us out there with antique rifles. I need submachine guns."

Anna sat up, rubbed her eyes and massaged the skin over her forehead.

"New factories are springing up across the East," she said. "They are churning out all kinds of things now. You will have new equipment soon."

"I will be dead before any of it arrives. Meanwhile, the Americans and the British are offering us everything: Thompson guns, Sherman tanks, Spitfires. The railway that comes down from Norway is still open. Why are we delaying?"

"Listen to you—a major talking like a general!"

"I talk to all kinds of people. The British are offering to supply us. Why are we dithering?"

"Because the boss doesn't want to stand there like a beggar with his hand out!" she snapped. "Perhaps you would like to go and argue with him."

"No. That is what I want you to do. That is your work now. It is in the East. Go."

"How dare you presume to give me orders? A little major! I am the eyes and ears of the Soviet worker. I will have you—"

She was shouting and bit her lip. Vassily's sister was washing the dishes in the kitchen next door, but the noise had stopped. The sister knew they were sleeping together but never mentioned it.

"Your true colors," Vassily said bitterly. "This is the only reason I went to bed with you. I was afraid of a firing squad if I refused."

Anna gasped and clutched at the bedclothes. Then she narrowed her eyes. "I see what you're doing. It won't work."

"I want you gone by the time I get back," Vassily snapped, rising to his feet.

"I am telling you this won't work. I am not going to get angry."

"You are too old for me. I need a younger model."

"It's not working, Vassily Andreyevich. I know that you have feelings for me."

She got out of the bed, went to him and reached up to touch his face. He tried to recoil from her but did not pull back far enough.

"No," he said. "No more of that." Anna did not know whether he was addressing her or speaking to himself. "I am a soldier again. In this room, I was your physician. Whatever happened here stays locked in the room. Now I want you to get your things and go." He was trying to sound angry but his voice was trembling.

"Look at you," said Anna. "My poor boy."

When he came back to the house after dark, she had gone. The bedroom door was locked and the key was on the kitchen table, next to a brief note informing Vassily that she had taken his sister east with her. They went all the way to Samara on a government train and Anna kept her safe by her side for the rest of the war.

By the summer of 1942, the Soviets had pushed Army Group Centre all the way back to the outskirts of Smolensk. Vassily was in the rear when a convoy of troop carriers arrived, carrying fresh recruits. He hailed one: "Come here for a moment, my well-fed child. What do you have there?"

"Anti-tank launcher, Comrade Major. We've all got one. Present from Mr. Churchill."

Vassily nodded approvingly, running his hands over the barrel. "Thank God for the British," said the young soldier, eagerly.

"The British," said Vassily sternly, "are capitalist, imperialist swine, whose day of reckoning will come. After we have gutted the Fascist beast."

The soldier's face fell, and he stuttered. He did not know how to respond. Then Vassily grinned. He winked at the boy, thumped him on the shoulder and pressed the weapon back into his hands.

37

It was the morning of Tuesday, September 26, 1961, the day before they were all due to fly out to Spain. Everyone was supposed to be working together now, sharing the MGB rooms on the second floor of the Kremlin, but Karpov made it clear that Vassily would not be allowed to set foot inside the door.

Karpov sat hunched in a chair in a private office just off the main room. He was looking at a map of the Moscow district on the wall. He had not slept or shaved. Oleg cleared his throat. Karpov did not look up. "They have brought the maid back in," he said politely. "If you want to watch."

"What is happening with our little English prince? Any sign of him?" Oleg shook his head in silent apology.

"What about the King?" said Karpov, after a long pause, his voice weakening again as it had in the presence of the chairman of the Politburo.

Oleg said: "No more news."

Karpov looked at the map on the wall again. Oleg had the horrible idea that his boss was fighting the urge to weep, but Karpov suddenly roused himself, snapped upright and marched past Oleg out of the room.

Karpov tramped down the corridor and opened the third door he came to. When he walked into the room, Masha, the maid, cried out: "No."

"Out," said Karpov, hoarsely. Simonov left the two of them alone together.

"Do you know about me?" Karpov asked her. Masha could not speak but she nodded.

"I had a girl who looked like you," he said. "I built a cage for her. She died before I could use it. Would you like to try it out for me instead?"

Masha wanted to shake her head but she could not. She shivered uncontrollably.

"You were telling him about the night the chairman came to Anna's house. You said they finished a bottle of brandy between them and he had to sleep on the sofa in the living room."

"Yes, Comrade." She stammered the word a little.

"Sergei was there too, wasn't he, that night?"

She nodded, biting her lip.

"Was he drinking too?"

Masha shook her head. "He rarely drinks at home. I've only seen Sergei really drunk once in all my time with the family."

"What was the occasion?"

"He was with Vassily Andreyevich."

"Those two together? Surely not. They are unlikely drinking companions."

"It was about a week or so before—"

"Be precise!"

She stammered again. Then her eyes lit up and she said: "I know exactly when! The night of the October Revolution dinner last year. Sergei brought Yulia home early."

"I was at that dinner," said Karpov, with a warning note in his voice. "Sergei was not at all drunk that night."

"Not when he came home with Yulia. They were with Vassily Andreyevich. Sergei said he was sorry to drag him away from the party and make him drive them home. It was Vassily's birthday and Sergei insisted he come in for a drink. I don't think they really knew each other. Both of them were just being polite. But they started drinking and they ended up talking all night."

Karpov nodded. "Anna stayed at that dinner at the Kremlin alone that night. I remember."

"She came back in the early hours. She was not at all pleased to see Vassily. He left immediately. He embraced Sergei like a brother at the door and Anna's eyes nearly came out of her head! She turned her tongue on Sergei when he had gone."

"I can imagine. But what on earth does a genius like Sergei find to talk about with a slime like Vassily, for the whole night?"

"I could not hear everything." Masha cast her eyes down to her hands, which were gathered in her lap. "They mentioned your name many times, Comrade Chief Administrator. I think they talked about Yulia. At one point Sergei shouted something like: *What future does she have here?* I think he meant his daughter."

"Sergei was agitated."

"Yes."

"Did he mention anyone else?"

"He talked about his deputy, the other comrade professor. He was worried about him. I think he was asking Vassily Andreyevich for help."

Karpov blinked. "His *deputy?* Are you talking about that Karelian fool?" He saw that the girl did not understand the word and said: "Never mind." *I must have spooked that snooty swine,* he thought. *It was just before the Revolution party. He went blubbering to Sergei. But what did I do at that dinner?* It was a blank.

Karpov rested his chin on his knuckles for a moment and considered the girl. She could not meet his gaze.

"How was Sergei feeling the next day? Suffering?"

"I don't know. He stayed up all night, hunched over a chess set. His wife was not happy with him."

"I should think not. But then, a week later, the shoe was on the other foot, wasn't it? His wife was drinking like a sailor with the leader of our great nation. Sergei refused that honor."

"He did not drink with them. He went to bed early and he was up and out of the door the next morning before I woke. He had already gone around the house clearing away the empty bottles."

"Clearing away the bottles. Indeed. Tell me this. Did the chairman bring anything with him when he visited that night?"

Masha managed a nod. She began to stammer again and he interrupted her.

"Was it a bag—like a doctor's bag? Old and worn?" She nodded. "There was something in there, wasn't there? And you looked?"

"Yes," said Masha.

"It's all right. I don't blame you. The leader of the Soviet Union in your house. You were curious. You took a peek. He was passed out on the sofa and you were cleaning around him. Something like that?"

"Something—something like that."

"What was it?"

"A document. I flicked through and I saw that it was military and it scared me and I did not read anything. I swear on the lives of my parents. I put it straight back."

Karpov ran a hand over the stubble on his face. He could threaten her, but it would make no difference. She could hardly be more scared. Still, at least he knew her parents were still alive. That could be useful.

"Do you remember if anything was written on the front of the document?"

She looked him in the eyes for the first time. She said eagerly: "It was strange because it was just one word. One black word in all that white space. It didn't say 'top secret' or anything like that," she added desperately.

"And what was the word?"

Karpov knew the answer already. He could picture the document. The last time he had seen a copy, it was being returned to a safe in a newly refurbished meeting room in the Kremlin.

The chairman's secretary put it back and locked the door of the safe, in accordance with the strict protocol that Karpov had drawn up personally. He had expressly forbidden anyone to take copies of the document out of that room, as a matter of state security.

"It was a word I didn't understand," said Masha. *Rhinemaiden.*

The others were waiting for Karpov in the operations room. They had been watching the interview with Masha through a two-way mirror.

Four desks were arranged around a big table. The MGB had a Xerox 914 photocopier—the only one in the whole of the Soviet Union. They had made copies of various pages from the newspaper that Michael had given to Vassily in Vienna, and these sheets of paper were laid out on the table. There was a wooden chessboard in the center with the pieces set up as though a game was in progress.

Everyone was standing: Oleg, Simonov, Berg and Kasha, the girl who had sworn into Anna's face on the Moscow metro almost exactly two months earlier. She was wearing a headscarf today too, and a shapeless thick gray woolen dress that covered her from the chin to the ankles.

Karpov took all of this in and said quietly: "She had the key to the whole thing hanging around her neck all the time. It took me two minutes to find it. You have been fiddling around with her for weeks. Explain."

Simonov looked around to see if any of the others were going to rescue him. They were all studying the floor. He swallowed and said: "Comrade Chief Administrator. It was the maid who first alerted us to the significance of the newspaper. And she has provided a lot of information about the British boy. Naturally, there are limits to her knowledge. She does not understand English . . ."

"She knew more than she realized. You have been too soft."

"We made the judgement that the girl would not respond well to pressure."

"Everyone responds to pressure!" Karpov roared. A little noise—the tiniest of whimpers—escaped from Kasha. Her hand wanted to rise to her mouth but she controlled it. It took Karpov a while to recover his composure and no one spoke.

"Keep pressing the maid," he said eventually. "She will know more. Take the gloves off. No limits. Have we got anything else out of the newspaper column?"

Simonov said: "We are combing through every word, every letter, as we speak. The cryptographers are crunching every possible combination."

"That means no. Have we made enquiries at the offices of *The Times* in London? I thought we had a connection there."

Oleg swallowed and said: "The King—"

Karpov raised a hand to silence him and closed his eyes. He gave the impression that he was struggling with something immensely painful. When he opened his eyes again, he looked the girl in the headscarf up and down. "I can never remember your name. They keep you away from me, don't they?"

Kasha's eyes were locked on a spot twelve inches in front of her feet.

"You are obviously trying hard to make yourself unattractive. Congratulations. You have succeeded."

When she didn't answer, Karpov said: "How are you finding the temperature in these nice new offices, my girl?"

"The temperature, Comrade Chief Administrator? It's—it's good." Oleg winced. You never actually answered questions like that.

Karpov looked around at the others. "It's good, she says. Perhaps it's too warm, if anything. Maybe it's making you all sleepy. Perhaps a colder climate would sharpen the mind." Kasha closed her eyes.

"Perhaps you think," Karpov went on, "that we closed all the camps when the Boss died? Maybe you think there's no gold left in the Arctic. I can assure you that there is, and they can always make room up there for a few guests."

Simonov said: "Comrade Chief Administrator, we are straining every muscle and sinew to interpret the very worrying chain of recent events. Every lead is being followed assiduously."

When Karpov screamed again Kasha could not prevent both her hands from flying up in front of her face. "Twenty-four hours! There are less than twenty-four hours before we fly out there. I want something good by then, or it's the gold fields for all of you. Results, or Kolyma."

38

VOLGOGRAD OBLAST, RUSSIA, 1920

"Cossack," shouted Maxim Karpov's mother. "Animal."

Maxim's father was crawling toward the front door of the house, watched by his wife and four children. Georgiy Karpov's eyes could no longer focus, but he dragged himself with determination across the rough wooden boards of the porch using his knees and elbows. How had he found his way back to the house in this state, along the unlit pot-holed road? The unerring homing instinct of the chronic drunk, decided Maxim. It was the summer of 1920 and he was ten years old.

"Marry a Cossack," said Georgiy's wife. "Oh, my mother and father."

The first story of the house was stone. Everything above that was wood. Maxim shared a bed with his brother on the ground floor, in a room that doubled as the kitchen. His parents and the girls slept above them. There was an attic room at the top, which the children were not allowed to enter. The pipe from the stove ran straight up through all three floors. In the winter they pulled the beds close to the pipe. Not too close, or you burned yourself.

As Maxim lay beside his brother that night, he saw his father creep down the stairs and pad into the room. Georgiy was searching for something in the kitchen cupboards—the ones he had made with his own hands out of pine the year before Maxim was born.

Georgiy left the door of the top cupboard open, then bent down to look in the bottom one. When he straightened up, he banged his head hard on the sharp edge of the open door above. He did not cry out, but sank on to his haunches and spread the fingers of one hand wide over the top of his skull. Maxim had never seen a man look so much like an ape. He watched his father turn toward the bed and screwed his eyes up tight.

The next evening, Maxim and his brother, the two girls, his mother and his grandparents all had to stand outside in the yard. Georgiy took off his shirt and handed it to his father.

Then he removed his belt and gave it to the priest. He was wearing his new leather boots and riding breeches. Stripped to the waist, his father could have been a wrestler or a circus strongman. It was after the harvest and the men from the district had spent the last week tossing bales of hay high up to the top floor of the barns that dotted the fields. The men coiled themselves and bent their legs then suddenly uncoiled, snapped straight and twisted, all at the same time, and the heavy bales sailed into the air over their heads without effort, again and again.

The Cossack men of Maxim's youth were wiry and strong, with sharply etched abdominal muscles. It was something he thought about increasingly as he became older, and watched his own body deteriorate into pudginess. It added to his lifelong conviction that he was a changeling—that the family he had grown up with were not really his blood relations.

His father knelt low before the priest, touching his forehead to the ground, and the priest commenced to whip his back with the belt. The sound of it was hard to bear and it was not long before Maxim's mother cried out. His grandfather looked at her and silenced her with a harsh word. Blood coursed down his father's back.

Sobriety did not improve Georgiy's mood. He did not like to see his younger son when he was with his friends—the boy's puniness and timidity were an embarrassment.

Maxim was playing with the neighbor's child in the yard one day when he thought no adults were around. He happened to be swearing loudly when his father emerged from the privy behind him. Maxim was cursing gleefully at the other boy and did not see his father until it was too late. He received a cuff around the side of the head that laid him out in the dirt and made his head ring for days.

Four families shared the wooden washhouse. It stood in a compound surrounded by a high pine fence behind the Karpovs' yard. The men and women used it on alternate days. On Sunday morning, his sisters went to wash with Yekaterina, the oldest girl from next door. She was fifteen and had a woman's breasts.

There was a knothole in the fence, in a section covered by a holly bush. No one could see Maxim as he stood on tiptoe and peeped. On that morning, the door of the washhouse swung open and a big cloud of steam wafted out, drifting away over the yard. Maxim saw his sister in her undergarments, pinning her hair. Then, miracle of miracles, Yekaterina walked past her, bare-breasted.

Her hair hung down behind her. She was singing something and trying to get the others to join in, waving her hands in the air, like a conductor. Her torso was as perfect as a statue of a Greek goddess. There was a fever in his forehead and a metallic taste in his mouth.

Maxim reached inside his trousers and moaned. His desire was mixed with anger: the girl's wantonness was responsible for making him lose control of himself like this. A hand with a formidably strong grip seized him by the shoulder blade. When she pulled him out from behind the bush, Maxim's mother could see the bulge in his trousers.

His father's voice was very level. "So," he said. "You have decided to become a beast?" Maxim did not reply. "Human beings do descend to the status of beasts sometimes. It is a sad fact. Perhaps we should keep you chained up in the yard from now on, like Zhuchka, and throw you scraps."

The boy was so afraid that it was effectively a physical illness. He thought: I am going to be sick. I'm going to faint. Why can't they see I'm unwell? Why does no one call a doctor?

His father said: "I am going to show you. I will show you."

Maxim could never quite remember the next few minutes in their entirety, although fragments surfaced in later life. He recalled being held down by his male relatives, and appealing to his grandfather for mercy, and seeing the old man shake his head. Karpov remembered looking back over his shoulder and seeing a great black figure, exaggerated to huge proportions in his imagination.

The figure extended an arm and there was something in the arm that formed a straight line, pointing down at the boy. In that moment the shape was not that of a man but of a creature with monstrously long limbs. Maxim remembered the shock of the bucket of icy water they dumped on his back afterward, and he remembered watching a sheet of blood mixed with water run across the ground. It was his own blood, and the sight of it made him retch.

After the beating, he crept around the house like a cat. He could hardly hold himself upright, but he was obliged to be quick on his feet whenever he saw his father.

When the period of penance was over, Georgiy began to drink again. One evening, Maxim came into the kitchen and his father was sitting with two other Cossack men. Georgiy did not see the boy until one of the men said something. Georgiy glanced over his shoulder and, without hesitation, picked up a small metal saucepan from the table and flung it at Maxim. It was not supposed to hit him, but it did.

The boy wept afterward, reflexively. He also began to think very quickly and clearly. He began to believe truly that, sooner or later, his father would kill him.

The Bolsheviks had their office on the main street, directly opposite the barracks. It was the only part of the village lit with gas lamps. All the buildings were made from wood. In a different time, it might have been beautiful. Later, when Karpov watched films set in the American west in his private cinema, the clapboard houses of the frontier towns reminded him of the southern Russia of his boyhood. The Bolsheviks called the building their "shop front." Local people were supposed to come in and pass on information about the Cossack rebels, or air grievances with the way the district was being governed. No one ever did.

The political commissar, Balakin, was behind his desk reading a novel when Maxim walked in. An older man—an army officer—was sitting by the corner stove, cleaning a pair of boots. Kudinov's uprising the year before in the neighboring district of Rostov had shaken the Reds, and both men kept their rifles close to them.

Balakin stared down at the boy as he removed his hat. The commissar had very intense eyes that disturbed people. He always looked a little drunk. Maxim pulled out the White newspaper and laid it on the desk. Balakin's eyes became even wider than usual.

On the front page was a caricature of Lenin. The Soviet leader was reaching out with impossibly long arms to strangle an elderly peasant. A cartoon Trotsky lurked behind Lenin, his face squashed and Satanic. There was a Star of David around his neck and he rubbed his hands together.

Balakin looked up at the boy. "Where did you find this?"

"I know the man who makes them. He has a printing press set up in his attic. He also has an illegal still up there."

"Take us to him."

"First I need to know what will happen to him, and to me."

The army officer had put down his boots and walked over to the desk. He eyed the newspaper with interest. There was a hint of amusement in his face.

The officer said: "If you are really talking about a man printing this stuff and distributing it, the sentence is death by firing squad."

The commissar said quickly: "There will be a reward for you if you help us."

"I will need a place to stay."

Both men stared at him. They made him say it again.

"This isn't a hotel," said the officer. "Come with me for a walk outside. We will discuss this like two men and get to the bottom of what this is all about."

"Wait," said Balakin, excitedly, raising a hand. "Why do you need somewhere to stay?"

"Because the man I'm talking about is my father."

The commissar's face broke into a gleeful grin. The officer turned pale.

At the execution, Karpov tried to look but he had to turn away at the crucial moment, and he threw up against a wall. Balakin slapped his back. The army officer had his eyes closed.

The three walked back across the street from the barracks to the Bolshevik headquarters. Soldiers were holding back a crowd of local people. Karpov's mother and grandfather were at the front. When the old man saw the boy, he began to scream obscenities. Karpov could not hear the exact words. His grandfather suddenly looked much older. He shook his fist at Karpov.

After that the soldiers let the boy stay in the guardhouse. He polished boots and was supposed to fetch food and cigarettes, except that the shopkeepers refused to serve him, and the other children spat when they passed him in the street. Karpov added the names of everyone who insulted him to the deportation lists.

His knowledge of local affairs made him useful to the Bolsheviks. He obtained the names of Cossack men who had gone away to join Kudinov's rebellion so that measures could be taken against their families. A letter came from Moscow that referred to the young boy's efforts obliquely, without mentioning his name, and with that slender shoot of official praise came Karpov's first experience of power.

On his twelfth birthday, Karpov presented himself to Balakin and asked him to write a letter of recommendation to the national police cadet training college in Petrograd. Balakin sneered at the boy's presumption. Karpov gently let it be known that he had been a witness to sordid bourgeois crimes among the men of Balakin's command. He might, under certain circumstances, be obliged to report these lapses of discipline to a higher authority.

At the police college in the city that had just been renamed Leningrad, Karpov was one of the slightest and weakest boys. He quickly established himself as someone to be feared. He specialized in collecting written evidence of the other cadets' misdemeanors.

In his final year, a wretched classmate called Vitaliy fell in love with a younger boy and declared his feelings in letters that came into Karpov's possession. Vitaliy pleaded with Karpov, falling on the floor before him in abjection. Vitaliy had a twin sister.

The oldest boys were sixteen now, and they cut a dash around the city in their black uniforms. Karpov took Vitaliy's sister out on a Saturday evening. Everything proceeded exactly according to convention. He bought her Syrniki with jam and Napoleon cake. They walked stiffly around the fairground on Admiralty Square, arm in arm. They spoke only occasionally, and very formally.

After they dined, Karpov took a room in a house in the Vasileostrovsky district. There was a handbasin in the corner and he waited outside and smoked while the girl cleaned herself. His knowledge of the female body was scant, and he did not fully understand what she needed to do.

When he went back in, she had arranged herself for him on the bed. He turned her over roughly and the sight of her exposed buttocks and her cries of shock and outrage touched something white-hot inside him.

He beat her with his belt, feeling a sense of slow unfolding ecstasy. He entered her clumsily and ejaculated almost immediately. Afterward, the look on his face made the girl shrink from him, pulling the bedclothes around herself. She told her brother that she feared Karpov would murder her if there was a second assignation.

The following week, the day before his class was due to pass out of the college, Vitaliy jumped from the palace bridge into the deepest part of the river Neva.

39

LONDON, 1961

Greta slept badly in an unfamiliar room. They came to her every night now—the dead.

It was the last week of September 1961 and she had moved her things into Johnny Jensen's flat in Covent Garden. When she came back on the third night he opened the door for her at the top of the stairs, his face the color of ash.

Greta said: "There's no need to look so terrified, my little friend. It's only for a week. I promise your virtue is safe."

Johnny said: "Someone's here for you."

Yakuv's eyes burned up at her from the sofa where he was lounging. Then he cast them mournfully over the chaos of sheet music and empty coffee cups that covered the table in front of him.

"I spoke to the Lithuanian envoy. An old acquaintance. He told me curtly that you were no longer resident at his embassy. He refused to give me your new address, but I made enquiries. Your landlord here was kind enough to invite me in."

Johnny's face colored. Greta said: "It's all right." When he didn't move, she said: "Please."

The Norwegian picked up his trumpet from the armchair and said: "I'll be in my room if you need me."

"Splendid fellow," said Yakuv, when Johnny had left them alone together.

Greta said: "I had a row with the envoy."

"Old friends like you? Falling out? A pity."

"He doesn't like the way I talk to his hulking sons. He doesn't approve of some of my methods, or my choice of targets. He thinks I'm going to bring the wrath of the police down upon us, and that the British will kick him out of his townhouse."

"This is what happens when you put a fox in a kennel. He gets too comfortable."

"I work better alone anyway."

"No Mindaugas?"

"Not for this job."

"What about me?" Yakuv asked lightly, looking at his cuticles. "When will you let me settle our debt?"

"There is nothing to settle. We've been through all this. They were already dead by the time I got there."

It was a long time before Yakuv could speak and his voice was different. "They were *Jews*. I didn't believe you. I left them to their fate."

"It wouldn't have made any difference."

Yakuv stroked his beard with his fingertips for a little while. Then he leaned forward and tapped his knuckles on the table. "I hear things about you, little vixen. You've been poking a bear with a stick. It's coming out of its lair at last."

"It's true that I'm hunting big game."

"And did you give a thought for what might happen afterward? Did you think you would just be able to come sauntering back to work for us as though nothing had happened?"

"It doesn't matter. Everything ends on Friday."

"Where?"

"Spain."

"What do you need?"

She raised an eyebrow and Yakuv smiled.

"Did you know that my queen in Jerusalem was our ambassador to the Soviet Union in the forties? It left her with a deep and abiding hatred for Stalin and all his crew. She has empowered me to offer you logistical assistance: a car, firearms, travel documents. All deniable, naturally."

"Naturally. All right. I could make use of a couple of passports. I'm taking a young man with me."

"Is that wise?"

"He will only make his own way there anyway. I would rather know where he is."

Yakuv shrugged, then got up abruptly. "Let me know what you need. You will have it within twenty-four hours."

"Thank you. And please don't be angry. I have to do this one on my own. Wish me luck for Friday."

"You?" he said, walking toward the door. "Luck? All right, then. Good luck and long life."

"And *what*?"

"Long life."

She waited until he had shut the door and his footsteps were descending the stairs before she threw back her head and laughed long and loud.

40
SPAIN

Vassily was the first of the Russians to arrive in Valencia. he sat on a high stool in a bar in Cabanyal, reading *Las Provincias* with an expression of distaste. It was the quiet time between the beer and snacks of mid-morning and the hour of the aperitif.

A young man came in, stood at the bar two yards away and ordered a *cortado* in serviceable Spanish, took notes and coins from his pocket and started counting them on top of the bar. He did not acknowledge Vassily and Vassily did not look up from his newspaper. When the barman turned his back on them to make the coffee, the young man pushed a scrap of colored paper down the polished wood toward Vassily.

The Russian took a square piece of paper from the inside pocket of his linen jacket and laid it on the bar as well. When pushed together, the pieces formed a red and white ten-ruble banknote that had been cut in two, slightly off-center to avoid desecrating the face of Lenin. The serial numbers on both halves were the same. Vassily folded them away in his pocket.

The young man paid with Spanish coins, then drank the *cortado* in one swallow. When they went outside, the heat, the bright blue of the sky, the sea tang in the air and the life and energy of the streets hit them, like a wave. Vassily smiled his wide-open peasant's smile and turned to the young man. He had been with the woman and the pram at the airport in Vienna. "So," said Vassily, "the Bulgarian State Circus is in town."

The young man had reserved a hotel in the Carmen district that the Bulgarians had used before. There was a café on the ground floor of the building and four rooms for rent on the floor above. The woman who ran it had inherited the place from her parents. She had been married to a North African Communist who blew himself up while trying to infiltrate the Algerian nationalist movement in 1956.

The woman did not openly declare her sympathies, but she often took in officials from the Soviet Union and its satellites at preferential rates. She paid them many small kindnesses.

You went through the café and walked up a small flight of stairs at the back and there was a heavy door you had to get through to reach the corridor where the rooms were. They liked the security of having an extra door with a lock between their rooms and the street.

Karpov and Oleg were to sleep in single beds in the largest room, just off the staircase. Anna and Yulia would share the room at the back with the red-haired Bulgarian woman who had been pushing the pram in Vienna. All the others, Russian and Bulgarian, had to doss down as best they could in the two rooms between.

Anna and Yulia swept into the city by train. They were supposed to show themselves openly. They walked out of the magnificent station and made their way through the heat north into the Carmen. Anna tried to link arms with her daughter as they walked but Yulia pulled away from her.

Only one man followed them on foot, very discreetly. Vassily saw to that. He had no control over the manner of Karpov's arrival. The chief administrator's men had tranquillized him for the flight to Marseille and he had spent the night sleeping fitfully in the back of a cramped Simca they had hired. Karpov was disoriented and as crabby as a tired baby when the car wove its way through the tiny streets of the Old Town in the early hours of Thursday morning. Oleg and Temir had to hold him up as they got him from the car to the rear entrance of the hotel.

It could have been worse, thought Vassily. A passer-by would have thought he was an old drunk being helped to bed. A professional would have made him a long time before he was finally squeezed, cursing, through the back door.

There were four teams, doing six-hour shifts. They had three cars between them and a good Czechoslovakian VHF field radio system. The plan was simply to allow Anna and Yulia to be seen and to wait for someone to approach them.

Anna exploded when they told her what they wanted her to do: "I'm not just going to sit in the window like a whore in Amsterdam!" At this point Vassily expected a nasty crack from Karpov but none came. In truth, the chief administrator appeared to have little spirit left. He hardly spoke to the others, and refused to leave his room in the hotel for any reason. His hands trembled when he performed small tasks.

Vassily slipped out early on the Thursday morning without telling anyone where he was going. Oleg shoved him up against the wall when he returned. Vassily said: "Calm down. You'll make yourself sick." Oleg cocked a fist at him and Anna had to lunge between them in the corridor as they bristled and swore at each other. Suddenly she clutched her head and slumped against the wall in a kind of swoon and Vassily caught her, glaring at Oleg.

He laid Anna on the bed in her room and the Bulgarian woman fussed around them, looking for painkillers. Yulia sat on her own bed with her knees drawn up to her chest, staring silently at her mother. The rule was that the Bulgarian woman never left Anna and Yulia in the room by themselves. But Vassily broke the glass he was filling with water, and the woman ran downstairs to get another from the bar.

When she came back up and pushed open the door, Vassily had dragged Yulia off her bed and pulled her close to her mother. He was holding her arm tight and all three of them were whispering fast. They stopped instantly when the Bulgarian woman walked in. She only caught one word: *vera*. Trust.

Thursday afternoon stretched out long and lazy and the street outside teemed with tourists and local people laden with bags from the market. A girl sold flowers at a stall right opposite the ground floor window of the café where Anna now sat. She had rested on her bed for half an hour, then insisted on taking over from Yulia.

She was pretending to read a novel, which had been selected for the big, bold Cyrillic letters on the cover. A tiny old blind man was selling lottery tickets and cigarette lighters from a tray around his neck in the street outside. He called out every minute or so in the Valencian dialect.

The woman who owned the place was fussing behind the bar downstairs. Vassily had wanted to sit behind her on a low chair, where he would be close to Anna but hidden from the street by the bar. Oleg objected. He was still angry with Vassily. In the end, both men sat together behind the door at the top of the stairs, watching through a crack. If Anna stayed by the entrance, they could see the back of her head.

"You're a fool if you think we haven't already been made," said Vassily. "There are only two possibilities: Sergei is on his own out here—or he's got British intelligence or God knows who behind him. Either way, they're smarter than us."

Oleg said: "You'd know all about British intelligence, wouldn't you? Don't think we've forgotten about you. Wait and see what he does to you when we get back."

Vassily pulled away from him. Oleg grabbed the sleeve of his suit jacket and snarled, "You don't wander off on your own from now on."

The front door of the café opened and both men craned their necks to see through the crack what was happening. The little old lottery man had opened the front door and was groping his way in, prodding at the floor with his white stick. The woman behind the bar clicked her tongue at him.

"You're worried about my safety," whispered Vassily to Oleg. "That's very touching."

"I don't have any customers for you," said the woman who owned the hotel to the blind man.

"Or could it be that you don't trust me?" hissed Vassily with a smirk. "After all we have been through? It's like a knife in my heart."

They could not see the blind man now from where they were, but they could hear Anna talking in Russian.

"This lady does not speak Spanish," said the owner to the lottery seller gently. "She will not be here when they draw the numbers." She was steering the man gently back to the door.

"I'm sticking to you from now on," whispered Oleg. "You don't shake me off."

"Vassily," said Anna.

"All right, but I've only got a single bed. I hope you don't still snore."

"Vassily!"

He ran out into the street after the blind man and there was no sign of him in either direction. There was no way a man could move that quickly if he was shuffling along with a stick. Vassily bought a single rose from the flower stall and asked the girl if she recognized the lottery seller. No. He was not the usual one who sold the tickets in this district.

Vassily handed the rose back to the girl, went inside and plucked from Oleg's fat fingers the book of matches that had appeared on the table in front of Anna. It had a black horse on it, and the name of a famous café on the Plaza de la Virgen. There was a single Russian word handwritten above the horse's head: *polden*—midday.

"So, it's noon tomorrow," said Vassily. "It will be hot by then."

He followed Oleg up the stairs and watched as the big man started banging on doors and shouting orders.

"I mean, do what you want," said Vassily, "but there's no point in trying to sniff around the café now. Whoever this is already has the drop on us and they're going to see us coming a mile off."

Oleg glared at him, then came over and snatched the book of matches out of his hand as though Vassily had illegally appropriated a piece of Soviet state property. Vassily shrugged his shoulders as if to protest his innocence.

He went back to the door at the end of the corridor and settled himself on the floor, sitting cross-legged. He could see the back of Anna's head through the crack. He glanced down at the Swiss watch on his wrist. He missed the Strela. It was his talisman, but if you wore a Strela chronograph on a foreign job, you might as well have a sign hung around your neck with "Russian Intelligence" written on it.

Well, Vassily said to himself, I've done everything I can. All the pieces are in place.

41
LITHUANIA, 2004

Lunch arrived in the café by the castle in Vilnius: salad for Indrė Žukauskienė, and Samogitian pancakes with cream for Greta. "I can't be bothered to pick at my food anymore," the old woman said. "It's one of the compensations of old age. There are very few."

They had been talking without a break for several hours and Indrė had filled her notebook. It was good to pause for twenty minutes and collect her thoughts.

After they had finished eating and the waiter had cleared away the plates, Indrė took a photograph out of the leather organizer and said: "I can't wait any longer to ask. Who is this handsome fellow?"

The young man was sitting. He wore high leather boots, rough breeches, a tunic and a black cap, like a Russian sailor. He had pushed the cap back and was chewing a stem of dried grass. A tall boy with big, rough hands. He seemed pleased with who he was.

"I don't know about handsome," said Greta, holding the picture out at arm's length. "He was quintessentially Lithuanian—as tall as a tower, with that cherub's face. Not exactly good-looking. Why are you laughing? Am I describing your husband?"

Indrė nodded guiltily.

"Well, you know what they're like. I don't suppose they've changed much. The women here are so beautiful, but the men are not often handsome. So they have to have something else about them, don't they? This one had the fine old sense of humor that the country people used to have—where you always make yourself the butt of the joke. We laughed all the time."

Indrė had one eyebrow raised.

Greta said: "You're too polite to ask. I'll tell you anyway: yes, he was my first. The girls always made jokes about me being a seductress, but it wasn't true. I had no real experience of boys before I met this one. Give me the map there. We were around . . . here. The woods were teeming with people coming and going at that time—bumping into each other on the forest paths. There were German patrols in the area, and different kinds of partisans: Soviet fighters, people who had crossed over from Belorussia. There were supposed to be some Jews who had broken out of Fort Nine near Kaunas, but we never found them. We thought we were some canny operators by then but, by God, this boy and his friends got the jump on us. I was napping and one of the girls was supposed to be standing guard and she suddenly felt a gun barrel brush the hair away from her neck. We stuck our hands up. It was a miracle that they were Lithuanians."

"So, this was the partisan band that you joined up with in 1942? And was he the leader—the boy in the photograph?"

Greta snorted. "Certainly not. This lazy little princeling was the leader's son. And, yes, they let us join. Eventually. We spent the first few days as prisoners with our hands tied. Can you guess why?"

Indrė shook her head.

"Well, they had been stalking us for hours, close enough to listen to all the nonsense we were talking, and . . ."

Indrė's eyes widened. "You weren't . . ."

Greta nodded. "We always spoke German when we were alone together. Can you imagine how hard it was to convince them we weren't Nazi spies? Of course we told them our names and our life stories, and he sent people to make enquiries about us. He was obsessive about security."

"The boy's father? You said he was the leader? What was his name?"

Greta grimaced, as though feeling a twinge of pain from an old injury. "I still can't say it out loud. I don't know why, after all these years. A kind of superstition. We addressed him as 'Colonel.' That was his rank in the old army of Lithuania—the free Lithuania that lasted for a while between the two world wars. When the Russians came in 1940, they tried to convert some of the regiments into Soviet units. I don't think it was a success—like dragging donkeys uphill, I imagine. But a few officers, like this man, went along with it. On the face of it, he appeared to have become a loyal Red soldier, meekly accepting orders from Moscow. All the time, he was planning. Making friends, buying guns—or stealing them, hiding them. And thinking, thinking, thinking. I don't know if I can describe him to you.

"He was not as tall as his son, and he was slight and very frail by the time I met him. He had the wasting disease that cannot be cured. Nowadays he would be in a wheelchair. He was out there in the woods, hobbling along on crutches on the good days, being carried around on a stretcher on the bad ones. When he was really weak, they laid him by the fire and he rolled on to his side and poked a stick in the soil, drawing diagrams. We sat there with our legs crossed. It was a schoolroom. Like this."

She picked up a pen and began to draw parallel lines on a triangular white napkin.

"This is a salient, now it becomes a breakout. Here comes the counterattack. Here are the supply lines. Now the breakout is encircled. This is how German infantry fight—always moving, circling, circling, outflanking. But with a sharp stick in the mud, or the ashes of the fire, all scratched out at the end. He was the one who really taught me my trade. I had always been able to shoot straight, but now I became a really effective sniper. I learned to read the weather properly. When the sky is blue on a winter morning, it is an anticyclone. The high pressure means you must aim a little higher, but no wind will disturb the bullet's path."

"I believe I know who this man is," said Indré gently. "Was he the husband of—"

"Please," said Greta, putting a hand in the air. "I have never uttered her name either. I should have realized all these people would be known to historians now. But I made promises, back then. Humor a foolish old woman."

"I was thinking of a publication," said Indrė, very gently. "Called the *Free Fatherland*."

Greta nodded. "Perhaps you know more about those two than I do. I suppose they were the mother and father of the whole resistance movement, in a way. You are right: my colonel was the husband of the schoolmistress who produced that newspaper. She wrote most of it herself in an attic room by the light of a single bulb. She lived alone with their youngest son in a place not far from where I grew up—luckily for me. I went to her for help at a time of great need. She took me in, and it was my privilege to watch her at work one night. The newspaper was a great thorn in Stalin's side. Her honesty and eloquence were more dangerous to him than an armored battalion.

"The colonel and the schoolmistress made elaborate plans for a Soviet occupation. He was a man of vision. He foresaw from the beginning that the Germans would lose the war. Stalin would beat them back, invade Lithuania again and would never be dislodged willingly. His wife would keep the voice of the Lithuanian nation alive until the Western allies came to our aid. Until we were liberated, it would be better for her if the husband were dead. If he had been martyred in the war against Fascism, it would put the schoolmistress beyond suspicion when the Russians took over. He thought he would die either in battle out in the woods, or that he and the elder son would fake their own deaths and disappear. He spoke about being reunited again with his wife and the younger boy one day in a free Lithuania, but I think he had resigned himself to never seeing them again. He carried this sadness with him always, the way you carry a glass of something you do not want to spill."

"It's incredible to me that you knew these people. They are figures from legend. But so are you."

"I don't know, looking back, if we pulled off any really legendary exploits. We sniped, and ran, and hid, and ambushed staff cars when we got warning of them. We could not trade punches with an armored division. There were always reprisals against the local people too. I wonder how many of them thought we were heroes."

"There's a story about the group blowing up a train full of German soldiers."

Greta shook her head. "Not quite. That was us—the three girls, a couple of days after we left the others." She dabbed her mouth with a napkin. She picked up the one on which she had drawn military diagrams in pen, and screwed both into a ball. "We stayed with the group for nearly two years and the first year was wonderful. That is when these photographs were taken. Then some people left and others joined. We began to argue among ourselves about what to do.

"The colonel's strength was fading and he could not impose his will on the new people. He was playing a double game all the time—accepting help from the Soviets, but planning to fight them when the Germans were pushed out. We were getting news from the east then—the Nazis were on the retreat, falling back to the river Dnieper. For the first time, I began to understand that they would lose in the end. Others in the group were passionate Stalinists who could not fathom why we did not want to join up with the larger bands who were being more regularly supplied by Moscow. Then there was a student, a lunatic who decided our real enemies were the Poles! He thought the Germans and the Russians would come and go and we should concentrate on attacking Polish resistance fighters. It became this shifting cast of oddballs, and there were endless, pointless debates about every move we made."

"It sounds a bit like my office."

Greta chuckled. "I pray you get to work for someone like my colonel one day. His voice was the great thing. Like the voice of God. I cannot mimic him. He pulled off a great coup in the first week of 1944. He got hold of a great deal of explosives, which had been stashed away in a quarry up in the north. He wanted to use it straight away. The obvious target was the main railway line from Kaunas to Vilnius. By then I was his chief ally in the group, along with a man called Mindaugas, who became a lifelong friend.

"The others wanted to save the explosives for later. They wanted us to bide our time and wait until the Germans were in full retreat before we popped our heads up and started doing some serious fighting. They thought we'd stand a better chance of survival, and be hailed by the local people as liberating heroes. At the time I thought them pitiful cowards. So that is how things were in our little family at the beginning of 1944. I had had about as much as I could stomach.

"Then the colonel's son did something very foolish. He was a joker, as I told you. Sometimes he went too far. He made a remark I didn't like one day, and I slapped his face. So, we weren't talking. And then he went away on a job with Mindaugas and Vita. I think they had gone to the outskirts of Kaunas to meet a man who brought us news from the city. They had stayed the night together, and when they all walked back into the camp, I could see something was wrong. I could not get it out of her at first.

"She told me he had tried to kiss her and she had pushed him away and he called her something unpleasant. She was so ashamed—of herself, of course, though she had done nothing wrong! Women! I do not think now that the boy meant to cause any great harm. He was a simple animal, the kind who likes to fish, and smoke, and flirt with girls, and lounge around like a cat in the sun. He could be wonderful company but he was not a serious man like his father.

"I remember marching up to him as he lazed by the fire. I said: "Do what you want, but keep your hands off her if she tells you no."

"He said: "She didn't mind, really. Show me a virgin who does."

"I kicked him and he growled and said: "Do that again. I'll kick you back."

"Mindaugas was nearby, cleaning a rifle, and I remember him looking over like this and saying, *very* quietly: 'No, you won't, my boy.' They looked at each other for a while and I said: 'You can watch your mouth from now on too.'

"The boy laughed, and it wasn't a nice laugh. He said: 'I called her a Jew. She is a Jew.'

"I said: 'She is worth ten of you.'

"For some reason, this made him furious. He jumped up, grabbed hold of my pack, lifted it up and shook it. 'Look how much you girls carry compared to us. I'm loaded down like a pit pony while you three waltz around. My father treats you like princesses.'

"It was a sacred rule that you did not touch anyone else's things without permission. He did it to infuriate me. He picked up the Schmeisser then, which was always leaning against my pack. I said: 'That's mine. If you touch that it's like you put your hand between my legs.' Of course he gave a great laugh and started rubbing his paws all over the barrel. I pulled out my Luger and stuck it in his face. We were standing there and all the others had started to gather around.

"Mindaugas spat on the ground and rolled his sleeves up. Vita was in tears. She thought it was all her fault. I heard the colonel's voice behind me, like a noise coming up from the bowels of the Earth. 'What is this madness?' He came tottering toward the fire, walking like a drunkard. It was the first time I had seen him walk without a crutch for months. I remember that I said: 'We are leaving.' It just came out of my mouth, but as soon as I said it, I knew it was the right time. As the three of us were walking away down the trail the colonel called me back. He had packed sticks of explosive, wires and detonators into an oilskin bag. He gave it to me and we both nodded. That was all. I could hear his voice behind us as we rustled away through the young oaks. He was stripping the skin off his son's back, going around the clock face of insults: *Motherless. Worthless. Fool of a boy . . .*

"We blew up the track just east of Kaunas a few days later. We were heading in that direction anyway. He had explained it all to me and I wanted to do it while it was fresh in my memory. We set everything up and waited for something to come. If you're going to blow a railway track you may as well get a train into the bargain. It began to rain and we lay on the muddy forest floor, watching the water soaking the sticks and the wires. The cold sank into us as we lay there for hours, as miserable as you can imagine. We were alone again, with only half a plan. I was sick and tired of it all.

"I was convinced that the charge would not ignite now in the wet. Nothing would happen when I pressed the wires together, but some- one on the train would surely see the explosives and we would have to run for our lives with nothing to show for it. At least it was beginning to get dark. I think I may have dozed off, because I remember one of the girls shaking my shoulder, and a train was almost on top of us. I could see it from our position but there were no windows to tell what kind it was. When I touched the ends of the two wires together the ground beneath us heaved as though an angry god had pounded it with his fist. We pressed our faces into the soil and covered the backs of our heads with our hands, because even at that distance, chunks of glass and metal and God knows what else came raining down on to our backs. There was thick white smoke, and I could hear men groaning and crying out. We crept as close as we dared, but what we saw sickened us, and we turned and bolted like foxes."

"You must have found out later what you had done. It was quite a famous incident."

"So I believe. Although I understand that fewer men actually died than is supposed. About a dozen. Many more were injured, of course, and the track was broken for weeks. They were fresh reserves, being sent to the fighting near Smolensk. I believe we saved a good deal of Russian lives on that day."

Greta shuddered slightly. "That is how I choose to think about it, anyway.

"The partisans had been quiet for a little while, but the thing with the train set the country all around ablaze. I'm afraid we did not care. We thought it was time for our old friends to do some fighting. And the Germans did not have the men to go around burning villages in revenge by then. It was 1944, early spring, and the Red Army had already pushed west into Estonia. It was not a rout yet, but we saw German deserters for the first time—men on their own, fleeing westward through the woods. Broken men, with no fight left in them. Even those who were still armed fled from us like chickens. Grown men running from teenage girls!

"And we were leaving the Kaunas district anyway, picking our way east. Yes, toward the front line! It must sound insane to you. But we knew the full German retreat would wash over us sooner or later, wherever we were, and I had a place in mind—a place I had been dreaming of. Also . . . I feel now that something was always pulling us east, drawing us toward Vilnius."

"What was the place you had in mind?"

"An island in a boiling sea. A little paradise. My uncle's cabin. I had been there once when I was small, with him and my father. A little place for hunters to lie up, but in a good deal of comfort. My uncle always had rich and powerful friends he wanted to impress, so he had really bought the place to host weekend parties. Men out in the woods, pretending to hunt and drinking all day instead. Making grand plans, no doubt, for the future of Lithuania. They saw themselves as the natural leaders of the country, him and his friends.

"The main problem was finding it. I had a vague idea of where it was, but it was well hidden, close to the Rūdninkai Forest. We crept nearer, as spring turned to early summer. I must have driven the girls mad, leading us on marches that led nowhere, circling back on ourselves, climbing any hill we could find so that I could try to get my bearings. The location was so perfectly secluded, you see. It could have been made for three girls desperately trying to avoid men and tanks. Eventually we got to the little range of hills and I knew we were close."

Indrė did not want to interrupt, but she slid the tip of her finger southwest from Vilnius and indicated a spot on the map.

Greta nodded. "The hills rise up so suddenly from the plain that they look as if they were made by men. There was a local legend that the ancient people piled the soil by hand to build a fortress on it. The highest point is an outcrop that hangs over the valley and gives you a marvelous view up and down it from east to west. It is flat and almost bare on top, like a viewing platform. It was almost impossible to climb up from the valley side then because there were brambles and thorny bushes choking the bottom of the slope, like a green wave half a mile thick. I suppose armor could have crashed through, or men with flamethrowers, but why would they bother?

"If you looked up from the valley, there was no sign of human life. The cabin was on the other side, set in a dip below the top of the hill. It rested on a shoulder of it. It was screened with trees and invisible from any angle. There was a narrow track that led there from the west, through thick pine forest. It was difficult enough to find. You could just about pick your way there from the east, following a gully made by a stream, but you would have to know the country like the back of your hand to find that path, and be as surefooted as a goat to follow it. The cabin was so well hidden that we stepped out of the trees and gasped with astonishment when we saw it right in front of our noses. We reached out and touched the wooden walls to make sure they were real. Everything had been shut up and bolted with padlocks, but my memory had got us this far and it did not fail us now. I found a key under the chopping block in the woodstore."

Greta smiled at the memory. She sat back in her chair for a while, basking in it.

"And it was comfortable in there?"

"Soft beds! A bath! It was as though a djinn from the Arabian nights had picked us up and flown us to a sultan's palace. There were lots of bottles in the main room, and little things that men like to eat when they are drinking together. There were chocolate bars, the first we had seen since the winter of 1941. And real black tea, and tobacco, and salted nuts, which in those days came in little metal cans.

"I remember us sharing out the almonds, savoring each one slowly. We had not eaten well for weeks but we knew that you must never bolt food, even when you are mortally hungry. Each almond was as rich and satisfying as a fillet steak! When we walked into the bedroom, something stopped us in our tracks and made us cry out with horror. I believe it reduced all of us to tears. Can you guess?"

Indrė shook her head quickly, her eyes wide.

"A full-length mirror! You cannot imagine the state we were in. I was not a vain girl, but my teeth and hair were in a terrible condition and I cried for what the years in the woods had done to me. I was about to turn eighteen, but I looked much smaller and younger. Vita was a little older, and Riva was nearly twenty. She was the only one who did not look famished, but she was not happy with her face. She was one of those girls who is always fighting a battle against their eyebrows. The eyebrows had won. I remember her saying: 'Well, girls, I think we have solved the mystery of why the Germans have been running away from us.'"

"And you stayed there until . . . ?"

"Until the end."

"It must have been getting on for June 1944, when the Allies landed in Normandy. You must have begun to think that you might survive after all."

"I think I dared to hope then, when we settled into the cabin. It was hard to imagine anyone finding us there. But we lived in the moment, the way an animal does. When you are out in the woods, you do not think you will live to see the end of the week."

"Did the girls know? How fortunate they were? To have survived?"

"A good question. We had heard news, of course, when we were with the others near Kaunas, of the camps and ghettos. People who had seen some of the horrors for themselves told us stories. But I am not sure if any of us truly believed it all. The scale was so hard to take in. We thought that the rumors must be exaggerated. How could we imagine an evil so absolute, so meticulous?

"My eighteenth birthday came and we drank the place dry! The next morning, we regretted it. We went up on top of the hill and looked out into the valley through the bushes. It was alive with men streaming west. They were in full retreat. We hardly dared patrol the woods around us now because we saw large groups of deserters every day. Sometimes the men were on their own, and they had those silly half-smiles that soldiers wear after they have surrendered or run away. Mostly, we left them alone. Occasionally there would be a fellow who had something we needed: a weapon, or boots small enough to fit one of us, if we padded them. Sometimes we would just stroll out and greet them in German, if they were unarmed. They were half cracked from shellfire, and they laughed out loud sometimes. They thought they were back in their home villages, chatting to farm girls. I remember one man who could not stop giggling, it all seemed so surreal to him. He was too loud, and would not be quiet, and we wanted his overcoat. He was still laughing when I pulled out my knife.

"By the first week of July, the woods all around were flooded with Germans trying to get away from the front, and we spent most of our time looking out from the hilltop. I think it was the eighth of July when the stream of men became a torrent flowing through the valley. We could see their faces from our little viewing platform. They were as gray as their uniforms. They walked with their heads down.

"Occasionally you would see an officer on horseback, shoving the fellows on foot to the side as he raced westward. All that day, around the eighth or the ninth, we heard the sound of artillery fire creeping closer, like approaching thunder. Suddenly, up on the ridge on the other side of the valley, you could see black shapes moving. It was the first time we had laid eyes on the Russians. We gasped, and held each other tight. We felt that the end had come at last."

Greta, Vita and Riva lay in the undergrowth on top of the hill and watched the remains of Hitler's Army Group Centre file into the valley below them until it was choked with Germans at the narrowest part.

They could see Russian artillery moving on the opposite side of the valley. *Katyushas* mounted on trucks were being wheeled into position. By early evening, they bristled in a long line along the high ground. The girls had heard tales of this weapon from retreating Ger- man soldiers they had questioned but had never seen it up close before. The rocket launchers looked like black pipe organs.

They could just make out the commanding officer, a little stick figure in a Russian cap walking along the opposite slope. They heard a faint cry from the man's direction, which was picked up and repeated all along the Russian line. They saw the officer raise his hand high in the air. He brought it down in a sudden chopping motion.

The noise took a while to reach full volume. It was like one of those queasy machines that produces music at a fairground. The sound was like the snarling and yammering of cats, mixed with the whoosh and roar of fireworks, and a drumbeat of thumps underneath from the impact of the rockets.

The curtain of explosions crept close to the base of their hill, but the girls did not know it. They were all on their hands and knees by then, with their fingers jammed in their ears. Even with the tips pushed in as far as they would go, they still felt the vibration of the impacts passing through their bodies.

The barrage went on for longer than they thought possible. When it was over, they lay on the forest floor panting and blinking. No birds sang for a long time. When they crawled forward and looked out through the brush again, they saw that the ground of the valley floor had been thrown up and agitated everywhere. Later, they would have to creep down to pick through the bodies and scavenge for ammunition and other supplies. "Not yet," said Greta. "I can't go down there yet."

"What in God's name was that?" asked Vita.

"The Fascist serpent. The Russians are breaking its back at last. We are watching the death throes."

They walked back down to the cabin gingerly. Their bodies were sore all over, as though they had been on a punishing march with heavy packs.

"We need hot tea," said Greta. "The real thing, not pine needles. Let's finish that black stuff."

She went to the wood store and gathered an armful of chippings for a fire. The girls had gone inside. They did not leave the door open for her. She had to hold on to the wood with her forearms and shuffle up to the door awkwardly so she could turn the handle without dropping it all. She pushed the door open, cursing the girls for their thoughtlessness.

They looked up at her at the same time. They were sitting next to each other on the sofa, their hands in their laps. A man in German uniform was lounging opposite them in the armchair. His hands were behind his head and his boots were resting on his backpack.

"I didn't mean to frighten the girls," said Greta's uncle, as the two of them smoked outside later. He had taken the Luger out of his belt and stowed it in his pack. He had changed out of his uniform, but the splendid double-breasted field- gray overcoat hung from his shoulders.

She saw that he had ripped all the badges and insignia from the coat, so that his division and unit could not be identified. He read her mind and said: "I had nothing to do with all that nonsense. With *them*, I mean," he added, with a nod toward the cabin. "I'm just a simple fighting man."

"What happened to your gorilla?"

"Viktoras? Not everyone managed to break out. Some stayed to cover the retreat."

"He's Lithuanian. Loyal until the end."

"A bloody fool until the end!" Greta's uncle shook his head and gave a long whistle. "I can't believe you've kept those girls alive all this time, though. You'll have to put them in a museum somewhere. Or a zoo. It's a shame it's not a boy and a girl, really."

He saw the expression on her face and put up a hand in mute apology.

She said: "Laugh if you want to. I wouldn't, if I was in your shoes. How is your future looking?"

He shrugged his shoulders and looked away west, putting a hand over his eyes, then glanced back at the cabin and jabbed his cigarette toward the door.

"Those girls. What do they know about their parents?"

"Nothing. And we've been trying not to think about it for three years."

"Well, their father died exactly as I predicted. Shot in the street by a Russian commissar. He was trying to stop them looting."

"Don't say anything. Let me tell them."

"All right. What about *your* father?"

"Shut up about him."

He looked at her with compassion for the first time. "Sooner or later, you're going to have to hear it."

"Not from you. Shut your damned mouth. Not another word."

He raised both his hands in surrender and smiled. "I'm too tired to fight. I'm going to stay for one night, with your permission. I'll have a proper rest and leave late tomorrow."

"It's your place. Do what you want."

"What do you do about a lookout?"

"One of us watches the path all night. We set up on the corner over there. Don't worry about it. You sleep. Save your strength."

"You haven't changed, Zofija. You are the same good girl, full of kindness. God knows I don't deserve it."

"I just want you out of our hair and gone tomorrow, that's all."

Greta stole out at midnight and went in the opposite direction to the one she had indicated to her uncle. She headed uphill, pulling herself up the slope with arms and legs, cresting the sharp ridge, then slipped and slid down a goat track next to a steep gully, dry at this time of year. Very few people would know this way out. She waited behind a thick fir tree at the bottom of the ravine.

He came with the first light and she had to stop herself crying out because his silhouette and his gait, arms swinging easily, were exactly those of her father when he sauntered out in the early morning for the hunting. Her uncle was wearing a peasant's cap that had been hanging in the woodshed and there was no sign of the gray coat. His pack was on his back and the Schmeisser was hanging from it.

She stepped out and pointed the rifle at his heart. "Falcon," he said. "Little *falcon*."

"No more talk. Put it down carefully. Get the ammunition out. The Luger too."

"You can't leave me with nothing. You may as well just shoot me. I'll never get through."

"Take it all out slowly and put it on the ground."

"Zofija, I need a pistol."

"So you can creep back in and murder us?"

"You're not being rational. I'm going west as fast as my legs can carry me, until I feel an American cigarette between my lips."

They looked at each other for a long time. She slid the bolt back with her thumb. He said: "Do you know their mother is still alive?"

"Liar!"

"She was alive about a month ago. In a labor camp in Vilnius. She was in Kaunas, but they moved a lot of them over here. She must be one of the last ones left."

"As if you care enough about any of those poor people to find out something like that."

"I don't care. One of my . . . colleagues was talking about her and I remembered the name. She was a famous beauty before the war. I saw her on stage once."

Greta's thumb was still on the bolt. Both her hands showed white as they squeezed the rifle.

"We'll never get through. There's a sea of Russians between here and Vilnius."

He shrugged. "You might have a small window. They are massing all their artillery before the big drive toward Germany. It will take them a few days. They overreached themselves yesterday and they know it. I could have taken those *Katyushas* with forty good men."

"The Luger."

"There might be a tiny corridor open between the lines. I have a map here. I can show you the best way."

She lowered the rifle an inch or two.

"This is madness. At least pack a proper bag."

"We are going now."

"I should never have told you about this and your father at the same time. It was too much. You are both out of your minds."

"Talk if you want, but you'll have to walk at the same time."

"At least let's take some more ammunition. Wait for me!"

"Catch us up."

The sisters strode away. They had their rifles and the clothes they stood up in. Greta grabbed a few things from the cabin and ran after them without locking the door.

Riva pushed them hard all that morning. They would go northwest, through the heart of the Rūdninkai Forest, then due north into the southern suburbs of Vilnius.

They refused to stop. The girls ate chocolate as they walked. Greta had never seen them with that look in their eyes.

"Don't eat all of it," she said. "We don't know when our next meal will be."

"We'll hit the edge of the city by the end of the night," said Riva. "People are still living there. We take what we need. We kill anyone who gets in our way."

"He said we should stay out of town overnight and see what's happening in the suburbs first. They might encircle the city suddenly. We could run into a whole division."

"He told you that, did he?" said Riva. "Your precious uncle." Greta was silent.

"I wouldn't have let him go," said Vita, quietly. "A man wearing that uniform."

"I'm sorry," said Greta. "I did not have it in me to shoot him."

They trudged along through a sea of thin birches. The ground had been rising steadily for some time and their breathing was labored. They were walking along the top of a high weald that fell sharply down to a muddy forest stream on their left. They could see a stone bridge at the bottom of the slope.

Greta said: "Let's stop for a minute while we have the high ground. We'll have to rest at some point. We're going to need some energy when we get there."

"You sun yourself if you want," said Riva. "We are pressing on."

They heard the noise of propellers and all looked up at the same time. An aircraft was approaching from the east—a big clumsy supply plane, not a fighter. They flinched as it trundled noisily above them. Something square and heavy fell from it. There was a loud flapping sound as the parachute opened. Greta grabbed hold of both girls.

The square thing seemed to be coming down right at them and they tensed themselves to run. Then they saw it would miss the tops of the trees where they were standing by a few feet and that the wind was blowing it away from them. They could see it clearly now: a wooden crate the size of a small car.

They heard the crash as it hit the uppermost branches of a patch of big beech trees over to their right. Greta climbed the first few branches of a tree nearby and could see the parachute a quarter of a mile away. The wind had carried it further than they had expected. They had really believed it would land on their heads.

Greta looked at the girls desperately. "No," said Riva. "We're pressing on."

"But that must be a Russian drop for partisans! It's probably full of tinned food and guns."

"Absolutely not," said Riva, but, like a small child, Vita tugged at her sleeve. Riva looked at her and the hardness in her eyes dimmed. The two sisters hugged.

"I'm tired too," said Vita. "And Greta is right. We need to eat."

Riva was sobbing now. "It's all right for her! She blocks everything out. She's forgotten her family. I'm not a machine. I can't stop caring about our parents."

"Stay with her," Greta said to Vita. "I'll go and have a look."

"*Schatz*," Riva gasped, realizing what she had said and hearing the quiver in Greta's voice. "*Schatz*, I'm sorry. I didn't mean any of it." She reached out with both arms.

"I'll be back in twenty minutes," said Greta. "Don't move."

* * *

The crate had survived the fall without splitting open. She ran a hand over the rough, thin pine boards that held it together. Then she patted her pockets, feeling for her father's hunting knife. It was the last thing she had snatched up before dashing after the girls. She could stove in one of the planks with the knife handle, then worm the good stout blade into the gap and prize the wood apart.

She was circling the crate when a slight girl of about the same age stepped out from behind a tree and trained a machine pistol on her. She wore wide-legged trousers made for a man and had her hair up in a scarf. They stared at each other. A man was trudging up behind the girl, also carrying a pistol.

"Throw that gun down," said the girl. "You fucking throw yours down."

"You can't fight all of us. You might get one but—"

"I'll get both of you before I hit the ground."

"Stop," said the man with the pistol. "I don't think she's an SS general. Do you, Comrade?"

He had thick black curly hair and a beard. He was wearing a long soldier's overcoat. He came up the track slowly and kept his gun pointed at the ground. "No one is going to shoot anyone. For the moment. But this is our territory and this is our stuff, so who the fuck are you?"

He sounded very tired and very nasal. He had a heavy cold, at best. "A Lithuanian," said Greta.

"I didn't think you were Jewish. Unless you looted a peroxide factory."

"I'm not Jewish but my friends are. If there's no help for us here, I need to get back to them."

He shook his head. "Impossible. Never heard of such a thing. The Lithuanians I know? They kill Jews with pitchforks. You're not going anywhere until you tell me why you're blundering around out here."

Greta swallowed hard and said: "The other girls are looking for their mother. We heard she was in Vilnius. In Vilna, I mean."

He grinned. "Well, you're definitely not Jewish. 'Vilnius,' indeed! But what do you mean, the *other* girls? All of you are female? Impossible."

The girl in the wide trousers gave him a black look and said: "I've heard of them, Yakuv. Three sisters going around the woods shooting up Germans. Didn't you blow the train line?"

"Near Kaunas? Yes."

The man called Yakuv had a wide sardonic smile on his face. "Stories spread like lice out here. You said something about your friends' mother. What's her name?"

"Klara Klausner. She used to be an actress." The girl and the man exchanged an unreadable glance. Greta said: "Well? What does that look mean? Is she alive or dead?"

"It's been a while since we had contact with people in Vilnius. We were in the ghetto there and decided to make a break for it. Not a minute too soon. It's possible that a few are left alive there but I wouldn't hold out too much hope. I won't be able to find out for a day or two. You'd better go and get your girls. We can't hang around here all afternoon. What other weapons do you have?" he added, with a covetous look at the Schmeisser.

"What's it got to do with you?"

"I want to know what you're bringing to the table."

"Who said anything about us eating at your table?"

His face clouded with incomprehension. "How many did you say you were?"

"Three."

He laughed. "How long do you think three of you are going to last out here without our help? Don't tell me you don't want to throw in with us. We've got tents. Sleeping bags. Machineguns. The Russians are raining this stuff down on us like sweets at a wedding."

"And what are you giving them?"

He shrugged. "Loyalty, for now. We have all made the partisans' oath—*to fight the Fascist serpent with no regard for our own lives.* We'll see what happens when the war ends."

"We won't fight for the Soviet Union."

"And how can you speak for the others? I thought they were Jews—or is the story changing now?"

"Stalin killed their father. They won't fight for him."

The man nodded. He stroked his little beard. The hair on his head and face was improbably well groomed for a man who lived under canvas. "We can worry about the rights and wrongs of everything later. For now, we take guns where we can get them."

As he said "guns," all three stiffened at the sound of sustained automatic fire in the distance. Greta spun round. They heard the crack of rifles and another burst of automatic rounds. It came from the direction she had come.

"Oh, no," she said. "Oh, Christ." She turned and looked at the man. "I think it's my girls. Help me."

He shook his head. "Absolutely not."

The girl in the headscarf cried out: "Yakuv, they are Jews."

"So she says! But what are the chances? Jews and Lithuanians joining up together? Like a wolf making friends with the chickens. You know what they did to my sister, her pious Christian neighbors?"

"Of course I know," shouted the girl. "You've told us a hundred times. But can't you hear . . ."

Yakuv was talking in a very loud voice, to neither of them. There was a strange look in his eye. "Waited until she had given birth," he said. "So they could bayonet the baby in front of her. Laughed at her screams. Threw them in the gravel pit together."

"I'm going. Shoot me in the back if you don't like it," said Greta.

No one shot her, but they did not follow her either.

She crawled close through the slime of the leaves and could see that the Germans had laid Riva and Vita out next to each other, with the head of one beside the feet of the other. They are pretending, thought Greta. They are acting.

There were six men wearing the uniform of the Wehrmacht, and a motorcycle leaning against a birch tree. The men were all talking loudly and gesticulating. They seemed to be having a disagreement.

The girls are playing dead, thought Greta. They have been taken prisoner and ordered to lie perfectly still. They have been knocked unconscious. They have been drugged and have fallen asleep.

One of the men knelt next to Vita's head and opened her mouth to peer at the teeth inside, the way that country people look into the mouths of horses. When the man let go of her jaw, her head flopped to the side so that it was as if she were looking straight at Greta. The face was unreal, like that of a mannequin in a shop window.

Greta bit her wrist and her body bucked and convulsed, but she did not let a sound escape from her mouth.

Two of the men got on the motorcycle and rode away, roughly in the direction that Greta and the girls had come that morning. She waited until the sound of the engine had faded completely. The sun was high in the sky. She was thirstier than she had ever been in her life. Three of the remaining men sat in a line on a fallen beech tree. The fourth man assembled a fire and hung a tin from three leaning sticks to heat water. Greta propped herself up on one elbow and tossed a stick grenade, keeping her arm straight and stiff. She was expecting a cacophony of shouts and gunfire, but there was no sound until the thud of the explosion.

She got up and ran at them and saw that the man who had been heating the water was closest to the grenade when it went off. He was no longer a man.

The three soldiers sitting on the log had been tipped back off it by the blast. Two of them got up quickly. They were standing close together and they tried to dodge apart but she dragged the Schmeisser from right to left in a long burst that knocked them both on their backs. The fourth man lay cowering on the ground with his hands pressed over his ears.

She made him throw her his canteen and she drank the contents with a grimace of displeasure, because his mouth had tainted it with the sour taste of tobacco. He watched her drink with his hands raised.

She said: "Do you have those little tools? The spade things?"

"Of course."

"Then dig. Drag the bodies over here and dig a hole."

"How big? How big should I make it?"

"Deep. Wide enough for two bodies."

When he heard the number two, some of the tension went out of him and he could breathe more easily. He dug quickly. She sat on a fallen log and covered him with the Schmeisser all the time. When he had nearly finished, he said: "I have a family. I have a photograph of my children."

"Shut up," said Greta.

He pulled the girls' bodies in and began to pile the dirt over them. Greta gave a stifled cry and he stopped for a second, closing his eyes, clearly waiting for a bullet.

Greta said: "Continue. Finish." It was not her normal voice.

They stood for a moment and looked down at the graves. He was sweating very freely and his hair was matted. He wiped it out of his eyes with the back of his hand. He said: "They took us on. They fired every bullet they had. But there were six of us. It was over in seconds."

"Will your friends come back for you?"

"They said they would. It's hard to say. The Russians are very close now." He nodded to the east. You could hear shellfire and the *Katyushas* in the distance.

Greta said: "Kneel." The man screwed up his face as though he had been punched and she added: "We are going to say a prayer." He went down slowly on his knees, tired in the joints now and wincing from the effort.

Greta came up behind him and he closed his eyes again. He was expecting a head shot but she stuck the knife deep into his neck. It went all the way in easily, slipping into the gap between the clavicle and the scapula.

The soldier's mouth opened wide, but no sound came out. He had the eyes of a man being electrocuted. As he collapsed on to his side, he stared up at her and she came close to him and pulled the knife all the way out of him.

"Did you think I would waste time on a hole for you?" she said. "When the birds and wolves could have you instead? They will eat your eyes first. Jew. Killer. Child. Killer." With every word, she stabbed him.

She went on stabbing the man for a long time, until she realized he had died some time earlier and that she had been out of her mind for a little while. She saw that she had pierced and slashed him with the knife so many times that the wounds could not be counted.

The Earth continued to turn. The sun reached its highest point and descended. The sound of shellfire crept closer.

Greta lay on her side, her eyes open and unblinking, the moisture from the forest floor soaking into her clothes. She sensed the pulsing energy that was in the ground below her and watched the small wriggling things at work among the leaves and fallen timber. She heard the birds squabbling for territory in the upper branches and listened to the squirrels shrieking as they chased each other in crazy circles. All she could see in any of it was murder and death.

She stood up with aching slowness, like someone who has been in bed with a fever for weeks. She held out her hand and grabbed the trunk of a slender birch for strength. She felt the curling paper of its bark brushing against her skin. She traced a line of running sap with her finger and dug the nail into a pool of resin that had hardened like amber.

Greta heard the motorcycle a long time before she saw it and had time to settle herself into the roots of a vast beech tree that hung over the edge of the slope going down to the bridge. The Schmeisser was almost empty so she took the rifle that looked the cleanest and rested it on top of a broad shoulder of wood. Most of her body was protected by it. The bridge at the bottom of the slope was made of thick gray flagstones. The sides were high and the walkway was so narrow that two people would struggle to walk across side by side. The motorbike rider would have to slow down to get over it safely.

He approached more quickly than she had expected. She snatched at the shot and thought she had missed him. Then she saw the bike swerve and topple and he came off it straight back. There was something playful about the way he fell with his arms thrown up, like a child flopping backwards on to a hotel bed.

The rider lay sprawled for a moment and she saw him lift his head and look down at his legs. He didn't understand why he couldn't move them. Two men ran up from behind and each hooked a hand under one of his armpits, dragged him back thirty yards and sat him up behind another big beech. There were deep grooves in the thick mud from the tracks of the motorcycle and the weight of the man's body where they had dragged it.

One of the soldiers peeped out from behind the tree, looking for her, shielding his eyes with a hand. She fired again but it was too far away and she could not see where the bullet had struck.

She could see other soldiers now, moving carefully from tree to tree. There was a two-man machinegun team and about six riflemen. She thought she could make out the shape of an armored vehicle a long way behind them through the trees, but nothing came up and there was no more engine noise. She guessed that the Germans had come on the back of a horse-drawn cart, sending the motorcycle ahead as a scout.

One of the soldiers who had rescued the rider ran out from behind the beech and made for the bridge. He almost came right up to it but he stopped and knelt behind a thick silver birch. His head was hidden but she could see one shoulder with the marks of an officer on the strap, the tip of a machine pistol and one of his boots.

He was the only man she could see who was wearing a soft cloth cap instead of a helmet. The rest of the soldiers had settled themselves into cover now and they were very still and quiet. The officer dashed out from behind the silver birch and made it over to the high stone side of the bridge. She fired and very nearly hit him. She saw a puff of white dust where the bullet struck the top of the stone parapet.

A shell landed, a hundred and fifty yards to the right of the bridge. It threw a shower of black mulch from the forest floor high into the air. She saw the officer cower so low that he almost touched his forehead to the ground. She switched out the magazine quickly, her eyes fixed on him. If they come at me, she thought, I'll empty the rifle at the bridge as they cross. If any of them make it over I'll pull out both pistols and charge straight at them downhill. I'll take some of them with me. I don't think we'll be apart for long, girls.

The officer stayed still for a long time. Then he shouted up toward her, cupping his mouth with one of his hands: "Where are my men?"

"Dead," she replied in German, shouting with all her strength to make the sound carry down the slope.

The officer thought about this for a while. Then he said: "I need their rifles and helmets. We are coming up."

Greta shouted: "This is Soviet territory. Anyone who crosses that bridge dies."

The man said: "How many of you?"

Greta called back: "A whole division. Coming up behind me now." Well, it was almost certainly true.

The German shouted: "I don't believe you. You're not even Russian, are you?" He stood up very slowly and she slid the bolt of the rifle back but did not fire. He put his pistol in its holster and showed her the palms of both gloved hands.

"I think you're on your own up there," he shouted. "Throw down the rifles and we'll let you go."

"I need those rifles. They're marking my sisters' graves. Come and take them if you want them."

She fired at a patch of ground just in front of him, reloaded and fired again to show how quickly she could do it. The second shot hit the same spot as the first. The German ducked back behind the stonework.

Greta could see half of his head and that he was nodding. He turned and she heard him call to someone behind him: "I should have such a sister." A voice shouted something urgent in response and the man laughed grimly.

Another shell landed, slightly closer, and the officer flinched again. After the noise of the impact faded, he stood up tentatively. He showed her that his hands were still empty. Then he peeled off his gloves and held them pinned under one elbow. He began to clap his hands. He clapped slowly at first and she couldn't make out the sound very clearly. Then the other men joined in.

They stood up one by one and applauded. Their faces were very grim and they did not cheer or whistle. She stood up too, showing herself against the skyline: a lone girl with a German rifle. The men clapped until another shell landed in a stream seventy yards behind them with a massive flat slapping sound, and they were sprayed with muddy water.

The officer roared: *"Gehen wir."* His squad began to run back the way they had come, skirting the edge of the new shell hole. The man peered up at Greta for a while, his eyes very narrow. Then he saluted sharply, turned and ran after his men.

When Greta finished speaking, her fingers were interwoven and her head was bowed. She looked up at Indrė Žukauskienė and saw that the young woman was crying silently.

"Did you ever find out what happened to your father?" Indrė asked.

"I believe he was taken by the NKVD a day or two before the Germans came, and died on the way to Siberia, on the train journey, as many others did. This will sound so strange, but I never *wanted* to find out all the details. Part of me always carried around the idea that he might have survived somehow, even though I knew it was absurd. There is even a part of me now—the little girl part—that thinks of him as though he is still alive. At my age! Isn't it ridiculous?"

"And . . . their mother?" Greta shook her head gently. "I'm so sorry."

"Paneriai. It was at Paneriai. They found her close to the top of the pile. She was naked."

"Forgive me. I don't know why I'm crying. It's just . . . it was all for nothing. Everything you went through. There was never any hope—"

"No!" Greta almost shouted it and she brought the edge of her hand down so hard on the table that the plates and glasses jumped.

"You don't understand. She was *naked*. The early ones were fully clothed. They only started to strip them at the end. She was almost at the top. She must have died right at the end."

Indrė had her face in her hands. Greta reached out and took hold of her wrists.

"Don't you see? It might have happened just a few weeks before we arrived. Perhaps only a few days. We could have made it there in time. Who knows what was possible? It was worth it. There was still hope. There is always hope."

42

SPAIN, 1961

The colossal bell of the cathedral of Our Lady of Valencia tolled at eleven in the morning on Friday, September 29.

Sightseers milled around the Plaza de la Virgen. The people who stood peering up at the magnificent entrance to the cathedral or sat sipping iced *horchata de chufa* under umbrellas around the square did not know that their numbers were swelled on that morning by six members of the MGB, the Ministry of State Security of the Soviet Union, and an equal number of their counterparts from Bulgaria's KDS, the Committee for State Security.

They were posted in locations that gave them a view of the main routes in and out of the square and of that ancient and venerable Valencian institution the Caballo Negro café. A car was parked in a street close by containing a VHF radio transceiver crammed into a leather suitcase. Some of the operatives carried smaller radio sets in satchels or handbags.

Half a mile to the northwest, Maxim Karpov lay on his back, like a corpse, on the bed in his hotel room. Oleg stood nearby, holding his head in his hands. Temir paced up and down the landing outside, making the floorboards groan.

"That bastard," said Karpov weakly. "This time he's finished."

Oleg said: "We don't know he was behind this. Yulia could have decided to run for it herself."

"Alone? In a foreign city? You fool. Vassily is making his move."

"He was still here when we found the balcony doors unlocked. Why didn't he go with her when she went?"

"Not brave enough to jump!" sneered Karpov. "Much better to sneak out later while we were all distracted. Where is that Bulgarian slut?"

"I sent her out with one of the teams. It's not all her fault. I mean, she must have slept through the noise. But Berg was supposed to check the locks in all the rooms before lights out. He obviously didn't."

"Or Vassily gave Yulia a key to the balcony. What about the Devil's Mother? Where is she?"

"Getting ready to go. Still crying about Yulia. I told her to pull herself together."

"Crocodile tears. She's in on it."

"I don't know," said Oleg. "I don't know what to believe any more. But I know that it's past eleven, and if we're really going to go through with this thing without the girl, we've got to get into position now. Me and Temir, at least. We are needed out there."

Karpov raised his head from the pillow and glared at him. "And leave me here alone? Is this all part of your plan?"

Oleg struggled to keep his voice steady. "I don't have any plan. I follow orders. But it's time for us to move."

Karpov rolled to one side, using an elbow to lever himself up. "I'm not going to loaf around out there in the open. We'll all go together, in half an hour. The square is five minutes away."

He sat up and rubbed his face. A folding map of the city was spread out on the table between the two beds. The VHF transceiver on Oleg's bed started to buzz.

Oleg reached for the handset, saying: "Me and Temir need to be there if something happens. With Vassily missing . . ."

"No more smooth talking," said Karpov. "It's a bullet for him—"

Oleg actually dared to raise a hand sternly to cut off his master, and Karpov was so shocked that he fell silent. Oleg had the receiver to his ear. It was a big Bakelite device, like a civilian telephone.

"It's Vassily. He says he's found Yulia. They're in a café in . . . Beni-Maclet?" Oleg scrabbled for the map. "He says he had a hunch she would go there and he didn't have time to explain. He wants me to come and bring her in. He doesn't think he can handle Yulia on his own."

"Handle Yulia," said Karpov, moistening his lips with his tongue. Then his expression twisted into a sneer. "He had a *hunch?* Does he think I'm a simpleton? This is all some kind of scheme. He's trying to drag us away from the square. Send the Bulgarians. Team One."

Oleg frowned. "That's only three people. And this is Vassily. If he has got some kind of trick prepared . . ."

"All right," said Karpov, irritably. "Take Temir and go. Bring the girl back here." He suddenly looked up. "Wait. Is he trying to get you away from me?"

Oleg sat there cradling the receiver in both his hands, one palm still covering the mouthpiece.

"Is he still there?" asked Karpov. "Ask him . . . ask him what she is wearing."

She was at a corner table, her hair covered with a scarf. Her back was to the door. Vassily bought a drink at the bar, walked around her and peered down to check that it was really her before he sat down.

"Have you tried this stuff—the *horchata?*"

"No. I thought it sounded bizarre."

"It's an acquired taste. How is your orange juice?"

"Curdling in my stomach."

"I know how you feel."

"I don't believe you."

"Oh, I still get the nerves, after all these years. Every single time."

Neither of them wanted to touch their drinks. He looked over her shoulder at the door. "Do you remember London?"

"Vaguely." She looked at him sullenly. "Did you know my father was going to jump over the fence that night?"

"Of course not! I knew he was planning some kind of move but I didn't know exactly what he would do or when. He caught me by surprise. I had to think on my feet."

"You weren't the only one!" She took a tiny sip. "You knew he was alive, though, didn't you, Comrade? And you did not tell me." Each word dropped out on to the table, like an ice cube being spilled from a glass.

"It was for your own safety," said Vassily. "Everything we are doing is for you and your safety, even if seems the opposite."

He looked at the door again and his expression changed. He reached forward and took one of her hands in his. "Things are moving quickly now and I don't have time to explain. Just think of how it was in London. You trusted me then, remember?"

"Yes."

"Do you still trust me?"

"Certainly not."

Vassily grinned his peasant's grin. "*Statuettochka*. You have learned something. Now keep talking for me. Don't turn around."

A vast hand spread itself over her shoulder and she did not need to turn to see who it belonged to. When she stood up and looked past Oleg, she saw two Simcas parked outside and a small group of men and women standing around them, looking in various directions. She did not see Karpov until they went out and Oleg walked her to the car, pushing her head down to steer it under the doorframe as she climbed into the back.

Karpov was looking away from her out of his window, watching the people passing by on the street. "You should have taken the flowers that night," he said.

Yulia heard Vassily cry out from the pavement. "What are you doing? I'm coming with you. That's what we agreed. I gave assurances . . ." She saw a young man put the heel of his hand against Vassily's chest and shove him away from the cars.

Oleg said: "Leave him. For now."

As the Simca she was in rolled away, Yulia saw Vassily standing alone on the pavement, they made eye contact and he shouted a single word at her: "London."

Oleg let the Bulgarians pull ahead of him and the two Simcas went along in convoy. Oleg drove and Temir was in the passenger seat. Yulia and Karpov sat in the back in silence, staring straight ahead.

He did not paw or molest her in any way. Somehow that made it worse.

As the cars passed the Royal Gardens, Karpov said: "You stay by my side from now on. Your mother is going to keep the appointment at midday. You and I will observe from a safe distance and we will see what transpires. There are some things I can promise you, though. If Vassily is foolish enough to show his face again, this will be his last day on Earth."

He watched her stiffen slightly and his mouth curled into a smile, his first in three days.

"Whatever happens, at least one of your parents will be in safe hands at the end of today. We may go back to Russia immediately, or I may keep your mother and father somewhere neutral for now. There is an investigation in progress. They will provide critical evidence." Yulia kept staring ahead silently.

Karpov said: "Your parents' fate will depend on the testimony they provide to my investigators, as well as . . . the friendship that develops between you and me."

His hand finally crept on to her thigh, as she had known it would. She forced herself not to react. They had headed west on the ring road that followed the course of the river, from one to twelve on the clockface of the city, and were passing the medieval tower at the top of the Carmen.

"A political conspiracy is like a cancer," said Karpov. "Left unchecked, it spreads through the whole system. Your parents' role will soon become clear. If someone even more senior was involved, I will get it out of them. The punishment will fall where the blame lies. If the entire body of our great workers' nation has become infected, I will not hesitate to remove the head itself. There cannot be any weakness at the top at a time like this, when our enemies' boots are on our neck."

Yulia's face was unreadable. Karpov softened his voice. "Of course, enemies sometimes pose as friends. It is easy be taken in by honeyed words, when you are young and naive."

She did not move a muscle in her face. "I will find him," said Karpov. He was starting to get annoyed. "Your boyfriend. Our little prince."

Yulia blinked, once, in a leisurely way. Her eyes looked straight ahead. Both cars had come off the ring road and were on a slip road that followed the south bank of the river.

Karpov glanced at the men in front, moved his lips close to her ear, and whispered: "I'm going to make him watch when I fuck you. He is going to stand in the corner, like a waiter. He will hand me things when I ask for them. Afterward you will both thank me. You will get down on your knees and kiss my hand . . ."

As he said "kiss," a Saab GT750 hit the Simca in front, almost head-on. Both cars were traveling at about thirty-five miles per hour, and the impact stoved in the front end of the Bulgarians' car completely. The car carrying Yulia and Karpov ploughed into the back of it and pushed it along for a few seconds with a rending, howling noise.

Of the three vehicles, only the Saab was fitted with seatbelts.

Oleg had headbutted the steering wheel and blacked out instantly. Temir had fended off the onrushing windscreen with the heel of one hand and had had the presence of mind to yank the handbrake up with the other. Their car pushed the one in front around its rear axle and went past it for twenty yards before coming to a grinding halt against the stone parapet of the bridge.

Temir was dazed but moving. Oleg was folded motionless over the steering column. It looked as if he was hugging it with both massive arms. Temir looked around and saw that Yulia and Karpov seemed unhurt. Karpov was gabbling something at him but the awful noise of metal against metal and stone had left his ears ringing.

Temir pushed open his door. The Saab had bounced off the first Simca and rolled for thirty yards before coming to a halt on the other side of the road. It was sitting there now, steam erupting from under the bonnet. Temir could not see who was inside.

The car carrying the Bulgarians was about halfway between them, turned around in the road, and it blocked his view. Then he saw a woman get out of the Saab.

The crash threw Greta and Michael forward violently in their seats. The world was knocked off its axis for a few seconds. She recovered more quickly than he did.

She undid her belt, reached into the leather satchel around her neck and pulled out a Baby Browning and a revolver. She folded her arms over her breast, holding the two pistols, to make a cross. She closed her eyes and spoke loudly in Lithuanian: "Now walk with me, my sisters."

Michael started at the sound of her voice. His eyes were unfocused and his head was ringing. She tapped the barrel of the revolver against the glove compartment in front of him.

"There's another in there," she said. "Only for emergencies. Stay here and don't move."

The Bulgarian who had been driving the first Simca stirred in his seat. His forehead had spiderwebbed the windscreen. Blood flowed freely down his face. He looked out of the window and saw her coming at him. He pushed open the door with his last strength. She shot him twice in the middle of the face.

The man and woman who had been waiting for Vassily in the airport in Vienna, posing as young parents, were slumped in the back. Neither reacted to the shots. The woman's head was almost down between her knees and her long hair, dyed dark red, was trailing on the floor of the car.

A bullet shattered the Simca's rear window, and Greta crouched. The bulk of the car was between her and the one behind. She dropped down lower, putting her ear against the asphalt, looking under the belly of the Simca toward the other one.

She could see two pairs of men's feet, one next to the second car, the other walking slowly in her direction. She fired twice along the flat plane of the road surface, hoping to pick up a ricochet. She saw the walking feet stop and do a sudden dance, but neither man fell or cried out. There was no sign of Yulia.

Greta laid one pistol flat on the ground, reached into the satchel and pulled out a green cylinder, about the same size as an aerosol can of paint. It had "WP" and "No. 80" printed on it.

She threw the can into the back of the car, angling it down so that it hit the floor hard between the legs of the motionless Bulgarians. White smoke filled the car, then began to billow out of the open door.

A dense cloud drifted from left to right across the road, obscuring Greta from view.

She picked up the gun again and ran over the road to crouch next to the wheel of a car parked on the other side. She strained to see through the thickening smoke. She cracked off another shot in the direction of where Temir had been standing.

There was a cry from her left. The Bulgarian woman with the red hair had got out of the car and was crawling toward the middle of the road on her hands and knees, like a pilgrim inching toward a shrine.

The woman was on fire. The white phosphorus was burning her all the way down to the bone. She was close enough for Greta to shoot, but ammunition would become a problem soon. Greta set her face hard against the piteous screams. On the far side of the cloud of smoke, the Russians heard the noise but could not see who was making it.

When she came at him through the smoke, they were so close that they could have touched each other's fingertips with their outstretched arms.

Temir's body was angled away from her. He did not spin quickly enough. She shot him in the belly and he dropped his gun.

Greta pulled the trigger of the Browning again at point blank but it clicked empty. His giant hands grabbed at her.

She tried to club him over the head with the butt of the revolver but he blocked the blow and took both her wrists before she could fire again.

Her arms were raised high in the air and his hands were locked on to her wrists. He groaned and she sensed his weakness and drove at him. Still, he did not let go and they stepped back together stiffly, like tango dancers, until his back hit a rough brick wall with the Martini logo painted on it.

The letters were in blue and white, a yard tall. Temir's head was against the loop of the letter *R*. He was grimacing with pain but he still had both her wrists. Her right arm, the one that held the revolver, was locked at the elbow and the barrel of the gun was pointing straight up at the sky.

He was bleeding freely now. Greta heaved and the barrel of the revolver began to turn, like the hand of a clock going back the wrong way.

Now the gun was pointing straight up at the midday sun. Now it was at eleven o'clock, angled toward the first *i* in the word *Martini*. Now the *t*. Temir was straining with his last strength and the barrel wavered like the needle on a speedometer.

Greta's face was so close to his that they could have kissed. She roared at him, like an animal, the veins bulging in her face.

The barrel of the revolver reached the haze of down that grew around his left earlobe. Now it hovered close to the very edge of the back of his head.

Now it pointed at the top of the skull, into a nest of thick black curls slick with pomade. She fired and he went limp and slid straight down the wall. There was a thin spray of blood across the *M* of *Martini*.

Karpov cried out. He had dragged Yulia out of the car and had his arm around her neck and a gun to her head as he backed her away from Greta. He was trembling violently, looking back and forth from Greta to Temir, who was slumped in a heap against the wall. Yulia tried to shout but her voice was muffled by Karpov's forearm. The Bulgarian woman had stopped screaming.

Greta said: "Let her go." He shook his head. She raised a finger to her throat and made a cutting motion. "Don't you remember me? I'll open you up again. Like a can of stinking fish."

Greta sensed the movement from her side and heard the whipcrack sound and whirled around too late. She knew she had been shot but the pain did not register immediately. Temir was still pointing it at her—a tiny pistol that had been strapped around his ankle. She knew there was another bullet in it.

She saw his eyes roll in his head for a second and the arm that held the gun wavered. Then he recovered himself and his eyes focused again. The gun was pointing at her chest. When a second shot came, Greta shut her eyes tight.

She opened them slowly and she could see that Temir was dead now. His head had snapped to the side and something terrible had happened to it. The pistol had fallen from his splayed fingers.

Michael stepped slowly into her field of vision. He had the gun in one hand. He had taken off his glasses and was holding them in the other. They were still held together by tape. He walked very softly from toe to heel, keeping the gun trained on Temir all the time.

Greta swayed and blinked at Michael: she was seeing him as he really was for the first time. Then a body hit her and knocked the breath out of her lungs.

Karpov had shoved the girl at her with everything he had, then turned on his heels. Greta stumbled as she took Yulia's weight. She fired at him with one hand but it went wide.

Karpov was heading for the bridge that led back into the city. A crowd of people were hunkered down around the junction of the road and the bridge, cowering below the stonework or behind cars that had stopped. Greta did not want to fire in their direction.

A great shuddering cry came from Yulia, and Greta pulled the girl's head close to her shoulder and held it tight.

"Did he hurt you?"

"He was going to."

"Not anymore."

She staggered, and Michael ran to her side. All three looked down and saw a cluster of small spots of blood between Greta's shoes. She had turned pale and one hand was clutching the bullet wound in her side.

* * *

Sergei had aged visibly. His hair was completely white now. But as he strolled out of the darkness of the café, he looked tanned and rested, like a man enjoying a well-earned holiday.

He wore gray-blue slacks and a white short-sleeved shirt, open at the neck. He had no hat, and the waiter put up an umbrella for him before he sat. It was just a little early for an aperitif, but he ordered one anyway. The waiter poured a generous measure of blood-red vermouth into a square glass that contained a single cube of ice and a twist of orange.

Above the crowded *plaza*, the great cathedral bell began to chime for midday.

The Caballo Negro was in the southwest corner of the Plaza de la Virgen. Anna walked into the square from the northeast. She descended the steps and crossed the marble alone, walking slowly with her head down.

One of the Bulgarians was sitting on the edge of the fountain in the middle, pretending to read a newspaper. He was close enough to touch as she walked by. She saw another man called Berg but did not acknowledge him. Six more Russian and Bulgarian men were sitting at cafés at intervals all along the western side. Their heads turned as Anna walked toward her husband.

Karpov came all the way down the long street named after Saint Anne into the north side of the square at an awkward, lopsided shuffling run. He was drenched in sweat, but he could not take his jacket off: there was a gun under the arm.

He seemed bewildered by the noise of the streets and the strangeness of the language all around him. He paused to get his bearings, putting both hands on his thighs and panting like a dog. He looked around the square frantically, then saw them: Sergei and Anna sitting opposite each other in the far corner.

They seemed to be talking very calmly. Everyone who was watching took a breath. Berg stood up slowly and dried his hands on the front of his trousers. Then Sergei leaned forward, almost spilling the drink in front of him. He raised a hand to his wife's cheek. She was speaking animatedly now. Berg began to walk toward them. He could see other Russians and Bulgarians doing the same.

Sergei took Anna's face in both his hands. She stood up to lean closer to him and her chair fell on to its back. Berg broke into a run. When he was ten yards away, he could see that Sergei had something clamped between his teeth: the bright red end of a plastic capsule.

He bit into it and lunged at his wife. Their lips locked together. Both were standing now, and the vermouth glass rolled off the table and smashed. Sergei and Anna abandoned themselves to the kiss, their arms flung around each other. Berg heard someone shouting, "No!" in Russian.

He turned his head and saw a disheveled Maxim Karpov lolloping toward them. When he looked back, Sergei had sat down heavily in his chair and his head was nodding. Anna was leaning on the table with both hands. She swayed and collapsed slowly, pulling the tablecloth soaked with spilled vermouth on to the marble flagstones.

Greta had led Michael and Yulia at a furious pace down through the Carmen, ignoring the blasts from car horns and police sirens behind them.

They got halfway to the *plaza* and then she stopped and leaned against the doorway of an apartment building. Michael made her sit on the front step and an old woman who ran a fruit stand came over and spoke to her in Spanish.

Greta sat with her legs wide apart, on the edge of consciousness. A pool of dark red blood formed on the step between her feet. She waved Michael and Yulia on, screaming a Lithuanian obscenity at them when they hesitated.

Berg stood over Anna and reached down to take her pulse, but a repellent chemical smell hit his nostrils. He recoiled and backed away from her. Waiters who had come out of the dark interior of the café were shouting.

The sound of a police whistle came from the square behind. Karpov was ranting: "They cannot die. I need them. Do something."

One of the waiters started forward toward the bodies and Berg panicked and pulled an automatic pistol out of the underarm holder beneath his suit jacket. The waiter jumped back and stuck up his hands. He was shouting in the Valencian dialect.

Karpov heard a whistle again and turned. All around the square, a crowd of tourists and local people were staring at the scene unfolding outside the café. Karpov saw Yulia and the English boy running down the steps on the other side of the fountain.

Vassily was on the left, staring straight at Karpov with an unreadable expression. Karpov did not see the young woman with the blonde hair come into the square from the north, walking unsteadily with short, stiff steps and holding her side with both hands. On the pavement close to him, Anna twitched suddenly and Karpov lurched away from her.

The waiter was still shouting and pointing at Anna. Berg was waving his pistol around and Karpov could hear cries and exclamations from people on all sides.

A man wearing dark glasses and the uniform of the Policía Armada walked purposefully toward the café. He gripped a pistol in both hands. He barked a few words as he drew near them. Berg pointed his automatic at the sky.

Karpov put his hand inside his own jacket. He fumbled with the button that held the holster closed. The policeman shouted something else, a longer phrase in Spanish or Valencian.

Berg stared at him blankly. The man was clean-shaven under his police cap and he had a handsome face, though marked from adolescent acne. Berg levelled the gun at him and there was a flat pop. Berg hit the marble pavement hard.

Karpov was still fiddling with the holster under his arm. The officer fired again. He held his gun in one hand now, and one of his eyes was closed.

The bright blue Spanish sky filled Karpov's vision. Then a figure loomed over him, blocking it out: it was like a man, but monstrously large and black. One elongated limb extended itself toward his face.

"Father," said Maxim Karpov. "Please, Father."

When the two shots rang out, Yulia lost the scream that had been building inside her. Michael had his arms around her middle but she scratched him with her nails and broke free.

The policeman went stalking off into the darkness of the café, shouting for a telephone. Vassily watched him disappear, then went and squatted next to Anna with a napkin from one of the tables pressed over his mouth and a handkerchief in his other hand. He wiped away a trail of drool that ran down from the side of Anna's mouth. He did it so carefully that he did not smudge her lipstick.

Sergei was still sitting in the chair, his head hanging back, his eyes looking lifelessly up at the perfect blue sky.

Vassily went over to Karpov and crouched beside him. One of the Bulgarians drifted across and stood close by, staring after the policeman. Vassily tugged at the man's arm and he looked down and saw that the Russian had his fingers pressed against Karpov's neck and was shaking his head solemnly.

"It's all over," Vassily told him. When the Bulgarian man hesitated, Vassily shouted: "Get going, you fool! It's everyone for themselves now!" He watched the man sprint away, then looked around the square carefully. All the other Bulgarian and Russian faces had disappeared. He saw Yulia running toward him and he held up a hand as if to warn her off.

He felt Karpov's fingers curl around his other wrist. The chief administrator was lying still but his eyelids fluttered weakly and his voice came up faintly. "Vassily. Help me."

"I can't," Vassily began. Yulia had almost reached them and he started to rise to his feet, but Karpov held on to him like a drowning man.

"Rosinka!" Karpov hissed. Vassily stared at him. "Rosinka. Your sister's place. I will hang her from that cherry tree at the end of the garden. The boy and the girl next to her. If you don't get me out of here."

Vassily looked at him in silence. Then he said: "I just meant that I can't treat you without medical supplies. But the woman is coming now. I've arranged everything."

"That policeman . . ."

"I will take care of him."

Karpov breathed out slowly and deeply and Vassily felt the grip on his wrist slacken. He stood up and went to where Yulia was bent over her mother. He took hold of the girl with both arms and pulled her away from Anna. The chemical smell made his eyes burn and he clamped a hand over Yulia's mouth. She started fighting him but he ducked, placed a shoulder against her hipbone and scooped her up in a fireman's lift. He ran back past Michael, shouting: "Come on!"

Nausea washed over Karpov as he lay alone on his back with his arms by his sides. He did not hear Vassily, and he did not have strength left in the neck or abdomen to lift his head from the marble and peer down at his belly, so he could not see the spreading red stain on his dirty white shirt. Neither could he see Greta walk the last fifteen swaying paces toward him and lower herself slowly on to her knees beside him.

It will be all right, Karpov told himself. He had lost control of his emotions briefly, but the moment had passed. It was not real—just a nightmare from childhood. The man who had shot him was a Spanish police officer, and he would not finish off a wounded man in front of a crowd of witnesses. Now Vassily would find a way to fix things with the local police. And no enemy could attempt another attack under their noses, in the middle of the crowded square.

Someone was coming to treat him. That red-haired woman, he thought. She must have escaped from the car crash, like I did. Vassily would supervise her, no doubt. He would do the right thing, as he had all those years ago in Lithuania. Karpov had doubted him for a second, but it turned out that he was not such a tough customer after all. He responded to a little gentle coercion, just like everyone else in the world. It was an infallible law that had guided Karpov all his life. Karpov did not open his eyes when he felt the woman's fingers probing him. My life, he thought bitterly, in the hands of that Bulgarian sow. Still, she would follow orders. It would be all right.

Greta checked Karpov's heartbeat, then undid the top button of his shirt and exposed his neck. There was a long scar that ran down from below the right ear. She ran a fingertip down it. She was extremely pale, and hesitated for a moment as a shudder of pain passed through her.

One of the waiters took a step toward her but the policeman came strutting back out of the café with a broad white tablecloth folded over one arm and he yelled at all the onlookers to get back.

Greta recovered herself, dumped her bag next to her and rummaged in it. The smell of the filthy pavement rose up and hit her. The policeman got down on one knee, shook out the white tablecloth with a flourish and held it up around Karpov's head, like a nurse screening a patient from view.

Greta bent down so that her face was close to the motionless man. No one could see exactly what she was doing, but she might have been giving him the kiss of life.

Karpov stirred slightly when she touched him but did not open his eyes. She took out her father's hunting knife carefully so that most of it was hidden under the sleeve of her coat.

"Bring the others back," Karpov muttered. "Do you see them?"

"They scattered like chickens. They will pay for their cowardice. Call them on the radio. Drag them all back here. Someone must find a stretcher. Fetch me some water first."

"Do you see them when you are lying in bed at night?"

It was not the voice he was expecting. He opened his eyes but his pupils were dilated and he could not focus on her face.

"What are you talking about? Did you hear what I said? Get me some water, then call the others on the radio. The water first. I am burning."

"You will burn forever soon."

He was trying to process what she had said, and to place the strange voice. He could not move his head but his eyes flickered all around. He saw that someone was holding up a white cloth, but the man was facing away from them and he could not see who it was. He looked at the Gothic gate of the cathedral and the Star of David that was carved into the stonework above the door. His eyes returned to Greta and she watched his pupils change shape, like a camera lens, as he finally brought her face into focus.

She had smiled when Karpov opened his eyes. It was a beautiful smile, that of a saint, or a child. She was stroking the bone handle of her father's knife with her thumb, running it over the raised area where the image of St. Michael was engraved.

He is awake, she said silently. *Thank you. You have always protected me. Thank you, for this last grace.*

Karpov said: "You. Always you." A numbness was spreading through his lower body, and he could not move his arms. But his mind was racing furiously, crossing continents, scanning the wide Ukrainian steppe and the dark forests of Samogitia, spinning backwards and forwards across the decades, watching the gray faces flash up one after another, the endless roll-call of the dead.

"Is there anything you want to say?" asked Greta.

He managed to twist the corners of his mouth into an awful approximation of a smile. When he spoke, it was with a grotesque, ingratiating tone.

"You don't want me! I know what you really want. I can give you Germans."

"Germans?"

"I have dozens of them on my books. Half of my ballistic missile unit. The key nuclear people. They all belonged to Hitler once."

"And these are men you know well?"

"I lifted them myself in '45. I have worked with them for years. They were committed Nazis. Jew killers. We grabbed all the rocket scientists we could find. Intelligence officers. Valuable people."

"You would deliver them to me?"

"I will serve them up on a platter. I will put the hoods over their heads myself."

Greta nodded. "You were the same thing all along," she said, as though speaking to herself.

When he heard the tone in her voice, the corners of his mouth dropped. Karpov saw her open the folding knife. He tried to say the word *pazhalsta*, but it trailed off into a stammering, blubbering mess. His eyes filled with tears.

"Are you begging?" Greta asked. "You always do, at the end, don't you? You hard men."

A high-pitched, quavering wail rose up from the back of his throat.

She asked him again: "Are you begging for your life, Comrade?" He managed to form a single syllable and spit it out: *"Da."*

Her face became very hard. She put it close to his and said: "We never begged." She took the knife six inches to the side then drove it into his neck firmly and surely, without crying out or making a violent movement.

The tablecloth hid the sight of the knife sliding in under Karpov's chin, all the way up to the guard. No one else heard the click as the point of the blade bit into the top of his spine.

Karpov did not move his hands or make a sound. A tremor passed through him and one of his feet fluttered convulsively.

The policeman laid the tablecloth carefully over Karpov's face and upper body and helped Greta to her feet. They did not speak. She nodded at him and he bowed his head formally before turning away from her.

He went back into the café, shouting something incomprehensible at the pale, staring waiters. They backed away from him and he strode past the bar with the huge signed photograph of Joselito reaching out to touch the tip of the bull's horn above it and went through the swing doors into the kitchen.

He walked straight out of the back of the café where they piled up all the rubbish, sweeping off the policeman's hat and jacket. He stuffed them into one of the bins, turned left down an alley so narrow that a stout man would struggle to pass through it, and emerged on a broad shady street where a car was waiting.

He shouted something at the woman in the driver's seat and she had to turn so she could hear with her good ear.

Vassily was taking the steps down to the same street at a fast trot. Michael struggled to keep up with him, even though the Russian still had Yulia over his shoulder. You could see the muscles of his arms and upper back through his shirt.

A woman was revving the engine and, in the back, a man reached out to push open the door on their side. The man helped Vassily bundle Yulia into the car. She was limp and her eyes were rolling in her head.

Vassily turned to Michael and saw that the boy's eyes were on her. Michael didn't see Vassily hit him. One second, he was standing up, leaning to look into the back of the car, seeing Yulia's head lolling and the man with the pockmarked face holding it carefully, the next second he was sitting bewildered on the pavement.

Michael tried to get up, but his legs would not obey him. Vassily bent down to him and took his jaw between his thumb and his fingers. He peered into Michael's eyes, like a doctor trying to see right into the back of them. Then he slapped Michael's face, not gently but not viciously.

Michael heard someone shouting and realized it was his own voice. He was cursing his legs, trying to stand up and failing. His jaw throbbed, and the scratches Yulia had left on his face burned. He rolled himself over and he was on his hands and knees as the car pulled away from him, heading north out of El Carmen toward the road that ringed the city of Valencia.

43

LONDON

"Dad? What is *Rhinemaiden*?"

Sir Stephen Fitzgerald flinched as though he had been stung by an insect. He looked over both his shoulders. They were sitting at a table outside a big brash pub in the middle of Victoria station. It had a façade like a timbered Tudor mansion, made of fiberglass. The tables were out on the station concourse, so that people running for their trains walked right behind you as you sipped your drink. The vice admiral had chosen it deliberately.

Michael smirked. His father looked at him acidly and reached out to pour stout from a large bottle into a glass for his son.

"I thought you were going to answer all my questions," Michael said.

His father looked up at the big board that showed the departure times of the trains. "I don't know about all of them. Not if you're getting the five o'clock to Dover."

Michael said: "Let's start with an easy one. Why are you dressed like a theater impresario?"

Sir Stephen was sitting in full view of the commuters who flowed in and out of the station. One leg was thrown over the other. He wore a good suit, a Crombie overcoat with an ostentatious velvet collar, and a bright yellow silk scarf with a bold geometric pattern. A huge red carnation poked out of the breast pocket of the coat.

"I was turning into an old hermit. It's good to get out and see some life."

"Where have you been hiding? In an underground bunker or something?"

"Suffolk, mostly. There's a place I like out on the coast. We used to go there with your mother when you were very small. She loved the beaches. You won't remember."

Michael was sipping his drink. He shook his head.

"I don't suppose you have any memory of her."

Michael said: "That word you showed me—the one that must not be uttered out loud. I didn't find out anything in Germany, did I? I failed you miserably. Did you get to the bottom of it in the end?"

His father tugged at an earlobe and pouted slightly. "I can't say whether that word you mentioned means anything to me or not. Even if it did, I wouldn't be able to discuss it with you."

"I won't tell anyone. And I might be leaving the country for ever anyway."

The vice admiral was not a man given to extravagant displays of emotion. He studied the beermat on the table for a while as though it were a lost miniature by Hilliard.

Michael said: "Don't you have anything to say about that?"

"Let us suppose that I heard something," said his father, slowly. "Not actual classified material, of course, just one of those rumors that fly around the pubs near St. James's Park sometimes."

"Rumors. All right."

"Well. We all know that the Soviets made plans to invade Western Europe. Naturally, the attack would come through Germany."

"All right."

"Let us speculate that the Russians believed they could overrun us and our Allies and reach the river Rhine in a very short period. Let us say . . . seven days."

"Good Lord," said Michael, quietly. "Is that all?"

"They would launch nuclear attacks simultaneously against a number of Western countries, but not the other atomic powers. They believed that Britain and France would not retaliate with nuclear weapons unless we were bombed first."

The vice admiral paused as an announcement came over the station loudspeaker. They both drank.

"Now let us suppose—and this is all rumor and conjecture—that the Allies got wind of all this, with a lot more detail. Imagine if we knew exactly when the hammer would fall, and which divisions would be placed where."

"We could stop them in their tracks," said Michael.

His father shook his head. "We would never have the numbers. The Soviets are always fighting the last war in their heads. They have more tanks than you would believe, in case Hitler and his panzers rise up from the grave. That is not the war we would give them."

"What do we do?"

"Well, as I say, I am simply speculating. Here is a possibility: let us say that when they invade, we give them exactly what they want. We give up Germany. The Allies simply retreat, seemingly in disarray. Instead of seven days, the Warsaw Pact forces reach the natural barrier of the Rhine in three or four days. The river in the north and the Pyrenees in the south form a new Iron Curtain across Europe."

Michael snorted with laughter. Then he saw the expression on his father's face and the laughter died. "You can't be serious," he said.

"As I say, I'm indulging in idle speculation. But imagine if our intelligence was good . . . and continued to be so *after* the invasion. We would have a stay-behind network scattered through Germany. That would give us the location of all those Russian and Polish, Czech and Hungarian soldiers. Can you picture it? The world stunned by this great advance, Britain and France appearing to squabble with each other, as usual, each secretly suing for peace with Moscow, the American politicians dithering, worrying about their voters. Meanwhile, the Russians are consolidating. They garrison all those troops in a few obvious places."

He held Michael's gaze without blinking. "Stuttgart. Munich. Nuremberg. Aachen. One of the greatest assemblies of troops the world has ever seen, concentrated in a string of West German cities."

Michael saw it: waves of men and armor sweeping across the green plains of the Rhineland. The thunder of shellfire. Blinding flashes lighting up the horizon from end to end. "All right," he said. "You give up the center of the board. Then what?"

"A nuclear strike on those cities I mentioned, and on the troop corridors that run between them. Based on detailed intelligence from stay-behind agents. Britain and France and America suddenly acting in concert. One great salvo with every warhead available."

"No. All those civilians."

"It would have meant the end of the threat from Russia forever. And, yes, the end of Germany as we know it. A chessboard being swept clear of pieces. A terrible thing to contemplate."

"Germany would be uninhabitable," said Michael.

"The world would be a very different place. Are you going to have another of those?"

"No thanks." Michael felt queasy. He had had enough beer. The flower shop on the other side of the station was closing and the woman was pouring water from a bucket down a drain in the middle of the concourse.

"Hang on," said Michael. "What would have happened to all those stay-behind agents, calling in the strikes? They would never have survived."

"How strange," said his father, "the way young people see things. Michael, there are always people in this world who are willing to give up their own lives for something greater. There are more of them around than you would think. You might even have met some today without realizing it."

"Did you know about the Russian plan before you sent me to Germany?"

"Certainly not. We had the name—and a few hints from various sources. There were clues sprinkled around: things hiding in plain sight. I was still trying to piece it together when you flew to Berlin. In the end, it took a frank conversation with someone who had detailed knowledge of the Soviet plan to give us what we needed."

Michael was rubbing his head. "Someone from their side made contact?"

"There was an individual who had wanted to talk to me for some time. They could not do so safely when Colin Sinclair was . . . still in action."

Michael breathed in. "That was going to be my next question. What happened to him?"

The vice admiral kept his voice very neutral. "It was the coroner's firm verdict that he took his own life, Michael."

"I don't mean that. I mean why did he . . . do what he did?"

"His wife suffers from a rare disease of the nervous system. The treatment is very expensive."

"Money? It's as simple as that?"

"He would do anything to keep her alive, I imagine. I don't find that hard to understand. Do you?"

Michael drank thoughtfully.

"Poor Colin's tragic *suicide*," said the vice admiral, "meant that my contact in Moscow could speak to me candidly at last without fear of the news dribbling back to their colleagues."

Michael's eyes were trained on the tabletop. "Sinclair's death saved many lives," said Sir Stephen, carefully. "Do you follow?"

His son did not answer, but a kind of tension that had been in his face appeared to slacken.

Sir Stephen said: "The conversation the world needed took place eventually, at five minutes to midnight."

"And they just told you the whole thing?"

The vice admiral barked with laughter. "Of course not. My source revealed just enough of the Soviet battle plan to allow us to form a strategic response. Their aim throughout, I think, was to preserve the balance of power, not to fatally weaken their own side. It was like catching a glimpse of a couple of the cards in your opponent's hand. It was enough. Later, I flashed some of our cards to certain people in the Soviet command structure."

Michael was nodding. "Getting hold of the plan wasn't enough. They might still have invaded. You had to let them know we had read it, and that we had thought of a way to hit back at them."

"I had to hint at that possibility. I don't think they were in too much doubt by the end. I was able to have a frank exchange with someone on their side. Sometimes that is all that is needed. Of course, the demise of Maxim Karpov made all the difference. Despite some strong words, my opposite number had as little appetite for thermonuclear war as I do. We understood each other perfectly, I think." He leaned back in his chair. "I wonder how many of the world's problems we could solve, if I could sit down with the chairman of the Politburo of the Soviet Union once a month over a bottle of beer or two."

"Vodka for him, I should think."

"Very good brandy, I believe, is his tipple. I picture him sometimes, you know, when I'm at my desk. I imagine him sitting opposite me. What would he do? What is he thinking? I am not sure I have ever guessed correctly."

Michael sat back in his chair. "I think that's what happened with Vassily and Sergei. They had a frank conversation one night. They bared their souls. That's what started the whole thing."

He scanned the vice admiral's face for any clue as to what those names might mean to him. His father's expression was inscrutable. It was worth a try, thought Michael.

"Do you think the danger has really passed?" he asked his father. "I know that's what the newspapers think."

"The Soviets are having to rethink their tactics. The chief administrator was the driving force behind the invasion plan. Naturally, his supporters are in disarray now. We judge that there is little stomach for war in the Politburo in his absence." Sir Stephen shrugged. "Who knows how things will look next year? You can be sure that the Stalinist faction will regroup. There will be other Maxim Karpovs. I could say more, but . . ."

"There are so many things I don't know," Michael said, with a sigh. "I feel like your friends never took that coal sack off my head. I've been blundering around in the dark the whole time."

His father said: "You could find out just a little more about your own role in the affair, if you looked at the raw classified material. But then you would have to come and work for me."

Michael gaped at the vice admiral. The old man was inspecting his fingernails. "You can't mean it? Pulling strings? It's against every principle you've ever taught me."

His father chuckled: "You're right, naturally. It would be indefensible. Except for the unfortunate fact that you were bred to this kind of work. *Only once in a thousand years is a horse born so well fitted for the game as this our colt.* I am only asking you because I know what you will say."

"I have to go to her," said Michael. "She needs me." He looked up at the station clock and began to gather his things together.

"I can see from the look on your face that Yulia is quite a girl. I'm not surprised. Her mother was a remarkable woman."

"Oh, no, for God's sake! You can't just drop something like that in when I'm running for a train!"

As he stood up, his father said: "One more thing. Do you remember when we talked about revenge?"

"*Stalin will avenge us.* How could I forget?" He was putting on his jacket.

"You were right and I was wrong. It doesn't achieve anything." Michael's eyes narrowed.

"The man who killed your mother. No. Wait. *Wait.* I could have found him. The airman who dropped the bomb that night. I had access to their records. I could have hunted him down and killed him with my bare hands. And I would probably have got away with it. I thought about it. But I knew it would consume me. It would poison my whole life. Do you see?"

"Not really. Why are you talking like this? Something's wrong, isn't it? Why are you dressed up like that? And that flower . . ."

"I'm enjoying life at last, Michael. I've been hidden away, like an antique, for long enough."

"Are you sure you're going to be all right?"

Sir Stephen rose to his feet and took hold of Michael's shoulders with both hands. "Of course. Go to her."

People were looking at them. "Go," said the vice admiral. His grip was like a steel trap. "Go and get your girl."

They were not the sort of men who could hug each other.

44

MOSCOW

The young army officer, Andrey, married his betrothed, Xenia, on the Saturday. Today was Monday, but Vassily still had the ghost of a hangover and snatches of folk songs from the wedding ringing around his head. He had acted as toastmaster, under the watchful eye of Andrey's mother. He was forbidden to make any jokes about the bump in the bride's belly.

Vassily would stand godfather to the child if it was a boy, according to the Orthodox tradition. He had sold everything that might connect him to the Valencia affair, gathered the money and put it into an envelope for the bride and groom. It came to more than a month's wages.

It was a fine country-style wedding, with all the old customs observed. The ransom for the bride. The bitter vodka and the kisses that sweetened it.

The groom wore black boots and breeches and a red silk tunic with a sash around the middle. Most of the other men were in army uniform. The old soldiers told Vassily stories about his father. The young ones leaped and danced on their haunches and turned somersaults.

He had taken his air hostess with him. It was the first time they had appeared in public as a couple. She charmed everyone. Vassily remembered her face as they danced together at the end of the night, glowing with happiness, the room whirling behind her. He forced his attention back to the grim-faced men who were sitting in a circle around him.

The supreme commander of the Workers' and Peasants' Red Army said: "Blood demands blood. We must retaliate."

Vassily, the chairman and Simonov looked at one another but stayed silent.

"Nothing less than Soviet honor is at stake," Marshal Cherkezishvili went on. "Am I the only one who feels this? Comrade Vassily Andreyevich. You will agree with me when I say that Anna Vladimirovna was a beloved daughter of the Moscow regiment. The army does not forget the days of '41 when she stood alongside us on the barricades."

"What are the ordinary people saying?" asked the chairman. It was the new weekly meeting, when representatives of the Kremlin, the armed forces, the MGB and the recently expanded Fourth Directorate came together to discuss the most pressing matters of state security.

"You have probably seen the newspaper articles yourselves," said Vassily. "Some of them have been well received. The feeling is that two Soviet heroes have been murdered in a Fascist country, and a good man seriously injured. The identity of . . ." he glanced down as if checking his notes ". . . Michael Fitzgerald has so far been concealed from most of the world. There is, of course, widespread speculation that foreign spies were involved in the events in Valencia."

"Three," said the chairman, gently. "I'm so sorry?"

"Three heroes of the Soviet Union died. You said two."

"My apologies, gentlemen. Comrade Simonov's late predecessor was of course a hero and an example to us all."

The awkward silence that followed was broken eventually by the chairman. "I may as well tell you that there is no realistic prospect of repatriating the bodies. You may remember that I denounced Generalissimo Franco in no uncertain terms from the floor of the United Nations last year. The timing is most unfortunate. There has been no official cooperation on post-mortems, funeral arrangements, forensic investigation. And I know of no one with contacts in Spain who can help us unofficially."

They all considered this gloomily. Then the chairman appeared to make a sudden decision and turned to Simonov. "What are the tactical options? What does the MGB say? It is you who would carry out an operation, as a matter of honor, not our distant neighbors."

Vassily smiled and inclined his head.

Simonov said: "I have prepared a paper. We judge that there are three viable options. One: we bend our efforts to tracking down the Baltic and British agents who appear to have had a hand in this affair. When we find them, we make an example of them."

"Expensive," said Vassily. "And difficult. One, at least, is a serious professional. It could take decades."

Simonov glared at him above his spectacles. "If I might be permitted to continue without interruption. Option two: dedicate more resources to finding the fugitive Yulia Sergeiovna Forsheva. This would give us our best chance of answering the troubling questions that hang over this debacle. Indeed, if we do not find the girl, there are elements that are likely to remain a permanent mystery."

He glanced at Vassily as if expecting another interjection, then went on hurriedly: "Three: we continue to pursue investigations, but we make retaliation the immediate priority. Naturally, while the tensions of recent months have eased somewhat, we would want any response to be measured and proportionate." He coughed. "Sir Stephen Fitzgerald was almost certainly at the root of this *konspiratsia*."

"I understood," said the chairman, "that this particular old fox went to ground some time ago."

"There has been a curious development since Valencia," said Simonov. "We have received excellent intelligence from London that Sir Stephen has come out of hiding and is to be seen openly traveling to work at the offices of the Admiralty at the same time every morning. He appears to be taking no security precautions whatsoever."

"What do you mean—no guards?"

Simonov coughed again. "Not even a driver. He takes the London Underground alone with a carnation in his buttonhole."

The chairman stared at him. Simonov said hurriedly: "I did not believe these reports at first either, so I took pains to have them verified. It is frankly hard to interpret Sir Stephen's behavior. Our understanding is that he began to hide his whereabouts in response to the

Lithuanian threat. It could simply be that he considers that threat to have vanished now."

Vassily said: "But he must realize there is a threat from us. Does he think we'd take this lying down? He'd be a fool to show himself now."

Simonov nodded vigorously. "It is almost as if he is taunting us."

"No," said the chairman. "I don't think so. I believe I understand him. But then, unlike you, I have children. What do you say, Cherkez-ishvili? You are a father."

The marshal raised one unruly eyebrow and gave the merest of nods. "I think you are right."

Simonov looked helplessly at Vassily and they shrugged at each other in a rare display of solidarity.

"He is not mocking us," said Cherkezishvili. "He is offering himself to us."

The chairman cleared his throat. "Simonov, how are operational conditions in London?"

The new head of the MGB said: "Comrade Chairman, the service is ready to act at your instruction as ever. We are the strong right arm, and you are the brain. Our reach is as long as it has ever been." He did not quite click his heels under the table.

The marshal rolled his eyes and glanced at Vassily, expecting a sardonic smile. But to his surprise, the newly promoted chief of the Fourth Intelligence Directorate, as immaculately dressed as ever, did not appear to have been listening to Simonov.

Vassily was looking away from the table where the four men sat and out of the window, an expression of intense emotion on his face that was impossible to interpret.

45

LONDON

He stood at the edge of the platform, leaning on his umbrella, like an aged knight resting on his sword after a long battle. It was the first station at the east end of the Central Line and only a few commuters were waiting for the early train.

He boarded the first carriage and sat next to the doors. The only other passengers were two men with golf bags who walked past him and sat on the opposite side near the door that led to the driver's cab. One of the men gave him a shy half-smile, and he responded with a curt nod. The three saw each other every morning but, because they were English, they never spoke.

If the golfers had broken with convention on that morning and introduced themselves, then asked for his name and profession in return, the full answer would have been *Sir Stephen Fitzgerald, KBE, CB; Vice Admiral of the Fleet; Director, Naval Intelligence; Head of Planning, Defense Intelligence (Soviet Attack).*

The vice admiral had the usual tussle with his *Times.* His eye skipped over the bridge and chess columns, which might have been written in foreign languages as far as he was concerned, and alighted on the cryptic crossword.

Nine letters, he thought. Something, something. *A king. In the event of a cold snap.* What the devil did that mean?

The golfers got off at Debden and he did not look up from the newspaper as they walked past. He was alone in the carriage until Loughton, when three or four people got on. A big man came and sat two seats down, shifting his bulk into the ungenerous space between the armrests.

A cold snap, thought the admiral. Frost, snow, ice. The big man was fishing in his pockets and Sir Stephen felt a twinge of annoyance. He did not like to smoke on the Underground, and he did not see why others could not wait, rather than gassing their fellow passengers.

He looked over at the newcomer and could not help noticing his cheap, shiny, boxy suit. The shabbiness of the man's clothes contrasted sharply with the admiral's fine overcoat, bright silk tie and fresh carnation. A commercial traveler if ever I saw one, thought Sir Stephen. Poor devil. Good luck to him trying to sell things to housewives. A great brute like that, with an ogre's face.

The man was staring straight ahead, and his lips were quivering. He appeared to be experiencing some kind of crisis as the train slowed down before Woodford. Michael's father had seen men with that look on their face during the war. Poor chap, he thought.

Sir Stephen turned back to the crossword. One down was almost certainly "sable," not "black," so one across must begin with *S*, he thought, so he crossed out the *B* and penciled in the new letter. He had the sudden thought that the man two seats away was trying to offer him a cigarette. He was holding something out toward him. Now it was right in his face. Sir Stephen turned and saw that the object was a large cigarette lighter.

It is nothing, the admiral thought. All my life, I have carried this horror of it. And when it comes at last, it is nothing.

He knew straight away that the spray contained a nerve agent, and that very soon, he would not be able to move. He didn't try. The newspaper had fallen right next to his face and he saw the texture of the paper in astonishing detail: the way the individual fibers were woven together, like cloth; the blurring around the edges of the letters that had seemed so sharply defined when they were at arm's length.

It's just that you would rather not be alone, he thought. But, then, you would not want him here to see it either. Not like this. Would the boy ever fully understand him? Not yet, thought Sir Stephen. He's too young. I should have written that letter. I thought there was still time. My boy.

The police sergeant made a puffing noise and scratched the back of his neck, then walked out on to the platform and placed his helmet firmly back on his head. He kicked his black shoes against the door of the train because he had trampled a red flower that lay on the floor among the mud and the cigarette ends. The torn petals were pressed against his soles.

The platform was full of people now and the station staff were holding them back. The doctor was still inside the train, sitting on a seat and filling in a form. They had put a tartan blanket over the body. The sergeant looked at the crowd building up on the platform and blew out another breath. The Central Line would be backed up all morning and a lot of people were going to be late for work. He hated these jobs.

The station guard came up to him and said: "What do you think it was? Heart?"

The sergeant said: "Good Lord. How on earth should I know?"

The guard said: "Heart, I reckon. What was he trying to say, at the end there?"

"Blowed if I know," said the sergeant, testily.

"I thought it sounded like someone's name," said the guard.

46

SWEDEN

That same morning, a fisherman was rowing Michael across a narrow strait to an island in the Baltic Sea. All the local boatmen would take you over for five krona. They came if you whistled from the pier.

"You should have been here yesterday," said the man. "It was like bathwater. I take people in a circle around the whole island when the weather is better. Twenty krona. Do you know we are in international waters here? It doesn't belong to Sweden. That's why it doesn't appear on a lot of maps. Twenty. How about tomorrow, if it brightens up?"

"I'll see how I'm fixed," said Michael. The man helped him get off with his bag.

"I'll do it for fifteen," the fisherman called, and Michael waved a hand in the air.

The Russians had arranged themselves in the great hall as if for a portrait, although no photographs could be taken of them. Sergei and Anna sat on high-backed chairs at the far end of the room, like a king and queen holding court.

Yulia stood behind her parents. She wore a long black dress with white circles around the neck and sleeves. She played with her hands and chewed her lip when Michael appeared in the doorway. Her father looked up at her and was about to encourage her to go to him, when he realized that she was not waiting for his permission but was simply paralyzed by emotion. She is a woman now, Sergei thought. She will never ask for my leave to do anything again.

When Yulia ran to Michael, she grabbed the lapels of his jacket and pulled him to her roughly. He almost lost his balance.

Johnny had come back from the mainland with champagne. He walked around to the back of the house where a stream fell steeply in a manmade channel that had once turned a mill. He rested the bottles in the water, and within moments they were icy to the touch.

All the men stood up when Greta arrived. Nobody knew what to say. She dumped her big leather bag on the floor with a thump. The others were all staring at her and she smiled brightly. "Well. Is there anything to drink around here?"

Nobody answered and she said: "Either there is or there isn't—it's a yes or no question." And everyone laughed and Johnny lunged forward to pick up her bag.

They all got roaring drunk in the evening and there were gramophone records, and parlor games. Michael saw Johnny and Greta alone together in the kitchen, talking about nothing. They were eating each other with their eyes, but he did not see them kiss.

In the hall, Sergei recited some lines of Pushkin:

> *Don't you want to share the passion*
> *Of this moment with a friend?*

Anna rolled her eyes disapprovingly, but you could see that she was secretly proud of him. There was a clamor for Michael to follow suit, but he refused absolutely to recite anything in Russian.

He dredged up some English poetry instead:

> *Or who, in Moscow, toward the Tsar,*
> *With the demurest of footfalls*
> *Over the Kremlin's pavement, brigh*
> *With serpentine and syenite,*
> *Steps, with five other generals . . .*

Much later, he found himself nodding off in his chair. Anna had gone to bed. Yulia and Johnny had a chessboard set up in the corner of the hall. She was showing him how she had fought the great Szekeres to a standstill. She was the only one who was not drinking, and she was talking animatedly.

Johnny was trying to follow the moves, but the champagne and brandy were getting the better of him and his eyelids were fluttering. Michael must have nodded off for a while, because when he came round he realized that Greta and Sergei were sitting at the same table as him, talking in low voices. He stayed slumped in his chair and did not open his eyes.

Greta said: "Thank you for the invitation. I'm sorry it took me a while to join the party."

Sergei chuckled. "I am glad you could join us. It would not have been the same without you."

They laughed and he said: "I will try to think of a way to repay you, when we are more settled. We're all feeling a little disoriented."

Greta said: "It's a strange thing to be blown around like a wildflower seed. I know how it feels to lose your identity. Of course, my nationality was taken from me. I did not give it up willingly."

"Countries survive in people's hearts," said Sergei. "Lines and colors on maps mean very little. Nationality is an idea."

"And will you take a new one?"

"Who could take a mistress after such a wife? I'm looking to found a new nation somewhere. A republic of three."

"Not for long," said Greta, and Michael guessed she was nodding or gesturing toward him, although he was careful to keep his eyes closed and show no reaction.

"I think he is a good boy!" said Sergei in a whisper, and Michael heard them chuckle.

"What will you do now, my Queen of Cats?" the Russian asked, suddenly serious. "Johannes tells me you plan to retire. I cannot imagine you knitting by the fireside for very long."

"I don't know if I can change my stripes now. I have been out in the forest all my life. And there is still work to do."

"Wars never really end. But you can turn your back on them. You can come in from the dark woods for a little while." He leaned in close to her. "There must be something I can do to help, after everything you have done for us."

Greta exclaimed suddenly because Johnny was staggering over toward their table. He was falling-down drunk by then, and he dropped to one knee next to her chair. She pulled his head toward her breast. Michael saw through one half-open eye that one of her hands was covering Johnny's ear.

Greta said: "This one I will take, as part payment for my services."

"Only part?"

She made sure her hand was completely over Johnny's ear and said: "Karpov told me something, just before he died. He said there were still a lot of Germans in the Soviet ranks. Men who had been seized at the end of the war and made to work for the Soviet Union. In the nuclear program, the space program?"

"He spoke the truth. I know many men like this."

"I'm going to need you to write their names in a notebook."

Greta said it very lightly and gently, but everyone who was listening knew that it was not a request.

The next morning, Michael slept late. He had stuck to champagne and wasn't exactly hungover, but his head and limbs felt heavy.

Outside, it was a brilliant day, the wind blowing in strong off the water. Johnny was sitting on a bench beside the gravel path that ringed the house. He was fooling around with his trumpet but not playing seriously. Yulia had found a croquet set and was hammering hoops into the lawn. Greta was with her. She had never heard of the game.

"The air here," said Johnny. "You don't breathe it. You drink it like milk."

"This was your mother's place?"

"I suppose it's mine now. I don't come back often. I don't like rattling around on my own."

"It doesn't look like you'll have to, now," said Michael, as Greta wandered over toward them. She was wearing a long black leather coat.

"We're taking it slowly," said Johnny, quietly. "I'm still terrified of her. It's like sharing a bed with a Bengal tiger. She says she's going to change career. We'll see."

Greta was drawing near. Michael shielded his eyes with his hands and said to her: "You're not a gold digger, are you? Not going to murder him for this place? Slip some arsenic in his aquavit?"

"That's much too subtle for me," said Greta, and mimed hitting Johnny over the head with the croquet mallet.

"See that?" said Johnny. "If you find me dead on the lawn, you'll know who to thank."

"Don't be ridiculous," said Greta. "With all this water around? If I do it, my poor boy, they will never find your body." And she kissed him on the forehead and went back into the house.

Yulia was still out on the lawn, trying to smack the ball through a hoop with great determination. Johnny said: "You got a good one there. That was one of the great seductions. I'm proud I played a small part in it."

"I'm not sure I seduced her really."

Johnny creased with laughter and clapped Michael on the knee. "Of course *you* didn't seduce *her!*"

Michael glared at him. "I'll get to the bottom of it, you know. I'll piece it together. I was trying to work on everyone individually last night."

"Let it go." said Johnny. "You'll never know everything. Accept it. Be happy. She loves you."

Yulia was concentrating so hard on her croquet stroke that she didn't hear Michael come up behind her. She jumped when he put his hands around her waist. He squeezed her a little and she said: "You had better not be rough with me. I am having your baby."

Michael searched for words. She pinched his cheek hard with her finger and thumb. "All right? So, no more horsing around."

"Germany," he said finally.

"Giraffe."

"What?"

"Like a giraffe. With the long neck. It takes a while for the thought to reach your brain."

"That first night was all it took."

"There is no need to look so pleased with yourself, my boy."

"I think I already knew inside. I felt something, all that time we were apart." She burst out laughing, and he colored, and said: "Well, of course it sounds stupid when you say it out loud."

Yulia pinched his cheek again, not gently. "Better not try to be romantic, English boy. Leave it to the Italians."

They kissed seriously until he pulled away from her and looked back at the house guiltily, in case her parents had come outside and were watching them.

"It is too late to worry about that," said Yulia.

The wind was blowing in stiffly off the water and they kissed again. The rushing air was clean and cold against their skin and it filled everything with the promise of health and life and renewal.

EPILOGUE

It was 1966, and the music had changed. people said the clothes had changed too, but that wasn't true for everyone. Men like Oleg Kozlov dressed in much the same way as they had always done. Oleg needed a week in bed after Valencia, with concussion and cracked ribs. He managed to spin it out for another fortnight, malingering in the military hospital near Berlin, feigning confusion and fatigue. When he finally faced the investigators in Moscow, the interview was surprisingly perfunctory. Everyone else involved had already given slightly different accounts of the events in Spain, and no one could work out who to blame.

The job in London was presented as a chance to redeem himself in the eyes of the MGB. Oleg accepted it without hesitation, then spent twenty minutes vomiting in a toilet cubicle. A cloud of despair hung over him on the day he boarded the Underground train at the unpronounceable station where London's suburbs met the Essex countryside. He had convinced himself that he would foul the whole thing up. He would catch the wrong train. He would exclaim loudly in Russian at the pivotal moment. He would point the fiddly lighter device in the wrong direction, spraying nerve agent into his own unlovely face. He would kill the wrong old man.

But all went well. When he returned to Moscow, there was an envelope on his desk containing the offer of a job in Paris with full diplomatic cover, a grace and favor apartment and a place at an international school for his son.

Oleg inspected the flat first, so when his wife arrived, he was able to show her around with the offhand air of man unfazed by such luxury. He pointed out the landmarks you could see from the balcony. He turned the taps on and off, making a joke about French plumbing. When his wife failed to laugh, he glanced over and saw that tears were cascading down her face. It was the beginning of a new golden chapter in their marriage, all the sweeter for being unexpected.

Professional life was quiet in Paris. French intelligence seemed to be staffed exclusively by Corsican Mafiosi who had graduated from the hard school of Algeria. They were very tough and the simple rule was that you did not fuck with them. So Oleg interviewed the dreamers and the crazies who walked into the Soviet embassy, offering to defect. He performed routine administrative tasks, delegating as much paperwork as possible to the intense young men who worked under him. He was still obliged to travel occasionally.

On this particular day, he needed to make a brief trip to a private bank in Zürich to resolve a problem relating to clandestine payments— the eternal headache of every intelligence service.

He arrived at Orly two hours before the flight so that he would have time for a serious lunch. There was a quiet Italian place he liked to use on the top floor. A pretty Sicilian woman of around forty was usually serving. She wasn't there today. Oleg had the waiter pour him a beer. Then he ordered gnocchi with sorrel sauce, a sandwich on the side and a large portion of French fries.

"I'm probably not pronouncing any of that right," he said to the waiter.

"I wouldn't know," the man replied. "I'm Spanish, not Italian. I'll get them started on your order."

Oleg drained the beer and listened to the radio. He didn't like the new stuff much. Everything was very aggressive now. As he finished the beer the waiter spread the plates in front of him. Oleg smothered the gnocchi in Parmigiano-Reggiano. A rich smell rose from it. Something rebelled inside him and he felt sick. The food was fat and white and slick with oil. He turned up his nose and pushed all the plates away from him. The waiter came over to ask if he wanted another beer and said: "Is everything all right with the food?"

"It's fine," said Oleg. "I'm just not hungry." He suddenly gave a snort of wild laughter. He looked up at the man and beamed. "I'm not hungry!" He almost shouted it and the waiter laughed too, nervously, then found something else to do at the other end of the bar.

The Spaniard came back a minute later with a glass of sparkling wine in his hand. "From the young lady," he said. "It's her birthday. She's treating everyone." Oleg had been gazing into the middle distance, and took in the group of air hostesses at the other end of the bar for the first time. Their skirts were very short. Now this was one modern trend he could get on board with. How could he not have noticed them? I must be unwell, he said to himself.

Oleg took the wine glass and raised it in a salute to the air hostess at the center of the group, a tall, dark-haired woman with a very wide mouth. She smiled and raised her own glass. He took a big mouthful.

He thought about his son. When the boy was born, the doctors had said he would not make it past five or six. Now he was finishing high school, and the kink in his spine was no longer noticeable when he walked. He was sixteen, spoke French well and had begun to swagger a little around the girls. He will do better than I did, thought Oleg.

He finished the rest of the wine. They were playing a song with a sinuous, eastern modal melody, and he felt a sudden shudder of dislike for the music and looked for the barman. But there was no one behind the bar now.

Oleg looked down at the gnocchi and saw that shiny lumps of fat were congealing. A second serious wave of nausea passed through him and he gripped the edge of the bar with both hands. That awful song, Oleg thought.

"Are you all right?" It was one of the women, at his elbow now. He waved at her and nodded but as he did so, his vision sagged and surged and the room changed shape slightly. He had to hold on to the bar tightly to stop himself falling from his chair. He looked at the woman next to him and was about to say something in reply but stopped. She had spoken to him in Russian.

All the other women had disappeared. The barman had gone too.

It was just Oleg and the woman from the airline. But was she really a hostess? He realized that she was not wearing a proper uniform like the others. She had a blue jacket and blue skirt that looked like a uniform from a distance. She had dyed her hair dark and covered it in a headscarf with a floral pattern. She wore large sunglasses. When she took them off, Oleg saw the bright green eyes and felt a flash of recognition. His knuckles were white and the muscles in his forearms shook as he gripped the end of the bar.

Greta nodded. She reached for something in the inside pocket of her jacket. "It's time, Comrade," she said.

ACKNOWLEDGMENTS

Love and thanks to everyone who helped me write this story in difficult times: Simona, Nikita, Mum, Dad and Roy; Arzu Tahsin; Martin Williams, Georgina Lee, Kieron Bryan, Ed Howker, Ed Gove, Gregory Thwaites; Anna Gineotis, Luis Marchal and Jesus Campon; Tod Cury, Adrian Winbow, Zarah Fernando. This book would not have been possible without editors Bill Scott-Kerr and Eloisa Clegg, and my agent, the incomparable Julia Kingsford.

ABOUT THE AUTHOR

Patrick Worrall was educated at a comprehensive school in Worcestershire and King's College, Cambridge. He has worked as a teacher in eastern Europe and Asia, a newspaper journalist, a court reporter at the Old Bailey, and the head of Channel 4 News's FactCheck blog. *The Partisan* is his first novel.